TULIP MURDERS

A Novel in the Johnson & Wilde
Crime Mystery Series

ANDY GRIFFEE

Copyright © 2024 Andy Griffee

All rights reserved

The characters and events portrayed in this book are fictitious. Any similarity to real persons, living or dead, is coincidental and not intended by the author.

No part of this book may be reproduced, or stored in a retrieval system, or transmitted in any form or by any means, electronic, mechanical, photocopying, recording, or otherwise, without express written permission of the publisher.

This book is dedicated with love and affection to my brother and sisters, Simon Griffee, Lorraine Wheeler and Janice Watt.

TULIP MURDERS

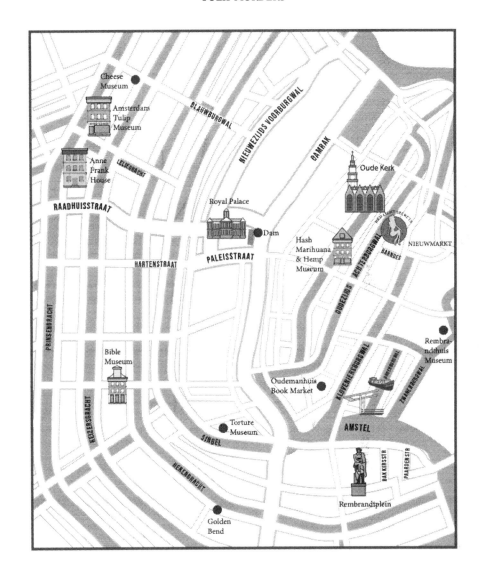

ANDY GRIFFEE

CHAPTER ONE

Willem Haecht's muscle had been for hire for eight years and it showed in the way he moved. His powerful shoulders rolled as he walked and his eyes were half closed in a quietly threatening observation of his fellow human beings. 'Private security consultant', he would mutter through clenched teeth whenever his mother called him a bouncer. He headed for a bar at the end of his shift at Amsterdam's Red Light Secrets Museum of Prostitution. His place of work nestled among the countless sex shops, window prostitutes, peep shows, brothels, coffee shops and drinking dens of the bustling district of northern Wallendeel.

The work was easy but dull compared to his first two years as a bag man for a German pimp. The man had spotted Willem in an amateur cage fight and used ready cash to tempt the 18-year-old away from the mouldering flat that he shared with his mother in a run-down tower block.

He soon became known to the zedenbrigade or vice squad after beating up a rival pimp over a business deal which went wrong. He spent a week in police cells until his victim unaccountably dropped the complaint. But he was picked up six months later when a girl he had been told to rough-up dropped dead of a heart attack a few hours later. His lawyer managed to get the murder charge reduced to manslaughter and then to serious assault, but he still spent four years in prison. Whilst inside, he became part of an all-white gang. Initially, it was purely an act of self-defence. But he was soon caught up in the struggle for racial supremacy among the different groups of inmates. His release on parole was welcomed by the prison's governor. Getting rid of Willem Haecht could only help to reduce the simmering tensions that exploded into violence in his overcrowded cell blocks. Haecht walked out of custody and into a hostel for newly released prisoners and then into a semi-respectable job at the world's first museum dedicated to the world's oldest profession.

The hours were steady and the pay sufficient to feed, clothe and house him. He had other priorities now. Haecht would wander around the numerous rooms of the once-famous brothel, making sure that the tourists and most particularly the stag-parties behaved themselves as they took their selfies and listened to audio stories from Inga, a prostitute for 15 years who was billed as Amsterdam's most famous lady of the night. It was the hen-parties that gave him most trouble. Over-excited groups of British women in fancy dress cackled with laughter and often tried to grope him in the darkness of the rooms. He would sometimes detach one and take her back to his one-room apartment. They were usually too drunk to give him any real satisfaction, but at least they were free, he reflected to himself.

Willem himself was feeling pretty drunk now. As captain of the *United Football Club*, he had insisted two senior 'players' match him drink for drink as they sank ten fluitjes of beer followed by several glasses of caipirinha, a strong Brazilian cocktail. The pathologist would subsequently record a very high blood-alcohol reading.

The trio had sat in a corner and quietly plotted their next 'game' – which was to be an attack on a Muslim community centre. The gang had taken their name from the bodyguards of Winnie Mandela who had terrorised Soweto in their trademark orange and green tracksuits. Willem revelled in the irony. The three men, all in their twenties and all with criminal records for violence, discussed the team list, transport arrangements, timing, facial coverings and weapons of choice (baseball bats). The attack was aimed at dissuading the locals from voting in the fast-approaching general election for the Dutch House of Representatives, and the trickiest discussion centred on how to get this message across. In the end they agreed on a variety of crude sentences to be spray painted on the interior and exterior walls of the target building.

The excitement of the discussion combined with the alcohol and a lack of food had gone to his head. It made him sway slightly as he emerged from the overheated bar into the coolness of the spring evening. He pushed a pair of wraparound Oakley sunglasses over his nose in spite of the approaching darkness and began to steer himself south along the Oudezijds Voorburgwal Canal, towards the quieter part below the bridge between Damstraat and Oude Doelenstraat. He cursed the slow-moving crowd of pedestrians as they meandered along the famous street in the opposite direction to him. He calculated ninety per cent of them were sightseers and only ten per cent were serious customers of the area's world-famous sex services.

After passing the bridge he realised he should have used the bar's toilets. The pressure on his bladder was becoming intolerable and he certainly wouldn't be able to reach his apartment without relieving it. A dark pedestrian alleyway appeared on his left and he veered sharply into it. He could just make out a collection of rubbish bins at the far end. After feeling his way there, he turned to the wall, pulled out his penis and sighed gratefully.

At precisely the same moment, an ambulance drew slowly to a stop at the entrance to the passageway. The driver stayed in his seat while two paramedics jumped down from the rear doors. They were wearing protective helmets and medical face masks covered their noses and mouths. They manhandled a stretcher from the rear of the vehicle and moved swiftly into the alley. Haecht had his free hand on the wall to stop himself swaying and was concentrating on his aim. He only became aware of the men's approach when they were less than five metres away. He tensed, sensing an attempted mugging, but then relaxed when he saw the paramedic uniforms. But wait. Why were they in the alley with him? Had there been someone else lying prone among the dustbins? He was still shaking his head in an attempt to work out what was happening when the taser hit him squarely in the chest. The burst of electricity sent an excruciating pain shooting through every part of his body, contracting his muscles, stunning his brain and turning his legs to jelly. He collapsed into his own puddle of urine and writhed for a few seconds until a syringe was stabbed into his neck. Its contents rendered him unconscious almost immediately. He was quickly rolled onto the stretcher and loaded into the back of the ambulance before it moved slowly away without activating its sirens or lights. It had been stationary for less than two minutes.

Sunrise in early April takes place in Amsterdam shortly before 7am and it was an hour before this on the following morning that the body was discovered. The Oudezijds Acchterburgwal is one of the oldest canals in Amsterdam, dating back to the medieval period. The DHL Express had used its *'floating service centre'*, otherwise known as a boat, to deliver parcels across the city for more than a decade. Couriers on bikes and electric vehicles met it at key hubs to carry its contents for the final mile to their destinations. On this particular morning, the man at the helm was Michiel van Diest. The 60-year-old veteran skipper of tourist boats thought he had seen most things during a lifetime on the city's waterways. When he had passengers instead of parcels, he would tell them about the fifty cars and the one hundred pedestrians pulled out of Amsterdam's canals each year. However, he had never seen a sight like this before.

He had only glanced to the port side for a moment, but it was enough for him to slam the engine into reverse and manoeuvre closer to the side. The body of a young man was draped over the mooring rope of a small launch. His head hung slightly down but was prevented from lolling completely forward by his hunched shoulders. The mooring rope spanned the front of his chest and ran under both armpits. His arms fell forward so that he was suspended awkwardly with everything below his midriff hidden below the surface of the water. Van Diest took a photo of the body on his phone and texted it to his manager at the central depot along with his location and an urgent request to telephone the police.

The Scene of Crime officers were forced to board a police launch to get to the body. They discovered large plastic ties had been used to fix the limbs to the mooring rope. But in some ways, it was the uniformed officers on the towpath who made the more surprising discovery. An empty wine bottle had been placed on the ground immediately above the dead man. In it was the slender stem of a tulip carrying its flower well clear of its leaves. Rubber-gloved hands placed the bottle and the flower into a large see-through evidence bag which eventually joined the corpse of 26-year-old Willem Haecht at the police morgue.

It was there that an astonished pathologist identified it as a perfect example of Semper Augustus, the most famous tulip in the history of horticulture. The flower had fiery ruby-red flames on a white background. The woman eagerly summoned the Amsterdam police force's senior murder investigator and pointed to the tulip with shaking hands.

'Even in the seventeenth century, few people would have ever seen this flower,' she said. 'Most often, the two colours of broken tulips run in long continuous strips down the petals. On this one, as you can see, the colour breaks into flakes that are all symmetrical.'

'So? It's a fancy tulip,' shrugged the detective. She was quietly amused at the younger woman's excitement.

'No. You don't understand.' The scientist opened the reference book in front of her. 'Look for yourself. This was one of the rarest tulips ever known. People would pay a fortune for just one of its bulbs. It was almost impossible to cultivate. This was the scarcest and most beautiful tulip in our country's history. Everyone thought it was lost long ago.' She stabbed a forefinger at a painting in the book. 'Don't you see? No-one has seen this tulip for nearly 400 years!'

CHAPTER TWO

'Oh, my goodness, she's beautiful,' exclaims Nina as she descends into the wide, light-filled saloon of our holiday home. The houseboat is called *Flora* and comprises a rectangular wooden box, roughly the size of two shipping containers, mounted on a raft. Eddie, my little brown Border Terrier, shoots in front of her to begin exploring its nooks and crannies. We could have booked into one of Amsterdam's quirky little boutique hotels but after living on a narrowboat in England for eighteen months, I was keen to stay afloat if we could.

First impressions are encouraging. Lots of bleached blonde wood with shimmering reflections of sunlight on the water bouncing onto the ceiling, generous expanses of soft seating with highly coloured cushions and a very modern kitchen area. Somewhere up front, behind that door, must be the bathroom and two bedrooms.

'Oh, how lovely, flowers!' says Nina as she bends to inspect a vase of ink-coloured Queen of the Night tulips.

'That's nice of them,' I say moving forward to inspect the contents of the fridge. 'And a welcoming bottle of wine too,' I add approvingly. I pour two large glasses while Nina disappears behind the door to the bow and I slump into a very comfortable armchair. This craft is very much a houseboat with no engine but large picture windows and every modern comfort. She is probably twice as wide as *Jumping Jack Flash* but at least my own floating home could make it to a mooring under her own power. However, our new temporary boat and its location look very promising. We are moored on the relatively short stretch of the Groenburgwal Canal which is picturesque, tree-lined and relatively narrow. It is also very central and we are tied up close to the canal's junction with the broad expanse of the Amstel River. The taxi from the train station dropped us off opposite Christ Church, as per our instructions, and the bulk of one of the first neo-Gothic churches to be built in the Netherlands now towers over us – just as the website promised.

'All okay?' I ask as Nina and Eddie re-emerge.

'Perfect. Nice comfortable beds and a big powerful shower.' She grabs her glass and collapses onto the sofa. She is immediately joined by her doting four-legged fan.

'He'll need a good stretch in a bit,' I say nodding at the panting dog. The journey on Eurostar has taken us just under four hours but Eddie has been no trouble, curled up on Nina's lap or occasionally snoring on the floor under our table.

'This was such a good idea,' says Nina, looking out of the window as a small motorboat goes past. 'Isn't the light just lovely?' She has spent most of our journey pouring over a map of the city and cross-referencing it with a guidebook while simultaneously making lists. She loves to do her research and I love to study her doing it.

'We needed a break.' In truth, we are both tentatively feeling our way back to the friendship we enjoyed before our arrival in Oxford, just after Christmas. Nina, herself a young army widow, had tried to help a grieving young American student whose girlfriend had been murdered. She had become very close to him in the process. Feeling lonely and abandoned, I had fallen into a brief relationship with a Thames Valley policewoman. My journalistic instincts had unlocked some painful secrets. But when the truth came to light, there were tragic consequences. We were both badly bruised by the episode and this holiday is an attempt to rebuild our relationship. Not that there has ever been a *'relationship'* as such – unrequited love on my part plus a shared history of entanglements with some unsavoury characters during our travels. Nina raises her head with its short crop of black hair and gives me a level stare with her big dark eyes.

'I'm determined to enjoy myself Jack Johnson. And you are ordered to do so too.'

'Aye-Aye captain.'

She wrinkles her neat little nose in distaste at my nautical banality - just as she did when she first came to my rescue on the Stratford Canal. I had done a deal to try out *Jumping Jack Flash*, a 64-foot-long hire boat with a view to buying her as my home after a ruinous divorce. However, I had been let down by a friend and was struggling to master the boat until Nina appeared out of nowhere and volunteered her services. 'It's very good of you to have me along,' she says with a smile.

'Yes. Well, it's nice to be able to afford it.' Our recent adventure in Oxford ended with me receiving an unexpected financial windfall.

'Well, you're the one who has been here before. I expect you to be a knowledgeable guide.'

My previous trip to the city had been with my ex-wife Debbie. It was one of number of half-hearted attempts to save our marriage and it had rained a lot. 'You're the one who has been doing all the research. However, you have to admit, I got the accommodation right.'

Nina clinks my glass with hers. 'I do. But come on, let's give this dog a walk.' We drain our glasses, slip Eddie onto a lead and head outside. Nina immediately leads the way towards a wooden drawbridge which spans the canal just to our stern. There is a T-shaped metal structure in the centre of the bridge which has a large rectangular weight at one end and chains at the other. It's easy to see that as the weight descends to street level, it would pull the drawbridge vertical to allow taller vessels to pass underneath.

'Ingenious,' I say as we begin to cross it.

'Romantic,' you mean.

'Er … what?'

'This is a Love Lock Bridge.'

'What's one of them then?'

'Look over there.' She indicates the metal chain link fencing of the bridge which has several bicycles propped against it. It's festooned with padlocks and then I notice whole bunches of them attached to other parts of the bridge, like elaborate fungi climbing up and across the bark of a tree. Thousands of padlocks have been attached to each other and they have mushroomed into enormous clumps of metal. 'It's just like the Pont des Arts in Paris. Couples attach padlocks to the bridge as a gesture of love for each other and then they throw the keys into the Seine.'

Having moved closer I can see that many of the padlocks have names scrawled on them. 'How bloody daft is that?'

She digs an elbow into my side. 'It's not daft. It's romantic. Although, actually, it is causing a bit of a problem. The French government became worried that the sheer weight of the locks might cause the bridge to collapse. It took them all away a few years ago but since then about a million have been put back. They reckon that's about 45 tons of extra weight!'

'Madness,' I say, shaking my head.

'There are Love Lock Bridges in Venice too. The Ponte dell'Accademia is one. But the Venetian authorities got very uptight about the risk to the old wooden bridges. They tried to stop shops selling padlocks. Then they ran a campaign aimed at the lovers themselves. They distributed leaflets which said, *'Your love doesn't need chains'* and *'Venice doesn't need your garbage'*.'

'What is this?' I ask laughing. 'Your specialist Mastermind subject – Love Lock Bridges of the World?'

She shrugs her shoulders. 'Actually, Alan told me all about them when we went to Venice for our honeymoon.'

Dammit. I silently curse myself for inviting the confidence. Alan was Captain Alan Wilde, Nina's husband who was killed in a fierce firefight with the Taliban just six weeks after their marriage. Nina still wears the platinum wedding ring he gave her. Her anger and grief have been overwhelming and prevented her from returning the love she knows I have for her - although she has given me hope more recently. She seems to sense my thoughts and transfers Eddie's lead to her other hand so she can link one arm through mine.

'Don't worry,' she laughs. 'There's probably an age limit for leaving love locks and you'll definitely be over it!'

'Ouch. Right, first drinks are on you tonight for that.' At 31, Nina is 15 years younger than me – another reason for my occasional bouts of lovelorn melancholy or jealousy. 'That's if they believe you're old enough to drink.' An elbow digs sharply into my side once again.

We walk on towards the Old Centre, through the lovely late afternoon sunshine, enjoying the sights of the tall terraced canalside homes and dodging the bicycles which arrive silently and surprisingly from all directions at the road junctions. Later, after completing a large circular walk, we stop off at Wertheim Park to let Eddie run free for a while. We are both moved by a memorial in the park which is dedicated to the millions killed at Auschwitz. Six large cracked shards of glass lie flat on the ground and reflect a shattered sky which covers a buried urn that contains the ashes of the dead from the concentration camp. A glass legend reads *nooit meer aushwitz*, 'Never Again, Auschwitz'.

Back on the boat, Nina is reading a paperback subtitled *A History of the World's Most Liberal City* and occasionally breaks off to tell me things as I struggle with the remaining cryptic clues on the back page of my English newspaper. We are in no hurry to leave our houseboat on the first evening of a two-week holiday, but eventually hunger sends Nina out with Eddie and she returns with some fried chicken and Belgian frites slathered in mayonnaise. If I ever find myself on death row, my last meal will include Dutch mayonnaise. We wash our chicken and chips down with the remainder of our complimentary bottle of wine.

'Don't make any arrangements for dinner tomorrow,' I say as Nina yawns and folds down the corner of a page. 'I booked a table at the Waldorf Astoria on Herengracht for eight o'clock while you were out.'

'Ooh, lovely! I can dress up a bit.' She sees me frown and moves across the boat. 'Don't worry. Just make sure you comb your hair and wear a clean and ironed shirt with a jacket and proper trousers. I don't want to eat alone.' She ruffles my mess of overlong curly hair and leans forward to plant a kiss on my cheek. 'Goodnight Jack.' Then we head for our separate bedrooms with my disloyal little dog trotting faithfully behind Nina.

CHAPTER THREE

Dr Beatrix van der Laen might be approaching her sixtieth birthday, but she was finding it hard to stop a childish giggle bubbling to the surface. As Commissioner in charge of Amsterdam's murder squad, she relishes the challenge of bringing killers to justice and every instinct is telling her this latest case is going to be a cracker. She allows herself a little smile instead, coughs, adjusts her wire-framed spectacles and nods at the young man sitting opposite her at the large conference table.

'First slide please, Robert.' 'Was slide the right word?', she wonders to herself. It used to be, but she has no idea if it is still appropriate for a PowerPoint presentation. Ah, who cares? Beatrix is one of those lucky people who find it easy to shrug off any concern about what people think of her. She has followed her own star ever since she inherited a healthy bank account and a large townhouse on Prinsengracht, the outermost of the city's four main canals. She had been just 23 at the time of her father's death but she completed her PhD in psychology and immediately joined the city's police force where her sharp brain, independent spirit and cheerful demeanour saw her rise quickly through the ranks. She likes men and has enjoyed many trysts over the years, but she remains unmarried and is content to share her beautiful home with a condescending Persian cat.

Beatrix sees the young man look to the bulky person at the head of the table for a reassuring nod of agreement. It makes her sigh inwardly. Robert Fruin is the opposite of her, forever seeking approval and worrying about the opinion of others. You can see it in his over-careful appearance. He is wearing an expensively tailored blue suit over a light blue polo shirt that is open at the neck. She has no idea how he keeps the shadow of six o'clock stubble on his jaw at exactly the same length each day. His glossy black hair is always immaculately trimmed, and his impeccable nails also suggest regular visits to a professional manicurist. Beatrix thinks he is very good looking with his strong jaw, high cheekbones, lively intelligent eyes and slim, athletic figure. She might even have tried to bed him if it wasn't for the fact that he was her deputy, and gay.

The Regional Chief Commissioner looks in turn at Robert, the Head of Public Affairs sitting alongside him and then Beatrix before giving his assent. A head and shoulders photograph of Willem Haecht appears on the screen at the far end of the room.

'So,' begins Beatrix. 'Who? What? Where? When? How? And Why? Let's start with who? Twenty-six-year-old Willem Haecht, a security guard at the Red Light Secrets Museum of Prostitution. A year ago, he finished a four-year stretch for beating up a working girl who had cheated on his boss at the time. She died shortly afterwards. Material found at his flat suggests he had an unhealthy interest in anti-Islamic activities and far right politics.' She nods at Robert again and he taps his laptop with a forefinger to change the picture to one of Haecht's body hanging across the slanting mooring rope.

'Where and When?' says Robert. 'He was abducted from an alleyway off Princenhofst at 10.35 pm and found like this in the nearby OZ Acchterburgwal canal, opposite Barndestag the following morning. Yesterday, at 6am.'

'Right near to the Five Star Erotic Theatre,' adds Beatrix. 'Although I can't say it appears to merit being called either *"Five Star"* or particularly *"Erotic".*'

'Cause of death?' asks the Chief Commissioner. He is used to her humour and knows that it hides a deeply serious person with an excellent mind.

'The How?' replies Beatrix. She knows she could be sitting in the overweight older man's chair instead of him, but she despises office politics, loathes budgets and prefers to stay at the sharp end of operational policing.

'Preliminary post-mortem results suggest he was tasered in the chest and then injected in the neck with Special K,' says Robert. The Chief Commissioner frowns.

'Ketamine,' explains Beatrix. 'He'd have been unconscious within 30 seconds.'

'But that didn't kill him,' continues Robert. 'That was an overdose of digitalis. It's a plant-based poison which would have stopped his heart within seconds.'

'From the foxglove,' smiles Beatrix. 'I have some in my garden. Quite lovely.'

'He had been drinking heavily. We don't know who with, or where yet, but hopefully he paid with plastic.'

'That is slightly less interesting than how he was abducted and how the body was placed in the water,' says Beatrix, leaning forward. 'Show the video'.

A CCTV image appears on the screen. The camera seems to be placed across the canal. Robert presses play and the four people in the room can clearly see the highlighted figure of Haecht swerve into the alley. The action is followed shortly afterwards by the arrival and departure of the ambulance and its crew.

'It's very professional,' observes Robert. 'They move fast, and their faces are hidden at all times. The ambulance was stolen a couple of hours before the hit. Its plates were changed and then it was abandoned in Vondelpark. It's with forensics now but I doubt they'll get anything from it. You can see the men are wearing medical gloves.' He returns to the image of the dead man suspended in the water. 'What we can't work out is how they manoeuvred the body into this position.'

Beatrix taps the table to emphasise her points. 'It's right in the heart of De Wallen, busy all night and swamped with cameras. He is abducted alongside one canal and dumped in another, barely 150 metres away as the crow flies. Did they do it straight away? Or did they park up somewhere, finish him off and go back just before sunrise when it was quieter? The team is still going through all the footage, but this particular place seems to be in a blind spot at water level. And so up he pops without anyone noticing and strapped to the rope with plastic ties. It's almost as though the body has been carefully arranged too. But at the moment, we have no idea how ... or why.'

'And then there's the tulip,' says the Head of Public Affairs.

Beatrix frowns at the interruption by the sharp-faced little man. 'Let's stay with Haecht for the moment. Obviously, we're talking to his workmates and tracking down his friends, looking at his computer. All the usual stuff. But this doesn't feel personal. And it also feels too elaborate to be criminals settling scores with each other.' She grins at the others. 'It's a good one alright. And, of course, the flower takes it to another level.'

Robert shows a picture of the Semper Augustus on the screen. It is standing upright in a green wine bottle. There is a moment of silence as they all take it in.

'There are millions of people all over the world looking at that photograph,' says the Head of Public Affairs in an awed voice. 'I know you wanted to keep it quiet for now,' he acknowledges to Beatrix as she shakes her head. 'But once the press had the tip-off, it was impossible.'

'It didn't come from my team,' says Beatrix flatly.

'Nor mine,' says the Head of Public Affairs. He shakes his head in wonderment. 'Semper Augustus. The rarest and most valuable tulip ever cultivated. Last seen in the first half of the seventeenth century. It's gone crazy. It's on the front page of almost every newspaper in the world and every single television channel is going mad. It's the top trending subject on all social media. How did it survive? Could it be cultivated again from scratch? What is it worth? I was told that one particular tulip expert sat in a television studio at NOS NL for eight solid hours doing interview after interview.'

'I heard a grower on the radio this morning estimating that it's worth a million euros,' says Robert.

'Where is it now?' asks the Chief Commissioner. 'Not replanted in your garden, I hope Beatrix?'

'It's still at the lab,' she replies, smiling politely at his attempted joke. 'They're very excited.'

'I hope they don't damage it. I've had a request to pass it on to the Ministry of Agriculture when we're finished with it. I think the Minister wants it for a photoshoot.'

'Anyone would think there was an election coming up,' mutters Robert quietly.

'The question isn't just how it survived for four centuries,' says Beatrix firmly. 'It's also why anyone would place it near the body of an inconsequential young man like Willem Haecht. We are going to have to dig very deeply into every aspect of his life.'

'There's the other botanical connection with the killing,' says Robert, steepling his long thin fingers and looking around the room. 'The digitalis that was used to kill him. As Beatrix said, it's the generic name for foxglove plants which contain toxic alkaloids.'

'What are you saying Inspector?' asks the Chief Commissioner. 'That we have a group of crazed killer-botanists at large in Amsterdam?' The Head of Public Affairs gives a little snort of laughter. 'That's not to be repeated to the press. Understood?' adds his boss, suddenly looking serious and pointing a fat forefinger at the little man.

'Of course not. But we do need a public relations strategy for this. It's huge. Are you planning on a press conference Beatrix?'

'Not yet,' she says firmly. 'Just issue the statement saying we want anyone with relevant information to get in touch. It's going to be hard enough as it is working in the middle of this tulipmania.'

'Alright then,' says the Chief Commissioner, clapping his hands together. 'Keep me posted and you can have a meeting whenever you need one.' He stands, as do all the others except Beatrix. 'Tell me if you need more people and I'll try to keep the press, the politicians and the First Chief Commissioner off your back as much as I can.'

Robert and Beatrix gather their papers and laptops together and take the stairs down from the fifth-floor conference room. They continue past the second floor, which houses the rest of their team, and stroll over the pedestrian crossing in front of the ugly red-brick police headquarters on Elandsgracht. They walk to the nearby canal and Beatrix lights herself a small cigar. She considerately blows the smoke out over the water, taking care to keep it away from Robert's face.

'You're genuinely excited, aren't you?' asks the younger man.

'Of course. We can only do our best – but that usually is sufficient. If you're too tired or worried to handle a case like this when it comes along, you might as well give up.'

Robert shakes his head in admiration. 'I wish I could stay as cool and cheerful as you. What's next?'

She takes another pull on the cigar. She tries not to inhale these days, but she still loves the smell of the smoke as she exhales. It reminds her of her beloved father. 'We shall have an end-of-day debrief and see what the team has found out. We can decide on the duties of the night shift and then go home for a good night's sleep. No point in being too tired to think clearly. And you can get home to that husband of yours.'

'I told Jan I might be working late. Maybe I'll stop off at the pool on the way.'

Robert is a keen swimmer and finds that a hundred lengths recharges his mind at the same time as they tone his body.

Beatrix sighs. 'And I suppose I won't be able to cycle to work for a while. The boss doesn't like the press photographing his senior murder detective on two wheels in the middle of an investigation. He says it gives the wrong impression - a lack of urgency. So, I have to sit in the back of car going nowhere fast instead.' She flicks the stub of her cigar into the water and they turn to make their way back to her team's offices. A man and a woman suddenly block their path. 'Dr van der Laen,' says the man, brandishing his phone under the detective's chin. 'Is there anything you can tell us about the Tulip Murder?'

'Do you know any more about the Semper Augustus?' says the woman urgently. She is holding a pen expectantly poised above a spiral bound notebook.

Robert moves forward with an outstretched arm to clear them away, but Beatrix extends her own hand and restrains him. 'It's okay Robert, they're just doing their job.' She looks at the pair of reporters calmly. 'Now my dears, I'm running a murder inquiry and trying to have a quiet smoke with my colleague here. If there is anything that we want to tell you, we'll do it through the press office and we'll tell everyone at the same time. After all, it wouldn't be fair of me to give you a scoop now, would it? So, do yourselves a favour and stop hanging around here. You'll get the same answer from all of my team - only they might not be as polite as me.'

'Can I have a picture?' asks the male reporter, raising his mobile phone up to face height. He knows that Beatrix is sometimes referred to as 'The Queen' by rank-and-file officers on account of her name and the extraordinary similarity in looks to the former monarch of the Netherlands who abdicated in 2013.

'Of course, my dear.' She zips up the gilet she is wearing over her linen trouser suit and plumps up her blonde-grey hair. She poses with a sweet smile and then leaves them standing on the pavement. 'Come on Detective Inspector Fruin, we have work to do.'

CHAPTER FOUR

The six 17th and 18th century merchants' palaces which comprise Amsterdam's Waldorf Astoria Hotel are immaculate from the outside. The paintwork looks recent, the stone looks scrubbed, the brasswork is polished and the windows are shining. The hotel's buildings stretch impressively along a substantial length of the Herengracht, or The Lords' Canal, with a double staircase sweeping elegantly up to the main entrance. Two uniformed doormen in bowler hats open both doors and bow their heads as Nina precedes me into the marble floored lobby area. I see them exchange a quick glance at each other. They have much to appreciate.

Mrs Angelina Wilde looks stunning in a little black dress, high heels and a single choker of pink pearls. She has been to a hairdresser after our tiring morning at the monumental Amsterdam Museum where she insisted that we get a proper introduction to the history of the city. The crowds and the sensory overload had sent me to my bed for a luxurious afternoon nap with Eddie. Nina said we could both be heard snoring in tandem.

I ask another flunkey for directions to the bar and he insists on escorting us to *The Vault*. It must have been the treasure room for the Mayor of Amsterdam when he lived here because we pass through a thick metal strongroom door at its entrance. I am more interested in the liquid treasure lined up behind a gleaming dark wood bar which is flanked by rows of highly polished glasses. Two flutes of chilled champagne are soon bubbling nicely in front of us. Yes indeed, Sir does have a table for two booked for dinner in the restaurant this evening. Cheers.

'I could get used to being rich,' I say, leaning back into the comfort of my armchair, sipping my drink and trying not to admire Nina's crossed bare legs too obviously. 'You look fabulous by the way. You'd make a bishop kick a hole in a stained-glass window.'

'Sorry?'

'Raymond Chandler. He said a blonde in one of his books would *"make a bishop kick a hole in a stained-glass window".*'

'But I'm not a blonde.'

I sigh. 'Yes Nina. I had noticed that. Chandler could turn a phrase. He said another character – it must have been Philip Marlowe - felt as *"inconspicuous as a tarantula on a slice of angel cake".*'

'Yes well, talking of being inconspicuous, you could at least have shined your shoes.'

I look guiltily down at my scuffed old brogues and automatically try to shine the top of the right one on the back of my left trouser leg. I notice the barman in his ridiculously smart black waistcoat, white shirt and black tie giving the hint of a smirk. No doubt, he thinks I am punching considerably above my weight. 'Sorry...' I mutter, and then think better of it. 'No sod it, I'm not sorry. That's one of the joys of being rich. You don't have to give a toss what other people think.'

Nina dabs her moist lips with a napkin which leaves a trace of red lipstick on the thick linen and smiles. 'I'm not sure your windfall makes you qualify as rich, Jack.'

'Well, I feel it,' I say stubbornly. 'But that's probably because I'm dining out with you rather than the size of my bank account.'

Nina affects the voice of a Southern belle. 'Why sir, that is a mighty gallant thing for you to say. You are a gallant gentleman, sir.'

'Wrong part of America,' I say laughing. 'If you're going to channel Audrey's Breakfast at Tiffany's look, you should be speaking like a *'Niew Yoiker.'*

She pokes out the tip of her pink tongue at me and bends over a search engine on her mobile and taps away. 'Ah here it is. Scott Fitzgerald. *"The rich are different from you and me. They possess and enjoy early, and it does something to them, makes them soft where we are hard, and cynical where we are trustful in a way that, unless you were born rich, it is very difficult to understand."* That's what I find so interesting about this city,' says Nina, returning her phone to a little clutch bag. 'There was no real history of aristocracy here, or even royalty. They built the city on land stolen from the sea and its prosperity came from trade and the most successful and richest merchants ran things. It was very meritocratic in its own way.'

'Well look around you Nina,' I say as we take our places under chandeliers in the hotel's magnificent restaurant. 'If the Dutch are meritocratic, it didn't stop the richest living like princes, did it? The early Dutch might have built their wealth from nothing. But their sons and daughters inherited it. I think Papa Hemingway had it right? The only difference between the rich and the rest of us is that they have more money. I don't think it pays to romanticise them too much.'

The food and wine are exquisite, the service attentive without being fawning and the company sparkling. Nina is on fine form as we name our favourite paintings from the morning, begin to plan an itinerary for the rest of our break and laugh at some of the absurdities of our recent adventures. However, I notice Nina avoids any reference to our recent time in Oxford and I am careful to follow suit.

We are just examining the dessert menu when a nearby door swings open. It is clear from comings and goings throughout our meal that it leads to a private dining room. Occasional glimpses over the shoulders of waiters suggest that, unlike the largely white and very modern restaurant space that we are in, the adjoining room is wood-panelled and hung with old oil-paintings. Gales of raucous male laughter and shouting emerge every time the door is opened for more silver trays of food or more bottles of wine and spirits.

'Talking of the rich, it sounds like they're having a good time,' says Nina as she points out an item on the menu to our waiter.

'We are very sorry if it should disturb you madam,' he says quietly. I find it strange that so many Dutch seem to speak English with an American accent. It must be the impact of US television shows. 'Perhaps you would like to move to a quieter table?'

'No, no. That's fine thank you. Have you chosen Jack?'

We are just finishing our coffee and I am contemplating a whisky nightcap in *The Vault* when the door of the private dining room bursts open again. Our alcohol intake has been pretty modest so far - two champagne flutes and half a bottle of Chateau de Saint-Martin each. The same cannot be said for the guests in the private dining room. While the waiters refreshing the food and drink have been careful to enter and leave as quietly as possible, an occasional dinner-jacketed guest has forcefully banged open the door to weave his way to the lavatories. They invariably leave it ajar until their return so that the party's noise bursts in on the quiet murmur of the restaurant for increasingly lengthy periods. The restaurant's manager is clearly concerned about this. He orders someone to close the door with increasing regularity and once, he even condescends to do it himself.

'I'm just going to freshen up,' says Nina. 'Won't be a second. Maybe you can order a taxi back to the boat Jack? I don't fancy a return trip in these shoes.'

Nina is just coming back to the table when the dining room door is thrown open so suddenly that I am surprised it stays on its hinges. A bear-like man with a large paunch and a square shaped head stands swaying in the doorway. He is holding a bottle of vodka by its neck down to one side of him. There are beads of sweat on his brow and the redness of his face contrasts sharply with the grey-white colour of his hair. This thick hair is side-parted and swept back in a quiff, but some strands have fallen forward across his eyes. His bow tie hangs undone, and the top two buttons of his shirt have also come adrift, revealing a small nest of curly white chest hair. His head seems unable to remain still on his neck, constantly rolling to left and right as though striving for an equilibrium all of its own. I can't ever remember seeing a man so inebriated and still standing upright.

Nina has frozen at the sight of the man but, as I return my gaze to him, his glassy eyes seem to come into focus on her and then onto her empty chair. The low hum of conversation from the other tables has fallen silent while a loud hubbub is still emerging from the private room.

'Lovely lady,' he booms, 'Please take your seat. Here I hold it out for you.' His accent is East European, his voice thick and slurred. He lurches forward in a sudden rush which ends when he puts a meaty hand on the back of Nina's chair. The other still holds the vodka bottle. He scrapes back the chair. 'Please. I insist for the beautiful lady.'

Nina exchanges a look with me and then slides into the chair. A young waiter appears near our table and is hovering anxiously in case he is needed.

'There,' says the man with a lop-sided smile. His puffy eyes are just slits now and I genuinely wonder if he is about to pass out. But instead, he drops his head down to the same level as Nina's and stares greedily down into her cleavage. A bead of sweat on his forehead threatens to follow his gaze. 'Are you comfortable now? Have I made you comfortable, beautiful lady with the lovely neck? A neck like a swan. Maybe you give me a kiss to say thank you, eh? What do you think?'

Three things then happen in quick succession. The young waiter moves forward and puts a hand on the man's nearest arm. He is a foot shorter, probably half the weight and thirty years younger than the dinner guest who reacts by sweeping his own arm outwards, straight and back. I think it is a very inebriated attempt to free himself of the waiter's grip, but the arm keeps swinging and the forearm connects with the young man's face. It sends him sprawling, backwards onto the floor. Now the big man is holding the bottle upside down like a club as the remaining vodka pours out onto the thick carpet. He is looking wildly all around him, poised to retaliate.

That is when the third thing happens. Two more large men appear in the dining room's doorway just as I am rising to my feet.

These two are younger and shaven headed. They show no sign of being drunk and seem to size up the situation in seconds before swiftly moving forward onto either side of the man. They each grip him firmly, one hand on a bicep and the other under an elbow and simply lift him off his feet and backwards through the open door which slams shut behind them. There is a stunned silence and then, in what feels like slow motion, people begin to move and talk again. The dazed waiter is helped to his feet by two colleagues. I move over to kneel by Nina's chair to check she is alright. Behind her, I see the manager reopen the dining room door and hurriedly slide into it sideways.

'Well, Jack. You certainly know how to show a girl a good time.'

'You've only been in the city for 24 hours and you've already got men fighting over you.'

'Only some men. I notice you didn't get involved.'

'It was all under control. And I had a bit of coffee left to finish.'

'Well, let's get back to the boat then, shall we tiger?'

'Yes, this is a bit of a rough dive, isn't it?'

However, before we can move the restaurant manager re-emerges from the dining room with another man. He flicks a finger in the air and a spare chair materialises at our table for two. The second man sits down on it and brushes some imaginary dust from his lap. He is wearing a velvet dinner jacket with a conventional thin black tie. His hair is closely cropped with a pronounced downward V-shape at the front that descends into the centre of his forehead. He has a neatly trimmed moustache and a beard which is shaped to a point below his chin, repeating the shape of his widow's peak. I feel as though I have seen this face before and then realise it looked out at me from countless paintings at the museum this morning. I estimate him to be in his late fifties.

'Sir. Madam,' he says looking at us each in turn. The manager is standing respectfully behind our new table companion, his hands clasped together meekly in front of his groin. 'I am the host of the small dinner party taking place next door and I take full responsibility for the actions of my guests. I am told these actions were unforgiveable and I wish to extend the most fulsome of apologies to you both – and particularly you madam. I am told my guest made a very unwelcome overture to you of a ... of a sexual nature.'

'I think it is the man himself who should be apologising,' I say.

'No,' says Nina quickly. 'I think it's best for him to stay where he is.'

'You're right,' I add. 'But it was the waiter who was physically attacked. Maybe you should be worrying about him.'

The newcomer nods seriously. 'I shall certainly make amends with him. And I would also like to compensate you for your ruined evening. Please,' he says turning his head to speak to the manager behind him, 'make sure the account for this couple's dinner is added to mine.'

'There's no need to do that,' I say defensively, but Nina jumps in again.

'That's very kind of you. Thank you.'

'You are English?'

'Nina Wilde and Jack Johnson,' says Nina. I notice that the man doesn't reciprocate with his own name.

'May I offer you a brandy perhaps. To ease the shock?'

'I'm not in shock but I would like a brandy. Jack's more of a whisky man.'

'A Remy Martin then. Two of them. And, let me see, shall we say a Chivas Regal?' There has been no consultation. This man is obviously someone who is used to making decisions and getting his own way. 'Actually, I'll have a Highland Park please' I say, purely out of devilment.

The man smiles and shrugs. 'Of course. You are here for pleasure, or business?'

'A two-week holiday,' says Nina.

'Although I may try to get a travel feature out of it,' I add.

'Jack's a journalist.'

'Really? I do hope I can persuade you to avoid writing about this unfortunate incident. It would be unfair on a splendid hotel and their staff don't you think? I am equally hopeful you will not feel the need to report this to the police. It is only too obvious that my guest has had far too much to drink. He will be mortified in the morning.' The manager himself returns with our drinks on a small silver tray and then retires out of earshot. 'To forgiveness?' He raises his glass expectantly, the question hanging in the air.

'To forgiveness,' says Nina and moves in to clink his glass while I do the same.

'Your English is excellent.'

'Thank you. I had a very traditional education, and I am told it is slightly too proper and should be more colloquial, more conversational. However, it is what it is.'

'Is it a special occasion?' I ask, nodding at the firmly closed door of the private room.

He shrugs. 'Not really. A little politics and a little business.'

'And a lot of drink,' says Nina with a smile to soften the observation.

We briefly discuss where we are staying, what we plan to do and when we must return. Finally, he sighs, drains his brandy and rises to his feet. 'Now, I am afraid I must return to my guests and oversee an orderly dispersal. It has been a pleasure meeting you both and I apologise again. May I?' He reaches across to lift Nina's hands to his lips and kisses it. Then he turns to me and shakes my hand, but he seems to have a sudden thought and doesn't release it. 'In fact, I have a sudden idea. You are guests in our lovely city, and you have been more than a little accommodating. Of course, the best way to see Amsterdam is from the water but then you have to share a boat with other tourists and pay such exorbitant fares. I own a comfortable motor launch. Perhaps I may take you both out on a little tour tomorrow? It is the least I can do.'

'That would be really lovely,' says Nina, looking at me.

'Um, yes, sure, thanks very much,' I add.

'Excellent!' he says releasing my hand. 'Now you write down where your boat is, and I shall pick you up from there. Shall we say 11am?' I write the address of *Flora's* mooring on a page of his small leather notebook, and he exchanges it for an embossed business card. He stands, bows his head slightly to each of us and returns behind the door to the private room.

'Well,' says Nina, draining her glass. 'That all ended rather interestingly. What's his name?

'Tulp,' I read from the card. 'Cornelius Tulp.'

CHAPTER FIVE

At the same time as Jack and Nina walked back to their boat, a newspaper columnist called Jan Goessens was also making his way home. Goessens had begun his evening with an obliging stranger in the cabin of a sauna in the Old Centre and then moved on to Club Church, a cavernous club where he had propped up the bar to watch a men-only dance party getting underway. There was an underwear-only dress code in place, but some of the men were breaking the rules by wearing tank tops and others were breaking the rules by dispensing with their pants altogether.

After half an hour, he decided he wasn't in the mood for partying. He had a slight headache and it was a very young crowd. He put his three-piece cashmere suit back on and retrieved his valuables including a pocket watch on a silver chain. Goessens toyed with the idea of calling in on Turkish Afet and letting her go to work with her paddle - but dismissed the idea with a yawn. He was tired and a little unfit, anxious about his rapidly thinning hair and growing paunch. A 55-year-old man like him needed to go to the gym more often, drink less, eat well and look after himself properly. He would call it a night and make an early start in the morning on his think-piece for that week's paper. The upcoming election meant that his editor was showing a closer interest than usual in his output.

Goessens's comfortable flat was situated in the Southern Canal Belt and he decided the stroll would do him good. He barely noticed his surroundings, the other pedestrians or the yellow street-sweeping machine that was working close behind him. He stopped briefly on the bridge across the Amstel to admire the view and then moved on towards Rembrandtplein. He was thinking about how to pitch an article on the history of the integration of Jewish people into Dutch society.

The common belief was that his country had been the benign and tolerant exception in a Christian Europe that either ejected the Old People, as they were called in Amsterdam, or kept them in humiliating ghettos. And yet, you didn't need to scratch far beneath the surface to find examples of 17th century Dutch laws against them. They were not allowed to enter certain trades or seek converts and a Jewish man could not have a sexual relationship with a Christian female. He therefore believed the Jews weren't wholly absorbed into domestic Dutch culture right from the start. Rather, he would argue, they remained part of an independent Dutch Jewish culture – Jews first, and Dutch second. It was a historical trend which, he would say, was reinforced by the arrival of Ashkenazi Jews in much greater numbers. These newcomers built their own synagogue and created their own autonomous educational institutions and burial societies. They had their own dietary regulations and they ran a Yiddish press. They dressed differently from Dutch men and women and spoke their own language.

Guessens had decided he was the man who was going to set the record straight. He would repeat the claim of one Holocaust survivor that the Anne Frank industry was the biggest public relations exercise ever carried out on behalf of an entire country. It left the impression that the Jews were all in hiding during World War Two, and that the entire Dutch population was in the Resistance. He would call this what it was, thought Guessens. A whitewash. Modern historians were beginning to write about this airbrushing of Dutch history, but it was him, Jan Goessens who would write the seminal article setting the record straight and hail it as a lesson from the country's past to inform its present and its future.

He would remind his readers that the Dutch, who had declared themselves neutral, quickly folded in the face of Hitler's invasion. Members of the Dutch Nazi party, the NSB, actually lined the streets to welcome the first German soldiers into Amsterdam. The 80,000 Jewish population of Amsterdam plummeted to only 5,000 by 1945. His article would stress how many of the Dutch authorities enthusiastically co-operated with the Nazis – organising special long 'holiday' trains to the camps, impounding radios and bicycles, carefully mapping the distribution of Jews throughout the city and sacking all Jewish teaching staff from the university. He had discovered that there were only 60 German officers posted in Amsterdam during the war - and the Dutch did the rest of the dirty work themselves. Dutch police took part in the biggest raids on Jewish homes or hiding places. The Frank family had actually been arrested by three Dutch policemen, and one of them continued serving in the city's force until 1980. One Dutch civil servant even invented a counterfeit-proof personal identity card to help Berlin's occupation of his country. Much of this inconvenient history had been brushed under the carpet after the war. It didn't suit the approved narrative of heroic resistance to the Nazis and punishment for doing so. But the people who had helped to run the city for the Germans were needed for its reconstruction and to rebuild the shattered economy.

Of course, he didn't condone the holocaust. He would need to be careful to stress this point. But the actions of the so-called collaborators during the war supported his thesis. This was what happened when new arrivals into a society didn't bother to assimilate into it. They would eventually be rejected by the majority during periods of immense social upheaval. And now it was happening all over again. As he walked home slowly, he mentally bent and shaped his argument so that it would support his conclusions. Immigration was bad for Dutch society and bad for the true Amsterdammers. We must be less of an easy touch with our benefits and our social housing, or these new incomers will reap the whirlwind when the majority lose patience with the aliens living among them. His mood had lifted as he mentally mapped out the bones of his article. There would be a backlash of course. There always was. But his editor would be supportive. It was all good for his profile.

Guessens had nearly crossed Remblantplein, a small square with a statue of the famous artist at its centre, when he became aware of the street-sweeping machine parked sideways and directly in his path. He was vaguely aware that the noise of its engine and its circling brushes had been with him for a while. One of its crew was dressed from head to toe in orange overalls with a baseball cap covering his head and a facemask covering his mouth and nostrils. The man stepped in front of Guessens with an outstretched arm. The workman didn't want him to go near the business-end of the vehicle and was diverting him to the safety of its rear. Guessens shrugged, put his hands in his jacket pockets and made the short detour. He was to regret that simple action because it left him powerless to struggle when the rear doors of the machine swung open in his face. Two men, also dressed in orange, were crouched in the box-shaped rear of the lorry. They yanked him off his feet and into the empty darkness before he could come to his senses. The crewman outside slammed the door shut and moved quickly to the driver's seat where he turned off the brushes and put the engine into first gear. A pair of knees and two strong hands pinned Guessen face down in the dust and dirt of the metal floor as the vehicle left the square. The second man, who was wearing a head-torch, pressed the contents of a syringe into his neck. The torch was still on as Guessen closed his eyes and felt an overwhelming blackness sweep through him.

CHAPTER SIX

This time, Dr Beatrix van der Laen and her deputy Robert Fruin are among the first police officers to arrive at the location of the body. They arrive just before dawn, straight from their respective beds and without breakfast. Once again, the helmsman of an early working boat has spotted a body hanging limp across a mooring rope. This one is located on the broad expanse of the Kloveniersburgwal which flows south to the Amstel River from Nieuwmarkt, one of the city's oldest central squares. The corpse is suspended between two boats near a road bridge and directly opposite a large performing arts theatre.

The senior of the two detectives is nursing a cardboard cup of coffee in both hands as she watches Scene-of-Crime specialists in all-white suits lay the sodden corpse out on the towpath and busy themselves over it. There is an early morning breeze fluttering the plastic police tape and a light rain has begun to fall. 'They said it would be sunshine and showers,' she mutters to herself. 'Just our luck to get the showers.' She thinks about sending Robert to her car for an umbrella but then decides that would be an abuse of power and does it herself. When Robert approaches her, she moves it to one side so he can share it.

'His wallet was in his suit pocket with quite a lot of cash and all his plastic. He's Jan Goessens, born 55-years-ago. He lived on Keizergracht. Running the checks now. Time of death – 5.30am. Or at least that's when his silver pocket watch stopped working.'

'Not necessarily time of death then,' says Beatrix. 'Time of immersion in the water.'

Robert concedes the point with a polite tilt of the head. 'Let's have a look then.' The pair make their way over to the body which is stretched out on its back with arms akimbo. She frowns at the pale puffy flesh of the face and the open staring eyes. 'I'm sure I've seen him somewhere before. Jan Goessens…'

The pathologist stands up to face them, pulling rubber gloves from her hands and freeing some dark curls of hair from under her hood as she does so. 'Hello Beatrix. Robert. Pretty sure he didn't die from drowning. I'll know for sure after I open him up. Plastic ties were used again and there's at least one puncture mark on the neck, just behind and below the ear, same as the last one. I'll run some tests to identify it as quickly as I can.'

Beatrix nods her thanks, bends both knees and crouches for a closer look at the features of the late Jan Goessens. She's sure she has come across the name before somewhere. Then she stretches upright with a grunt and takes a sweeping look at the surroundings. Impressively large buildings sweep along both sides of the canal, although it is nothing more than a watery cul-de-sac. She knows it was originally dug as a defensive ditch but lost its purpose when the city wall was taken down to make way for houses. During the war, it became a border for the Jewish quarter, separating it off from the rest of the city on behalf of the occupiers, the Germans. And now it is the location of the latest Tulip Murder victim.

Ah yes, the tulip? Could it be? She looks around her again with real purpose and Robert quickly catches on. 'You think there could be another Semper Augustus?' he asks.

'Why not? Everything else is the same. Round up a few uniforms and have a look.'

She watches Robert marshal five officers and take them a hundred metres further up the canal. Then they stretch out across the road and walk in a line until they are a hundred metres past her. She sees Robert turn and shrug with both arms raised. Then she looks across the road at the theatre. It is a grand building with large arched windows on the first floor and two entrance doors on either side of a six-columned classical portico. A man is opening one of the doors from the inside and pinning it back. She checks her watch. Eight o'clock. They have already been there an hour. Beatrix crosses the road towards the rectangle of light and sees from a plaque that the building is a deconsecrated church. Beatrix nods at the man, collapses her umbrella and wanders into a large marble-floored reception area which has more columns rising to a high ceiling. But it isn't the grandeur of the entrance hall which catches her eye. It is the painted metal buckets filled with mixed tulips which flank the reception desk. She walks over to the first and peers at it closely. Then she does the same with the second bucket. The member of staff materialises in front of her and coughs. 'May I help you?'

She looks up at him and smiles. 'Yes, you can. I am a police officer and I am going outside to fetch my colleagues. In the meantime, you are to watch these flowers. You are not to touch them, and you are not to let anyone else near them. Is that clear?'

The man creases his forehead at Beatrix and then looks at the crowded bucket of mixed blooms. Suddenly his eyes open wide and he leans forward so that his head is almost directly above them. 'My god! Is that ... is that the famous tulip? Another one?'

'Yes,' says Beatrix. 'I very much think it is.'

Unfortunately, for the police, the discovery means that within half an hour a crowd of several hundred people is milling excitedly outside the theatre. Beatrix had failed to warn the member of staff not to use social media during the sixty seconds she was gone. His photograph is quickly picked up by his colleagues and shared further. Within five minutes an excited breakfast radio presenter is telling the city about another astonishing discovery of the long-lost tulip. The police press officer, who is just finishing his night shift in the headquarters building, is overwhelmed with enquiries from the rest of the press and media. The crowd shows considerably less interest in the black van which takes the body of Jan Goessens away than the single flower hidden in the centre of a mixed bunch of tulips that has been found in a bucket in the theatre's reception area. Every time the main door opens or closes, it surges forward for an attempt to see beyond the two officers standing guard.

Beatrix is annoyed at herself. She should have stayed with the flower and telephoned Robert to join her. Now she has this ridiculous circus to contend with. Robert brings her another cup of coffee, courtesy of the chastened member of staff.

'The office says Jan Goessen is a newspaper columnist. Very outspoken and very right wing.'

'Of course,' says Beatrix, who is annoyed at herself all over again. 'I knew I'd seen that face before. He has a photo by-line at the top of his column.' She pulls a face. 'I couldn't stand him. He was a racist shit-stirrer… may he Rest in Peace. How are we doing with CCTV?'

Robert shakes his head in frustration. 'The cameras on the front of the theatre are all pointing down across the entrance rather than across the canal and there's nothing on the other side as far as we can see. And the staff can't explain how the flower got there. There was someone on the desk until 10pm last night, but she says she was very busy and distracted after the play ended. There was quite a crowd in the foyer and someone could have easily slipped it into the bucket without her noticing.'

'So, what do we have? Another victim with right wing political views. We can probably assume he was snatched off the street again, but we don't know where or when. He is knocked out or even killed by an injection again. And he is discovered in the same position and held in place in the same way, with plastic ties. The killers, or those who disposed of the body, have once again been very careful to avoid the street cameras. Meanwhile, a second flower that no-one has seen for a very long time is left nearby.'

Robert coughs apologetically. 'The Chief Commissioner wants a briefing.'

Beatrix sighs. 'Of course he does. Alright, tell them to spread the net wider for cameras. And ask if there's a back door or some way we can leave quietly with this damn flower.'

CHAPTER SEVEN

I am dozing in the warmth, idly contemplating the ripples of water that are reflected on the wooden ceiling above me, when Nina's head peers around the door. Her hair is wet and her running singlet looks pretty damp too. 'Come on Jack, you lazy sod. It's nine o'clock and the day is wasting. I've already been out with Eddie and I picked up some breakfast from a stall on the corner. Coffee's in the pot. I'm off for a shower.'

I pull on a towelling robe and discover a plate full of raw herring and another much smokier fish in the centre of the dining table. A bowl of pickles sits nearby with a loaf of dense-looking brown bread. I wolf down half of Nina's bounty, help myself to some cheese from the fridge and then pull out my laptop to see what has been happening in the world.

The BBC News website is usually my first point of call and one headline immediately catches my attention. The banner tells me it was posted an hour ago and the location tag says Amsterdam in red lettering. The photo illustration is the flower of a beautiful red and white tulip and the headline reads: **'Missing tulip found again by Dutch police after second killing.'**

I open the text and read about Semper Augustus, a rare

'broken' tulip that was thought to be extinct and which has now reappeared on the streets of Amsterdam on two consecutive days alongside the bodies of two men. The dead men were found attached to mooring ropes in the city's canals. The rediscovery of the long-lost tulip has amazed the Dutch public and created echoes of the tulipmania which swept the country in the early to mid-seventeenth century and caused unprecedented levels of financial speculation over the precious bulbs. Some are estimating that one bulb of the rarest and most beautiful tulip in Dutch history could now be worth more than a million euros. I whistle softly. A million euros for a single flower bulb.

'What's that then?' asks Nina, appearing behind me. She is wrapped in a large bath towel and rubbing her short crop of hair with another.

'Look for yourself.' She bends over me and stares at the screen while I try not to inhale her aroma of sandalwood soap and apple shampoo too obviously.

'Wow. Amazing. I wonder how it could just reappear like that. It's lovely.'

'Yeah. Feels odd though. Two killings - and yet it wouldn't have made the news in the UK without the rediscovery of a certain type of tulip.'

'That's journalists for you! Did you enjoy your herring and smoked eel?'

Smoked eel? So that's what it was. 'Yes, really fresh. Thanks.'

She starts to help herself to some while remaining standing alongside me. 'Why don't you see if our friend from last night is on there? What was his name, Tulp?'

I retrieve his card from my wallet on the table. 'Cornelius Tulp. The rest is all in Dutch I'm afraid.'

'Google him,' orders Nina. 'Cornelius Tulp, Amsterdam.'

I do what I'm told and a long list of entries cascades onto the screen. Many of them are in Dutch but Wikipedia comes up trumps with an English translation.

'Cornelius Tulp,' I read out loud, '(born 27th April 1966) is a Dutch businessman and politician. He has been Deputy Leader of the Born-Again Party since he jointly founded it in 2019. Tulp owns several large businesses in the technology, pharmaceutical and property sectors and is a key financial backer of Born-Again. He wants to increase the party's number of seats in the House of Representatives and many believe he wants to hold the balance of power by joining forces with the Party for Freedom, which was founded by Geert Wilders in 2006, and other right-of-centre parties. Tulp, who is a Roman Catholic, has campaigned to stop what he views as the 'Islamisation of the Netherlands', and supported Wilders when he compared the Quran to Mein Kampf. He wants all immigration from Muslim countries stopped and backs banning the construction of new mosques...'

'What?' interrupts Nina, frowning with her arms folded. 'And this is the guy who is taking us out for a jolly in his boat this morning?'

'Well, you seemed pretty happy about it last night,' I remind her.

'But look, he's a fascist.'

'Looks like it. And he'll be here in just over an hour, so you'd better get dressed.'

'We can't go,' she says, sitting down and folding her arms.

'We are going,' I say with a grin. 'Think of the copy. Don't you see? I'll be able to sell this as a feature back in the UK. My boat trip with the Dutch would-be answer to Donald Trump. Christ, even their surnames sound similar. I can make something out of that.'

'Well, I'm not going.' I know the stubborn set of Nina's jaw only too well but this time I am not going to give way.

'Oh yes you are. You owe him for saving you from that drunk last night. You're the one who accepted his kind offer. We both owe him for our dinner. And...'

'And what?' she demands.

'And I shall need someone to take lots of sneaky photos of us both. So go on, get dressed.' I yank her upright and bundle her backwards into her bedroom with Eddie yapping at our heels while she protests loudly.

It has stopped raining by 11 o'clock and the sun is shining in a blue sky scattered with cotton-ball puffs of cloud. There is still a bit of a breeze as we sit on the roof of our boat and wait for Cornelius Tulp. The early morning rain means Nina has decided she doesn't need to water the wooden box of tulips that sits between us. 'Seriously Jack?' she asks. 'Are you really going to try to get an article out of this guy?' I notice that we have dressed similarly. We are both in black jeans with white shirts, blue crew neck jumpers and white trainers. The coincidence makes me pleased – which I recognise is pretty ridiculous.

'Yes. We told him I was a journalist last night. Maybe that's why he invited us. Maybe he wants a bit of publicity. It doesn't mean we have to like Tulp or his views. Treat it like work. Journalists have to sup with the devil occasionally – but don't worry, we'll use a very long spoon.'

'Well, I'm not a journalist,' she replies with a pout.

'Today you are. Today you're my temporary intern.'

'In your dreams,' she says, but we are both distracted by a shout as a highly varnished launch motors towards us from under the Love Lock drawbridge. Tulp is at the stern with both hands on the roof of a small cabin while a much younger man and woman are standing side by side behind a windscreen at the helm. The boat glides alongside our houseboat and the woman loops a rope around one of our stanchions.

'Good morning,' hails Tulp with a smile and holding one hand up expansively. 'Please come aboard. We are ready to go.' He shakes both our hands as we step down into the boat's cockpit. 'This is Pieter and this is Anna. They are our crew for this morning.' We shake hands although I notice Tulp doesn't bother to tell the hired help our names.

'Jack and Nina,' I say, trying to make up for the omission.

Pieter and Anna are a fit and healthy-looking pair in their early twenties with the same striking blonde-white hair and they are dressed identically in blue shorts, white sweatshirts and blue boat-shoes. Tulp, who is wearing a yacht-club combination of chinos, blazer and polo-shirt, says 'Let's go!' and the launch accelerates impressively to complete a U-turn in its own length. He ushers us through the little cabin and back out into the open-air stern where we sit on a leather banquette. He takes a sideways seat just under the cabin roof.

'She's beautiful, isn't she?' he says, stroking the gunwale. 'One of the classic Riva boats used as water taxis in Venice. She was built at the Sarnico Shipyard on Lake Iseo and she runs on a Chevrolet 5 engine. Five point seven litres! I had her brought to Amsterdam on the back of a lorry and fully restored by the best Dutch craftsmen. Solid mahogany.'

'You must have used a lot of varnish,' I say, raising my voice above the deep throb of the engine. The rich brown woodwork is shining like glass and someone has polished the chrome-work as though it was their family silver.

'And you, my dear, you look as though you were always born to ride in such a boat. You are like George Clooney and his wife at the Venice film festival, or perhaps Audrey Hepburn and Gregory Peck!' I see Nina giggle in spite of herself. She slips on a pair of sunglasses and strikes an exaggerated theatrical pose. We all laugh. 'And now, perhaps, it is not too early for an aperitif whilst we see the city from the water – just as it should be seen.'

He clicks a finger at Anna who is standing to attention alongside Pieter at the wheel. She immediately forages in a cupboard and brings three glass beakers to the stern. 'Gin and tonic. Perfect to sip as we go along,' says Tulp enthusiastically stirring his lemon and ice with a plastic stick. 'Did you know it was we Dutch who invented gin? In 1650 a doctor in Leiden was the first to infuse juniper berries into distilled spirits – and gin was born. Proost!'

'Cheers,' I reply, and we all take a sip. It's strong stuff, probably a half and half mix.

'In the early days it was graded jong, oud and zeer oud. That means young, old and very old. We exported millions of gallons of the stuff.' He winks. 'We told the world it was good for their stomach and kidney ailments.'

'But bad for their liver,' adds Nina.

'Ha, ha. Exactly! But by the time they discovered that, it was too late! They were addicted to the stuff.'

'My grandad kept Somerset cider in a shed,' I tell them both. 'There were two labels on the barrels. *"Black-and-White"* and the better stuff, which he called *"Colour"*.' Tulp looks puzzled.

'There are two levels of television licence in the UK,' explains Nina. 'Black-and-white and colour. He was copying that.'

'Ah I see,' laughs Tulp again. 'I thought you were making some kind of racial joke.'

Nina gives me a sideways grimace as Tulp smoothly slips into his tourist guide act, pointing out various points of interest as we make our way along the Herengracht canal. The almost continuous monologue makes it difficult for me to begin any conversation about his politics, but Nina takes the opportunity to take pictures of us both after swapping seats with him. At one point, early in our trip, Tulp points out one particularly grand house.

'That is actually my home. It has been in my family since the 17th century. I am a lawyer and a businessman from a long line of doctors and merchant traders. But we have always been involved in politics too. This stretch of the canal is called 'The Golden Bend'. You will see that the people who built these houses for themselves bought two adjoining lots so their homes could be as wide as they were high. All the other canal homes in Amsterdam are very narrow – just over nine metres. This was strictly enforced.'

I notice a small arched entrance at water level under Tulp's home. 'Is that a boat house?'

Tulp wags his finger and smiles. 'Ah, the observant journalist. Yes indeed. Thanks to my ancestors, I have one of the only homes in Amsterdam with a built-in garage for my boats. I keep my water taxi in there.'

We meander back to the Amstel along the parallel Keizersgracht Canal. I assume we are being returned to our boat. It's frustrating. So far, we have been unable to have any kind of meaningful conversation which might lift an article beyond the travel section of the Sunday papers.

Tulp is pointing out a distinctive dark red streetlamp and boasting that Amsterdam was the first city in the world to have an official lighting plan. Hardly surprising, I think to myself, when a false step in the dark could plunge you to a watery death. Nina senses my growing anxiety but then Tulp himself comes to the rescue. He examines the expensive gold Rolex on his wrist, then puts a hand on each of our knees and looks at us in turn.

'Now, Jack and Nina, I was due to be back in the office, but it is such a glorious spring day. I haven't been out in the fresh air for a while. I wonder, shall we go over the Het IJ and have lunch on board my other boat? We shall be more comfortable over there. Or do you already have plans?'

'That would be lovely,' says Nina quickly. Bless you, I think to myself. We need more time to get some decent copy. But, in truth, it isn't too much of a sacrifice. Tulp has been an engaging and knowledgeable guide and I think Nina has been enjoying the envious stares of pedestrians as we cruise by. Extending our morning for lunch on board an even more comfortable boat, with the chance of a proper interview, doesn't sound like too much of a hardship. The body of water called the IJ, which was previously a bay alongside Amsterdam's waterfront, is choppy after the calm water of the canals. But the 250-horsepower engine gets us quickly across and into a marina which has been created on a spit of land alongside a wide canal.

Tulp, Nina and I have all stood in the boat's stern for the crossing and we are still on our feet as we motor slowly towards a beautiful white boat tied to a pontoon. 'Niko,' says Tulp proudly. 'Built in your home country at West Cowes on the Isle of Wight in 1963.'

Niko is a classic gentleman's motor yacht which I estimate to be more than 60 feet in length. She has carefully balanced proportions, an expansive aft deck and a commanding bridge which makes her look like a proper little ship. A line of ten port holes run along her side hinting at comfortable accommodation within. This is a boat which could easily take you on a worldwide cruise – providing you could afford the fuel and the crew that is.

'She was originally based in the Solent, then she was a family yacht in Corfu with a professional two-man crew. After that she spent some time on the French Riviera with the fast set and then she came back through the canal system and across the Channel to Falmouth in Cornwall. I bought her there and paid for a big refit before she came to Amsterdam. We have direct access from here out to the North Sea.'

'She's really beautiful,' says Nina, and I can tell she isn't just being polite.

'Thank you, my dear,' says Tulp patting her hand. 'And so are you.

Although I think you know that, and Jack definitely does. Come along. Lunch!'

Having disembarked onto the pontoon we are soon sitting around a polished cherrywood table in the light-filled main saloon. Blue curtains frame the large rectangular windows. Pieter pours chilled white wine into three Riedel glasses while Anna unpacks five large sandwiches from a wicker basket and places three of them on plates in front of us. Tulp tells us they are Broodjes, traditional Dutch sandwiches filled with a combination of meats and cheeses. A bowl of pickles sits in the centre of the table.

'It is only a picnic I am afraid,' says Tulp, 'But then, we all ate too well last night did we not?'

'Ate *and* drank too well,' observes Nina with a cocked eyebrow.

'Ah yes. I am afraid Leonid disgraced himself,' says Tulp sadly. 'I hope this little trip helps to make up for your ruined evening.' His mobile phone begins ringing just as he has finished his Broodje and he is wiping his chin and little pointed beard with a napkin. 'Excuse me a moment.' He takes the phone out onto the deck and begins talking urgently in Dutch.

'You're going to need to get a move on if you want that interview,' hisses Nina. Pieter appears briefly to top up our wine glasses and then vanishes below decks again.

'Plenty of time,' I say confidently. 'You heard him. He's taking the afternoon off to spend more of it in your beautiful company.'

But Tulp looks uncharacteristically serious when he returns. 'Forgive me. I am afraid some business has come up which means I need to return home at once. We shall drop you off at your boat, of course.'

'Oh,' I say quickly and glancing at Nina, 'I was hoping you might do an interview with me. For the UK press. We didn't realise who you were until we looked you up this morning.'

Tulp's smooth demeanour doesn't falter for a second. 'I thought you might. This was half in my mind already. That is why I gave you my card. But I'm afraid my time is pressing now and an interview in the UK press won't do much to help Born-Again in the election. Forgive my directness.'

'Just ten minutes?' asks Nina.

'We must leave immediately I'm afraid.' Nina has now adopted the look of a crestfallen puppy. How can she make her dark eyes look so huge? 'Well,' he concedes, 'perhaps I can share some thoughts with you as we make our way back. After all, they say there is no such thing as bad publicity, don't they?'

I quietly reflect to myself that whoever *they* are, *they* are badly mistaken. We are quickly disembarked from *Nico* and back on the Venetian launch where Pieter helms us past the rows of moored boats and back onto the wide waterway. Tulp is sitting opposite me, inside the cabin and out of the wind as I switch on my phone's voice recorder and hold it a foot away from his mouth. He doesn't bother to wait for the first question.

'For centuries, our country has welcomed communities of newcomers and made them part of our national success story. But our liberal tradition and respect for intellectual freedom is now blowing up in our faces. We had been a pale white country for centuries, and we prospered. But it all changed in the second half of the last century. We were forced to give up our colonies in the Dutch East Indies and 300,000 Indonesians arrived. We coped. They opened restaurants. At least they spoke Dutch. But then in the 1960s tens of thousands of migrants arrived from Turkey and Morocco. They were badly educated with low incomes and we had to build places for them to work in places like the Bimmer – I am sorry, I must call it Zuidoost now – as if changing the name changes anything.' Tulp is no longer charm and good humour personified. He is looking angry and his blue eyes are unblinking.

'Then 300,000 came from Surinam in South America when it became independent during the 1970s and slowly the great exodus of ordinary Amsterdammers began. In just twenty years, 400,000 ordinary working Dutch families and their children abandoned our city for good. Then the jobs disappeared, and the immigrants were left unemployed. Crime rocketed. And now it is happening all over again as the Muslims come across the Mediterranean in their little boats and threaten our society. If we do nothing, the Islamic culture will gain the upper hand. We have been too tolerant. Too multicultural. That is why I have created the Born-Again party. The rest of our country has already woken up to this threat...' Tulp pauses to hold onto Nina's arm as the wash from a big ship sends our boat rocking. She quickly shakes herself free. The wind has risen in the last hour and the chop is considerably worse than before. Tulp is talking with a grim urgency.

'The voters in the south have supported Wilders and the PVV – The Freedom Party - so they are now the second biggest party in parliament. In 2019 the Forum for Democracy won the biggest share of the vote in the local elections. Now, I intend to make sure that Amsterdam wakes up too. If Born-Again does well, we could hold the balance of power to create a popular anti-immigration, anti-Islamic ruling coalition for the Netherlands and, frankly, this is long overdue. We must make the Netherlands Great Again!'

I try to ignore the frustration and anger which is etched in Nina's face during this polemic. 'So, in practical terms, if that happened, what differences would the people of Amsterdam see?'

'We must tear down the ugly grey apartment blocks that were built for the immigrants in our industrial zones. Our economy has changed. and we do not need these zones or this workforce any more. We can offer them financial inducements to go home if we have to. If the homes are not here, they will not continue to come. This is the time to raze these prefabricated concrete slums to the ground and replace them with high quality developments, million-euro townhouses. That is what must happen now for this city to prosper. Our stock exchange has overtaken London. We are Europe's largest share trading centre. We must become a top destination for business – for highly skilled and highly paid Europeans. Sony are bringing their EU headquarters here. It is the moment to reshape the infrastructure of our city again.'

'So deep down, it's just a grubby money-grabbing charter for property developers.' Nina's voice is shaking with pent-up emotion.

'I'm sorry?' says Tulp, who has been thrown off stride by the interruption. He is staring at Nina in disbelief.

'This morning you told us all about the rich merchants who built the canal district for themselves and pushed everyone else out whilst turning a nice profit. It's that all over again, isn't it?'

Tulp looks at me. 'Who is doing this interview? You or her.'

I open my mouth, but Nina is too quick for me. 'And you dare to wrap it all up in a load of political bullshit which is fundamentally racist. Rich ex-pats working for Sony are welcome, are they? But frightened refugees from war-torn countries aren't. Is that it?'

Tulp flicks one hand disdainfully. 'The tourist speaks. You should only voice opinions about things you know about, young lady.' I close my eyes. Trying to dismiss Nina rather than arguing it out is the wrong way to go. I sense my interview, such as it was, is now over.

Nina gets to her feet and points a finger at Tulp's face. 'People like you need to understand that welcoming new communities enriches your culture. It doesn't destroy it. We had a debate last night, about rich people. Jack and me. He thought you were different just because you had more money. But listening to you I realised something. When you're rich because your family has always been rich, you become careless about other people's lives. You lose your humanity.'

Tulp is now standing too. All traces of his easy charm and bonhomie have been replaced by a cold fury. 'You are wrong, and even worse, you are very rude. There is no excuse for such behaviour from a guest. Now you will sit here quietly until we drop you off.' With that, Tulp stalks to the bow, roughly pushes Pieter to one side and sits down to helm the boat himself. The bow of the boat rises as we immediately pick up speed.

I stop the recording and return it to my pocket. 'Nice one,' I say.

'Jack Johnson, don't you dare...'

'No,' I say hastily. 'I mean it. Nice one. I would have been seriously disappointed in you if you hadn't said those things.'

She gives a little smile. 'It did feel rather good,' she confesses.

'There's a time and a place for everything,' I smile back. 'And that was definitely the time and place!'

'But did I ruin your interview?' she asks.

I shrug. 'Maybe. Maybe not. Who cares? We're on holiday remember?'

CHAPTER EIGHT

In the event, Tulp is too angry to bother dropping us off at our boat – even though a cursory glance of my tourist map suggests it is on the route back to his palatial home on The Golden Bend. Pieter climbs up onto a jetty in the Oosterdok with one end of a mooring rope.

'Thanks for the trip, and for lunch,' I say awkwardly to Tulp as I pass behind the back of the helmsman's chair. Tulp remains stock still and staring straight ahead through the boat's windscreen. Pieter looks apologetic and gives us simple walking directions. 'It's really not far,' he promises, before scuttling back down on to the gleaming launch.

'Well, he's pretty thin-skinned if he wants to be a politician,' I say to Nina as we set off in the general direction of the Amstel. 'But you did give him both barrels.'

'He's as rich as Croesus,' says Nina. 'I don't expect anyone ever stands up to him.'

'Still, it was a nice way to see a bit of the city. And I might just have enough for an article.'

We stroll alongside the broad expanse of the Oudeschans Canal and pass a large 16th century tower which my book tells me was built to defend the harbour. It's not a particularly tall tower but it still stands out as a landmark among the surrounding houses. We swing right and are walking past a coffee shop which straddles the corner of two roads when a coincidence happens. It's the kind of coincidence that only happens in real life, rather than in books. I hear my name being shouted. A woman has emerged from the doorway of the Solo Coffeeshop and is hurrying towards me.

'Jack. Jack Johnson. It's you, isn't it?'

It takes me a moment to place the woman's cheerful round face in such unlikely surroundings. 'Su? Wow! It's great to see you!'

We pump each other's hands and hug before I I introduce her to Nina. 'Su Mortimer. Angelina Wilde. Nina. Su and I worked together in London for the same paper. She wrote and I subbed. What are you doing here?'

'Working. I moved here a couple of years ago with my Dutch boyfriend and I act as a stringer for the British press. I couldn't believe it when I saw you walking past. What are you doing here?'

I explain that we are on a fortnight's holiday and staying on a houseboat.

'Come in, please. You could be the answer to my prayers.'

We move inside the coffee shop. It's like an upmarket pub with lots of dark, well-polished wood. There are several booths along one side facing a long bar with traditional leather-topped stools. Su ushers us into one booth which has a jumble of papers on its table and an open laptop. 'Coffee? Tea?' she asks, pushing a menu towards us. 'Or you could have a space cake? They're a bit strong to be honest. Or a pre-rolled joint?' This is like being offered drugs by an eager-to-please sixth form prefect. Su has an open and honest-looking face which she always used ruthlessly to gain the trust of her interviewees.

I see there are three types of joint on the menu. They are Hash-and-Tobacco or Weeds-and-Tobacco for 4 euros a joint and something called Pure Amnesia Haze for 6 euros.

'Or there's weed you can buy by the gramme or 5 grammes,' continues Su. 'You can see them there. Sativa and Indica. That's made from the dried unprocessed flowers of the two different cannabis plants. They reckon Sativas gives you a mind high but

Indicas give you a body high. Hash is the strongest stuff – that's made from the resin of the plant. Sometimes it's named after the country it comes from. You can see Kashmir Pollen there. That's 14 euros for a gramme. Or there's Moroccan, Afghan or Lebanese.'

'I'll just have a beer thanks, Su,' I say, folding the menu closed.

'Sorry, you can't get alcohol in a coffeeshop,' she smiles, 'it's strictly prohibited. Soft drugs only I'm afraid.'

'Ok, a coffee will be fine.'

'Very wise. I never touch this stuff myself,' she says nodding at the weed and hash menu on the wall. 'I'd never get any work done. It's just that this place is convenient, and they let me work here. I live just around the corner.'

'Jack,' says Nina apologetically and covering one of my hands with hers. 'This stuff isn't for me I'm afraid. It smells like a cross between cat pee and a smelly armpit. Sorry, Su.'

'No worries Nina. Honestly. I suppose I've just got used to it.'

'You two have a catch up and enjoy your coffee. I'll get back to the boat and let Eddie out for a walk.'

'Eddie's my dog,' I explain to Su. 'Are you sure?' Nina nods, shakes hands with Su again, brushes my cheek with her lips and is gone. 'Sorry about that. She's a bit of a head-girl. And she has felt pretty strongly about drugs ever since a dealer pointed a double-barrelled shotgun in her face. But that's another story.'

'She's lovely,' says Su. 'How long have you been together?'

I shrug. 'Well, we're still just travelling hopefully really. Or at least I am.'

Thankfully, I'm rescued by a waitress and order two Americanos. We spend the next twenty minutes briefing each other on our life events of the last four years. I am reminded that Su had an English father and a Dutch mother and was bilingual as a child. She has clearly thrived since moving to Amsterdam with her boyfriend, a part-time model called Wilhelm.

In turn, I tell Su about my divorce, my decision to live on board a narrowboat, a little of my 'relationship' with Nina and our morning's meeting with Cornelius Tulp. 'Wow! You really got to meet him, did you? He's pretty secretive usually but I suppose he has to come out of his shell now that he's standing for election himself. I could sell the story about his drunken dinner party to one of the gossip columns here if you like? We can split it 50:50. I might even be able to place a piece about your boat trip with him if you let me have the interview.'

'We've promised not to mention the dinner party. But I'll think about the interview.'

'It is interesting though. The populist hard-right politicians have really got their tails up over here – just like a lot of other places. You can see them having an impact. Even these coffeeshops are having a hard time. Some of them in the towns are only allowed to sell to locals with a 'weed pass' now, and none of them is allowed to be within 250 metres of a school. Quite a few have been forced to shut. There's a crackdown in the red-light district too. A lot of the window brothels have been closed down and there's even talk of moving the whole thing.'

'I suppose it's giving you plenty to write about?'

'Too true. I'm drowning in work at the moment. It's gone mad. There's a lot of interest in these Tulip Murders back home and I'm struggling to cope with the demand.'

'I read about them on the BBC's website this morning. They sound intriguing.'

Su rubs the little scar above her top lip. It was the result of a childhood accident and a mannerism I remember with a smile. 'Intriguing is an understatement. Two right-wing sympathisers, one a thug and the other, a controversial newspaper columnist, are found dangling from mooring ropes with plastic ties at the crack of dawn and alongside them, a perfect example of a tulip that no-one has seen for nearly four centuries. Both men were left in the same pose. Look.' She swivels her laptop screen towards me. 'This picture is about to make the papers. Someone took it from a boat and eventually they got around to posting it on Instagram.'

The photograph shows the body of a well-built young man draped over a rope with his head falling forward and slightly sideways. 'Poor sod.'

'Turns out he was a member of a racist bunch of thugs who got their kicks attacking Muslim communities at the weekend. The police have been pulling the rest of his gang in for questioning.'

'Could the killers be Muslim extremists? Getting their own back?'

'It's possible. It's happened before. There was a populist politician called Pim Fortuyn who was anti-Islam and very loud about it. He was killed in 2002 by a left-winger. Then, a couple of years later, one of Fortuyn's supporters, a columnist and filmmaker called Theo van Gogh, was shot dead by a Muslim called Mohammed Bouyeri. But the backlash actually helped the right-wingers for a while. Some of Fortuyn's mates even made it into a coalition government.'

'Quite a hornets' nest here isn't it?'

'Mate, you don't know the half of it.' Su orders two more coffees at the bar and brings them over. 'Look. I've just had a thought. I'm busy feeding copy to London about the murders. The police aren't giving much away, which probably means they don't have a clue. But a couple of weekend colour supplements have asked for decent length features about the Semper Augustus. 'The Dutch Tulip – National Cliché or a National Treasure, or some such nonsense. I just don't have the time, but they'll pay well. Why don't you have a stab at it? I'd rather take a ten per cent commission than see the work go begging.'

'I'm not sure, Su. I'm supposed to be on holiday with Nina.'

'It'll take you half a day, a day at most. Just pop over to the Tulip Museum on Prinsengracht and find someone who knows what they're talking about. If you've got time you could get to one of the flower auctions or borrow my car and drive out to Keukenhof garden. It's amazing at this time of year. Millions and millions of bulbs in bloom. There's bound to be an expert out there for you to interview. And Nina would love it.' She can probably tell from my face that I'm tempted. 'Come on Jack. You'll probably make enough from one feature to pay for your entire holiday.'

'I'll need to talk to the boss first. Give me your mobile number and I'll get back to you.'

CHAPTER NINE

Father Nicholas Jansz van der Heck felt in the pocket of his woollen sports jacket and rubbed his plastic dog collar between two fingers. He always took it off when he came to sit in Amsterdam's first large public park, the Oosterpark. The sight of any single man sitting for any length of time near the large children's paddling pool would raise suspicions. But the sight of a priest doing the same thing could lead to challenges and even violence. He knew this from bitter experience. It had been like this ever since that accursed report which had dominated the national debate. It had revealed 1,800 reported cases of child abuse by Dutch Roman Catholic clergy or volunteers since 1945.

Nevertheless, he couldn't help himself. Roughly twice a month, but never on the same day or at the same time, the 70-year-old retired priest would return to a different bench by the pool. He would pretend to be listening to music or a podcast on his smartphone's earbuds. Unlike reading a book, this allowed him to half-open his eyes and watch the young children as they cavorted in the water during the spring and summertime. Sometimes the younger ones were completely undressed as they frolicked near the mushroom shaped play-fountain. He would limit himself to an hour before walking back to his modest home in the nearby suburb of Oosterparkbuurt where he would put his dog collar back on, cook an early dinner and switch his computer on. You could find anything on the internet these days if you knew where to look, but there was nothing like seeing these young angels in the flesh.

This time, the priest had chosen the late afternoon for his visit to the pond and the number of children was fewer than usual. But it was a different crowd of parents who would probably never have seen him there before. Most of them had set childcare routines and he was careful to avoid slotting into the same one too frequently. He knew he must tear himself away after another thirty minutes. Any longer might arouse suspicions.

He began to think about his sermon for the coming Sunday as he walked back across the large expanse of green. He may have been encouraged to retire by the Archbishop of Utrecht but that wouldn't shut him up. He was often asked to preach at one of the city's Roman Catholic churches. This was partly because of his public profile from the broadcasting work that he did on the city's television and radio stations. It added a touch of glamour to each church that invited him, and he was told congregations were significantly larger when they knew he was to appear among them.

The invitations to be a guest preacher also came because the priests of the city were worried. At 17%, Christianity was still the largest religion in the city and Roman Catholicism made up the largest part of that figure. He felt that this, in itself, was an astonishing achievement. The Netherlands had been a Protestant country for centuries and the Catholics had been tolerated, but certainly not encouraged, after the country's bloody wars with Spain. But it was his own church which had overtaken the Calvinists and the Protestants after the First World War. And now it was his church that was under the greatest threat. Islam represented 14% of religious worship in Amsterdam and it was still growing rapidly. It was widely predicted that it would be the city's largest single religious group within a few years. The Catholic priests of Amsterdam would never go as far as he did in his condemnation of Islam, but they were all too happy to host his fire and brimstone message from their pulpits.

The ageing priest limped slightly as he walked, but he betrayed few other signs of old age. He still felt vigorous and was confident he would live for many more years. His hair might be silver-grey now, but it remained thick and required regular trims so that he looked his best for his television appearances. He was frequently invited to take part in panel discussions where he would win applause and derision in equal parts from live audiences for his forthright opinions. He chuckled to himself. It gave him endless pleasure to know that he annoyed the Archbishop so much. The young fool should never have forced him to retire. He had no power over him now, short of seeking his excommunication by Rome, and most of the other priests would do all they could to let him continue preaching to the faithful.

He had decided to base Sunday's sermon on an ancient 7th century text called 'Concerning Heresy'. In it, St John of Damascus named Islam as a Christological heresy. This was truer now than it was then, he would thunder from the pulpit. He would release a text of his sermon to the papers in advance. That would stir things up.

The path from the paddling pool crossed a small metal bridge which bisected a long lake and then swung toward Oosterpark's southern perimeter. This was his favourite season of the year and he was pleased to see a small group of gardeners ahead of him spraying the flowers with some kind of insecticide. He liked to see the city being properly cared for and detested the graffiti that had sprung up everywhere in recent years – much of it in a foreign tongue. It was shocking. But what else could you expect when one in five Amsterdam residents hadn't even been born in the Netherlands?

The work gang was using an electric cart with a white plastic tank on the top and a big bucket area at its rear for grass cuttings and leaves. The three men were all wearing gloves and masks covered their noses and mouths, presumably to protect them from the chemical spray. One of them nodded as he approached and considerately switched his spray off. He smiled his thanks at the man. But when he was just two metres away from the cart, another of the men swung the nozzle up into the old priest's face and drenched him in toxic vapour. He instinctively opened his mouth to shout but the fumes overwhelmed him. His throat and eyes burned in agony as he was bundled off his feet and flipped headfirst into the open rear of the cart. The attack had taken seconds. The last thing he felt, as he lay on his back with a hand clamped over his mouth, was a sharp pain in his neck and the last thing he saw was the darkening sky as the bucket's lids were slammed down above him.

CHAPTER TEN

Dr Beatrix van der Laen had not been roused from her bed this time. She had been wandering around her large garden in a dressing gown with a torch and a pair of secateurs when the call came through. She had been cutting away dead wood from her shrubs and reflecting that her day job had very similar aims, dealing with the deceased and removing the diseased from society. The menopause was already disturbing her nights and the endless recycling of her thoughts about the Tulip Murders made it impossible to go back to sleep after 4am.

And so here she is again, fully dressed and standing on a canal towpath at dawn for the second morning in succession. Once again, Robert welcomes her with a large cardboard cup of coffee. She is alternating sips with puffs on one of her little cigars from the rear of a police-launch that is being held stationary under a bridge. A chain runs along the stone wall at one end. She is unsure what it is for. Perhaps to act as a grabline if anyone falls in? That's ironic, she thinks to herself. Because draped across the chain is the upper half of an elderly man with a shock of thick grey hair. She has recognised him straight away and the contents of his soaking wallet confirm it. It is Father Nicholas Jansz van der Heck, a well-known Roman Catholic priest who has used his retirement to become a ubiquitous rent-a-quote for the nation's media.

His eyes are still wide open and staring, as though in outrage, as two Scene-of-Crime officers in gloves and hooded white suits do their work from another launch. The pose is exactly the same as the others with both arms draped downwards over the chain which crosses his chest. Once again, the body has been fixed in place with strong plastic ties.

'Another extreme right-winger,' says Robert. She notices that his lovely eyes are slightly bloodshot with tiredness in spite of the injunction to her team to pace themselves. So far, the Regional Chief Commissioner has shielded her from the inevitable politics of two headline-grabbing murders. But now she knows he will be unable to say no to the First Chief Commissioner and the Minister of Security and Justice who will want the Central Unit of the Dutch police force to get involved. The official line is that it exists to support the ten regional police units of the Netherlands with centralised specialist services. More like get in the way, thinks Beatrix bitterly. She anticipates that the nature of the killings, and the profile and politics of the victims, means that the Special Interventions Division, which has the terrorism brief, will want to attach officers to her squad. They may even lobby to take over the entire investigation. She sighs and tosses the stub of her cigar into the dark water.

Robert has read her thoughts. 'The Central Unit could be helpful with the social media side of all this.' He has phrased the comment carefully because he is aware that however hard Beatrix tries, the world of Facebook, Instagram, Twitter and all the other most popular Apps are largely outside his boss's comfort zone. 'We just don't have the manpower, or the expertise, to be sifting everything that's out there at the moment. And it's going to get worse now,' he adds indicating the dead priest.

Beatrix nods back at him. 'You're right of course. Someone is taunting us with the way they're staging these killings. Three in three days. And two different types of fatal poison which are both derived from plants. I wonder what killed this one. Plus, the reappearance of Semper Augustus of course. They're doing it to get the world's attention. And now they've done that so successfully, maybe they'll tell us why.'

Her deputy shrugs and shivers at the same time. The sun isn't fully up and it's chilly on the water. 'Maybe. Or maybe they think it's self-evident. Maybe they're just sending a message that if you support hard-right causes or you are anti-Islam, you've got it coming to you.'

'Maybe. Anyway, I predict an urgent meeting this afternoon with a few more people around the table including the spooks from the General Intelligence and Security Service and a high-up from the Ministry.'

'Well, if they've been doing their monitoring job properly on potential enemies of the state, perhaps they can hopefully point us in the right direction.'

'I admire your youthful optimism, Robert. However, I think they'll be more inclined to kick in some doors than *'point us in the right direction'*. Have you sent someone to the priest's home?'

Robert nods. 'No news yet.'

'I wonder where they snatched him?'

'We're still checking but there were no overnight reports of anything suspicious. The same as the newspaper man. They must be fast and good. But we saw that with the first one.'

'Not good Robert. Fast and professional – but not good. Come on, let's find the bloody tulip.'

The launch takes them to some steps near the bridge and they climb up to street level. Police cars with their lights flashing have blocked off both ends of the bridge as well as the adjoining road and at least twenty uniformed officers are milling about, waiting for instructions. They put out their cigarettes at the appearance of the Commissioner and begin to shuffle around her. There is some stifled laughter when one of them mutters 'pay attention to Her Majesty Queen Beatrix now lads.'

'Alright you know the drill,' she says, raising her voice so they can all hear. I want the whole of the road on this side closed and I want two groups, shoulder-to-shoulder searching it from both ends. We're looking for a single red and white tulip – you've all seen the pictures – but if you find it, don't touch it. Just call it in. And keep an eye out for anything else that seems out of the ordinary.'

It takes thirty minutes before the officer in charge of the northern group comes crackling through on the police radio. Beatrix looks down the canal-side road and sees him holding an arm straight up in the air.

She sets off quickly with Robert and a white-suited officer hurrying close behind. As she gets closer, she sees that the sergeant in charge of the search party is pointing towards a window box on the roof of a moored boat. A selection of single-coloured red, yellow and pink tulips is planted in it and there, right in the centre of the display, like a queen in a gorgeous robe surrounded by her nodding courtiers, stands Semper Augustus.

The curtains are drawn and there is no sign of life on the boat. Beatrix calculates that she has a very short amount of time before news of a third Semper Augustus seeps out and a crowd begins to gather. Her mobile rings.

'Beatrix?'

'Good morning. Chief Commissioner.' She rolls her eyes conspiratorially at Robert.

'Another one I hear.'

'You hear correctly Chief Commissioner.'

'Exactly the same?'

'Exactly the same. They've told you who the victim is?'

'Yes. I can hardly believe it. An elderly Roman Catholic priest. It's very shocking.'

'A priest with an virulent anti-Islamic reputation and a high public profile.'

'Yes, yes, I know all that,' says the Chief Commissioner impatiently. 'And another tulip I suppose?'

'We've just found it in the last few minutes. On the roof of a boat not far from the body.'

'How long are you going to be out there?'

'I don't know. Another hour maybe.'

'Alright. Come and see me as soon as you get back. I think we're going to be getting a lot of help, whether we like it or not.'

'Understood. But we must stay in charge. It's all happened inside our patch so far. It's still our case.'

'Yes, yes. I'll do my best. Come and see me as soon as you can. I'll have someone sent along from the press office to say no-comment on the ground. But I think we're going to have to do a press conference later today.' Beatrix groans inwardly. 'And we'll need to keep the uniforms down there for the moment to control the scene. I'll send an inspector with a few more men.' He hangs up. Robert approaches and shows her the screen of his mobile.

'It's already out,' he says gloomily.

Sure enough, a local news website has a headline screaming: 'THIRD BODY, THIRD TULIP'. Beatrix looks around and sees a man and a woman in the upstairs window of a house on the opposite bank. The man has a pair of binoculars trained on them. His vantage point would also allow him to see the body being recovered from under the bridge. She raises the middle forefinger of her right hand and holds it up at the couple. Robert smothers it with his hand almost immediately. 'Not a good idea, boss. Think of the photograph in the papers.'

'You're right,' sighs Beatrix. 'Thank you, Robert. Not enough sleep but that's no excuse. Let's see if anyone's at home, shall we?'

They move to the stern of the boat, cross a small gangplank and rap on the door. A dog's bark is immediately heard from inside. 'I hate dogs,' mutters Robert. Beatrix smiles. Another reason she likes her deputy is their mutual love of cats. Robert and his husband have a sleek pair of Persians.

After a minute the door is opened by an attractive, slim woman with short hair and dark eyes. 'Yes, can I help you?' she asks politely in English as she picks up a scruffy little brown dog.

'We are police officers. Can we have a word?' replies Beatrix in her own flawless English. 'What is your name?'

'Me?' says the woman, somewhat startled. 'I'm Nina. Angelina. Mrs Angelina Wilde.' Then the woman turns to call into the interior of the houseboat. 'Jack. Jack. You'd better get up here. It's the police.'

CHAPTER ELEVEN

I am still in my bare feet as the two detectives take us outside to see an officer in a white coat busying himself around the flower box on *Flora's* roof. We stand a couple of metres away as he carefully parts the single-coloured tulips to show the white and red-streaked one in their centre. I take a quick snap with my mobile and then we all troop back into the boats interior and sit around the dining table.

The older woman shows us a warrant card to prove she is Commissar Dr Beatrix van der Laen. She tells us she is leading the Dutch police investigation into the recent killings – the so-called Tulip Murders. She and her sidekick, a younger smartly dressed man who could easily moonlight as a male model, turn down offers of coffee but wait patiently while I prepare a cafetiere for Nina and myself.

'The body was found at dawn, under the wooden drawbridge,' she says, nodding her mane of swept back hair in the direction of our canal's junction with the Amstel. 'And, as you have seen, the Semper Augustus was found on the roof of your houseboat just now.'

'You are on holiday?' asks the male detective. His long fingers hover over our guidebook and a folded city map on the table.

'Yes, we arrived two days ago,' I say.

'And we'll be here for a fortnight,' adds Nina.

'Did either of you hear anything during the night? Did the dog bark at all?'

We both shake our heads. 'No, nothing springs to mind,' says Nina who has Eddie on her lap. 'I slept really well.'

I shake my head to indicate the same answer. 'Eddie is used to a bit of noise on the towpath. We live on a boat in the UK.' I catch Nina looking at me. 'Well, at least, I do.'

'Whoever left the flower took quite a risk clambering over the roof of a boat during the night,' says van der Laen. 'Assuming that's what they did.'

'We didn't hear anything and Eddie didn't bark.'

'I watered the flowers yesterday evening,' says Nina. 'About eight o'clock. I'm pretty sure it wasn't there then.'

'Street cameras?' I ask.

The younger man gives me an appraising look. 'We're checking but even if there are any, the killers are being careful to hide their faces.'

'What do you do for a living Mr Johnson?' asks the woman.

'I'm a journalist.'

She rolls her eyes. 'Well, congratulations. You have landed yourself in the middle of quite a big story.'

'Jack has helped the British police a lot,' says Nina protectively.

'Is that so? I have found journalists to be slightly more of a hindrance than a help in my work. No offence.'

I glance out of the window and see a small crowd gathering. Word must be spreading about the discovery of a third Semper Augustus. The others follow my gaze and the two police officers exchange a frustrated look with each other.

The officer is right. We are now part of the story and I imagine my friend Su will be only too keen for us to find out what we can. I unfold the tourist map of the city on the table and mark the wooden drawbridge with an X. 'So, this is our mooring and the Groenburgwal Bridge is where the latest body was found. May I ask the locations of the other two?'

The male detective shakes his head in disbelief and laughs, but van der Laen is courtesy and good humour personified. 'Why not? Show him Robert. It's public knowledge and we have already disturbed the morning of these visitors to our city.'

The officer called Robert bends over the map with my biro. 'The first one was found here, in the water on the Oudezijds Acchterburgwal A young thug injected with digitalis – from the foxglove. The second was found here, on the Kloveniersburgwal. He was a newspaper columnist, injected with gelsemium, a highly toxic chemical found in yellow jasmine.'

'And now we have a Roman Catholic priest,' says van der Laen. 'Who no doubt has been injected with some other kind of poisonous plant.'

'It's strange,' I say.

The woman laughs. 'And that, Mr Johnson, I believe is what the English call an understatement.'

'No. Look at the map. The locations of all three bodies are in a completely straight line.' The others bend their heads over the table. I lay my biro across the three marks on the map. Then I hold my thumb on the plastic pen. 'And correct me if I'm wrong but they seem to be exactly the same distance apart.'

'A coincidence?' asks Nina.

'Surely you would expect them to be more randomly scattered than this?' I ask van der Laen. She has taken off her wire spectacles and is concentrating on the map. 'It has to be a coincidence,' she says, more to herself than to the rest of us.

'What possible other reason could there be?' asks Robert.

'The killer, or killers, are abducting individuals from the street?' I ask.

'We can't be sure,' he replies. 'The first one definitely. Yes, probably the other two as well. There was no sign of disturbance at their homes.'

'And they are carefully posing the victims in the same way and leaving the long-lost tulip somewhere nearby?'

'And they seem to be using plant-based poisons to finish their victims off,' adds van der Laen.

'It's all really considered and carefully planned, isn't it?' I ask. 'So surely this straight line linking the three on the map, and the equidistant spacing means something too.'

Nina and the two police officers are staring at me.

'If your theory is correct and there is a fourth consecutive killing, the body could be found here.' Robert has continued to draw the straight line and puts an X on the southwest corner of a green rectangle called Rembrandtplein.

'Or here,' says van der Laen, extending the line to the north.

'All the others have been found in water,' says van der Laen. 'Rembrandtplein is a busy town square. And the same distance in a straight-line north is … it's somewhere near the Oude Kerk. It's our city's oldest church.'

I shrug. 'Nevertheless, it might be worth keeping both areas under surveillance tonight – or having a few extra patrols in the area.'

I would expect a British police officer to bristle at the uninvited advice, but the detective just gives me a friendly smile and stands up. 'Thank you, Mr Johnson. You may have given us something else to think about. I don't think we need a statement from you if you heard nothing during the night. We have your details. Now we must get back to our headquarters. Good day to you. The crowd will go when we take the tulip away. We may have to remove the whole box for tests, but it will be returned – minus the Semper Augustus of course. I hope you enjoy the rest of your holiday.'

The door has barely closed on them before I have retrieved Su's number from my contacts file and rung her.

'Su? Hi. It's Jack. I think you'd better come over to our boat as quickly as possible if you want a head start on the third Tulip Murder.'

CHAPTER TWELVE

THE DUTCH TULIP – NATIONAL CLICHÉ OR NATIONAL CURSE?

As the rarest and most valuable tulip in history reappears on Amsterdam's streets alongside a macabre series of unexplained murders, **Jack Johnson** *reports from the city on the tulip's place in the Dutch psyche.*

'Tulips, quite simply, are sex on a stalk,' the attendant at The Amsterdam Tulip Museum tells me. Her excitement is, perhaps, understandable. The small museum, located in the exclusive Prinsengracht area of Amsterdam, is bursting at the seams with visitors. Tulipmania has returned to the city after almost 400 years along with Semper Augustus, the rarest and most valuable of tulips which everyone thought had died out long ago.

A huge blow-up photograph of the white flower with its variegated flame-red pattern has been put in the front window of the museum and new information panels are packing in the curious – tourists and locals alike.

'The tulip is an outrageously sexy flower,' continues our guide, holding up a wooden model of the flower which has been hastily painted to represent the rediscovered Holy Grail of the horticultural world. 'Look at it. It is both male and female. It has a full curve like the hip and buttock of a sex goddess. Cleopatra or Marilyn Monroe perhaps? The folded leaves around the swollen bud are vulval. And yet, at the same time they are overtly and precisely phallic. Like the glans or the tip of a penis. The tulip knows no sexual boundaries. It goes beyond the aesthetic.'

It's always nice to meet someone who is happy in their work. But the truth is that the Netherlands has had a love affair with the tulip for centuries. The country is the market leader for cut flowers and the tulip is one of its most successful exports. Daily flower sales in March often pass twenty million euros and 35% of all the globe's flower and plant exports pass through the Netherlands each year. They are worth 6.2 billion euros to the Dutch economy.

This passion for the tulip can be seen everywhere in the country's capital. As soon as you arrive at Schiphol airport or disembark from Eurostar at the Central Station, you can't escape it. It decorates every rack of postcards, every display of fridge-magnets and every shelf of the tourist shops. It is a big and blooming business.

The country's obsession with the genus Tulipa dates back to the first half of the 17th century when it became the first example of a speculation bubble in the history of mankind. The tulip was one of the earliest imports to the Dutch Republic, as it was known at the time. It arrived from Turkey and by the early 1620s it was the unrivalled flower of fashion and the costly habit of gentlemen botanists like Adriaan Pauw, the Pensionary of Amsterdam who planted out beds at his rural castle retreat in Heemstede. He used a mirror-sided gazebo to multiply their effect, making hundreds of rare tulips appear as thousands.

But professional growers quickly moved into the market, supplying a much broader range of stock including high-priced hybrids. Demand exploded as ordinary hard-working Amsterdammers gambled their livelihoods on buying bulbs which they hoped would develop into the most exotic and valuable varieties – the 'broken' tulips. These flowers had streaks of colour running across paler backgrounds and if some of these varieties came up in your garden, it was the equivalent of winning the national lottery.

Of these, the Semper Augustus became the most famous – mainly because it was the scarcest. It was believed that only 12 bulbs of the flower existed at one time and rumours abounded that the mysterious collector who owned them all was Adriaan Pauw. In 1637 one Semper Augustus bulb was supposedly advertised for 13,000 florins, the price of a very nice house and garden in the centre of the city. But that was also the year of the crash.

People began selling the paper rights to tulip bulbs, off-loading them for a quick profit. Sellers were dealing with stock they did not possess for prices they couldn't afford. Eventually, the authorities stepped in and ended the madness – but only after many people had been ruined.

And just as the economic bubble burst, growers began to realise that they could not maintain the 'broken' tulips for ever. Botanists now know that the patterns are due to a virus which infects the bulb and causes intricate stripes, streaks, featherings and flame-like effects. But the virus also weakens the bulb and eventually makes it stunted and weak until it has insufficient strength to flower, and it withers away. The phenomenon which created the rarest and most beautiful tulip bulbs was also the one which sealed their fate. Until now.

'Everyone thought the genetic line of Semper Augustus had ended centuries ago,' one grower told me. 'The only evidence of its existence is on paper drawings from the time. We are all in a total state of shock. This has enormous implications for our industry. We are desperate to know where these flowers have come from and how they have survived.'

However, the most valuable tulip in Dutch history has reappeared in the most shocking of circumstances. Single Semper

Augustus blooms have been deliberately placed near the bodies of three men killed on three consecutive days in the city.

Police think the victims, a nightclub bouncer, a newspaper columnist and a Roman Catholic priest, were all abducted from the city's streets and killed almost instantly with toxic plant-based poisons. Their bodies have all been draped over chains or ropes in the canals of the city and discovered at dawn in the same grotesque pose. And a Semper Augustus has been found near all of them – on the towpath, in the reception area of a theatre and on the roof of a houseboat (*see panel for an account of my close encounter with Semper Augustus*). The men all held anti-Islamic hard-right political views and there is furious speculation in Dutch newspapers that the killings have something to do with the forthcoming national elections. The police remain baffled.

But it is a sign of the country's tulip obsession that most of the chat dominating social media is about the reappearance of Semper Augustus rather than the killings. Has some horticultural genius managed to recultivate it after all these years? Have they even unlocked a way of defeating the virus and guaranteeing its future? And what is a single bloom now worth? Thirteen-thousand florins in 1637 is the same as just over one-and-a-half million euros today. Admittedly, that was at the height of a tulipmania that was gripping the city. But when you see the size of the crowds gathering now to catch a glimpse of a single Semper Augustus, you realise that tulipmania is back in Amsterdam with a vengeance.

Nina looks up from my laptop screen. 'You pulled that together quickly. What happens if there's another flower found in the morning with another body?'

I shrug. 'The subs in London will have to keep the piece up to date. Or Su. I'm not spending any more of my holiday on it.' Our morning had involved a dash to the Tulip Museum after the police had left and the crowd outside our houseboat had dispersed. I then spent all afternoon doing research on the phone and the internet.

'The woman at the museum was hilarious,' laughs Nina, 'you should have seen your face when she started talking about reproductive organs.'

'She was astonishing. I had no idea the tulip was part of

Amsterdam's sex industry!'

'Oh well, you'd better press send,' says Nina. 'And we can get on with our holiday.'

'And let Su and the subs do their worst,' I mutter to myself. Although I have worked as a sub-editor myself, I still have a writer's prejudice that my own copy is unimprovable. I attach the article to an email. Then I attach a smaller piece about the discovery of the flower on our roof, add the photo of it from my phone and send it all off to Su. It is early evening and my stomach is grumbling.

'Why don't we find something to eat in Rembrandtplein?' I ask. 'It's not far and it's warm enough to find a table outside with Eddie. It'll be interesting to see if the police have stepped up patrols there after our discussion.'

Nina quickly agrees and we stroll across the Amstel on Halvemaans Bridge and into the Rembrandtplein district just as the sky is darkening. We pause briefly on the other side and look back to admire the reflection of the lights on the far bank in the still black water of the river. The little town square is just one block in from the Amstel. We pay homage to the statue of the famous painter in the centre of the square and laugh as Eddie chooses to cock his leg on the plinth.

'He's clearly not an art lover,' says Nina.

'No. But a lot of the locals are.' I nod around the square where several artists are already at work or in the process of setting up their easels to draw its nightlife. The streets off the square are full of hotels and cafes. We quickly find an empty table, loop Eddie's lead under a leg and order two plates of steak and salad with a bottle of wine to share.

'Cheers.'

'Proost,' I reply.

'It's odd, don't you think?'

'What?'

'That the flower should be left on the roof of our houseboat. I mean, what are the chances of that happening?'

'I know what you mean. They had the whole city to choose from. But they seem to be plotting the location of the corpses very carefully for some reason.'

'The straight line...'

'Exactly. And the same distance apart. They placed the body under the Love Lock Bridge and I suppose we just happened to be moored nearby with a convenient box of bog-standard tulips on our roof.'

Nina looks around us. 'Well, I only saw a couple of policemen in the square so perhaps they aren't taking your theory very seriously.'

I shrug and take a large swallow of wine. "It wasn't a theory. Just an observation. And maybe they're all in plain clothes. They wouldn't want to scare the killers off. They'll need to catch them in the act.'

'It's amazing really.' She is running a forefinger around the rim of her wine glass.

'What is?'

'How you seem to be such a magnet for trouble. There's never a dull moment with you is there, Jack?'

'Is that why you love me?' I regret the words as soon as they are spoken and I can feel myself colouring up. Nina has never declared her love for me although I live in constant hope. The grief for her husband stopped her contemplating any new relationship for at least a year after his death - and then Oxford happened. I still can't believe I turned her away from my bed at the end of that particular saga. But I was determined not to exploit her confused and vulnerable feelings at such a difficult time. I trusted my instinct not to rush things. I can be so bloody stupid sometimes.

Fortunately, the arrival of our food helps to cover the moment and we are soon wiping up the meat juices with our bread. Nina spoke to her niece on the phone during the afternoon while I was working. She fills me in on all of Anna's news from Oxford University. As she talks, I reflect that as a single child with dead parents, she and Anna have become the closest thing to a family for me.

It is dark now and somehow the wine bottle is already empty. 'Shall we find a bar?' she asks.

I'm relieved that Nina is taking a more relaxed attitude to my alcohol intake than usual. She's definitely got the holiday spirit.

'Of course,' I reply.

We find an English-looking pub called The Old Bell on a corner of the square and Nina charms the guy at the door so that Eddie is allowed in to join us. I tie his lead to a bar stool and we both order large single-malt whiskies with a small jug of water.

'Here's to the rest of our break,' says Nina, clinking my glass.

'What are your plans afterwards?'

'I honestly don't know. I think maybe you were right. I need to give Anna a bit more space, so I think I'll move on from Oxford.'

I suspect she also wants to move on from sad memories of the place. I have similar reasons for also wanting to move on from the City of Dreaming Spires.

'Me too.'

'Where?'

My honest answer is 'wherever you are going' but it sounds a bit pathetic. 'Oh, I don't know. London maybe? It would be easier to find a bit of work there.'

Nina sips her whisky. 'Well, at least my flat fell through, so it's easy for me to move on. Maybe I'll just hitch a ride on *Jumping Jack Flash* with you and Eddie and see where we end up?'

I can't help grinning in spite of myself. 'You'd be more than welcome. You know that. Same again?'

We chat easily over a couple more whiskies. The loosely arranged plan has pleased us both, although there are deeper issues which are still going unsaid. Plenty of time for that, I think to myself. Eventually, Nina drags me off the bar stools and links her arm in mine for the short walk back through the square and across the river to *Flora's* mooring. Nina's right. There doesn't seem to be an unusually large police presence. I can only see two pairs of uniformed officers.

This time we stop halfway across the road-bridge to admire the city at night. 'It is incredible,' says Nina. 'To think that all of this was created out of a marshy wilderness that was constantly being flooded by the sea.'

I look west along the river to where a rubbish collection barge with its own little crane is moored to the bank. Some work lights are shining brightly and we can see men moving about among rows of neatly stacked plastic bins. I nod in its direction. 'Maybe they should have left it as a swamp? Mankind seems to make a mess of most places.'

Nina affects an Irish accent. 'Ah to be sure Jack. It's the whisky that's making you maudlin, so it is.' She hooks one arm through mine and we walk on across the bridge and back to our boat with Eddie happily trotting along at our side. Life, for the moment, seems good.

CHAPTER THIRTEEN

A few hours before Jack and Nina's night-time stroll, a small thin man was working two kilometres away in the Eastern Docklands of the city. Hans Grootveld reached up and pulled the rear door of his hatchback shut with a grunt. The boxes of books seemed to be getting heavier and heavier, but he was forced to admit it was more a case of him getting older and weaker as he neared his 80th birthday. He had parked as close as possible to his storage unit, but the five return trips had tired him out.

The books were destined for his stall at the weekly book market which took place at the Spui. However, his was the only stall among more than twenty-five which specialised in the politics of the far right. People often approached him with books they wanted him to find. But most of them were whinging liberal critiques of nationalism and populism, whereas he stocked books which would actually appeal to the true believers. Not that it paid very well. It was just his way of keeping the flame alive. It was also a means to an end.

The second-hand book trade also put him in touch with people who had a taste for a different type of merchandise which did earn him a decent income, although he preferred to trade it online. He could conceal his identity more easily on the internet and there was a huge global demand for his memorabilia linked to Adolf Hitler's Waffen-SS and other parts of the Nazi regime. That meant he could charge premium prices and even, occasionally, get a little online auction going between collectors in different countries.

There was nothing illegal about selling such things – not if they had been acquired legally. But that was the problem. Ninety-per-cent of Grootveld's stock had been stolen from small museums across the Netherlands. He had cautiously researched his vulnerable targets over a period of years. Then he used a false name and underworld connections to assemble a gang of professional burglars. He had given them the most specific instructions and rewarded them well for just a few months of work. Some of the raids were lightning-fast smash-and-grabs with doors demolished and less than six minutes spent inside the building. Others were quiet burglaries carried out in the dead of night.

None of the gang knew where Grootveld stored the proceeds of their crimes. But they had slowly accumulated into a highly valuable collection which he released onto the market in very small quantities that were spaced apart. At that very moment he had two buyers interested in some forks from the personal cutlery of both Adolf Hitler and the SS leader Heinrich Himmler. His SS uniforms and the uniforms of the Hitler Youth were also very expensive and popular. Then there were the parachutes, daggers, helmets, emblems, caps and binoculars which were all snatched from glass display cabinets. Canadian, French, English and American memorabilia had been ignored, but mannequins dressed in German clothing were stripped naked. In one raid, 15 dressed mannequins were taken in their military uniforms. The spate of burglaries even prompted the Arnhem War Museum to instal roadblocks so large that vehicles could not enter its site.

There had also been firearms amongst the various hauls. Grootveld knew he would need all of his wily business sense to fence a Fallschirmjagergeweher 42 (FG 42), a rifle that was used by German paratroopers that ought to fetch him a minimum of fifty thousand euros.

He returned to the lock-up one last time, switched out all the lights and set the state-of-the-art alarm system. No low-life burglar scum would get the better of him. He turned three different keys in the three locks of the solid steel door, looked up at the two cameras covering the entrance - which he could monitor via his smartphone - and shuffled slowly back to his car. He had an ache in his lower back from hefting the boxes. It was all getting too much for him and he was seriously considering abandoning the book trade. It had served its purpose and he fancied a quiet retirement now, with an occasional sale of his stolen memorabilia to supplement his pension.

The industrial estate was very quiet at this time of the evening. That suited him. He didn't want anyone from a neighbouring business to get too curious about his comings and goings or what might be stored inside the unit behind the piles of books.

So, he was surprised and not a little nervous when he saw a police patrol car slewed horizontally across the approach road to his business premises and blocking his exit. He could just make out a police motorbike propped on its stand behind the car. Two officers in peaked caps were sitting in the car but the motorcyclist was on his feet. He was wearing blue striped trousers tucked into big leather boots, a bright yellow blouson and a bright yellow crash helmet with a black visor that was pulled down. He was standing with his legs apart and holding a gloved palm in the air towards Grootveld.

'Shit,' said the old man. His mouth was instantly bone dry and he tried to hawk some saliva into it. Were the cops onto him? Had somebody blabbed to them? Had he made a careless mistake with a recent sale?

The motorcycle cop was now walking towards his car and making a circular winding movement with one hand. Grootveld obediently pressed a button to lower his driver's window. He expected the policeman to raise his black-mirrored visor to talk to him as he stooped forward. But instead, he simply reached through the window with his gloved right hand and yanked out the ignition key. 'Hey, what are you doing?' asked the old man.

Now the policeman reached back into the car with his left hand

and pushed it between the headrest and the back of Grootveld's bald head. 'What? What are you doing?' he shouted. But it was too late. The hand in the leather glove pushed his skull downwards and forward at speed. It crashed forcefully into the top of the steering wheel. The action was repeated twice more so that the old man's face and forehead was a mess of blood. There was no driver's air bag to save him as the engine had been switched off. Hans Grootveld was still conscious and groaning as he was lifted out of his car by the three men. The old man was no weight at all, and he was quickly bundled face down into the back of the police car. His nose, crushed and broken, was rammed down onto a see-through plastic sheet that was covering the rear seat. It was the last thing he smelt before he felt something sharp stab him in the neck.

CHAPTER FOURTEEN

Day Four. Tulip Murder number four. The body of a skinny old man hangs in the same pose as the others. It is slumped across a mooring rope on the Amstel River where the main thoroughfare of the Amstel Road runs along its bank. The police have sealed off the immediate area shortly after the junction with a smaller road called Bakkerstraat.

'The body was found by the owner of the record store.' Robert points across the road to the entrance of a shop which is half-way below the level of the pavement. It has a sign above the door that boasts about the 25,000 vinyl records inside. One of their team is taking notes from a man with a ponytail who is dressed in a denim jacket and jeans. 'He was taking a bag of rubbish over to the boat.' A large, unmanned rubbish collection barge is moored up and the body of the old man is suspended between its metal hull and the stone wall of the riverbank. Beatrix has already spent a few minutes staring down at the top of the man's bare skull. 'The wire to the camera above the shop's entrance has been cut.'

'And the flower?' she says. She hears the question come out wearily and makes a mental note to buck up. She needs to set an example and remain optimistic and full of energy for her squad.

But in truth, she is tired and worried. She had been forced to stop her car on the drive over when a rush of anxiety had flooded through her whole body and left her shaking and tearful. This had never happened to her before. Two hundred extra officers have been deployed in central Amsterdam overnight, but none of them reported anything relevant or suspicious. The pressure from the Ministry of Justice and even the Prime Minister's office was becoming intense. The locals might occasionally grumble about being swamped by tourists, but worldwide publicity of this sort was not to be welcomed.

'Nothing yet,' says Robert, scanning all around him again. 'We're still looking.' A crowd of curious bystanders is gathering at the cordons which have closed off the road. Car horns are sounding angrily in the background. Word is getting out again and they all want to see a tulip that might be worth more than a million euros. Although, thinks Beatrix, surely the more there are, the lower the value?

'Any identity yet?'

'We're going to have to get the barge moved,' says Robert. 'Or at least slacken her ropes and push her out from the wall. We can't get down to him any other way.'

Beatrix nods, shivers, and pulls her quilted coat tighter. 'We need a break, Robert. Where are the team on any connection between the victims?'

'Nothing. Far right politics but that's it. Still no evidence that they knew each other.'

'This is a small, crowded city. How can they snatch people without any witnesses?'

'They must be hiding in plain sight, Beatrix. They used the ambulance for the first hit. Maybe they've got their hands on other official vehicles, other uniforms. We're trying to find out whether the barge was already here or whether they shipped it onto this mooring.'

'It seems like they've been planning this for months. They know exactly what they need and how to get it.'

'And yet there isn't a sniff from our informers. They can't be local villains, or someone would know about it.'

'And how are they gaining from this? What is the motive? It can't be financial – and it doesn't feel personal, so it has to be political. Doesn't it?'

'And why go to the trouble of using different plant-based poisons? It's like they're flaunting their knowledge of toxicology. Foxglove, yellow jasmine and now oleander. God knows what this one will be.'

'The poisons must tie in somehow with the Semper Augustus,' says Beatrix. The pair of them know they are repeating a conversation they have already had several times, but they continue to work away at it, hoping for a spark of inspiration. 'Speaking of which, we need to find the flower before the crowds really start arriving. The last thing we need is some kind of riot in front of the television cameras.'

Uniformed officers have already been despatched to comb the area as increasing numbers of newcomers swell the crowds on the road at both ends. However, an hour passes with no discovery of the rare flower.

'Maybe they've run out of them,' mutters Beatrix to herself as Robert urges the senior uniformed officer to widen the search radius and start knocking on the doors of nearby houses. 'I doubt they've got a field full of the damn things.'

The Scene-of-Crime work party has also used the past hour to slacken the rubbish barge's mooring ropes and push it further out into the river. A soaking wet driver's licence is brought to Beatrix in an evidence bag. The dead man is seventy-nine-years-old and called Hans Grootveld. His address is in Oostpoort. She rings HQ to begin background checks and orders some officers to go to his home immediately.

She will call the whole team together this afternoon, she tells herself. They will systematically go through all they know about the four killings and then she will lead a brainstorm on possible new lines of enquiry. She automatically starts to scan the faces in the crowd. Has she seen any of them before at the other locations? Have they been stupid enough to return to the scene and enjoy the sight of the police flailing around uselessly? No. These people are professionals. They wouldn't be so careless. But even as she is thinking this, one face comes into sharp focus for her. It is the Englishman. Johnson. And his girlfriend is standing alongside him. He is looking straight back at her and beckoning urgently. She sighs heavily and begins to move towards them.

CHAPTER FIFTEEN

'Commissioner,' I call out, indicating the officer who is standing between us. 'Commissioner. A word. Please.' The detective called Dr Beatrix van der Laen taps a constable on the shoulder and indicates that he should let me and Nina through the cordon. We duck under the plastic tape and walk a short distance with her.

'Well, Mr Johnson. What can I do for you? As you can see, I am quite busy.'

'There's been another body. We saw the news on the internet first thing this morning.'

She indicates the activity going on all around us. 'I would have thought that was obvious.' She smiles tiredly. 'Even to a British journalist.'

'Is the body next to the rubbish barge?' I ask.

'Yes. They are recovering it shortly,' she says. 'But really...'

I interrupt her quickly. 'We may have seen them dumping it last night. We were walking back across the bridge, over there, and we stopped halfway across. I could see some workmen moving about on this barge. They had a few lights on and they were doing something on this side of the boat, by the road.'

The younger detective called Robert now joins us and hears what

I have said. 'What time was this?' he demands, his pen poised above a little leather notebook.

'About 11 o'clock.'

Nina nods in agreement. 'We were walking back from a bar in Rembrandtplein. I know we got to our boat at 11.15pm.'

'Did you see anything else?' asks Robert urgently. 'Did you take any photographs? What else can you remember?'

'I didn't take much notice,' I admit. 'We'd been drinking. I suppose I didn't think it was strange to see a rubbish barge working late at night. I just saw the lights and a few men moving around on deck. I'm pretty sure they had overalls on, with fluorescent yellow strips. But that's all.'

'Damn,' says van der Laen.

'But there's something else.' I pull out both sides of our tourist map and turn it to face them. 'Remember yesterday? I showed you the first three bodies were all found in a straight line running north to south. This one is too. Look for yourself.'

The two detectives bend to study the map where I have added a fourth X to mark the location of this morning's corpse. It is directly in line with the other three.

'But it's not spaced apart from the others in the same way,' she says.

'It's exactly half the distance of the others. The full distance would have been in Rembrantplein, like I said.'

'And the bar you went to last night. Did you say that was in Rembrantplein?' asks Robert. The older woman gives him a curious look.

'Yes,' I admit. 'We were curious to see whether you had stepped up patrols in the area last night. And you have to admit, we weren't far out with the location of this body. It was still on the straight line that connects them all. Surely, you have to take that seriously?'

The stately woman with her carefully sculpted hair fixes me with a steely stare. 'Oh yes. We shall take this very seriously, Mr Johnson. Robert, please arrange a car to take this pair back to HQ will you? We shall continue our conversation there.'

We are left waiting in an interview room for about 20 minutes with two undrinkable coffees that quickly go cold in their plastic cups. After a while, it gets a little boring staring at the room's only decoration. Two framed photographs of the former Queen, now Princess Beatrix of the Netherlands, and her son, the current King Willem-Alexander hang above the chairs opposite us. They are bisected by a no-smoking sticker. I assume the pictures have been put up as something of an in-joke because the former monarch really is a dead ringer for Dr Beatrix van der Laen. The regal woman in the photograph has enormous sapphires clipped to her ears and pearls around her neck. But she shares the policewoman's dimpled cheeks, piercing blue eyes and silver-grey mane of hair which sweeps backwards and upwards from a high forehead.

'Are we under arrest?' I ask the Queen's doppelganger as she sits down alongside her number two.

'If you were under arrest, we would be talking to you separately. For the moment you are simply helping us with our enquiries.'

'In that case...' I say, half-rising, but Nina puts a hand on my arm.

'Play nice, Jack,' she says quietly.

'Why have you brought us here?' I ask.

She steeples her hands and tucks them under her chin with both elbows resting on the metal table. 'The murders began on the day you arrived in Amsterdam. The third Semper Augustus is found on your boat. Then you notice a pattern to the location of the bodies. And finally, you just happen to see the fourth body being dumped on the Amstel. That's all quite curious, isn't it? What do you and your girlfriend think?'

'She's not my girlfriend,' I say at exactly the same time as Nina says, 'I'm not his girlfriend.' We sound like a couple of embarrassed teenagers. 'We're just friends,' I add lamely, 'on holiday.'

'Alright. If you say so. Please go over your movements since you arrived in Amsterdam.'

I give a brief account of everything that we have done with Nina chipping in. When she hears about the article I have written for the British press she asks to see it. I pull it up on my phone, open the document and they both read it in turn.

'It seems we are *baffled*, Beatrix,' says Robert.

'If you would like to give me an alternative description of the state of your investigation, I'll see that it is shared more widely,' I say defensively. Nina looks at me with a raised eyebrow and I realise I sound a bit pompous.

'And now we discover that you also go on a boat trip with the prominent right-wing politician, Cornelius Tulp?' says Robert. 'How would you describe your own politics Mr Johnson?'

I snort with laughter. 'You really are reaching, aren't you? I told you, we met him by accident after one of his guests spoilt our dinner.'

'My colleague asked you about your politics.' insists Beatrix.

'Oh God … I don't know. I'm a journalist. I agree with whoever it was who said whenever a politician says something, my first response is *"why is this lying bastard lying to me?"*.'

'He isn't very political,' confirms Nina with a smile. 'But he has a strong moral compass.' I look sideways at her and give her a grateful smile.

'Very well,' says Beatrix. 'I'm going to ask you to remain here while we run some background checks.'

However, the door opens just as she begins to stand. A younger woman enters and bends to whisper in Beatrix's ear. We are only a few feet away, but the briefing is in Dutch. I do make out the word 'Nazi' though.

'This is a joke,' I mutter to Nina once we are left on our own.

'They're just doing their job,' she says. 'And don't forget, they're unfamiliar with your talent for finding trouble. It takes a while to get used to it.'

We spend half-an-hour scrolling idly on our mobile phones. The hashtag #TulipMurders is everywhere, particularly as no Semper Augustus has been found near the site of the latest victim. Speculation is rife across all of social media and almost all of the comments are accompanied by a pink tulip emoji. It must only be a matter of time before it is redesigned in white with red streaks. 'Did someone find the tulip before the police?' is a common question. 'The killers must have been disturbed before they could leave the flower,' is another theory. 'Maybe there were only ever three of the flowers,' says a tulip expert and this is already being shared and retweeted thousands of times.

Nina shows me an English-language news website. The morning's victim has been identified as a 79-year-old antiquarian and second-hand book seller called Hans Grootveld, a widower who lived alone. A neighbour describes him as "*a bit of a loner and very security conscious*" and another stall holder at Spui Market reveals he mainly stocked books about nationalism and right-wing politics.

'An ultra right-wing bouncer, columnist, priest and now a right-wing bookseller,' I say. 'You can see why the police are interested in my politics.'

'You're not the only one joining those particular dots,' says Nina. 'Listen. "*It doesn't take a genius to see the common link between the #TulipMurder victims. They were all anti-Islam, anti-immigration and pro right-wing causes. Our country has always cherished its political and religious freedom. Our police and intelligence services should be turning Amsterdam upside down to find the religious terrorists responsible for these terrible crimes – starting with the places where the immigrants live.*"

'That is one confused person,' I say. 'They cherish their history of political and religious freedom but want to kick Muslim doors in.'

Eventually, it is Robert who returns to our room on his own. 'We are sorry to have kept you. You are free to go now. Thank you for your help. I hope you are able to enjoy the rest of your holiday.'

'What?' That's it? You haul us in here, question us and then just show us the door with no explanation?'

'Leave it Jack,' says Nina. 'Let's just get out of here.'

'The exit door is better than a cell door is it not?' says the Inspector. 'This way please.'

He escorts us to the front door of the police headquarters. But before ushering us through, he steers us towards a tall plump man in a blue double-breasted suit who unfolds himself from an easy chair. He peers at us through a pair of thick black plastic glasses.

'This is Archi Gupta Bhalla from the British Embassy. I'll leave you in his capable hands.'

Archi Gupta Bhalla shakes our hands and murmurs "*enchanted*" at Nina. 'Please, just call me Archi. There's a bit of a media scrum out front,' he says. His lips protrude slightly so that he looks as if he is permanently pouting. 'Lots of reporters and cameras. I think it might be best if we take the back door. My car is there.'

Archi is clearly familiar with the layout of the police station and seems to have a licence to roam. He takes us along various corridors smelling of bleach and then down a flight of stairs and out into a lower-level parking area. 'It'll be a bit of a squeeze I'm afraid but there's just about room for in the back for a little one. That'll be you I think, Mrs Wilde.'

'Where are we going?' I ask as I admire the vintage Porsche that he is ushering us towards.

He bends to straighten his tie in the reflection of the driver's window. 'I'll whizz you back to your boat if that's alright. Your dog will be wondering where you've got to.'

So, the man from the embassy already knows we are staying on a houseboat and that Eddie is travelling with us? He has obviously done his homework.

Nina squeezes sideways on the tiny rear seat while I belt up in the front. The drive to our boat only takes ten minutes but it is a fast and furious affair as we dodge trams, buses, bicycles and pedestrians at speed and with a liberal use of the horn. Archi maintains a monologue throughout a journey which is frequently interrupted by near misses.

'I run UK/Dutch police liaison over here, among other things. We had a call early this morning asking us to check you both out. Of course, it wasn't difficult with you being all over the internet. But I made a few calls to the British police forces you've worked with – just to be sure. Don't know why Beatrix and Robert didn't just google you for themselves. I see you've written a couple of books. Fancy having a go at that myself one day. They're nice people, Beatrix and Robert that is. Good at their job. Beatrix has run the murder squad in Amsterdam for about 15 years. She has a national reputation, international even. She's very well thought of. She's wrapped up a lot of famous cases. But she must be under a hell of a lot of pressure at the moment with these so-called Tulip Murders. Some of the press call her 'The Queen of Murder' because of her name of course, and she does look a bit like Princess Beatrix. That's the former queen. She abdicated; did you know? I think she quite enjoys the notoriety. Commissioner Beatrix that is. She's always been helpful to me. It's surprising how often a British tourist gets into trouble with the police over here. But then, we're the single biggest nationality to visit this city. More than one and a quarter million a year. LOOK OUT you stupid idiot! And they say the Italians are crazy drivers! Anyway, the ambassador told me to drop everything and help them out when the call came in. I expect he was shitting himself at the thought of a Brit being responsible for these killings. Especially if there's a whiff of political terrorism in the air. Whoops-a-daisy. Sorry about that folks. Cyclists. D'you know there are 800,000 bikes in the city centre? That works out at one per resident. And not a single bloody cycle helmet between them. It's madness. Anyway, it was quite interesting coming into their HQ today. Robert told me they're digging up all kinds of interesting things about the victims.'

Archi turns to look over his shoulder and make sure that Nina is listening to him. I only just resist the urge to grab the steering wheel. 'The first one, the bouncer, he was the leader of some kind of gang of thugs whose idea of fun was attacking Muslims at the weekend. Called themselves the 'football club', or some such nonsense. Then there was the newspaper columnist. He'd been using his paper to demand that the red-light district should be moved to the outskirts of the city. Turns out, he had pretty exotic sexual tastes of his own. Then they found tonnes of child pornography on the home computer of the priest. And they've just found a hoard of stolen Nazi memorabilia in a lock-up belonging to the bookseller who was discovered this morning. His car was abandoned nearby. Extraordinary! Oh, come on, move over, you stupid man! You'd better keep all that to yourselves for now. Chatham House rules and all that. But I'm sure it'll all come out soon anyway. We get all the British papers at the embassy, which is at The Hague by the way, and they're full of it too. Mostly because of this rare tulip of course. What's it called? Augustus something? I was briefing Beatrix and Robert about you when they brought in this morning's flower. Very pretty yes, I'll grant you that – but worth over a million euros? I think not. They couldn't find it at first. Did you know? Turns out the owner of a nearby record shop found it in a little pot on his doorstep. Stupid chap thought he'd hang onto it and make a fortune. They found it in a filing cabinet in his office. Now then, which is your boat? This one here is it? *Flora*? Fine. Any chance of a quick cup of tea?'

The man from the embassy makes a fuss of Eddie but is careful not to have him on his lap. 'No, no, little man. You'll get hairs all over my suit!' He gratefully accepts a mug of Earl Grey from Nina. 'No milk. Just a squeeze of lemon if you can spare any from the G&Ts.'

'What did you say your position is at the Embassy?' asks Nina.

Archi tips his head back and peers at her through his thick rimmed glasses. 'I don't think I did actually. I just sort of make myself useful. I'm a kind of consular attaché.'

'But you handle the liaison between the Dutch and British police?' I ask.

'Among other things,' he nods cheerfully, reaching for a biscuit. 'D'you mind if I have one of these? I had to skip breakfast in the rush.'

'Gosh,' says Nina. 'Are you some kind of spy? Like James Bond? You drive the right kind of car and you do dress very well!' She has made her dark eyes deliberately big and round. I can tell she finds Archi amusing and has decided to tease him. Archi, however, takes the enquiry very seriously.

'No, no, no. Not at all. Of course, I would love to be James Bond. Who wouldn't? What do they say? All men want to be him, and all women want to be with him! But I am a minor official of the British Foreign Office in the Netherlands. Please don't tell my mother that though! She is convinced that I shall be the next British ambassador in New Delhi and that all of our relatives there will be very impressed.' He gives a big-bellied laugh and Nina and I join in. 'And don't be fooled by my beloved car or my clothes. You don't buy them on the wages of a minor junior diplomat! My papa runs a big clothing company in Birmingham. He paid for me to go to a fancy school and on to Cambridge, and he still gives me an allowance, thank goodness.'

'But seriously,' he says folding his hands across his belly, 'I don't want another posting yet. It's a fascinating time to be here.

Politically, the place is on a knife-edge. Of course, it's famous for its liberalism, for cherishing individual freedoms and all that. And if that means treading a line between control and chaos, the Netherlands – and this city in particular – have always embraced a certain degree of chaos. Oh my gosh yes. Especially in the sixties. But the mood is shifting. Geert Wilders is pretty popular you know? He was actually convicted of racial discrimination and inciting hatred. But he denounced it as a political trial and he wasn't fined or sanctioned in any way. The liberals don't know how to handle him, or the other right-wing parties. So, Wilder's mob get the space to peddle their hate speech and grow in numbers. When the Party for Freedom became the third largest party it had the leverage to push through tougher immigration laws and they've been reminding people about that ever since. And now you've got The People's Party for Freedom and Democracy and Tulp's Born-Again bunch wading in. I hear you bumped into him. I'd love to hear more. It won't take much for a right-wing anti-immigration coalition to form the next government.' He pauses his political lecture to pop some gum in his mouth and then remembers his manners. 'I'm sorry. Would you like some? Here, take a packet why don't you?' He presses a small plastic bag into Nina's hand.

'Now I must love you and leave you. I need to get back to work. Thanks for the tea and biscuits. Here's my card. Don't hesitate to get in touch if I can be of assistance. I don't imagine the police will be bothering you again. Not unless you bother them that is. Ha ha.'

We shake hands and stand on *Flora's* stern to watch Archi roar off in his fast car. Nina opens her fist and we discover he has given her a packet of twelve tablets of 'refreshing' cannabis strawberry chewing gum. Then we have to hold each other up or risk falling overboard as we convulse with laughter.

CHAPTER SIXTEEN

I ring Su to check she can amend my article to include the fourth murder but decide not to tell her about our morning visit to police headquarters or the reasons for it. I know she would try to milk it, but Nina and I agree it was all a waste of time and not worth any additional headlines or unwelcome attention. As it is, a steady trickle of gongoozlers is still arriving at *Flora's* mooring to see where the third Semper Augustus was discovered.

'At this rate, there'll be a bloody tourist trail for the Tulip Murders complete with a special map, audio guide and souvenir postcard,' I complain as I pull our landside blinds down.

'Well, I for one wouldn't mind doing a few more touristy things instead of wasting time in a police station,' Nina replies.

We spend the next hour swapping ideas from Nina's tourist guide and my laptop and finally arrive at a list of things to do and places to see for the next few days. Top of Nina's list is the Rijksmuseum, an enormous national institution which, unsurprisingly, is located in the Museum Quarter. I see from its website that we are being encouraged to *"lean back and dive into"* a collection of more than 8,000 masterpieces from the Middle Ages to the 21st century.

'How can you *"lean back and dive in"* at the same time?' I ask grumpily. The destination feels to me like one we must tick off as a duty rather than something to savour.

'Jack! It would be like going to Paris and missing out on a visit to the Louvre!'

'That doesn't sound too bad an idea to me. Once you've seen one Mona Lisa, you've...'

'We're going to see some Rembrandts – and that's final.' Nina has been swotting up on Rembrandt ever since we decided to come to Amsterdam and has bought a heavy glossy book about the painter. 'I want to see *The Night Watch*, obviously, and his self-portrait – the younger one and the older one where he's dressed as the apostle Paul. I read somewhere that they've also got *The Anatomy Lesson* on loan. And we should try to see some Vermeer too. *The Milkmaid*, obviously, and *Woman Reading A Letter*.'

I sigh and resign myself to an afternoon in a crush of sweaty bodies, straining and standing on tiptoes to get a glimpse of Nina's greatest hits. I move my laptop's pointer around the screen.

'Bloody hell. It says we need to allow 4 to 5 hours and book in advance if we want a chance of seeing the Rembrandts.'

Nina pokes her head over my shoulder. 'That's 4 or 5 hours to see the whole museum. We can do the Gallery of Honour and Rembrandt and some other stuff in a couple of hours. Stop being such a grouch and book us in, Jack. This one is non-negotiable.'

Her jaw is firmly set and I know it's no use arguing. Amazingly, we manage to secure two slots for the afternoon, but I insist on a beer and sandwich lunch in a bar first. 'Eddie isn't too bothered about 17th century masterpieces and he'll need a stretch before we leave. Don't forget he cocked his leg on Rembrandt's statue.'

'Shameless,' declares Nina. 'Using your dog as an excuse for a liquid lunch. Just don't keep sloping off for a pee yourself once we're in the museum.'

The queue of people snaking up to the museum entrance looks tediously long but our pre-booked tickets allow us to quickly nip inside. However, it doesn't prevent a very English sense of guilt at queue jumping. Nina insists on hiring two audio commentary kits and we insert one earpiece each so we can still hear each other. We are soon standing in front of a painting called *The Night Watch,* which is enormous. We're told it shows a group of civic guardsmen about to set off on patrol through Amsterdam – a kind of 17th century Dutch Dads' Army. The central figure is dressed in a red sash and called Captain Banninck Cocq, which is pronounced Banging Cock by the audio guide. This makes me snigger like a naughty schoolboy.

'It's a bit bloody dark,' I mutter as the commentary, which has an American accent, tells me that this was deliberate so that the figures become dramatically spot-lit. We're told that this was one of the paintings in which Rembrandt re-invented the group portrait. Instead of ranking the soldiers in line, they are allegedly a disorderly group captured in action and doing things like loading a gun, waving a pennant and banging a drum. 'This is what makes the painting so unique,' I hear through my earpiece. It still looks pretty artificial and static to me. Nina is listening intently while I am keen to move on. There's only so much pleasure I can get staring at an overly dark painting of some blokes with floppy hats and dubious facial hair. I am also intensely irritated by the American pronunciation of Baroque as Bar-Roke.

The next painting Nina drags me to is a self-portrait of Rembrandt at the age of 22, before he moved to Amsterdam. A round-faced young man with a mess of red hair sits in dark shadow. I hear Nina give a little sigh of pleasure when we're told how he experimented with the end of his paintbrush to scratch lines in the wet paint to suggest sunlight catching his curls. Once more, I think he should have opened the curtains a bit more and let more light in. I leave her there to find a loo and agree to meet in front of another self-portrait – Rembrandt aged 55 and posing as the apostle Paul.

I stare hard at the face while the commentary witters on about more astonishing use of light and shade and the symbols of martyrdom in the painting. His bulbous pitted nose tells me that he was a bit of a toper, a suggestion reinforced by his round droopy eyes, creased brow and fleshy skin. He's obviously had quite a lot of life experience in Amsterdam since the earlier self-portrait. But Nina doesn't seem amused by this observation and the earpiece probably means I shared it more loudly than I meant to.

She drags me away and we set off in search of *The Anatomy Lesson*. This one is actually quite interesting. We are told it dates from 1632, so he painted it shortly after arriving in Amsterdam at the age of 25. It shows the naked body of a man with a discreetly placed loincloth being dissected on a slab. We're told he was an armed robber who was hanged for his crimes and then cut up in public. The painting depicts the city's annual public dissection by the chief surgeon who is pulling the tendon of an arm upwards with some kind of surgical instrument. A group of doctors lean over the body in their starched white collars or stare directly at the viewer.

'It's important to remember,' says the commentary, 'that Holland in the 17th century was largely a Protestant nation and the church was no longer a major patron. So, artists looked to the emerging professional and middle classes for patronage.' We are told that all of the dignified-looking men of the Guild of Surgeons who feature in the painting would have paid Rembrandt for the privilege, and that the Chief Surgeon, Dr Nicolaes Tulp would have coughed-up the most money for such a prominent place in the spotlight. Wait. What was that name again?

I push forward and stare at the painting's label on the wall. Sure enough, the painting's full title is *The Anatomy Lesson of Dr. Nicolaes Tulp*. Tulp. It's the same surname as Cornelius Tulp, our private tourist guide and co-founder of the Born-Again party. Could I be looking at one of his ancestors? I stare at the well-lit face of Dr Tulp standing alone on the right-hand side of the painting. The two men share the same shrewd eyes and very similarly shaped eyebrows and noses. The 21st century Tulp even has the same slightly upturned moustache and pointed beard as the painted man in front of us.

'Look,' I say to Nina. 'He's called Tulp. Just like Cornelius Tulp. Remember?'

'They certainly resemble each other,' she says. 'And didn't Tulp say he was a lawyer who came from a long line of doctors?'

'Oh well. I don't imagine we'll ever see him again to ask.'

I am forbidden from fleeing the vast and crowded treasure house for another two hours but eventually we emerge blinking into the late afternoon sun. Nina has hoovered up a thick pack of postcards from the museum's shop and is looking very happy. Visitors have apparently been asked to stop taking photographs and start sketching the art instead. I fear any drawings by me would have borne little resemblance to the great works of the Dutch masters. But they wouldn't have been shrouded in darkness either.

'That was brilliant. So many amazing pictures. I loved it, Jack. Which one would you like to take home?'

'Well, there isn't much room on *Jumping Jack Flash* to hang these kinds of paintings. And the insurance would be a bummer. But I think if I could have any of them it would be *The Threatened Swan*.' And it is true, I thought the life-sized mute swan flaring up into the air to defend its nest against a dog was pretty magnificent. 'But even that couldn't just be a great painting of a swan. It turned out to be some kind of political allegory.'

Nina links an arm through mine and is jauntily swinging her other arm in high good spirits. 'You're not as much of a philistine as you pretend to be, Jack Johnson. I thought I'd love the Rembrandts most, but in the end, I'll take a Vermeer home, please; *Girl With a Pearl Earring.*'

'Nah,' I reply, gently steering Nina towards the tables and chairs outside a nearby bar. 'I'll stick with the real thing.' She gives me a puzzled look. 'You know, the film with Scarlett Johansson in. Now then,' I add rubbing my hands, 'wine or beer?'

CHAPTER SEVENTEEN

Even the most casual observer would suspect that Lieutenant Colonel Willem Becker had been a military man at some point in his life. He still marched along the pavements near his home in the Vondelbuurt district of Amsterdam with both fists clenched, thumbs pointing straight at the ground and arms locked rigid. He held his head rigid too, although his eyes flickered from left to right as he constantly scoped his surroundings. His hair was still razored to a fine fuzz, the ironed creases in the trousers of his suit were razor sharp and his tie was immaculately knotted. He was a small man, just over 5ft 6 inches, but he carried himself with the natural authority of someone who had given orders for most of his life and expected them to be instantly obeyed.

Many of his men in the Korps Commandotroepen, or the special operations force of the Royal Netherlands Army, had well-toned physiques that towered above him. But even the company's most feared Sergeant Major afforded him the utmost respect. Like most of Europe's special forces, he was prevented from talking or writing about his most memorable operations – even in retirement. However, he had quickly found solace in old soldiers' regular reunions.

In fact, he had quickly assumed a leading role in their organisation after he had marched out of his base at Roosendaal for the final time, ten years earlier. At first, they had been slightly drunken and depressing affairs in isolated country hotels where they might also do a bit of target shooting or watch a war film. But then their get-togethers had acquired an edge after the weasel politicians tried to cheat 17,500 military personnel out of their rights by raising the state pension from 65 to 67. In doing so, they conveniently ignored the fact that most soldiers had been forced to retire earlier. Becker had run an efficient and persuasive campaign, marshalled a fund to take the issue to court and shone a spotlight on every MP from the ruling coalition who had turned down an opposition motion to plug the six-hundred-million-euro funding gap. The old soldiers won, of course, after a short sharp engagement and Colonel Becker was given most of the credit for the victory.

He saw how the campaign had given the men a new sense of purpose and self-respect and he relished being a combat leader again. And so, at each subsequent reunion, he purposefully introduced a political discussion and often invited a guest speaker. Invariably, they were from the right-wing of Dutch politics and they were pleased to share their private thoughts with such an appreciative and naturally secretive audience. The old soldiers echoed the politicians' despair at the state of their country and were only too happy to find a common enemy in the growing number of Muslim immigrants. They had to be held back, they muttered to each other, in much the same way that the early Dutch settlers found ways to hold back the flood of the sea.

Slowly and incrementally, 'The Colonel' as he was known, found himself shaping the group into a fighting unit again. They would each report back on different ways in which they had made the lives of their immigrant neighbours more difficult during the previous two-months. They would brag about an assisted property-eviction here, or a mid-night lorry dump of rubbish there. Many stood for election to their local councils and boasted of fresh opportunities to take the fight to the other side in a hundred different ways.

And now, Colonel Becker had another battle-plan taking shape. If the time came, and his country needed him, he wanted his unit to be able to act as a civil defence force. He had watched the television reports of fighting on the streets of America and if the same race riots came to the Netherlands, he would make sure that their voices would be heard and order would be maintained for as long as there was air in his lungs.

The Colonel's nostrils twitched and flared in anger. Someone, somewhere nearby, was smoking marijuana in Vondelpark. His regular late afternoon exercise march through the city's largest park was often spoilt in this way. He could cope with the cyclists, footballers and joggers who regularly used the park's 120 acres. They were just trying to keep themselves fit. But he detested the idea of sharing it with undisciplined dope-heads and he wouldn't hesitate to point patrolling police officers at the culprits if he had the chance. He paused to look carefully all around him but couldn't identify the source of the sickly smell. The good weather meant the park was still busy, even at this late stage in the day.

He resumed his one-man parade along the park's central path which bordered a long and beautiful lake. He often enjoyed the concerts which were staged in Vondelpark. It was a huge green lung in the centre of the city and he had been wise to buy his small and exceptionally neat house close by.

The inline skater was almost silent as he came up behind the Colonel at speed. He was travelling at about 15 miles per hour with both arms swinging powerfully up and back, up and back. His head was covered by a black skating helmet with a red chinstrap outside a black snood that covered the bottom half of his face.

The heavy left boot of the skater with its single metal line of wheels hit the unsuspecting older man just below his right knee, instantly breaking both the fibula and the tibia and sending him flying onto his face. The skater also tumbled to the ground but rolled expertly to cushion the fall and he was wearing thick protective arm and knee pads in any case. He was back up within seconds and bending solicitously over the prone and groaning man. Others nearby had been horrified to see the collision. Several were already beginning to make their way across to see if they could help. But they paused at the sound of a siren and stood still as a small ambulance raced along one of the park's walkways and pulled up at the scene.

Afterwards, as they told their loved ones about the incident, they wondered how the vehicle could have got there so quickly but at the time they just assumed its crew had been parked nearby and witnessed the accident for themselves. This, in fact, was actually the case - however they had also been given a ten-minute warning that the 'accident' was about to happen.

The small man lying on the ground in his suit and tie was rendered unconscious within sixty seconds of a masked paramedic bending over him. He must have banged his head in the fall. However, the bystanders took some comfort in seeing the skater join the man on the stretcher in the back of the vehicle. It was the least he could do. He would be able to escort the accident victim safely to hospital and contact the man's family. Reassured, they turned back to minding their own business. Once again, the siren of the ambulance blared across the park. But it was silenced as soon as it reached the long main road of Van Baerlestraat.

CHAPTER EIGHTEEN

Jack, Nina and Eddie are already on a coach heading to the Keukenhof Gardens when the Colonel's body is found at 10 o'clock the following morning. It is half in, half out of the water of the exclusive Herengracht Canal, directly in front of Amsterdam's Biblical Museum. The body is once again draped over a mooring rope, but this time it is largely concealed from view by the stern of a broad-beamed Dutch barge. A Semper Augustus has been found on the boat's stern deck, almost directly above the slumped head of the veteran officer. A fast-growing crowd has gathered less than 30 minutes after the discovery of the body and the flower.

'I want his photograph out to the press and media as quickly as possible,' says Beatrix to the force's Head of Public Affairs. 'You can name him and give his address. He was fifty-nine. I want to know where and how he was abducted. Someone must have seen something.' The sharp-faced little man nods and bustles off through the crowd.

'Ten euros says he's tied up in nasty right-wing politics and he's got a nasty little secret somewhere,' says Robert. 'And another ten says he's been killed with a plant poison.'

'I'll keep my money thanks. Any word from his home yet?'

Robert shakes his head. 'But there is something different about this one. It's not on the same North-South axis as the other four. But it is still on a dead straight line going west from the bridge by the English couple's boat – the site of victim number three.'

Beatrix lights one of her small cigars and looks at the map he has spread on the bonnet of a police car. 'How far is it between the two points?'

'About 700 to 800 metres – much farther apart than the others.'

Beatrix blows out some smoke and shrugs. 'So, they're tidy. They do things in straight lines. I don't see that it gets us anywhere.'

'It's curious, all the same,' says Robert.

She silently agrees with him but is frustrated that she can't understand the significance. She turns to a uniformed officer and snaps, 'You there. Do your job. Get those people farther back, will you? We haven't got room to breathe here for Christ's sake!' An angry flush of red has crept up the skin of her throat.

Robert lets his boss's burst of temper go unremarked. It's completely out of character, but she wouldn't be human if she wasn't feeling the pressure now. Politicians of every shade are pontificating about the killings – only too aware that the country goes to the polls in another ten days. Officials from the Ministry of Justice are virtually camped in police headquarters and every newspaper and television or radio news programme can talk of nothing else. Yet people are continuing to be snatched from the streets of one of the world's smallest and busiest cities and being killed and deposited in some kind of bizarre and ritualistic way.

At this point, a police motorbike siren shrieks briefly and the crowd parts to let it approach the cordoned area followed by a gleaming black Mercedes. The passenger in the limousine waits for the driver to open his door and then unfolds his tall frame and looks around calmly.

'That's all we bloody need,' mutters Beatrix.

The Dutch government's Minister of Justice runs a hand through his wavy blond hair and buttons his suit jacket. He waits deliberately for a television cameraman to position himself and give a thumbs up before striding purposefully towards the two murder detectives.

'Dr van der Laen,' he says, shaking her hand.

'Minister. This is my deputy, Inspector Robert Fruin.'

'Fruin,' he nods. 'Good morning. Victim number five, yes? I understand he was a military man.'

Beatrix shows the politician a driver's licence in a see-through evidence bag. 'Lieutenant Colonel Willem Becker, 59. He lived in Vondelbuurt. That's all we know at the moment. We're checking with army records and we've sent a team to his home. He was found in the same pose as the others by that barge and the tulip was found on the deck.'

'I'm going to make a brief statement,' he says nodding at the cameraman. 'I spoke to your Chief Commissioner on the way over. Is there anything else you can tell me?'

Beatrix sidesteps the question. 'We need to know if anyone saw him being abducted. I've released his photograph already. And I wouldn't talk him up too much if I was you. I'm sure we shall find something disreputable about him if the others are anything to go by.'

The Minister gives a business-like nod and adjusts his tie. 'Just catch the bastards will you Beatrix? And be quick about it. Good day.' He turns, strides over to the camera and talks into it briefly before his car sweeps him away.

'Be quick about it,' repeats Beatrix in frustration as the crowd refills the space left by the car. Many are lifting their mobile phone cameras in the air to capture a stretcher with the covered body on it being loaded into a black van. The pathologist stops by Beatrix and Robert. 'Syringe mark in the neck?' asks the policewoman.

'Yes, Beatrix. Just like the others. We'll need to do lab tests to identify the poison again. But there's something else. His right leg was badly broken. Both bones and very recently. I'll find out more when he's on the slab.'

'Could it have happened in the water?'

'It's possible, but unlikely I think.'

'Alright. Thank you. We'll keep that detail to ourselves for now,' she turns to tell Robert. But he has turned away himself to take a call.

'That didn't take long,' he says returning to her. 'They've found a small arsenal of guns in the cellar of his home. Pistols, semi-automatic rifles, a light machine gun – even a mortar and grenades.'

Beatrix sighs and pushes her hands deep into her coat pockets. 'Alright. We'd better go and take a look before the Minister decides to turn it into another photo-opportunity.'

CHAPTER NINETEEN

'You do realise this is the very best time of year to see the tulips?' says Nina, briefly raising her nose out of the guidebook. Our coach has already driven past some spectacular tulip fields divided into strips of vibrant colour which draw gasps of admiration from the passengers on our coach. We are on our way to Keukenhof Gardens which are about forty kilometres south west of Amsterdam. It bills itself as the largest flower garden in the world with more than seven million bulbs planted there every year. It is also sufficiently enlightened to permit dogs on leads and Eddie is already enjoying the attention of some children on the seat next to us. He really is a good-natured and friendly little soul – unless he comes across a squirrel.

'Listen,' says Nina. 'The bulbs are planted by 40 gardeners and donated by more than 100 growers. They synchronize the flowerbeds to make sure there are blooms throughout the park's 8-week opening period. They get an average of 26,000 visitors a day.'

'More bloody crowds,' I complain automatically. But actually, I am looking forward to this day trip. It'll be a nice stretch for Eddie outside the city and the online research for my article has sparked a real interest in the flower. I'm keen to find out more. I am even considering investing in some tulip bulbs to decorate the roof of *Jumping Jack Flash* when we get back to Oxford.

The crush of people at the entrance to the gardens is intense and Nina stoops to pick Eddie up at one stage rather than risk him being trodden on. But we are soon through the bottleneck and exploring the immaculate paths flanked with swathes of primary-coloured tulips. Each turn in the path reveals another breathtaking vista, particularly where beautifully tended moss green grass interspersed with flowerbeds runs down to large lakes that mirror the image of mature trees.

The tulips are on stalks and so are Nina's eyes. 'It's just incredible,' she keeps saying. 'We must buy some bulbs to take back.'

'I don't know,' I say. 'Having briefly owned a Semper Augustus, I'm not sure I'm happy to settle for second best.'

'Idiot. You didn't own it. It spent the night on the roof of your hired houseboat.'

I notice that some of the tulips we see appear to have the 'broken' type of decorated petal and one such group is labelled Rem's Sensation. This puzzles me as I thought the virus which created the broken patterns also caused them to die out. Eventually, after two hours of wandering around scenes which overwhelm our senses of sight and smell, we make our way back to a building with cafes and shops inside. It's time to worry about our sense of taste.

Unlike the Tulip Museum in Amsterdam, there does not appear to be any special celebration of the reappearance of Semper Augustus and I stop a young woman in uniform to ask about this.

'You are right,' she shrugs. 'We are a charitable foundation and at the moment our manager does not want to mark the reappearance of this flower. It is being left beside murdered people and that is not something we wish to celebrate. But if you would like to know more you should speak to Geert.' She points across the room at a middle-aged and balding man who is wearing a white laboratory coat and thick black glasses. 'He is our resident expert.'

We introduce ourselves to Geert. I flash my press card and ask if I can ask him some questions. I tell him I'm doing research for an article. Nina stifles a snort of disbelief, but the man gives a broad friendly smile and suggests we buy him an espresso in return.

Nina claims a table and I do just that.

'Ah yes, the famous Semper Augustus,' sighs Geert. 'I am hoping the Ministry of Agriculture will allow me access soon. I never dreamt it might be possible to see it in my lifetime. It is a truly amazing thing.'

'I'm a bit confused,' I say. 'I thought broken tulips were caused by a virus which eventually killed them off. But I've seen some today. What was it called – Rem's Sensation?'

Geert nods. 'Yes, it has a similar pattern to the broken tulips – but it is a stable variation and that's because it is the result of breeding and not a viral infection. Tulip collectors believe they are still a poor substitute for the rare cultivars like Semper Augustus, but of course, they are long-extinct - or we thought they were!' He shakes his head in disbelief.

'Do you have any theories how it might have survived?' asks Nina.

'Everyone in my world has been asking that question. When the broken varieties first appeared with their beautiful patterns – some of them were like flames and some were like feathers – the breeders thought it had to be caused by a special combination of growing conditions. They experimented with different types of soil and different depths of planting, they varied the manure, the watering, the light, everything they could think of. They even tried fertilizing their fields with pigeon dung or even plaster from old walls. Of course, it was all doomed because now we know TBV is to blame for broken tulips.' He registers my puzzled look. 'TBV stands for the Tulip Breaking Virus.'

'And this virus eventually weakens the bulb?' I ask.

'First it infects the bulb and breaks its lock on a single colour. The pattern varies depending on the variety of the tulip, the strain of the virus and the plant's age at the time it is infected. But yes, eventually the bulb gets weak and withers away.'

'Except, apparently, for Semper Augustus?'

'We didn't find out that a virus was to blame until the mid-1920s. It was an English scientist actually, called Dorothy Cayley. She discovered that the break in colour could be transferred by putting infected tissue from broken bulbs into healthy bulbs when they were dormant. She did the work in Norfolk you know. Have you ever been there?'

I shake my head. 'But how are the bulbs infected with the virus in the first place?'

'Aphids. The little green monsters. There are four different species of the insect that can pass it on. They pick up the virus in their mouths when they suck up sap and then they pass it onto the next plant they feed on. It's funny really. Aphids cause millions of euros worth of damage to the flower bulb industry each year and we are constantly researching how to detect the virus and how to prevent it with pesticides. But in the case of Semper Augustus, the aphids and their virus created a flower of quite incredible beauty and value.'

'So broken tulips aren't particularly wanted anymore?' asks Nina.

'The virus certainly isn't wanted because the bulbs eventually die. It's illegal to sell broken or infected bulbs in some countries like yours and the United States. And of course, they are completely illegal here in the Netherlands. We have more to lose than most if the breaking virus spreads to other flowers. The tulip is one of our main exports.'

'So how do you think these latest Semper Augustus flowers survived?' asks Nina.

Geert shrugs his shoulders. 'Your guess is as good as mine, dear lady. There are a few varieties of the older, truly broken tulips still in existence. Zomerschoon is one – but only because the worst aspects of the virus have somehow remained benign since 1620. Absalon is another – it's rare and dates from 1780 and it has gold flames on a dark chocolate brown background. We still don't wholly understand the science behind these survivors.'

'So, are you saying the virus could have somehow remained benign with Semper Augustus too?' asks Nina.

'I suppose it might be possible, but I seriously doubt it. Everyone at the time would have tried to keep on breeding such a valuable flower. But they couldn't. All the records say it died out. And anyway, how could anyone have kept such a secret for more than three centuries, nearly four?'

'What about Adriaan Pauw?' I ask. 'He was a famous collector, wasn't he? And phenomenally wealthy for the time. Maybe his family found the secret and they've kept it to themselves for all this time?'

Geert laughs. 'And now his descendants are scattering them around Amsterdam as funeral wreaths? I don't think so, my friend. But you're right. It's a mystery and I'm afraid I can't help you. Unless …'

'Unless?' say Nina and I simultaneously.

'Well, it's not my field but I know that the genetic code, the DNA of TBV, the Tulip Breaking Virus, has been partially sequenced to help with detecting it. It's supposed to be quite easy now to use various techniques – molecular, optical and serological – to spot it. Perhaps someone has done something very clever in a laboratory to develop the Semper Augustus again from scratch? Ach … I don't know! It sounds mad. But I must get on. It is our busiest time of year of course. It was nice to meet you both and thanks for the coffee.'

We watch Geert weave his way through the crowds. 'He's a nice man,' says Nina, as she gives Eddie a pat under the table.

'And very knowledgeable. But even he is baffled.'

The weather is forecast to be fine for the rest of the day and we have a range of optional times for our return coach trip. So, we stock up on sandwiches and go back outside into the gardens. Nina has noticed a boat trip on offer for visitors to traverse the tulip fields and we are soon gliding along a flooded ditch in an electrically powered whisper boat. The passengers are a mixture of many nationalities and individual headphones offer a variety of languages for a pre-recorded commentary.

At one stage it describes a stunning field of Queen of the Night tulips as we are motoring past it. The deep maroon colour of the petals make it the darkest of any tulip, we are told. 'Imagine what a disaster it would be if such a field became infected with the broken tulip virus,' warns the commentator in our ears. 'That is why Dutch growers who see a broken tulip immediately consider it to be garbage and a threat. If you find a broken tulip in your garden, remove it immediately to prevent the risk of spreading.'

'Gosh, I hadn't realised the broken tulips were so feared,' says

Nina as we disembark onto dry land. 'He made it sound like they're public enemy number one.'

'So not only is the Tulip Murderer wanted for being a serial killer,' I say. 'He's also wanted for keeping a broken tulip in a public place! That's probably even more of a hanging offence over here.'

Nina laughs and we make our way back to the coach and our return trip to the city. However, later that evening we hear more news that makes my words feel ill-judged and insensitive.

CHAPTER TWENTY

Neither of us feels like eating out or cooking for dinner so Nina suggests an online food delivery site which is linked to many of the city's best restaurants. We quickly find a Chinese eatery which is well-rated and start to examine the menu. 'It's always so tempting and yet it's always so much in reality,' complains Nina.

'Why don't we invite Su and her husband over for dinner then? It would be nice to meet up with them socially. And I owe her one for that article.'

Nina narrows her eyes at me. 'No, it's you who helped her out by doing it. Are you sure she isn't an old flame of yours?'

I grin. 'Are you a tad jealous, Mrs Angelina Wilde?'

'Don't be silly, Jack. I just want to know the lay of the land.'

'We just worked together.' I realise my brief affair with a woman detective in Oxford is the elephant in the boat at this moment.

'I'm off for a shower. You make the call and do the order. And you'll need to pop out for some more wine.'

'Do this, do that. And are you sure we aren't already an old married couple?'

Nina smiles and goes off to her bedroom. Su readily accepts an invitation to dinner but says her husband won't be able to make it as he's on an out-of-town photoshoot.

I order a Chinese meal for three and take Eddie out again to find a few bottles of red and white, plus a bottle of 12-year-old Yamazaki, because I deserve it.

I'm relaxing in a chair on Flora's roof with a generous measure of the Japanese whisky by the time Nina re-joins me. Her cropped hair still looks wet, but she looks elegantly casual in a moss-green linen shirt and white calf-length capri pants. Su appears shortly afterwards clutching a bottle of Burgundy wrapped in brown paper. The three of us relax and chat as quiet descends after the peal of the Westerkerk bells. The golden glow of a falling sun on the surrounding buildings makes it feel as though nothing has changed in centuries.

'It's strange. This city can be so peaceful and calm at times. In spite of all the bloody tourists. Oh sorry, I don't think of you as tourists. Sorry.'

'Of course, we are tourists,' says Nina smiling. 'There's nothing to be sorry about.'

I have resolved not to indulge in too many reminiscences with Su about working on our old paper. It would be too boring and rude in front of Nina. Su is sensitive enough to steer clear of the subject too.

'Peaceful and calm?' I challenge, topping up all of our glasses. We probably need to slow down on the aperitifs or our tastebuds will be too blurred to fully appreciate the Chinese meal. 'You must be joking. You've had four murders in four days remember!'

'Five in five actually,' says Su, sipping her drink. 'There was another one last night. A retired officer in the Royal Netherlands Army.'

'Bloody hell! We've been out in the tulip fields, so we haven't checked the latest news. Is it the same modus operandi?'

'A couple of witnesses came forward. It sounds like he was deliberately hurt by an inline skater and taken away from a park by a bogus ambulance crew. Same pose in the water. Same tulip found nearby. Nothing much yet about his politics but they found a pretty big collection of working guns and ammunition in the cellar of his home.'

I shake my head in disbelief. 'And where was he found?'

'On the Herengracht, opposite the Biblical Museum. It was a pretty appropriate place for a dead body!'

I duck downstairs to fetch my tourist map but Nina and Su follow me before I have time to return. The moon is rising now outside, and I can see that the streetlights have come on. 'Show me,' I say.

Su marks an X and a 5 to indicate the location of the body and I draw a straight line from the fifth location to the third location, the bridge near our mooring. 'It's another dead straight line,' I say, shaking my head in puzzlement. 'What are the chances of that being a coincidence?'

'So, you've got a right angle with a bit sticking out of the bottom,' observes Su, shaking her head. 'So what?'

'I don't know, perhaps there's something which connects all these locations. I point to each one in turn and refer to a scribbled list in my notebook. The first was found in the red-light district, the second was found outside a theatre, the third was at the Groenburgwal Bridge, the fourth was the Amstel and this one last night was here, in front of the Biblical Museum.'

'I'm sure the Dutch police have been asking themselves the same question,' says Su. 'It's certainly nothing that's glaringly obvious.'

'Well, Jack loves a cryptic crossword,' says Nina. 'And he loves any chance to *help* the police. At least that's how he sees it. The police don't always agree though.'

There's a knock at the boat's stern and Nina begins to clear the table for the meal. However, when I open the door, it isn't a motorbike delivery courier but Archi Gupta Bhalla.

He too is clutching a wrapped bottle of something and grinning sheepishly.

'Hello there! I thought I'd pop in to share a drop of some ridiculously expensive alcohol – if you're not doing anything special that is?'

'Great to see you, Archi,' I say, pumping his hand. 'You're just in time for a Chinese.' Archi is wearing another suit which looks made-to-measure at considerable cost. He has obviously come straight from work although I find it hard to imagine him in any kind of casual attire. I introduce him to Su and she remembers seeing him briefly at an ambassadorial reception for local journalists. He obviously can't remember her, but he regrets it with considerable charm. We are soon cosily ensconced in the soft-seating area, and sampling his offering of a velvety smooth Bordeaux.

We both enthuse about our day out at the Keukenhof Gardens and they listen with the polite but slightly superior interest of real locals. The arrival of a bag full of aluminium cartons of food is greeted enthusiastically though. As we tuck in, I tell the others all about the virus-carrying aphids which cause broken tulips, because, of course, I am now a world-leading authority on the subject.

'You heard there was another killing last night?' asks Archi as he bites into a spring roll.

'Su told us,' says Nina. 'An army officer, wasn't it? Found in the water again near a Bible Museum?'

Archi nods. 'Retired. And the word is he was building up a bit of a private army. Although I'm not sure whether he thought he'd be starting a revolution or stopping one.' He looks up at Su and me, suddenly remembering we are journalists. He coughs. 'Chatham House rules apply here I hope?'

'That means I don't report anything you say without getting your agreement first,' says Su, dipping her own spring roll in some soy sauce and nibbling its end.

'Yes. Right. Well, that's alright then, isn't it?'

I don't quite know what to make of Archi. He is obviously very bright and he talks fast, as though his tongue is trying to catch up with his brain all the time. And if he's acting as police liaison for the embassy, he is obviously highly trusted by his employers. Yet there is also something slightly naïve and unworldly about him too – an impression accentuated by his round baby-faced cheeks and thick schoolboy glasses. I wonder if he is lonely. He certainly seems to be enjoying himself now and shows every sign of being entranced by Nina. He bobs up and down to top up her glass and even fetches a cushion for her back without being asked.

Archi becomes more loquacious and keen to impress as we move onto our third bottle of wine. 'I shall get a taxi home,' he declares expansively. 'My diplomatic plates will prevent me from getting a parking ticket.' His tie is undone along with his top shirt button now and he has dispensed with his suit jacket to reveal a waistcoat that is straining under some internal pressure. 'But I must try to keep a clear head for the morning. I am doing very important work on these so-called Tulip Murders.'

I immediately sense Su's journalistic antennae twitching. 'Really? Care to share it?' she asks.

'Let's just say we have offered to assist the investigation and the offer has been accepted,' he says self-importantly. Then he wags his finger at us. 'But don't forget – Chatham House rules.'

Su widens her eyes a fraction at me. By any measure, this is a good story for her with plenty of sales opportunities in the British press. 'Yes,' I say carefully. 'The Met's murder squad has a lot of expertise. It makes sense to reach out to them for help.'

'No, no, no, no.' responds Archi immediately. 'This goes much higher than the Metropolitan Police.' He beams around the boat's saloon with evident satisfaction.

'It must be the British Secret Service then,' says Su.

Archi folds his arms and smiles enigmatically but says nothing.

'It could be,' I say disingenuously. 'But there would need to be some kind of suspected connection with UK-based terrorist cells for that to happen.'

Archi takes a generous slug of his drink and then pops some chewing gum in his mouth. I find this quite distressing. I really hate to see people masticating and I'm repelled by his cocktail of decent red wine with strawberry and cannabis flavoured gum.

'Are we getting warm Archi?' asks Nina.

I can tell Archi finds the thought of getting warm with Nina almost too much to bear. He coughs and stares into her big black eyes. 'No, Nina. I'm sorry to say Jack is not even tepid with his theorising.'

She follows up ruthlessly by placing a hand on his arm. 'Oh, come on, Archi. Give us a clue. They've promised not to report it unless you give them permission anyway.'

Archi points a forefinger in the air. 'This is true. You need to focus on the amazing amount of comment about the murders that is on the internet,' he says. 'There are millions and millions of observations appearing there, all of the time. It's a worldwide story – thanks largely to the reappearance of the rare tulip. Perhaps, among all of these oceans of data, there is a crucial piece of evidence that is going unnoticed?'

'GCHQ!' says Su at once.

'Of course,' I say. 'The Government's Communications Headquarters at Cheltenham. They're helping the Dutch to sift all the online traffic about the murders.'

Archi is smiling and clapping his hands slowly. 'Well done, my friends. You got there in the end.'

'And have they found anything yet?' asks Su. She tops up Archi's glass even though it is still half full.

Archi, still chewing his gum, leans back on the settee and spreads both his arms wide. He is relishing being the centre of attention. 'I am not privy to the exchange of any information like that,' he says, 'But I have put the wheels in motion today for this to happen. It was a good day's work, and my ambassador is delighted with me. And now I am celebrating with my new friends.' He beams at all of us.

'At this rate, you really will be the next UK ambassador in New Delhi,' says Nina.

'So, Archi, will you let me tell the GCHQ story?' asks Su as the laughter dies away.

The poor man suddenly looks panic-stricken. 'No, no, no, no – we agreed. Not without my permission Su.'

'But it's a good positive story for the UK government, isn't it?' I ask. Su shoots me a grateful look.

'Yes, yes, it is. Of course. But it would need to have approval by the Foreign Office's press office. You mustn't write about this. You promised.' Archi now looks like an overgrown schoolboy on the brink of tears rather than the next James Bond.

'Don't worry, Archi,' says Nina. 'They won't drop you in it. You won't, will you guys?'

'No. A deal is a deal,' I say firmly.

Nina looks hard at Su. 'No, I guess not,' she agrees resignedly. 'But I bet GCHQ announce it themselves tomorrow. As Jack says, it's good PR for them.'

'Look Archi,' I say. 'How about you give Su here a tip-off if you hear the co-operation is going to be formally announced.'

'That might be possible,' agrees Archi. But the exchange has clearly frightened him and he has decided it is time to pull himself together. 'And now I must be going. It was a delightful evening. Thank you for the meal.' He staggers slightly as he stands to put on his jacket. 'Perhaps I may use your bathroom before I go?'

'You two aren't going to drop him in it are you?' hisses Nina as the door closes behind him.

'No. Of course not,' says Su, shrugging on her coat and grinning. 'But I'll make sure he gets home safely now. He can share my taxi. Then he'll hopefully feel that he owes me one.'

'Journalists,' says Nina, shaking her head sadly.

Su and Archi eventually weave off into the night and I follow behind them briefly with Eddie for his night-time stroll.

Nina has cleared up the debris of our meal by the time we return and is curled up in an armchair with her new Rembrandt book. It really is a thick tome. She has it open on a glossy picture of *The Night Watch*. 'It's interesting,' she says, 'this book says the painting was a statement to the rest of Europe. In effect it was saying; *Here, we don't depend on kings or popes, or armies or hired guns; this is our town and we take care of it ourselves.*'

I pour myself an inch of whisky with a drop of water and slump into the chair opposite her. 'What else does it say?'

'Well, he really was the hot young artist in his twenties and thirties and everyone who was anyone wanted him to paint them. He used new techniques and that caught the mood of the time. Amsterdammers thought of themselves as innovators and liberals too. But this book reckons he fell from favour because his style was seen as a bit too emotional and dramatic for the Dutch - and he failed to suck up to his patrons. He got into fights with them about money and he had a pretty disastrous personal life. Eventually he went bankrupt and died at sixty-three.'

'He looked like he'd had a pretty hard life in the older self-portrait.'

'And then, ironically, his paintings became fashionable again in the nineteenth century - when the Netherlands was all about national patriotism and identity again.'

'And now history is repeating itself.'

'It's not just here though is it, Jack? People feel powerless in the face of global forces don't they? Global banking, global migration, global technology – even global terrorism. So, they panic and put up walls, or patrol the seas, and they try to reinforce their own nationalism and identity.'

'Which ultimately means having to define themselves as insiders or outsiders.'

'And woe betide the outsiders.'

'*Make America Great Again. Take Back Control.* Simple populist slogans repeated over and over and over again. I read an article recently saying it's all straight out of the Nazis' political playbook. I think it's also something to do with countries who had big overseas empires,' I add, sipping my drink. 'They have this rose-tinted view of their past glories – or at least some of their population do. And then that becomes an emotional call to arms when people are frightened.'

'I hadn't expected to find it here in the Netherlands though,' admits Nina.

'You thought it would be full of smiling people holding tulips, wearing clogs and living in windmills?'

Nina scrunches her nose at me. 'Well, it turns out even the tulips need to be protectionist doesn't it – or they risk becoming infected and broken?'

'Broken, but very beautiful,' I say wistfully, staring into the bottom of my empty glass and thinking the same description could be applied to Nina.

'And that, Jack Johnson, is the whisky talking. I'm going to bed. And so should you.'

I watch her disappear into her bedroom with Eddie dutifully trotting behind her. My beautiful, clever and troubled Nina. Once again, my mind returns to that night in Oxford when she had offered to come into my bed on the boat. Had I been right to send her away? It was the hardest thing I have ever done in my life. Would it ever happen again? And if it did, how would I respond?

I reach across to turn out the lamp on a side table. The tourist map is still open under it and I pull it onto my lap. Five bodies in five locations including one near our own hire boat and all connected by straight lines. Someone was trying to tell the world something and, so far, no-one understood what it was.

CHAPTER TWENTY-ONE

Two hours later, at just after 2am in the morning, a small blue motorboat glided quietly along a lengthy straight stretch of the Herengracht Canal. There were now more than a thousand police officers posted across the city centre with specific instructions to look out for anyone doing anything suspicious - like tying a dead body to a mooring rope or a safety chain and leaving a supposedly extinct tulip nearby. Officers in pairs spent the night patrolling the main waterways and others sat in their vehicles at most of the key road and waterway junctions.

However, Amsterdam is a 24/7 city and there was still occasional water traffic going about its business. One particular boat, named *Prins Hendrik* after a Dutch warship, was partially covered with a plastic canopy on a metal frame and quickly recognised by the local officers as a gin-and-tonic cruiser. Its job was to supply private groups of increasingly drunk visitors with huge balloon glasses of G&T and snacks as they meandered around the canals. This one had obviously been working late, deposited its last passengers and was now returning to its overnight mooring.

The helmsman of *Prins Hendrik*, who sported a full beard and glasses below a baseball cap, touched the peak of his hat and nodded to the policemen on the towpath as he passed down the centre of the broad canal. He stood at a wheel near the stern where a comfortable bench seat wrapped around him in a U-shape. A low table in front of him still sported a silver-coloured ice bucket and three rows of glasses. Five sausage-shaped fenders hung along each side of the boat and below them, on the port side, a woman's body was suspended by a rope under the surface of the water.

The extra drag was affecting the boat's steering slightly and the helmsman had to compensate for it to stay in a straight line. But the body was firmly clamped to the rope and the rope was firmly tied to the hull. The grim underwater cargo was invisible in the darkness to anyone on land, or even in another passing boat.

The boat, which had a quiet electric engine, glided under a large bridge carrying the Raadhuisstr, a road which leads to the Dutch Royal Palace, and turned left just before the next bridge. It was now on a short spur which crosses the three main canals. The house where Anne Frank hid from the Germans was nearby but at this time of night, the short stretch of the Leliegracht was tree-lined and very quiet.

The *Prins Hendrik*'s helmsman looked hard all around him and double-checked his location via the GPS on his mobile phone. Then he reduced speed to a tick-over and steered the boat to the starboard bank where he quickly made it fast to some railings and cut the engine. He reached under a bench, took off his glasses and quickly replaced his baseball cap with a full-face crash helmet. Then he reached up inside the front of the helmet from below and grabbed the beard. Both his hands were clad in surgical rubber gloves. Having tugged the beard forcefully down and out, he stuffed it into his jacket's pocket, tossed the glasses overboard and untied a rope on the port side of the boat.

He pulled it up for two metres, tied it off, checked quickly over the side and then climbed up onto land where a motorbike was parked nearby. He checked its registration against a text message on his phone and then stooped to pick up two keys from under the front tyre. He used one to unlock a chain that was wound around the spokes of the wheel and the front suspension forks. Then he used the other to start the engine before slowly moving off into the night.

Ten minutes later, two patrol officers used the same short stretch of road to cross over from the Herengracht to the Keizersgracht. They had been ordered to continue walking the same kilometre-long loop all night. So far, they had alternated between the port bank and the starboard bank of the canals and this time they took the port side of the connecting canal. This gave them a good view across the thin strip of water. One of them gave a sudden shout and pointed to the other bank. A woman's body was clamped to the hull of the little G&T tourist boat. The arms of a woman hung down on either side and the head was slumped forwards.

The officer immediately radioed headquarters while his partner raced back across the bridge. His 9x19mm semi-automatic service weapon was already in his hand as he approached the boat and looked down onto it. It was empty although the powerful torch in his other hand quickly illuminated the red and white colours of the single Semper Augustus tulip that had been placed in the ice bucket.

CHAPTER TWENTY-TWO

'We've got the CCTV from the opposite bank at last,' says Robert tiredly. He and Beatrix have now been on site for four hours, ever since they were roused from their beds and regretfully informed about the sixth murder victim.

The body has now been taken away, but the two of them are determined to capitalise on the early discovery if they can. They climb up into the back of a mobile incident room which is mounted on the back of a lorry. Two mugs of coffee are pressed into their hands. 'Alright, let's have a look,' says Beatrix.

One of many screens shows a black-and-white image of the boat being moored, the body being pulled up into view and the helmsman making his getaway. They watch it several times at normal speed and in slow motion. 'Alright, do your best to get a close-up of his face before the helmet goes on. There might be a second or two when he hasn't got the glasses on.'

'But the beard is obviously false,' says the unfortunate technician. 'And he keeps it on until the helmet is on.'

'Yes,' Beatrix snaps. 'I think I realised that. Just do your job. I want a decent image I can release to the press.' The man shrugs hopelessly and bends to his task. 'What the hell is wrong with me?' she thinks to herself. 'I'm going from nought to one-hundred miles-per-hour these days.' Beatrix takes a deep calming breath, counts silently to ten and then puts a hand on the man's shoulder. 'Just do your best, please.' The man nods respectfully. 'What about the motorbike?' she asks Robert.

'We've got a registration number from another camera at the end of the street – but it was stolen of course. Just like the boat. We're checking cameras at its usual mooring, but I doubt they've messed up. They're just too careful and too professional.'

The two of them move back out into the chill morning air. Light rain is forecast later but for the moment it is dry and cold and wisps of fog cling to the surface of the oily green canal water.

'Any word from her home?'

'We're having to tread carefully. The husband is there and he's in a bad state. He had offered to pick her up from the office yesterday evening, but she insisted on walking. He called us when she still hadn't come home by midnight and wasn't answering her phone.'

'And I suppose we told him to wait until morning?'

Robert nods. 'And even if someone saw her being snatched, like the people who saw Becker's fake accident in the park, I have no doubt the attackers were careful to hide their faces. Even if they've got clean records, they won't want them plastered all over the media.'

'Ah look. The boss is here after a good night's sleep and a hearty breakfast,' says Beatrix as an unmarked police car pulls up.

The Regional Chief Commissioner hoists his bulk out of the rear seat and they cross over to meet him. 'No crowds yet?' he observes, looking around him.

'It's a quiet street, sir,' says Robert. 'We've sealed off both ends and most residents aren't up yet. The body went an hour ago. But it's only a matter of time before word gets out.'

'What do we know about her?'

'Fifty-year-old Mrs Catharina Schrader, a successful and wealthy property developer who runs her own firm. Married with no children. She's got a big pad in Maarssen village and an office in the Baxter Building. She doesn't seem to have any obvious political affiliations, but she is a leading light in some kind of lobby group for property developers. She had a drinks party for clients at the office yesterday afternoon so didn't drive home. Her husband offered to fetch her, but she said she'd walk a little of the way to clear her head and then catch a taxi.'

'Maybe they snatched her in a taxi?' says the Chief Commissioner.

'We're already onto it,' says Beatrix. 'We're checking to see if any taxis were stolen yesterday.'

They all walk over to look down on the G&T boat. 'So, you think they brought the body here on the boat? Any decent pictures?'

'We know it for certain now. We've got someone doing their best,' replies Robert. 'The body was underwater and tied to the hull until he got here. Then he just pulled it up into view and tied it off. He's wearing a false beard, glasses and a cap and then he puts on a full-face motorcycle helmet before escaping.'

'Damn. And we had the place swarming with uniforms. Alright. Anything else I need to know?'

'The flower was left in some water in the ice bucket. It's been taken away for tests.'

'And the location,' adds Beatrix. 'It's another dead straight line going north from the location of the last body. We're still trying to work out if that's at all significant.'

'Alright. I'm going straight to the Ministry to make my report. I'll need to catch up with you again this afternoon. Keep me posted. I suppose you're turning the poor woman's life upside down as we speak?'

'Oh yes,' says Beatrix grimly. 'All the victims seemed to have had dirty little secrets. We don't know what Mrs Schrader was hiding yet. But we'll find out. I'm going to see the husband now.'

The Schrader's home is ultra-modern and minimalist with lots of leather and chrome furniture behind huge glass walls and expensive looking rugs on polished wooden floors. Mr Schrader is unshaven and hollow-eyed. He ushers Beatrix and Robert to an empty settee and introduces one of his wife's senior colleagues, Pieter de Hooch. 'I came as soon as Gerard called,' the man explains as he pours four glasses of water from a jug. 'This is just awful, just truly awful.'

'We are very sorry for your loss,' says Beatrix. 'However, we urgently need to know if anyone may have had a reason to kill Mrs Schrader. Did she have any enemies?'

The husband buries his face in his hands and convulsively sobs. De Hooch puts a hand on his shoulder and looks back at Beatrix. 'Enemies? I don't think so. Of course, you always have business rivals in our game, and you drive tough deals with builders and planners and so on. There's always a bit of friction. But no, I don't think Catharina could be said to have enemies. She was very well-respected.'

'She was on some kind of lobby group?' says Robert. 'Is that right? What was it lobbying about?'

De Hooch shrugs. 'A few firms have got together to threaten to pull their businesses out of the capital,' he says. 'And Catharina took a leading role. The rules for new housing projects are killing us. They insist 40% of all new homes are to be social housing and 40% mid-market. That leaves just 20% for high-end sale or decently priced rentals. The liberals have been making it economically unviable for us to build decent new housing. There's a housing crisis in this country – and yet the asylum seekers are being given priority. It's all madness and there will be a backlash, mark my words. Catharina felt passionately about this and was organising the industry's resistance.'

'Could this be the reason for her death?' says her husband, looking up at the two detectives. His face still wet with tears. 'I thought it was these tulip madmen?'

'Everything points to this being part of the recent sequence of murders,' confirms Beatrix. 'But we are still trying to establish the motive or find a connection. I take it your wife didn't know any of the previous victims?'

Schrader shakes his head. 'We've been following it all, of course. On the news and in the papers. But I'm sure she didn't know any of the others. It's madness. Why would anyone kill Catharina?'

Robert turns back to de Hooch. 'This lobby group she was on. Did it have any kind of public anti-immigration stance?'

The man shrugs again. 'The liberals and their rent-a-mob

loudmouths tried to accuse us of racism. Of course, there is limited space for new property developments in Amsterdam. But the demand is enormous – and that's partly due to immigration. The politicians think the answer is to try to distort the market – but they've gone too far. Nothing will get built unless things change.' He looks across at Schrader. 'Of course, we shall do anything we can to help you catch Catharina's killers. But Gerard needs to rest now. It's been a tough night for him.'

Robert takes the wheel to drive them both back to police headquarters. 'Six killings on six consecutive nights,' says Beatrix. 'We must look like idiots to the rest of the world.'

'These people are very well-trained and fanatical. They have to be. That still points to some kind of terrorist cell, doesn't it? All the victims are connected with anti-immigration campaigns or extreme right-wing issues so we should be looking at their natural enemies, shouldn't we? We need our intelligence chums to come up with something. That's where the answer lies, as long as these people manage to keep hiding their identity and not making any mistakes.'

Beatrix nods. 'Otherwise, we're just rolling the dice on a police patrol officer being in the right place at the right time for a change.'

CHAPTER TWENTY-THREE

Our alcohol-fuelled evening with Archi and Su prompts a lie-in for both of us the following morning – albeit in separate bedrooms. Eventually Nina is the first to rise and she brings me a large glass of water without being asked. 'I'm going out for a run with Eddie to clear my head. Bacon sandwiches in half an hour, please.'

I head for the shower and let the water pummel me for ten minutes before turning to fulfil Nina's orders. I'm enjoying the novelty of endless water and electricity as the houseboat is connected to mains supplies of both. On *Jumping Jack Flash,* I have to constantly think about where to top up my water tank or when to run the engine to recharge the boat's batteries.

Nina reappears carrying two cardboard cups of coffee and looking nicely flushed. She is only wearing a t-shirt, shorts and trainers so I imagine the dry sunny day beyond the boat's windows is also warming up nicely. 'Good run?' I ask, bending to give Eddie a cuddle. He's more interested in licking the bacon grease off my fingers.

'I called in for these,' she says putting the cups on the galley's dining table. 'The barista was a young American and he was chatting to another member of staff. 'It sounds like there was another killing last night. He was saying that the road at his home was cordoned off and he had to show his passport and leave his name with the police before he was allowed to go into work.'

'That's six in six days,' I say, buttering four slices of bread and forking the bacon onto them. 'It's crazy. The police must be frantic to make a breakthrough.'

Nina slathers her bacon in both tomato ketchup and Dijon mustard and then washes down a mouthful with a big slurp of coffee. 'God, I needed this. I may have to resort to some painkillers too.'

Having finished my breakfast, I pull out my laptop and find an English-language news website. It has a picture of a small gin launch and explains that the body was found tied to its hull by patrolling police officers. The dead woman has already been identified as a prominent Amsterdam property-developer and a Semper Augustus tulip was discovered on board the little motorboat. There are quotes from shocked residents in the small stretch of canal called Leliegracht where the boat and body were discovered in the early hours of the morning. However, there is no official statement from the police or the Ministry of Justice yet.

I retrieve my city map, which is starting to look a bit creased and careworn, and I find the relevant canal. The news story doesn't give an exact location for the body, but I draw a line north from the location of the fifth body, outside the Bible Museum and make it the same length as the distance between it and the location of the third body, the bridge near our boat. Nina leans over my shoulder to watch what I'm doing. 'I'm happy to bet the latest discovery isn't far from that X,' I say, pointing to my newest mark on the map. 'There's definitely a pattern here. But what the hell is it?'

'Well, it looks like a square is emerging with a bit of tail hanging down at the bottom on the right,' she says. 'So that would make a capital letter Q wouldn't it?'

I draw a tentative straight-line east from the location of my newest mark for the same distance again and then join the small remaining gap going south to make the square as Nina suggests. It does indeed look like the capital of the letter Q.

'I wonder what Q could stand for?' I mutter. 'Are the killers trying to tell us who is responsible do you think?'

'But don't you see Jack? If we're right, then we've predicted the location of the next murder. And if it's going to be 7 in 7 days, then it'll happen tonight somewhere near that spot.'

'And if it is a Q, then it probably stands for a Dutch word which we wouldn't know.'

'Not necessarily,' says Nina, her eyes widening. 'It couldn't be … it couldn't be Al-Qaeda, could it?'

I stare at her. 'Bloody hell. That would make sense. Wouldn't it? If they can take out the Twin Towers, they can easily bump off a few anti-Islamic fascists on the streets of Amsterdam.'

'Shall we take this to the police?' Nina looks slightly doubtful, and I am too. It still seems a bit of a stretch and surely, if it means anything, the police and the Dutch security services would have been on to it by now.

'Why don't we text Archi with this?' I suggest. 'He's running liaison between the Dutch police and GCHQ. If he thinks there's anything in it, he can pass it on.'

'Good idea,' says Nina. 'And in the meantime, maybe we should wander up to the top right-hand corner of our Q and have a look around?'

I peer closer at the map. My last X seems to be in the heart of the red-light district and close to a church called Oude Kerk. It looks pretty big on the map. 'Okay. If you're sure you don't want to soak up some more culture?' She wrinkles her nose at me and bustles off to shower and change while I compose an email to Archi with a photo of my map and send it off. I imagine he'll be nursing a sore head this morning too, although there is no sign of his fancy car so he must have collected it early to go to work.

I add a few remaining scraps of bacon to Eddie's breakfast bowl and then settle him down in his basket. He's too young for the sleazy sights I am expecting in the De Wallen area of the city.

The Oude Kerk looks vast when we finally approach it by foot and sure enough, it sits incongruously in the centre of Sin City. All around its mammoth presence, hookers are sitting in the street-level windows of the surrounding buildings. Nina is shaking her head in disbelief. 'I wonder who was here first?' she says. 'The prostitutes or the clerics?'

'They've probably both been here since the very start. Let's have a look inside,' I say. We pay our entrance fee, pick up an English language leaflet and head into the dark coolness of the massive interior.

'Oude Kerk is Amsterdam's oldest building and youngest art institute,' reads Nina aloud. 'It began life around 1213 – wow! It was just a wooden chapel at first and then became a stone church that was consecrated in 1306. The church has seen several renovations by 15 generations of Amsterdam citizens.'

'It was probably Roman Catholic to start with,' I say.

Nina nods. 'At its height it had 38 altars running during Sunday Mass, each with their own priest. It must have been busy in here. It says that the Calvinist Dutch Reformed Church took it over in 1578 after the Spanish were defeated. It was looted and defaced throughout the 16th century and at one stage it was just a place where locals gathered to gossip. Peddlers sold their goods and beggars slept here. Then it was reclaimed as a church.'

We look up to admire the high barrel-vaulted wooden ceiling and Nina reads on to discover that all of Rembrandt's children were christened in Oude Kerk. 'His wife Saskia was buried here in 1642,' she says. We find a small Rembrandt exhibition near her shrine in the Holy Sepulchre and learn that each year, on the 9th of March, the early morning sun illuminates her tomb and that an early spring breakfast event is held to mark the occasion. Nina seems to be quietly moved by the story.

There are also various contemporary art works on show, but Nina gives them only a cursory glance before leading us to the bell tower where I have to shell out more euros for the privilege of climbing 67 metres of narrow stairs.

'Not bad,' I concede breathlessly at the top as we look out across the city's rooftops and down at the canal which runs closely along one side of the church. 'I suppose if the killers stay true to form, someone's going to end up in the water down there tonight?'

'But surely, the police will keep this whole area under

surveillance?' asks Nina.

'Only if they pay attention to Archi and our Q theory,' I answer. 'Or if they've already clocked it for themselves.' Eventually, back on the ground, we make our way to the exit walking across a floor made up of gravestones.

'The whole church was built on a cemetery apparently,' says Nina. 'Although the mound they built for the foundations makes it the most solid ground in the city.'

'Well, let's hope there isn't yet another body to worry about in the morning,' I reply.

We walk out onto the cobbles in front of the church and pass a bronze statue of a young woman with an inscription which reads; 'Respect sex workers all over the world.' A red string bracelet has been tied around one of the statue's ankles. A few metres away, facing the church, flesh-and-blood sex workers in minimal clothing look blankly through their windows at us and the other passers-by. 'This is just so weird,' says Nina. 'It's like being in a human zoo. A zoo displaying human beings.'

We complete a circuit of the massive building before heading past a Prostitute Information Centre and continuing west to find somewhere for lunch.

CHAPTER TWENTY-FOUR

Dr Beatrix van der Laen's legendary good humour is under considerable strain. She has been up most of the night on a damp and chilly towpath and then spent all morning drawing yet another blank with her team on the latest killing. Now she has been summoned to the top floor of the Ministry of Justice and Security's building in the city. What a waste of time when she needs to be down on the ground making preparations for tonight.

Her immediate boss, Amsterdam's police chief, is sitting alongside her and doodling nervously, and sitting next to him is his immediate boss, the First Chief Commissioner of Police for the Netherlands. Various civil servants are also filling the seats around the conference table adjoining the Minister's penthouse office as well as the director and deputy director of AIVD, the General Intelligence and Security Service of the Netherlands.

They are all waiting for the Minister to arrive from his other office in The Hague, but there is little conversation, just quiet muttering between colleagues sitting immediately next to each other. Beatrix looks out of the window across the city. She wonders to herself how could they possibly justify calling this ugly building *Rembrandt Tower*. With a height of 135 metres and 36 floors, the office skyscraper has nothing whatsoever in common with the 17th century painter. She hates it with a passion and loathes being forced to visit it.

She had been a lower ranked detective in 2002 when an armed man had stormed the building and taken 18 hostages. She smiles at the memory of his grievance. He said he had bought a widescreen television to try to avoid the black bars when he was watching widescreen VHS tapes. However, the black bars remained and so he was very angry at the Dutch electronics company Phillips, which used to have its headquarters in *Rembrandt Tower*. Unfortunately for the man, Phillips had relocated just a few months earlier, but no-one had told him. The hostages emerged safely but the intruder shot himself dead in one of the building's toilets. It's a shame he didn't dynamite the whole damn building she thinks to herself as the room gets to its feet to greet the Minister. A couple of factotums are trailing anxiously in his wake.

'Good afternoon everyone,' he says, claiming the vacant chair at the end of the table. 'Please be seated.'

'Dr van der Laen. Please brief us all on the essential facts of last night's killing.'

Beatrix pauses a moment before speaking. She looks calmly at the faces that are fixed on her and sighs inwardly. Once again, she is the only woman at a table surrounded by the male, pale and stale. She remains seated but gives a succinct account of the victim's identity and background, the location of the body, how it was discovered and other relevant circumstances. 'In conclusion, the modus operandi appears to be the same as the other five; the victim had been engaged in lobbying against social housing which might have been resented by certain liberal or racial groups. But once again, the perpetrators have covered their tracks well and avoided identification via our street cameras.'

The Director of AIVD takes this as his cue. 'There is still no seriously credible claim of responsibility from any particular group, and we don't have any leads into any known organisations or cells.'

'And you have officers attached to the police inquiry?' asks the Minister.

The AIVD Director glances across the table at the three senior police officers and nods. 'We do, Minister.'

'And do you have any concerns about the conduct of their inquiry so far?'

There is a pause. It is always tempting to indulge in inter-departmental point-scoring. The man glances across at Beatrix. He still finds her resemblance to the country's former monarch uncanny. Uncanny and disconcerting. And they even share the same name! One of his predecessors had been heavily criticised for investigating relatives of Queen Beatrix after a rift in the royal family. The secret enquiries had been in response to a request from the Queen's office. The revelation had been embarrassing for both the secret service and the Queen. He shakes his head. 'Of course, we are all disappointed that the killers haven't yet been brought to justice yet, Minister. But no. At the moment we are all working well together and doing everything possible to bring these outrages to an end.'

The Minister steeples his hands. 'I have just come from a meeting with the Prime Minister. Of course, you can imagine how concerned we both are at the national and international reaction to these murders. Can you make any kind of educated guess as to who is responsible?'

The counter terrorism man sighs. 'They are obviously seeking maximum publicity for their actions. The tulips tell us this – although we still have no idea where the flowers have come from or how they have survived. Our joint inquiries have drawn a blank on that so far. The experts are baffled. We also don't know why the bodies are so carefully posed in the same way. Perhaps that too is just a ruse to seize the public's attention. The victims, as Dr van der Laen says, all seem to be associated with activities that would be consistent with the far right in our country – either overtly or secretly. Perhaps this means the killings are being carried out as some kind of Islamic or racial revenge. But the tulips and the plant-based poisons may also suggest an environmental terrorist group.' He shakes his head. 'To be absolutely honest Minister, we are struggling to make sense of it all.'

The Minister runs his hand through his thick shock of hair in frustration and looks around the room. 'I appreciate I must sometimes leave politics at the door in this role, ladies and gentlemen.'

'Lady, not ladies,' says Beatrix under her breath.

'But I don't need to remind you we have a national election looming. Chaos fills a vacuum and the government is genuinely disturbed by some of the extreme views being aired in the wake of these murders. It is making for a highly toxic and febrile atmosphere. Several groups have applied for permission to hold public demonstrations and marches through the city and I am very anxious about the potential for violence.'

'We will be ready for it, Minister,' says the Regional Police Commissioner.

'Really?' thinks Beatrix to herself. She has witnessed other protests in the city and knows it will take a concerted effort with water cannon, dogs and mounted officers to disperse large and angry crowds – especially if the anti-capitalism protestors join in the fun, as they always do.

'Thank you,' says the Minister. 'However, I cannot only worry about Amsterdam. If protests get out of hand in other towns and cities, our forces will be seriously stretched. We may need to ask for the help of the military. Make a note of that please,' he signals to a civil servant sitting on an easy chair behind him. 'Alright. Publicity. The latest summary please.'

A young man, probably the youngest person in the room, stands and walks over to a large flat-screen television mounted on a wall. 'The story of the Tulip Murders is everywhere. Of course, the initial focus was on the reappearance of the lost tulip. But now it is about the serial killers causing terror on the streets of Amsterdam and, I'm afraid, the inability of the authorities to catch them.'

The man in his sharp suit nods to a colleague with a laptop. The screen behind him shows front page story after front page story in quick succession. It pauses on the German tabloid newspaper Bild which has a picture of the tulip and a canal location and a headline which screams: "*TULIP MURDER No. 6!*". The story on the front page of The Sun, a British tabloid, is equally prominent: "TULIPS FROM AMSTERDAM? NO THANKS!" A cartoonist has drawn an outsized Semper Augustus with blood dripping from a petal and forming a red puddle at its base.

The screen shows several more until the Minister holds up his hand. 'I think we get the idea, thank you.'

'Every main television news programme across the world is following the story and, of course, the internet is swamped by it.' More images appear with screen grab selections of comments on Facebook, Instagram, Twitter and several more social media Apps. 'And as you say Minister, there is no shortage of individuals pointing the finger of blame at certain groups and cranking up the temperature. Some of them, of course, are politicians standing in the forthcoming elections who are trying to gain political capital.'

'Alright, that's enough. What precautions are we taking for this evening?'

The head of police for the whole of the Netherlands clasps his hands in front of him. 'I have drafted reinforcements into Amsterdam to support the city's force. We shall have more than 1,000 additional officers patrolling the city centre again tonight and helicopters on standby. All key road, canal and river junctions will be permanently manned from dusk until dawn. The thefts of any vehicles during today and tonight will be investigated immediately – especially official vehicles, ambulances, police cars or council vehicles and so on. The evening television and radio bulletins will be encouraging any member of the public who sees something suspicious to contact us immediately.'

The Minister nods. 'Let's pray your precautions are sufficient. Although they clearly weren't last night.' He smiles sardonically. 'This situation isn't only life-threatening. It's career threatening too. I hope I make myself clear.' An awkward silence and paper shuffling greets this statement. 'Alright, is there anything else?'

'Yes,' thinks Beatrix to herself. 'Let us get on with our bloody jobs.'

'Um, there is just one other thing Minister,' says a diffident grey-looking man. Beatrix recognises him as one of the Ministry's senior civil servants who rarely says a word in operational meetings.

'Well, go on.'

'Shortly before the meeting I took a call from my opposite number at the Ministry of Foreign Affairs. It appears the British Embassy has been in touch.'

'Something from their GCHQ?' demands the Minister hopefully.

'No Minister, I'm afraid not. However, they have passed on some analysis of their own in case it is helpful. It concerns the pattern of the locations of the murder victims. Perhaps we can have a look at the map they sent with it?' He too nods at the operator of the laptop and a map of central Amsterdam appears on the screen.

'They stress this is only a theory, but if you mark the locations of the murders and join the dots as it were, well it could appear that they are designed to form a capital of the letter Q. Obviously, the top right-hand corner of the letter is still missing at the moment but they were wondering if it might indicate the precise location of what might be the final killing – or at least, where the body of the next victim will be found. I'm not operational of course but as this has only just come in, I thought it might be worth sharing with the meeting.'

The Minister is sitting up straight now, staring at the screen. 'Good god! So, it does! A giant letter Q. What does it mean? Anyone?'

'The British also wonder whether it might possibly point towards the involvement of Al-Qaeda. The letter Q you see. Or the Quran perhaps?' He catches the eye of the head of AIVD and sits back. 'Or perhaps not...' His voice tails away.

'We'll take this away for further analysis Minister,' says the spymaster sharply. He doesn't know whether to be angrier at his team for failing to spot this before the British or at the civil servant for springing it on him during the meeting.

'Dr van der Laen? What about you? What do you think?' demands the Minister.

Beatrix stands and walks over to the screen. 'This latest position suggests somewhere near Oude Kerk,' she says. 'There's water nearby and that has been a common feature so far.' She turns to face the group. 'I certainly think there has to be some reasoning behind the pattern of the locations or they wouldn't be connected by straight lines going North-South and East-West. We mustn't be any less diligent in covering the whole city centre tonight - but I think it might be worth paying Oude Kerk some special attention while our AIVD colleagues explore the Al-Qaeda theory.'

'Excellent. Well said,' says the Minister beaming. 'Who knows, perhaps this meeting has achieved the breakthrough that is so urgently needed. I shall brief the Prime Minister immediately on the latest developments. Thank you everyone.'

Beatrix and the city's Chief Commissioner share a lift to the ground floor. 'Do you really think there might be something in this Q business Beatrix?' he asks her.

'Who knows?' she replies, looking for their car and driver. 'This latest theory may have come to us via the British Embassy – but I suspect I know where it originated.'

CHAPTER TWENTY-FIVE

Nina and I resist the temptation to spend the evening hanging around the Oude Kerk and settle down for a cosy evening onboard *Flora*. We assume the police will have swamped the area and agree that two English tourists aren't going to be much additional help. Nina has her laptop open on one thigh and Eddie is resting his chin adoringly on the other. I am re-reading a spy thriller and we are half-way through a decent bottle of Portuguese Douro. The wood-burning stove is blazing, and Mozart's flute concerto is playing softly in the background. Lights reflect on the water outside and bring a soft glow into the room. I sigh happily. 'This is all very hygge isn't it?'

Nina looks up and smiles. 'That's a Danish concept. But the Dutch do have an equivalent. There was something in my guidebook about it.' She taps away at her keyboard. 'Dutch version of hygge. Yes, here we are. The Dutch word for it is gezelligheid – a blend of simple pleasures: cosiness, togetherness, conviviality, jolliness and contentedness.'

'It sounds like a sneeze. Gezelligheid!'

Nina laughs and sips her wine. 'It says here that firstly you have to sit in semi-darkness with a lot of flickering little candles in glass holders so that it's impossible to read and you can barely see each other.'

'Ah well, we're not quite achieving peak gezelligheid then,' I observe. 'It sounds very bossy.'

'And apparently no house is gezellig without flowers. It says if you go round to someone's house for a gezellig evening, you need to make sure you take a bunch of flowers and a bottle. And if you're a non-drinker it says, don't be surprised to be told not to be so ongezellig!' She giggles. 'Not much chance of anyone saying that to you, Jack!'

'So, what would be the English version of all this?' I ask.

Nina shrugs. 'Hygge is supposed to be untranslatable from the Scandinavian. I suppose the closest we would get is cosy.'

I stretch, yawn and roll my head in a circle. 'Well, I hate that word. But I suppose it's what I'm suffering from. Cosy contentment. But we are supposed to be on holiday in one of Europe's most exciting and sexy cities. Are we being terribly boring do you think? Shouldn't we be out clubbing or something?'

Nina ruffles the mess of fur on top of Eddie's head. 'No, I'm fine with a bit of gezelligheid, thanks.' She returns to her laptop and I refocus on my book, but after ten minutes she exclaims, 'That's strange.' She unfurls herself, pads barefoot to her room and returns with her hefty Rembrandt book.

'What is it?'

'Come and look.'

Her computer screen has three windows open and the same image in all of them. It looks like a pencil sketch of a woman. She is wearing an ankle length shift of some kind and her eyes are closed. She is suspended on a vertical pole and there are two wooden beams protruding on either side of her head. A rope across her chest is holding her body in place and her arms hang down in front of it. Finally, a short axe is hanging down from one of the beams by her head. On each of the windows is the hashtag #TulipMurders and no other words.

Now Nina flicks through her Rembrandt book to a collection

of glossy pages in its centre and points to an identical image. Underneath it says the drawing is in the collection of the Metropolitan Museum of Art in New York but there is no more information about it.

'How strange,' says Nina. 'I wonder why someone would associate this Rembrandt sketch with the Tulip Murders and put it on social media?'

'Well, the pose is almost identical to the Tulip victims. Maybe someone just saw the resemblance? What's it been posted on?'

'Facebook, Instagram and Twitter,' replies Nina. 'I wonder...' She taps her keyboard and uses her forefinger to scroll around the screen. 'Yes. Here look. It's on TikTok too.' Someone called Troll has posted exactly the same image with the same hashtag but on this platform the head of the woman moves slowly from side to side, like a macabre metronome. 'I wonder why someone would take the trouble of posting it on every single platform. And I wonder who she is?'

'Why don't we ask Su if she's got any ideas?' I suggest. Nina forwards one of the images to Su via email and my mobile rings about ten minutes later.

'I don't know the image and I can't find anything out about it online,' she says. 'But I know someone who might be able to help. She's a Rembrandt expert based at Rembrandthuis – the artist's former house on Jodenbreestraat. It's a museum now with a big collection of his etchings. I'll give Jodi a ring and see if she can meet us in the morning.'

A text comes through half an hour later confirming a meeting with Jodi at 10 a.m. tomorrow morning. Nina is delighted. 'I really wanted to go there anyway,' she says, collecting Eddie's lead to give him a final evening stroll. 'It's supposed to be an exact recreation of his rooms based on an inventory of his things that was made when he went bankrupt.'

'Su will be hoping there's a story in this,' I say, rising to join her.

We lock up the boat and walk south, across the wooden drawbridge with its love locks and through the neighbouring roads. There are still lots of people about.

'Don't get your hopes up too much about this sketch,' I warn her at one point. 'I expect it's just someone who saw the similarity of the pose and posted it as a curiosity.'

'But then why didn't they say as much?' asks Nina. 'I should have looked to see what else Troll has posted in the past. I'll have a look when we get back.'

I can't work up much enthusiasm for her line of inquiry and I am more preoccupied wondering if the killers are going to complete their letter Q this evening. I wonder if Archi passed on our suggestion and if he did, whether the police are taking it seriously. Is there really an Islamic terrorist cell about to strike again? Oude Kerk isn't far to walk from our mooring but once again, we resist the temptation and after a while we turn back, retrace our steps and collapse into our separate beds.

CHAPTER TWENTY-SIX

Johan Munt was seriously looking forward to his evening's entertainment. The little boutique hotel on the southern end of the Oudezjids Achterburgwal canal was typical of its kind – quirky with tiny rooms, steep staircases and fitted with cunning space saving devices that frequently baffled foreign tourists. However, the shower had good pressure and he luxuriated under it.

Munt had just turned 40 but as he soaped his body, he congratulated himself on staying in shape, despite no longer being a professional football player. As a former Dutch international, he had endured rigorous diet and training regimes in order to remain at the top of his game in the soccer-mad country. He had been worried he would quickly go to seed after he retired. But a frequently used gym membership card and regular runs along the canals near his home had kept his stomach flat and his lungs working well.

He turned 180 degrees to let the water massage his back and shoulders while he rubbed some expensive shampoo into his curly locks. He wasn't losing his hair either, he thought to himself with satisfaction. Okay, the woman he was due to meet looked completely stunning in her photographs – and at least a decade and a half younger than him. But he felt reasonably confident she wouldn't be disappointed.

Of course, he had never been in the same league as his country's greats – Cruyff, Bergkamp, van Persie, van Nisterlrooy and van Basten. But his face and name were still well known, and it wasn't hard to get a reaction on the dating app that he regularly used. His profile picture helped. It showed him seconds after scoring a goal for the national side. He was celebrating, bare-chested and jubilantly waving his orange shirt in circles. The photographer had caught him roaring in triumph with his eyes shining and his mouth open. His biceps and abdomen looked ripped. Okay. It was 15-years ago now. But what woman wouldn't want a bit of that action?

But he also knew that he had to try harder since that ridiculous television programme which had ruined everything. He knew that when women Googled him, the first story to greet them would be 'the moment of shame' and that would put some of them off altogether.

A few years after his retirement, Munt had been invited to be a television studio pundit for an international friendly against England. He was nervous because he had hoped to build it into a regular and well-paid slot for himself. But the uppers and the brandy that he had taken before going live had affected him badly. The studio lights were hot, and the other pundits seemed to be getting much more airtime than him. He knew he was lagging behind the discussion and confused by the technicalities of the tactics being described. He was unsure how to contribute. The host seemed to be deliberately ignoring him. He grew petulant and then aggressive. And that is when he said it.

'There should be a limit,' he had interjected abruptly.

'A limit?' asked the host. 'What do you mean Johan? What kind of limit?'

'A limit on the number of black players in each international side.' Broadcasters abhor a silence but a long one definitely followed this comment.

'What? How can you possibly say that?' said the ex-player sitting next to him. His family were from Senegal.

'And not just international sides. All of our professional sides,' continued Munt relentlessly. 'There are too many foreign players in our teams. We need to rediscover our racial purity on the football field.'

Events were a bit of a blur after that. The other pundit had got to his feet and was angrily pointing in his face. The host had his hand pressed to his earpiece and Munt knocked over his glass of water as he lunged for it. Watching the replay, he realised that most of this went unseen because the director had cut away to some commercials. Nevertheless, he had been unplugged and unceremoniously bundled into the green room where a TV executive producer and the black pundit's wife hurled insults at him.

Munt's career in television punditry ended before it even began. However, his sense of grievance continued long after the incident. He realised his comments had not come from nowhere. He must have been unconsciously nursing this resentment throughout his career. And towards the end, he had seen the endless conveyor belt of super fit and ridiculously talented young black players running rings around him and decided it just wasn't fair. Where were they all coming from? Why was it allowed? Something needed to be done.

But as one door closed, another door opened. His television career may have been over, but a new lucrative side-line opened up. He discovered there was no shortage of political rallies, private club dinners, closed door meetings and 'special' hospitality events where he would be invited, for a fee, to expand on his anti-immigration theme. Of course, it helped that he already had a national profile. He found an agent who commissioned a writer to help Munt develop his thoughts which he then memorised as a provocative speech laced with a few jokes and footballing stories. Slowly, he began to earn a decent living on the Dutch talks circuit and recently he had been having exploratory talks with a couple of parties about standing for parliament. Yes, he felt things were going pretty well for Mr Munt after he had turned a disaster into a triumphant new start for himself. His life was back on track. In fact, it was splendid, and this evening was going to be a rewarding and well-deserved bonus.

The couple had quickly approved of each other's online profile and agreed to continue their correspondence in private. This had been less than a week ago, but their dialogue had quickly become teasingly erotic. Anna could give as good as she got and by the end of the fourth day erotic pictures had been exchanged which displayed a fair amount of bare flesh and very particular parts of their anatomy. Munt had invited her to his apartment, but she had called him a cheapskate and demanded a specific room in a particular boutique hotel with a good bottle of champagne and lots of flowers.

He stepped out of the shower, pleased that he had invested in the expensive gel which now perfumed the steamy air, and towelled himself down. Then he pulled out his mobile to make sure she hadn't cried off and, for the hundredth time, lingered over the pictures she had sent him. My god, he thought to himself, she was gorgeous. She had the looks of a high-class catwalk model. Her tits were small and tilted upwards, her legs were shapely and seemed to go on for ever. Soon they would be wrapped tightly around him. He couldn't wait.

Munt checked his watch. She was due in fifteen minutes. Should he get dressed again or receive her like this? He checked the coldness of the champagne and slightly rearranged one of the twelve pre-ordered bunches of flowers which decorated the room. He had just decided to get dressed again when there was a knock at the door. Christ. She was ten minutes early. He wrapped the bath towel back around his mid-riff and checked his reflection in the full-length mirror. The towel bulged slightly where he was already in a state of semi-arousal. Ah well, the foreplay would have to come later. They were planning on making a night of it anyway. And if it got a bit rough? Well, the rougher the better was his view.

He approached the door, holding the towel closed below his navel with one hand, He couldn't resist a quick look through the security peephole first. He wanted to see her in the flesh for the first time. But the corridor looked empty. There was another knock on the door. He fixed a smile on his face which he hoped was welcoming, but also cool, and reached up to the lock with his free hand to pull it open.

The moped had mounted the pavement and come to a stop on one side of the hotel's entrance steps. The rider, who was clad from head-to-toe in black leathers and a full-face helmet, walked to the large square storage box above the bike's rear wheel. He paused to send a text on his mobile phone before opening the lid and removing a cardboard pizza box.

He could see through the glass door that the young female receptionist was taking a call. He waited to watch her leave her desk. She was later to reflect that a guest ringing to complain about water coming through their room's ceiling would have probably used the hotel's internal phone system rather than an external line.

The moped rider crossed the reception area, pausing only to look up at a wall-mounted security camera and give it a thumbs-up gesture. Then he moved along a ground floor corridor, stopped to one side of the door to room three and extended his arm to knock with a gloved hand.

Holding the pizza box horizontal in front of him, he reached under its lid and grasped its contents. As the door swung inwards, the man in leathers stepped across to straddle the threshold. His left boot was extended forward slightly to prevent the door being closed in his face. But this turned out to be an unnecessary precaution.

The hotel guest facing him was clutching a towel around his waist with one hand and wide-eyed with surprise. He had clearly not been expecting a tall and broad-shouldered man in black leathers and a crash helmet to be proffering a pizza at him. 'What? No. There's been a mistake. I haven't ordered any pizza,' he protested as he took an involuntary step backwards into the room.

The delivery driver stepped forward into the gap, shouldered the door wide open, pulled a Taser from the pizza box and pulled the trigger. A compressed gas cartridge broke open inside the gun and shot its electrodes into the man's bare chest at point blank range. The charge flowed instantly into Munt's nervous system, flooding every inch of his body with the worst pain he had ever experienced in his life. It flung him backwards onto the floor of the hotel room where he writhed in agony as the door was closed and the tall intruder bent over him with a syringe. This too had been concealed in the pizza box. Munt's muscles wouldn't do what he wanted. He flapped and convulsed on the floor like a freshly landed fish. This made him powerless as the needle plunged into his neck and its contents were quickly emptied into his blood stream.

It would take just 30 seconds for the ketamine to do its work and render the ex-footballer unconscious. The intruder sat on the bed for 60 seconds, one heavy biker boot planted on the man's chest, just to be sure, and then retrieved the pizza box. He removed another syringe from it. This one contained a lethal dose of nicotine and he injected its contents into a neck vein before removing the last item that was hidden inside the box.

It was a single red and white broken tulip which he carefully positioned as the centrepiece in a glass vase that was already filled with white roses. He spent a moment fiddling with the arrangement and when he was satisfied, stood back to admire his handiwork. Then he replaced the Taser and the two empty syringes in the box. It took another five minutes for Munt's body to be arranged to the killer's satisfaction. Finally, he pulled out his mobile and took two pictures – one of the corpse and another of the tulip.

The reception desk was still unstaffed as he returned to cross the hotel's entrance foyer where an elderly Belgian couple were waiting patiently for someone to appear. They watched through the glass as he put the pizza box back into his plastic pannier and zoom away. Later, they told police that no, they had suspected nothing. Why would they? Although yes, perhaps it was strange that he was taking the pizza box away. Maybe the customer didn't want it after all? Or perhaps no-one had been in to receive it? The receptionist had returned from the silly trick that had been played on her. There was no water leaking into a room on the top floor. She checked the elderly couple in. No, they hadn't mentioned the delivery driver to the young woman. Why would they?

CHAPTER TWENTY-SEVEN

I check the local news websites as soon as my eyes are open the following morning and I'm surprised to see that no overnight killing is being reported. There is no account of a seventh murder in seven days or the discovery of a seventh Semper Augustus tulip. It's puzzling. I had convinced myself that the final part of the capital Q would be completed by today with another murder in the Oude Kerk area ending an entire week-long killing spree. I catch myself feeling slightly disappointed and immediately flush with guilt. It's surely a good thing that no poor soul has been violently despatched to meet his or her maker during the previous night.

Su is already sitting in Jodi Luiken's tiny office at the Rembrandthuis by the time we are ushered into it. 'Come in, come in,' says the Rembrandt expert, 'It's a bit of a squash but we'll manage. Coffee? Pull up a seat.' Her English is flawless but delivered in the usual sing-song manner.

We shake hands as Su introduces us. Our host is very friendly and very different from what I had expected. I suppose my clichéd image of a Dutch expert in Old Masters was a matronly figure with unkempt grey hair, wire-rimmed glasses and a fierce demeanour. Jodi Luiken is a very different proposition. I estimate her to be in her early thirties and she has the flawless white skin of one of Vermeer's maids, piercing green eyes and a glorious halo of red wavy hair that has been elegantly styled to fall just above a graceful and slender neck. She is wearing a shirt tailored out of a startling silver cloth which makes it shimmer metallically, like the skin of a fresh mackerel. Nina leans across to me and I bend my ear to her mouth. 'Close your mouth Jack,' she whispers. I frown at her and she smiles sweetly back at me.

Fortunately, Jodi doesn't seem to have heard and is busying herself with pouring out two more coffees. Then she slides a photograph towards us across her desk. It is the sketch of the dead girl hanging on the post.

'Su has explained why you are interested in this drawing so let me introduce you to Elsje Christiaens of Spouwen in Jutland. She was just 18-years-old when Rembrandt made this sketch of her corpse in 1664.'

'Just eighteen!' says Nina. 'What happened to her?'

'It is one of two Rembrandt drawings of Elsje kept at the Met in New York,' continues Jodi. 'The artist moved to the right of the body for the second sketch and drew her side-on. You ask what happened to her Nina? Well, I am sad to say she was sentenced to be garrotted on a pole here in Amsterdam until she was dead and then beaten on the head several times by the hangman with the hatchet that you see hanging beside her.'

'That's horrible, exclaims Nina.

'What did she do?' I ask. I notice Su has her notebook out and is scribbling furiously. As I predicted, she thinks there may be a story here.

'Okay,' says Jodi smiling, 'We are fortunate to know quite a lot about poor Elsje thanks to the investigations of Isabella van Eeghen, who is a specialist in the city's municipal archives. Elsje had only arrived here in the city fourteen days before the terrible events which saw her taken in front of the Alderman's Court. She had come to the city looking for work as a maid and taken lodgings in a room on the Damrak. But after two weeks, her landlady suddenly demanded part of her rent – money which Elsje had not yet earned. Early the next morning the landlady reappeared and threatened to take some of the girl's meagre possessions in lieu of payment. The court heard that Elsje refused and so the landlady began to beat her with a broomstick. Elsje fought back with a hatchet that was lying on a nearby chair and the older woman was knocked over by the blow, fell down a flight of stairs and lay there, dead. No doubt you have seen the steepness and narrowness of stairs in traditional Dutch houses. They are very dangerous.'

'Was she caught straight away?' asks Su.

'Not quite.' Jodi smiles sadly and sips her coffee. 'The court records state that she stole some clothes from the other lodgers and then fled. Some neighbours had been alarmed by the screams, but she said her hands were bloody from a nosebleed and then she made her escape. The neighbours found the landlady's body in the cellar and chased Elsje through the streets until she jumped into the river in panic. She was hauled out and taken straight to the court.'

'It seems an odd choice of subject for Rembrandt,' I say. 'He's almost acting like a 17th century press photographer.'

Jodi smiles. 'Who knows what was going through his mind? He was quite old and not very successful by the time he was rowed across the IJ to draw Elsje's body. He had lost this lovely house, and his second great love, Hendrickje Stoffels had died. Perhaps he identified with the young woman as a victim of harsh fate? Or perhaps he was trying to capture the much larger forces at work in Amsterdam through a small and very human story?'

'What do you mean Jodi?' asks Nina, leaning forward.

'Elsje was an immigrant who had come to the city looking for work. But she was far from alone in this respect. Between 1600 and 1650 the city's population rose from 50,000 to 150,000. That's a trebling of the population in roughly two generations. Tens of thousands of immigrants were arriving all the time from Antwerp and Portugal along with the Huguenots from France and itinerant workers from Germany. The city had changed enormously in Rembrandt's lifetime and perhaps he was trying to capture something of this in his old age?'

'So, we're back to immigration again,' I say.

Jodi fixes her amazing green eyes on me. 'What do you mean Jack?'

'Most of the victims of the Tulip Murders seem to have had some kind of connection with immigration. Or anti-immigration I should say. There was a thug who organised violent raids on Muslim housing areas of the city, a priest who gave sermons about it, a newspaper columnist who wrote about it, a retired army officer who was stockpiling guns for some kind of fascist militia and a man who sold right-wing books and collected Nazi memorabilia.'

'And a property developer who was lobbying for changes in the limits for new housing which could have disadvantaged poorer immigrants,' chips in Su.

'I didn't know that,' I say. 'But my point stands. Now you're telling us this image by Rembrandt, which has mysteriously and suddenly appeared across all of social media with the hashtag #TulipMurders, is a 17th century immigrant who was sentenced to death by the city's authorities.' Su is still scribbling away in her corner of the room.

'And yet whoever posted it didn't say anything about it. They didn't even say it was by Rembrandt,' says Nina.

'So, what are we saying here?' demands Su. 'That the image of Elsje was posted by someone close to the killers, or even the killers themselves, as a subtle message about why they're doing what they are doing?'

'That sounds a little incredible,' says Jodi. 'Why wouldn't they just explain their motives more directly?'

'You're right, Jodi,' I say. 'It is all pretty bizarre. Obviously, the people carrying out these killings are highly organised, even professionals perhaps. They've carried out six murders in six days and evaded capture in a city which is swamped with police patrols and security cameras. Moreover, they've done all they can to attract attention to what they've been doing.'

'The tulips?' asks Jodi.

'Yes, of course. Semper Augustus. They decorate the corpses with a long-lost and highly valuable tulip. The only reason to do that must be to attract the world's attention to what they are doing. And then they take the extra trouble and risk to pose their victims in exactly the same way as Elsje here! It's all very theatrical and dramatic, isn't it? And yet it took Nina to spot that these posts were the same as a photo in her art books. No group or individual has claimed responsibility. It's as though someone, or some people, are being deliberately baffling.'

'But why would they do that?' asks Nina.

'I honestly don't know. Possibly, to crank up everyone's curiosity in advance of the big reveal?'

'The big reveal?' asks Jodi. 'What do you mean?'

'The big announcement of who they are and why they've been doing this. Oh, heck. I don't know. I'm just thinking aloud.'

'Well, I do know one thing,' says Su. We all turn to look at her. She points at the photograph of the Elsje sketch and then at her notebook. 'This is a story.'

'Maybe,' I say hesitantly.

'No. Not maybe Jack. Certainly. Mysterious posts from an anonymous account suggest a particular Rembrandt connection with Tulip Murders. Does it suggest immigration is the key issue here? Are the killings motivated by race?'

'You won't quote me on that,' says Jodi firmly to Su. It is a calm statement rather than a question. I am quietly impressed by the beautiful Rembrandt expert.

'Don't worry Jodi. I won't quote you at all on the race issues. Just the facts you gave us about the drawing. The main thing now is that I need to get a response to this from the police. Are they already investigating the posts? And if they aren't, will they now? Either way it's a story. And it's yours truly who has brought them to their attention.'

I cough. 'Well, actually, it was Nina who saw them first, Su.'

'Happy to give her credit for that,' smiles Su brightly.

'Er, no thanks. Keep me out of it,' says Nina.

'Fair enough. An anonymous English tourist spotted them among the millions of posts.'

I realise Su has her teeth as firmly clamped onto this story as Eddie when he's wrestling me for one of his toys. 'Well, if you're going over to police HQ to ask them about it, I wouldn't mind tagging along,' I say.

'It'll be interesting to hear if they've followed up on your letter Q theory,' observes Nina.

'The letter Q?' demands Su instantly.

I sigh. 'I'll explain on the way.'

We stand to say goodbye and give our thanks to Jodi. Nina announces she's going to stay and have a proper look around Rembrandt's house. Jodi offers to give her a personal tour.

'Right then, Jack Johnson,' says Su as we begin walking west along the Herengracht. 'What's all this about the letter Q?'

CHAPTER TWENTY-EIGHT

Both Beatrix and Robert have suffered another sleepless night, tossing and turning in the expectation of a call to tell them of the discovery of another body in the Oude Kerk area and racking their brains why anyone would describe a large capital letter Q across their city in dead bodies. Beatrix has detailed one poor detective on her team to spend the entire night combing through a dictionary and the records of Amsterdammers whose names begin with Q. The two senior murder squad detectives had considered being part of the stake-out of Oude Kerk themselves but were ordered to leave it to the supervision of another senior officer and get some rest.

The non-appearance of another body is, therefore, something of a relief when they gather in the Chief Commissioner's office over coffee and pastries for breakfast. 'Perhaps they've given up,' he says, rubbing his meaty hands together and smiling hopefully at the other two.

'Or perhaps we focused on the wrong area and the call is yet to come in,' says Robert.

'Now, now, Inspector. Plan for the worst but hope for the best.

That's my motto.' He greedily helps himself to a third pastry. 'What do you think, Beatrix?'

Beatrix is lost in thought and twirling the end of a long string of pearls. 'I don't know. But one of you will turn out to be wrong.'

The two men look at each other. They are both quietly worried that Dr Beatrix van der Laen, the highly experienced, unflappable and brilliant murder detective isn't her usual self. She had startled her deputy by giving him a tight hug on arrival at the station that morning. 'Sorry. I just needed that,' she had said.

It's true that no previous case of hers has been caught in such a worldwide spotlight. But she has had to cope with the close attention of politicians before and her file of unsolved murders is a very thin one. She would usually back herself and her team with confidence - or cheerful insouciance at least. This time feels different. It isn't just the scale of it. It is the combination of the brutal efficiency of the abductions and killings and the showmanship of the murder scenes. The careful posing of the victims. The tulips. What are they up to? How can she break the pattern and bring this nightmare to an end?

Beatrix stands up and walks over to a map of the city centre that is pinned to a noticeboard. The Chief's assistant has marked all of the Tulip Murders on it with a small number denoting the sequence alongside a printed photograph of each victim. The Chief himself had joined the dots with a pencil and ruler to form a capital letter Q with the top right corner missing. The two men are quiet and watch while she presses a finger on 1, then 2, then 3 and so on until she gets to 6 in the top left-hand corner. She mentally recaps the key facts of each killing as she traces the murderers' route around the city, but she is still shaking her head in frustration when there is a knock on the door.

'Come in,' barks the Chief, brushing pastry crumbs from his fingers onto the plate on the desk in front of him. It is a uniformed inspector who runs the central operations team.

'Sorry to interrupt,' he says. His face says it all.

'Another one?' asks Beatrix. 'Where?'

The inspector walks across to the map. 'A small hotel on the Ouderzijds Achterburgwal – just there.' He points to a place on the map a short distance directly west of the second X on the map, alongside a narrow canal. Beatrix marks a seventh X on the map where his finger is. 'The call has only just come in,' adds the inspector. 'A hotel cleaner found the body ten minutes ago and the manager called us as soon as he saw the tulip. The room is locked and he's standing guard. I'm sorry.'

Beatrix puts a hand on his arm and smiles at him. 'It's not your fault my friend. Thank you for telling us straight away. Come on Robert. Let's go.'

'Brief me when you know more,' the Chief calls, somewhat plaintively, as she is leaving the room. Robert is following close behind but gives a backwards glance to see the Amsterdam police chief burying his face in both his hands.

A Scene-of-Crime team is already waiting for the two detectives in a van outside the front of the small hotel. Beatrix and Robert put on gloves, white suits with hoods and shoe coverings and join two other officers outside the door of room 3 with the manager.

'Wait here a moment,' she orders and nods at the manager to open the door. She takes a few steps into the room and stops to take in the scene without disturbing anything. Her first impression is a blaze of colour and floral aromas so strong that they penetrate her face mask. There are flowers everywhere. Vases of red, white and pink roses are on almost every surface along with red and yellow tulips. The smell is overpowering and even slightly sickly in such a modest sized room. There is a large bouquet of white roses in a vase on a coffee table and artfully placed in its centre is a single bulb of Semper Augustus. Everything is neat and tidy apart from a pile of clothes which have been flung onto a bedside chair. There are no obvious signs of a violent struggle.

Beatrix walks forward, past the end of the bed to the door of an en-suite bathroom in the far corner. It is wide open and she stands in the doorway. There isn't room for a bath but there is a small shower squeezed into the corner of the room. It has a door to the side and a large transparent piece of glass faces her. It doesn't quite stretch to the full height of the room and the head, shoulders and arms of a dead man protrude through the gap between the top of the screen and the ceiling. He has been lifted up and suspended so that his head and both arms hang forward, outside the shower screen. The rest of his naked body is suspended in the air and pressed flat against the inside of the glass.

The head is slumped forward, so she is forced to crouch on the floor to look up at the face of the dead man. He has tight curly hair and handsome even features. She realises with a start of surprise that she recognises him. Munt. Johan Munt. The footballer. She saw him play once at the Johan Cruyff Arena. She even remembers the fuss about his racist comments on a live television show. 'So, Johan,' she says quietly to herself. 'What have you been up to recently?'

She takes a picture on her mobile of the dead man and retreats into the corridor where she removes her face mask. 'Alright, it's all yours,' she says to the Scene-of-Crime officers. She shows Robert the picture on the screen of her phone and tells him who he is. Robert isn't a football fan, but even he has heard of Johan Munt. 'Wait here and see if they can find Munt's mobile,' she says. 'I'll go to his home and brief the Chief on the way.'

'Christ,' says Robert. 'That's all we need. A dead ex-international football player. Just when we thought this couldn't get any bigger.'

It takes fifteen minutes for the unit to establish that there is no sign of Munt's mobile phone but Robert's chat with the manager establishes that he had been expecting a guest. Munt had pre-ordered all of the flowers and the champagne. He had also booked the room and paid a deposit in his own name. 'She must have been someone special,' observes the manager. 'That's a lot of effort. A first date maybe?'

'It could have been a *he*,' says Robert matter-of-factly. 'Let's not jump to conclusions. Okay, let's see what you've got on camera.'

It takes half an hour to scan the archived footage from the camera in reception and a second one that covers the corridor outside room number 3. It is Robert who notices that the pizza delivery driver doesn't just arrive with a pizza box, but he leaves with it too. He also registers the thumbs-up gesture to the camera. Cocky. The same man is seen on the second camera knocking on Munt's door, standing to one side while it opens and then moving swiftly inside whilst simultaneously taking something from the box. He is seen leaving exactly 7 minutes and thirty-five seconds later. The man is completely anonymous behind his crash helmet. He looks broad shouldered and tall. The force's technical support team will pour over the video, but he doubts it will reveal anything. The moped, when its registration number is tracked and traced via cameras in the street, will almost certainly turn out to have been stolen.

The manager, who has been watching the footage over Robert's shoulder, notices that the reception desk is unmanned. He checks the rotas and calls the member of staff at her home. She tells Robert why she left her desk and he tries to reassure her whilst silently admiring the well-planned and carefully timed operation. They had removed any chance of the killer being accosted in the entrance foyer with the bogus phone call. He phones Beatrix to brief her about his discoveries.

'It would be nice to know who Munt thought he was meeting,' she says.

'I imagine his phone is underwater at the bottom of a canal by now.'

'And there's nothing here to help with that.' Beatrix has been prowling around Munt's very masculine apartment for the past forty minutes. 'He's got a laptop though. I'll bring it in. If we can manage to open it up, there's an outside chance that his phone communications were mirrored on it.'

'Alright boss. See you back at base.'

However, even before Robert reaches police headquarters, the hotel's manager has earned himself a week's salary with a tip-off to the newsroom of a commercial television channel. The man is already being interviewed on live television outside the hotel by the time Beatrice returns to her office. Several of her team members are clustered around a wall-mounted television to watch the breaking news. She sees the picture change to footage of Munt playing for the Dutch national side. They look up guiltily as she approaches.

'He was a bit crap anyway,' she says with a smile. Then she notices the little figure of the Head of Public Affairs hovering uneasily by her office door. 'Back to work, guys. Team meeting in an hour.'

'Hi Beatrix. Number seven eh? You'll need to do a press conference. Munt is a big name. The lines in the press office are going mad.'

'*Was* a big name,' she corrects him, swinging her office door open and claiming her desk and chair. 'Alright. But it'll need to be late afternoon. We'll give them some security footage of the suspected killer – and I can appeal for information about whoever Munt thought he was meeting. But there's precious little else to go on.' She looks up in annoyance. The man is still hovering in his doorway.

'There's something else, Beatrix,' he says apologetically. 'It may be nothing. But we've had a strange query from an English journalist based here in the city. It's about a sketch by Rembrandt of an 18-year-old girl who was executed for murder. Here. Look at the picture.

CHAPTER TWENTY-NINE

My late morning visit to police headquarters with Su is a frustrating one. We present ourselves at the front desk and ask to see someone senior on the Tulip Murders investigation, but we are fobbed off with a junior ranker from the press office. He promises to take our query higher but says everyone else is busy responding to a new development. 'Well, tell them I'm running with this tomorrow morning, statement or no statement,' warns Su. In reality, I suspect she is bluffing. She needs a line from the police to give the story legs.

'What's the new development?' I ask the young man. 'Another killing?'

'No comment,' he says sharply, although I can tell from his face that I've hit the bullseye.

'Oh, come on,' says Su in exasperation. 'If Jack's right it'll be everywhere soon.' But the man just points to the door and hurries off into the building's interior. 'I'll make a couple of calls,' Su tells me.

I wander outside and lean on a railing by the water. She re-joins me five minutes later. 'It's another one alright. In a hotel on the Old Side. And you'll never guess who it is.' The name doesn't mean anything to me but Su is almost hopping with excitement.

A taxi drops us off about 50 metres from the hotel. It's impossible to get any closer because a noisy crowd has gathered outside. It has massed into two groups which are separated by a line of police officers stretched between the hotel's entrance and the canal. Several cardboard and wooden placards can be seen and there is a lot of shouting and chanting. Someone has an ear-splitting air horn.

'Football supporters?' I ask Su, my voice raised above the din.

'No. It's politics,' she shouts back after studying the messages on the boards that are being waved around. 'The right are blaming the left and the left are blaming the right.' I notice that some of the banners in one group depict crude pictures of tulips dripping with blood. 'Munt's going to be a martyr for the hard right now, and the left are effectively saying good riddance to the racist bastard!' Many of the placards seem to have the logos of different political parties on them. The police line has forced them to group themselves into two distinct pavement coalitions.

A bottle suddenly smashes on the pavement in front of us. It has been lobbed over the police from the rear of the crowd of right wingers. A rising cacophony of police sirens suggest reinforcements have been called for. 'Look, Jack. You don't need to be here for this. I'll stay and get a few pics and some colour. I'll meet you back at the boat.'

'Are you sure you don't want me to watch your back?'

She grins. 'You're on holiday, remember? Go on. Piss off.'

Flora is barely ten minutes away, so I turn away from the demonstration and walk back to rejoin Nina and Eddie. The Netherlands is an interesting country, I reflect to myself as I thread my way through Oudemanshuisport and its arcade of book shops. I had expected to find a deeply liberal and tolerant society, at peace with itself and welcoming the world to the calm waters on its doorstep. But we had discovered turbulent currents near the surface and this recent string of murders is threatening to turn them into a maelstrom.

Nina is enjoying an early lunch on the roof of the houseboat and Eddie is watching her greedily. I tell her all about the new victim and the demonstration outside the hotel and she enthuses about Rembrandt's house and her personal guided tour. 'Jodi asked if we'd like to meet up with her for a drink before we go back. I said yes and she's given me her phone number. You don't mind, do you?' she asks teasingly. 'She is rather beautiful and clever. I thought you might enjoy it.

'Behave,' I warn her, ducking back downstairs. I find my tourist map and mark the location of the small hotel on it with a number 7 alongside the X. The location of the latest body definitely doesn't indicate progress towards a capital letter Q anymore.

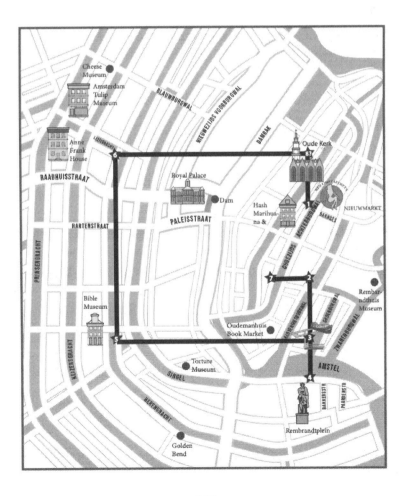

I stare at the diagram, much as I stare at my crossword clues, willing the cogs to turn and for it all to become clear. And suddenly it does. What if there isn't a line between the first and second victims? What if it's a gap? If that's the case, then I am no longer staring at a capital letter Q. No. Now I am staring at a potential capital letter G. Bloody hell!

I call Nina down from the roof and show her my latest calculations.

'It's possible,' she says cautiously. 'Are you sure there aren't any other possible permutations?'

'You're right. I need to go through the alphabet to make sure this is the only possible option.'

'You do that, Jack,' she yawns. 'It'll give you a break from your crosswords. I'm having a quick nap with Eddie.' Nina heads for her berth while I write out the alphabet in upper and lower case and use the pattern of the seven killings to try to form another letter. But it's no use. A capital letter G is the only possible option.

What can the G possibly stand for? An image springs to mind. It was a word on one of the placards at the demonstration. One of those alongside a bleeding tulip. It had the word GroenLinks on it. I pull out my laptop and google it. It's the name of the Green party in the Netherlands, founded in 1989 by a merger of four left-wing parties. I also read that it is known by the abbreviation G. I look back at my map of the murders. Yes, they could also form a capital L as well as a capital G. It could be a monogram of overlapping letters. Could it stand for the Links in GroenLinks, or for Labour or the liberal left? My laptop tells me GroenLinks has had some electoral success in the House of Representatives and describes itself as green, liberal and tolerant. A natural enemy, you would think, of the kind of people who had been turning up dead with a rare tulip alongside them.

Of course! The tulip. What better embodiment of the Greens than a rare and precious flower? And then there are the plant-based toxins. The seven victims had all, to my knowledge, been killed by poisons derived from plants. In effect, they were killed by nature, green in tooth and claw.

I stare at my diagram again. Am I looking at the 'big reveal'? Is this, in reality, a cryptic declaration of responsibility for the Tulip Murders by a gang of eco-terrorists?

I go and shake Nina awake and drag her, tousled and grumbling, into the boat's saloon. 'For God's sake Jack, I've only been asleep for five minutes.'

My fingers are trembling as I explain my theory. 'This has to be it doesn't it? There's no other explanation.'

'Make me a cup of tea, Jack,' she says, tracing her fingers through the alphabets to double-check my calculations. I do as I'm told while she remains bent over the table. She looks up and rubs her eyes as I return with two steaming mugs. 'You could be right. Or you could be on a wild goose chase again.' She giggles to herself. 'That's goose with a capital G of course!'

I shake my head in annoyance. 'But don't you see? I could still be right about Oude Kerk as the location of the next killing. It would form the top right-hand corner of the G. The last piece of the jigsaw!'

'Rather than the top right-hand corner of the Q. Yes, I know. I can see that. But I'm not sure the police will believe you twice.'

I realise I've already cried wolf. But I still feel I have to do my best to share my new theory with them. 'This points to some kind of ecological terrorist cell being responsible for the killings,' I say stubbornly. 'We have to do what we can to get them to consider it. I'm ringing Archi. And it ties in with the botanical poisons and the tulips.'

The man from the embassy is distinctly dubious at first. Robert has already told him, off the record, that he should have taken the Q theory directly to the police rather than feed it through the embassy's formal channels to the Dutch Ministry of Foreign Affairs. Just like the Director of AIVD, Beatrix hadn't appreciated the civil servant unwrapping the Q theory as a surprise present during the meeting at the Ministry of Justice. And the latest murder of the footballer had killed the idea anyway – much to the annoyance of His Excellency, the British Ambassador. Archi can't see how to even begin telling his boss the Q theory is now a G theory. And if the G theory turns out to be bunkum too, he fears his involvement in all this might be career threatening. All of this thinking goes unspoken, but Jack hears it anyway in Archi's hesitancy and doubtful prevarication.

'I just don't know Jack. It's just a theory, isn't it? There's no actual proof as such is there? It's ingenious of course. I'll give you that. But I'm not sure we should be taking it to the Dutch police again at this stage. I'm sorry. Look, I must dash I'm afraid. I've got a problem with an English stag party who all lined up to pee in a canal and then threw a local in the water when he complained. The Dutch don't mind them buying sex or having a joint, but they absolutely draw the line at urinating in public and giving their citizens a dunking. Catch you later. Love to the lovely Nina.'

Nina has been listening to our exchange through the loudspeaker on my phone. 'You can't blame him really, Jack. He's been burnt once.'

'God save me from bloody spineless bureaucrats,' I say loudly and crossly. 'I've a good mind to give this to Su and let them all read it in the bloody newspapers.'

Eddie gives a little yap. We both look to the open stern doorway where Commissioner Beatrix van der Laen is standing. 'No Mr Johnson. I know you are a journalist, but I really don't think that is a good idea. Do you?'

CHAPTER THIRTY

'Talking of journalists,' she says, advancing into the boat with her handsome young deputy immediately behind her. 'I'm told a journalist friend of yours has been making enquiries about a Rembrandt sketch?'

'How did you know she was my friend?' I ask.

'I spoke to her on the phone half an hour ago. She's going to meet us here as soon as she can.'

'Okay. Let's wait for her. But let me show you something in the meantime.' I talk Beatrix through my new G theory but I'm perplexed by her growing smile. 'Am I saying something funny?' I say curtly. 'I know I was wrong with the Q theory, but this all hangs together, doesn't it? You can't ignore it surely?'

'Calm down, Mr Johnson, I'm smiling because … well, why don't you tell him Robert?'

'We've had a couple of analysts brainstorming your Q theory ever since you mentioned it,' says Robert. 'They plotted the location of the latest killing and brought us exactly the same as this an hour ago.'

'Including the speculation that G stands for Green,' adds Beatrix, 'or the Greens.'

'So, you're taking it seriously?' I ask, while shooting a told-you-so look at Nina.

Beatrix raises both palms upwards. 'It's just guesswork of course. But it adds up to a definite-maybe when you take into account the tulips and the plant-based poisons.'

'So far, we've had digitalis – from the foxglove, and gelsemium – from yellow jasmine. We haven't gone public with the others, but our labs have also found traces of water hemlock, deadly nightshade, oleander and ricin, which comes from the castor oil plant. We're waiting for toxicology on the latest victim.'

I whistle. 'Someone must have one hell of a poison garden!'

'Hellish is an appropriate word,' says Beatrix. 'But again, there is something quite exaggerated about all this isn't there? Why are they taking the trouble to use such a range of plant-based poisons? It would take some very particular knowledge and expertise of course. But this is more than showing-off I think.'

'It could be to attract more attention,' says Nina.

'Precisely!' says Beatrix. 'They seem to want maximum publicity. As if the reappearance of Semper Augustus isn't enough. They want the whole world talking about what is going on, putting the puzzle together for themselves and coming to their own conclusions.'

'It's mad,' says Nina.

'This isn't the work of a lone psychopath,' says Beatrix, who takes a seat without being asked. 'For a start, there is more than one person involved. We know that from the video pictures of the fake ambulancemen. I think this is the work of a small and highly skilled team.'

'It is also very professional,' continues Robert. 'They've abducted seven people in seven days, some of them in broad daylight, in spite of widespread public alarm and huge numbers of police patrols.'

Beatrix nods. 'Everything points to it being political,' she says. 'Criminal and political.'

'So, if G stands for the Greens, and the tulip and the poisons are taken into account, you've got some kind of highly trained eco-terrorist cell wiping out a range of right-wing activists in the run-up to your elections,' I say.

Beatrix gives herself a little shake. 'I have enjoyed our little brainstorm, but I ask for your discretion at this moment.'

'But what about Oude Kerk?' I say urgently. 'This means it could still be the location of the next murder – maybe even the last. And if they maintain the pattern so far, it will take place tonight.'

'You'll leave that to us,' says Beatrix firmly. 'But you can be reassured that we shall take every precaution we can. Ah, this must be your friend Su Mortimer. Excellent. Please come in Mrs Mortimer, or is it Miss?'

'Just call me Su, Dr van der Laen.'

'Good. You wanted to alert me to this drawing that has been posted on social media. Is that the case?'

Beatrix opens a satchel and puts a glossy print of Elsje on the table.

'The pose is exactly the same as the Tulip Murder victims,' says Su, 'and maybe her immigrant status is relevant too. What do you think? On the record.'

The woman detective folds her arms and looks serious. She still looks immaculate but there is a darkness under her eyes that betrays long days and short, disturbed nights. 'You want a story, Su? A scoop? Is that it? Alright, you can quote me. Are you ready? I thank you for bringing this to our attention. It may or may not be relevant to our investigation. We would appeal for the person who posted the sketch to contact us, so they may be eliminated from our enquiries. End of statement.'

Su finishes scribbling in her notebook and looks up. 'Is that all?'

Beatrix smiles at her. 'Yes, that is all. But it is more than anyone else has, is that not so? Now it is my turn to ask a question. How did this come to your notice?'

'That was my fault,' says Nina immediately. 'I was just scrolling through the #TulipMurders hashtag and came across it. I recognised it from my book about Rembrandt.'

'And then the Rembrandt expert at Rembrandthuis, Jodi Luiken, identified the picture for us and told us the dead girl's story,' I add.

'And I brought it to you,' says Su pointedly. 'So, if it is relevant, I'd appreciate a bit more than you've given me so far.'

'If it turns out to be relevant, you'll be the first to know. But I don't want to see anything else from our conversation in the papers. Is that clear?'

'What else?' demands Su. 'What else have you been discussing?'

'Just that Mr Johnson's so-called Q theory no longer works in view of the location of this morning's latest victim,' says Robert smoothly. Beatrix is looking hard at me. The message is clear. She doesn't want anything about the new G theory going public. This must be because she is hoping the ambush the killers at Oude Kerk tonight. Nina also understands what isn't being said and puts a cautionary hand on my arm.

'That's right,' I say carefully. 'My Q theory is in the dustbin. So, your former Queen isn't a suspect anymore! Shame. It would have been a hell of a story.' The tension of the moment is broken by general laughter. Beatrix and Robert shake hands and Beatrix makes a point of squeezing mine and mouthing thank you before she heads back onto dry land.

Su is looking at me suspiciously. 'There's something else you aren't telling me,' she says.

'They came here because you took Elsje to them,' I reply calmly. 'And to put a lid on my Q theory in case I was still peddling it. Come on, cheer up Su. She's given you enough to run something. *"Police are examining a possible link between the Tulip Murders and a Rembrandt sketch of a dead girl. Murder detectives are appealing for the anonymous person who posted the sketch to come forward. Etc, etc, etc."* There isn't a paper in the Netherlands that won't take that angle, let alone abroad – especially with a picture of the sketch and the background you've got on Elsje.'

Su smiles. 'You're right. Thanks, Jack. I'd better get off and start selling. Stay in touch guys.'

'You just love it don't you?' says Nina as soon as we are on our own. 'You've got the bit between your teeth again.' She smiles. 'You'll never change.'

I pull a face. 'It was a bit annoying the police had already got there with the capital G.'

'Yes Jack. It's such a shame that you can't single-handedly wrap up a case which is dominating every waking thought of every law enforcement agency in the Netherlands.'

I choose to ignore her sarcasm. 'Su will kill me if she finds out I didn't tell her about the G theory.'

'And I will kill you if this takes over any more of our holiday. You did the right thing not to tell her. She'd have splashed it everywhere and wrecked any chance of ambushing the killers tonight. Anyway, it's still just a theory. And any connection with the Greens is even more of a stretch – until or unless they claim responsibility.'

'Yes, I know. Look, we can do whatever you want for the rest of the day. Even more paintings if we must. But this evening, we have plans.'

'Oh yes, and what do you have in mind?'

I point to my map and grin. 'We're going into the red-light district to see what happens when we find the G-spot!'

Eddie barks furiously as three cushions are hurled at my head in quick succession.

CHAPTER THIRTY-ONE

Daniel Raap adjusted the wooden butt of his hunting rifle so that it sat more firmly in the pit of his shoulder. The camouflaged tarpaulin sheet underneath him prevented the dampness of the earth from chilling his ancient bones. He still felt stiff though. He had only been lying in the same position for about an hour, but he had to admit to himself he might be getting too old for hunting.

It was a pity. He had only bought this manor house in the countryside outside Amsterdam because of the generously wooded private estate around it and the prospect of decent game. Most often, it was the warm dead body of a muntjac deer that he slung into the back of his little off-road vehicle. They would decimate his trees if he didn't cull them regularly. And his personal chef could work miracles with the venison from the stocky little animals. Sometimes though, he would shoot roe deer or fallow deer and on one glorious occasion, he had downed a wild boar and sent her piglets squealing away in terror.

He squinted through his telescopic sight at the centre of the small clearing where he had scattered a few deer nuts and waited. Raap knew he should be campaigning in the city with the election coming so soon. As co-founder and leader of the Born-Again party, and a former member of the House of Representatives, he already had a reputation and profile that was important to their cause. It was hard to start up again at the age of 70, but he had no regrets after splitting with bouffant Geert Wilders and his Freedom Party.

Of course, he still supported all of Wilders' views about the Moroccan immigrants who made the Dutch streets so unsafe. And he was quite happy with the Freedom Party's stance on pulling out of the European Union, banning the Quran and shutting down all of the mosques and fundamentalist schools in the country. That all made complete sense as far as he was concerned.

Raap adjusted his prone position again in an attempt to get comfortable and shook his head. He still couldn't believe that the liberals accused him of being intolerant. Yes, of course, most Dutch liked to regard themselves as the most tolerant and progressive people in Europe, maybe even the world. Why couldn't they see that the problem with immigrants is that *they* were the intolerant ones and that the values of liberal democracy were inherently in conflict with those of Islam? It was the foreigners who made their women wear the hijab and who were so opposed to sexual liberty. Why were the Dutch, and especially the Amsterdammers, so short sighted? He sighed. He would have to summon the energy to wake them all up. But not today. Today he was hunting. Tomorrow would do.

He just couldn't stand the rabble rouser Wilders, with his thick head of peroxide platinum hair. It was quite right to call him the Dutch Donald Trump. He was a populist ideologue who basked in the attention and had taken Raap's support and wealth for granted one too many times. The Freedom Party, known as the PVV, was a one-man political party in Raap's view and the far right in the Netherlands needed to broaden its appeal beyond Wilders if it was to win power. He knew that meant building a coalition because of the fractured nature of Dutch parliamentary politics. But why not make it a coalition of like-minded right-wing parties? There would be no dilution of their new laws then.

If Born-Again had to deal with Wilders one day, so be it. But he and Tulp would do it from a position of strength with their own followers. Their combined fortunes would ensure this was the case. After all, he had nothing else he needed to achieve in a long and successful life. And he had nothing else to spend his money on after selling his companies. It might have been different if he and Mary could have had children. But now she was dead, and he was wary of the gold-digging young women who pretended to admire his cadaver-like appearance and scrawny shanks. They were just after his considerable fortune.

Raap suddenly held his breath, and his rambling thoughts came into sharp focus on the scene in front of him. He knew he was invisible to the adult muntjac sniffing its way into the clearing. The brown and green of his hat and jacket allowed him to blend into the bushes and his powerful rifle and telescopic sight enabled him to be far enough away - but still sufficiently lethal. He had checked the breeze carefully and it hadn't changed direction, so there was little chance of being scented in his upwind position.

The crosshairs settled on a point just behind the front shoulder of the little brown deer. His finger tightened on the trigger. He knew he had to squeeze it gently so there was no kick to the barrel in the final few milliseconds. He tried to breathe in and out more deeply and calm his heart rate. God, this was so much better than endlessly dreary political strategy meetings and having to be nice to the army of people they had assembled to campaign for their new party. Even he recognised most of them to be mad, bad or just sad individuals. No, this moment in the hunt made him feel alive and virile again, tingling with anticipation as a powerful lifeforce flooded through his body.

His trigger finger paused. He froze as the deer looked up from the nuts and scanned its perimeter suspiciously. But then it ducked its head and began eating again.

At that moment, Raap's chef was a mile away, in the kitchen of the manor house and making final preparations for the old man's lunch. The window was open so he could enjoy hearing the birdsong as he cooked. Later, he would recall the shots as a double tap, with one following immediately after the first. At the time, he didn't consider it to be odd. He had never been hunting himself or he would have known that the two shots couldn't have come in quick succession from the same single-round bolt-action rifle.

In fact, the second shot came from a different gun. It fired a bullet which entered the back of Raap's thinly covered skull and shattered his brain to pieces.

CHAPTER THIRTY-TWO

A gaggle of Japanese tourists and their guide, two young male sex workers and a patrolling pair of police officers stand still and bow their heads respectfully as the long black hearse divests itself of its sad cargo. Four pall bearers, all dressed in black suits, black ties, and white shirts hoist the coffin effortlessly onto their shoulders.

It is a biodegradable coffin that is made from woven willow and covered with a profusion of beautiful spring flowers. Some of the tourists raise their phones to take pictures of it.

Three of the men are tall and strong looking, whilst the fourth is older than the others and has a large paunch. The quartet solemnly carry their burden through the front door of the massive church and along its considerable length. The coffin is on their shoulders and being steadied by their hands. This presumably explains why they are unable to remove their sunglasses or black fedora hats in spite of the sudden darkness of the church's interior.

There are many more tourists inside, but they fall silent as the procession goes slowly past them. The shiny black shoes of the four men are walking on a floor made up entirely of gravestones. Many are highly ornate and someone has counted 2,500 of them, under which are said to be buried 10,000 Amsterdam citizens.

This afternoon, another dead Dutchman is being brought to join them in the Oude Kerk, Amsterdam's oldest parish church.

The coffin is settled on the cold stone ground of a small side chapel which is suffused with multi-coloured light as the early afternoon sun streams through a stained-glass window. The men move to stand along one side of the coffin, facing the little altar with their hands clasped in front of them. They bow simultaneously and each of them picks a flower from the coffin. Then, they file out of the chapel and walk in a line, past the ornate stone font and the wood carved pulpit with its spiral staircase, back out of the church where they climb back into the hearse with its mirrored windows and drive slowly away.

No-one questions the presence of the coffin. Some tourists notice it and some even take photographs of it. The tour guides have seen many coffins lying in repose at the church before a funeral service takes place. They think nothing of it. At one point, a curious seven-year-old wanders over to the casket and spells out the ten letters printed on a small white card. D-A-N-I-E-L-R-A-A-P. But then she is pulled away by her mother.

Slowly, as the sun begins to set, the number of tourists dwindles, the attendants at the art exhibitions pack up their explanatory leaflets and leave and a security guard begins his final checks before locking all the doors.

Outside the church, a small regiment of plain clothes detectives has moved into position all around it and along the adjoining stretch of canal. Some pretend to be artists, others have commandeered first floor rooms above the neighbouring sex shops and more are perched at bars or on moored boats. All of them are expecting a long night - but they have been carefully briefed by Dr Beatrix van der Laen and her deputy to stay alert. She has told them this may be their last chance to catch the killers in the act.

The security guard has climbed wearily to the top of the church's tower to satisfy himself that it is empty. Whilst he is up there, a couple arrive at the main door of Oude Kerk, just five minutes before its formal closing time. They have immediately been recognised on a monitor in the rear of an unmarked lorry which is parked nearby. This is the mobile control unit of the police operation and Dr van der Laen is hunched forward, closely watching the couple on the screen.

'What the hell are they doing here?' asks Robert, who is standing immediately behind her.

'Pick them up and bring them over here when they come out,' instructs Beatrix tersely.

Meanwhile, Jack and Nina are walking around the perimeter of the church's interior for the second time during their stay in Amsterdam. This time, however, it is much darker and emptier. The muffled noise of the city's traffic is the only sound to disturb the oppressive silence. They are both silent too. Are they struck dumb by the oppressive weight of historic events that this church has witnessed? Or is it a sense of foreboding that this place of death and remembrance is about to welcome another poor soul into its keeping?

The sound of the guard's steps echo in the vast space before he appears and immediately sees the couple. He barks some Dutch at them and then switches to English after they shake their heads. 'We are closing the church now. You must leave immediately, please.' He points urgently to the exit. The guard is anxious because he has been told that some police officers will double-check the rigour of his final tour of the building today, before the doors are firmly locked and the alarms activated.

The couple nod and begin to make their way back through the church. As they approach the font, the man moves to one side of it and the woman to the other. It is made of white marble fashioned into an octagon with a carved base of flowers sitting on a pillar that has four oversized metal acorns at its feet. Nina is about the same height as the font, but Jack is about a foot taller and he glances down into its baptismal bowl as he passes.

His shout brings the security guard running towards him. All three look intently into the bowl where four crimson and white Semper Augustus tulips are lying across each other.

The guard's excited message on his radio is quickly relayed to Beatrix who takes less than three minutes to join the group at the font. She has Robert with her but everyone else has been ordered to wait outside and guard all the exits.

'My God! Four of them,' she says, before turning to Jack. 'Why are you here?'

Jack shrugs. 'Wrong place at the wrong time. We just thought we'd have an early evening drink and see the G-spot before turning in. And then we stumbled across the flowers.'

'The G-spot?' says Beatrix, stony faced. 'That is not so funny Mr Johnson. Alright, if the flowers are here, there must also be a body nearby. An eighth body. Although god knows how they pulled this off.'

'I've already been everywhere…' protests the guard. 'Unless…'

'Unless what?' snaps Robert.

The man's eyes are wide in amazement. 'Unless the body is in the coffin?'

'What coffin? What are you talking about?'

'Bodies do tend to be in coffins,' observes Nina drily.

'Come. Come with me.' The guard ushers the little group into the side chapel where a willow basket festooned in flowers is lying on the floor in front of the altar. Robert kneels to read the label in the gathering gloom.

'Hell's teeth!' he says, looking up. 'It says Daniel Raap!'

Beatrix closes her eyes, as though trying to cope with a sharp and sudden pain. 'Alright, I want a news blackout on this until we know more.' She points to the security guard. 'You, you stay with my team for the moment and no phone calls. Understood?' The poor man swallows and nods fearfully. 'Robert, get Scene-of-Crime in here quick. I want this coffin opened and the body identified fast. No-one else is allowed in the church until I say so. You two, come with me.'

We traipse outside after her, pausing by the bronze sculpture of the female sex worker with her red string ankle bracelet. Beatrix speaks quietly and urgently to another member of her team before climbing into the rear of a lorry that is kitted out like an office and parked in a little side street. She orders everyone out and points to two chairs in front of her.

'Who's Daniel Raap?' I ask.

'An elderly billionaire businessman and a former member of the

House of Representatives. He sold his companies and helped to found Born-Again with Cornelius Tulp. He was the leader of a new and very right-wing party that is standing in this election for the first time. If it is him in the coffin, it's a spectacular coup and it will also be incendiary.' The door of the lorry is opened and a note is passed up to Beatrix. 'It seems he was reported missing by his staff late this afternoon. He had been out hunting at his place in the country. It's almost certain to be him then. He fits the profile of the others alright.'

'But why the change of tactics?' asks Nina. 'The others were all found in the early morning, and in the same pose as Elsje.'

'Perhaps they realised we would be onto the eighth location by now. They changed tactics to avoid getting caught. They killed Raap, if that's who it is, during the day and brought the body here in broad daylight. They knew we would be mounting a night-time operation and concentrating on the water. The four tulips feel like a final flourish don't you think? And in terms of importance, Raap was a much more considerable figure than the others. And if this completes the G, it makes quite a finishing statement.'

'And there's the coffin,' says Nina.

'What about it?'

'Biodegradable materials. Excellent Green credentials with a capital G.'

Beatrix nods. 'I wonder what poison they used this time.'

The door swings open again but this time it is Robert. 'They've opened the coffin in the church,' he says, glancing across at us.

Beatrix waves a hand. 'It's okay.'

'It's Raap. He was dressed in hunting gear, but he had his wallet on him and we all recognised him anyway. Only this one is different.'

'Why,' demands Beatrix.

'He wasn't jabbed with a poison. Or if he was, it probably didn't kill him. He had the back of his head blown off.'

'So, the hunter became the hunted! Alright Robert. Thank you. I'll need to get back to HQ to brief the team and the Chief and prepare a press announcement. Talk to the officers who went to Raap's home. See what his staff are saying. Did they see any strangers around this morning? And I want the calibre of that bullet and the type of gun as soon as possible.'

'What about us?' I ask.

'You can go back to your boat. But I am asking you not to tell your journalist friend about any of this. Not yet anyway. We may face some serious demonstrations, even rioting, now. The right wingers have a significant new martyr and the anti-capitalist mobs will be celebrating the death of one of their bogeymen. We need some time to prepare. There may be lives at stake. I appeal to you.'

'Yes. Alright,' I say immediately. Beatrix nods her thanks. She is controlled and automatically making decisions with authority, but she looks pretty devastated. I reach out to put a hand on her arm. 'It's not your fault, Beatrix.'

'Thank you. But we should have got them this time.' A light suddenly comes on in her eyes. 'Of course, they could have hired a funeral service to deliver the coffin to the church. But they would have needed papers and an explanation. And there may not have been time to organise all this if they killed him earlier today. I wonder if they stole a hearse and delivered the body to the church themselves? In which case,' she says excitedly, 'we must have them on camera somewhere!' She stands up. 'Go. You go home. Please. And stay quiet. We have a lot of work to do.'

CHAPTER THIRTY-THREE

Nina and I are only too happy to stay quiet but several thousand people in Amsterdam and the rest of the Netherlands have other ideas. The story of Daniel Raap's murder dominates the television evening news programmes. It turns out to be too big for Beatrix or anyone else to keep a lid on it for long. The television news reports show pictures of the entrance to Raap's country home with police guarding a large pair of gates and the exterior of Oude Kerk. It also contains a graphic map of the location of the Tulip Murder victims across the city and animates to stress the outline of a capital letter G. We don't understand enough Dutch to follow what is being said, but there seems to be reaction from a wide range of politicians and their body language varies from anxious denial to furious outrage.

The response is almost instantaneous. A toxic mix of far-right, far-left, pro-Islam and anti-capitalist protestors take to the streets of Amsterdam along with all those who just fancy causing a bit of mayhem as night descends. The first we know about it is the steady increase in the number of police sirens as they race to trouble spots across the city. Shortly afterwards, a police helicopter starts circling close to our houseboat with a powerful searchlight and it is joined by others, presumably carrying news cameras.

It is midnight, and Nina and I are still glued to a continuous news channel on our boat's little television and watching in fascination as crowds of demonstrators square up to each other as well as the police. The riot police are better equipped than the stone-throwing protestors. The officers are wearing black protective helmets and carrying round wickerwork shields covered in black cloth. They also have long flexible truncheons. But they seem to be hopelessly outnumbered. We see fireworks exploding in their ranks and petrol-filled bottles bursting into flames.

Some in the crowd are chanting and waving placards and almost all of them are wearing balaclavas or woolly hats and scarves to disguise their identities. The smashed glass of bus shelters and shopfronts is strewn everywhere and at one point, a waist-high barricade of bicycles is piled across a bridge where a stand-off ensues. The television cameras show firemen trying to extinguish flames that are blazing in several upside-down cars. They are being pelted with stones as they try to do their job.

'Bloody hell,' says Nina at one point. 'I thought the Dutch were a placid people.'

'Most of them are,' I reply. 'But you get crazies like this in every country.'

The momentum of the protests seems to swing at around two o'clock in the morning as increasing numbers of riot police make concerted attempts to break up the crowds or snatch and arrest the most prominent troublemakers. At one stage the cameras show a line of mounted police on horses charging to clear a square and another shows a large black lorry with two water cannons mounted on the roof of its cab. The pressure from the jets knocks several demonstrators to the floor and gives others a good soaking.

Finally, the action seems to be concentrated on one big square where a thin blue line of riot officers is trying to keep two angry crowds apart. The police are easy to identify due to the fluorescent yellow band across the shoulders of their blue blouson jackets, but they look as though they are perilously outnumbered. Then it all changes again as the officers put on face masks and tear gas is fired into both sides of the square. Most of the demonstrators turn to flee as police reinforcements charge among them from adjoining side streets.

Gradually, the coverage scales down to show the wreckage-strewn streets, and switches to commentators and their interviewees back in the studio. I turn the television off and open my laptop. The demonstrations have already made the BBC News website in the UK.

'Wow. It's not just happening here in Amsterdam. There are reports of riots in Eindhoven and Rotterdam too. It says the far right believe Raap was murdered by Islamic or environmental terrorists and the left say this is what happens when you stir up unrest with populist propaganda. Meanwhile, everyone else is blaming the government for its failure to stop the murders and control the situation. It's all pretty toxic.'

Nina gives a big yawn. 'It all has to be connected with the elections, doesn't it? It's all been so carefully planned and that must include the timing.'

'I'm sure you're right. But it's a high-risk game, isn't it? Why would a terrorist cell wipe out eight right-wingers in this way? Surely it'll just cause a wave of sympathy for the right-wing parties at the election and achieve the opposite of what they want?'

Nina yawns again. 'Search me, Jack. But I need to get to bed. It's been a long day.'

'I'm still a bit wired,' I say. 'I'll give Eddie a little stroll before I turn in.'

'Okay, but be careful, and lock the door behind you,' says Nina, moving towards her bedroom.

I fix a lead to Eddie's collar and head off into the city. It isn't long before I come across the first signs of damage. Workmen have already been called out and some are fixing wooden boards in place where shop windows have been smashed. I pick Eddie up to carry him over the broken glass. A small mini-market looks as though it has been looted. Its shelves are empty and a wire screen designed to safeguard a display of spirits is hanging by one hinge.

All the bottles have gone. On another street, a recovery vehicle is winching the burnt-out remains of a car onto its wheels. The air is full of the smell of burnt rubber and a helicopter is still buzzing around overhead. I feel as though I am walking through the wreckage of a Middle Eastern warzone rather than a European tourist city.

In one square, council workmen are trying to stem the flow of water from a stone fountain that has been broken into pieces. Fragments have been used as missiles by the crowds. The squads of riot police have gone but there is still a substantial police presence on the streets – either patrolling on foot or cruising past slowly in cars. The sight of Eddie seems to reassure them and I am dismissed as a rubbernecker.

Eventually, we wander into the large open space of Dam Square. I recognise it as the site of the final big confrontation between the two factions. Several street-cleaning vehicles are working alongside gangs of men with shovels, brushes and electric carts. The faint smell of tear gas is still in the air. A tourist information panel tells me that this square, which is at the heart of the city, has been a magnet for social and political activities and protests for centuries. It may be a convenient meeting point for throngs of tourists now, but it reverted to being a battleground of ideas again tonight. The Royal Palace sits on one side of the square and I wonder if King Willem-Alexander is still in residence. He was probably whisked away at the first sign of trouble on his doorstep. It would certainly have been difficult for the reigning monarch to get a good night's sleep.

I turn with Eddie and we begin to thread our way back through the streets and along some of the canals. We stop at one spot for Eddie to cock his leg against a tree and I stare across the water at the row of gabled brick houses opposite me. The homes are dark or shuttered and it is a very peaceful scene after the dust, noise and artificial lights of the clean-up activity in the public spaces. The narrow buildings rise up five storeys into the night sky, their roofs hidden by decorative bell-shaped gables. They are so narrow and close together they make me think of a line of football players forming a wall to defend a free kick, their shoulders hunched and their hands lowered to protect their private parts.

For a moment I feel a pang of envy. I enjoy living on *Jumping Jack Flash* and I relish the chance to move my home occasionally. But it must be nice, I think, to be surrounded by the solidity of a brick home – especially one like these. And it would be nice to share such a space with Nina – as a couple. Could that ever happen? This wishful thinking dominates my thoughts until I am crossing the wooden drawbridge with its love-token padlocks near our mooring. I pause to admire the view along the canal. The next thing I see makes me freeze.

The figure of a man is hunched near *Flora's* stern door. His coat collar is turned up and he has a woollen beanie on his head which is bent close to the door handle. Who the hell? A flurry of thoughts rushes through my head. Is it one of the protestors, still at large and determined to cause trouble? Or could this person be connected with the murders? My blood runs cold. Has the killer who left a tulip on the roof of our boat returned for some reason? And Nina is on board, asleep, alone and unprotected. I have one immediate thought. I must close the gap between the would-be intruder and myself as quickly as possible. I release the lead on Eddie's collar and begin to run towards the boat, my arms and legs pumping. My eyes stay fixed on the man's back. Eddie is sprinting ahead of me now. Thankfully he isn't barking and the man remains unaware that we are bearing down on him.

He's just ten metres away when I realise the most important question is whether I am about to tackle a killer armed with a knife, or even a gun? I am completely unarmed and more than slightly lacking in combat skills.

I am just about to raise my voice in challenge when Eddie registers the figure on the boat and starts barking and bouncing on all fours. I watch helplessly as the brave little dog leaps forward and jumps down onto the stern. But instead of a snarling, teeth-bared, all-out attack, he stands on his hind legs and repeatedly tries to jump up into the man's arms.

The figure straightens and turns his face towards me. He is grinning broadly. 'Hello, Jack. Thank Christ it's you! I've been calling through this bloody keyhole for ages.'

CHAPTER THIRTY-FOUR

'Will? What the hell are you doing here?' Eddie has now been scooped up by my oldest and least reliable friend and is eagerly trying to lick his face. I first met Will at boarding school, and he has been letting me down ever since. In fact, I would never have met Nina in the first place if he hadn't reneged on an agreement to help me with the first few days of ownership of a narrowboat after my divorce.

Will is a professional actor who enjoys middle-ranking success on theatre tours and the occasional television series. However, he enjoys spectacular success with the opposite sex who are mesmerised by his film star features, muscular body and little-boy-lost demeanour. He pulls off his beanie and shakes out his blond curls as Eddie continues to lick his face. 'Hey, little man. I'm pleased to see you too but enough with the face wash please!' He puts Eddie down onto the deck and advances to give me a hug. 'And it's great to see you too, matey.'

I am dazed with surprise. 'Will. It's almost four a.m. and we're in the middle of Amsterdam. What the hell are you doing here?'

He grins, showing his regular white teeth and trademark dimples. 'I always know how to make an entrance don't I? I remembered you saying you were coming over here for a couple of weeks with Nina. You sent me a picture of the boat with its details, remember? Then a gig fell through at short notice yesterday, so I thought I'd join you for a mini-break. Just a couple of days. I hopped onto Eurostar and here I am. You don't mind, do you?'

This is characteristic of Will. He lives for the moment and eagerly embraces any opportunity for entertainment which passes his way. It ought to be frustrating, but I have learned to live with it, and time spent in his company usually turns out to be fun.

'I couldn't see a bell or anything, so I was trying to rouse you to let me in. Where's Nina then?'

'She's asleep on-board and I've been out for a walk. There were some street riots earlier tonight and I wanted to see the damage for myself.'

'Well come on then, let us in. I'm dying for a sandwich and a beer.' He is soon settled with both in an armchair while Eddie stretches out at his feet. 'My taxi driver said something about it all kicking off tonight. What's that all about then?'

'Don't you ever read the papers?'

'Only if they've given me a good review,' he grins, taking a huge bite of bread, cheese and pickle.

'Keep your voice down. You'll wake Nina.' It takes me the best part of the next hour to tell Will about the eight Tulip Murders, the Semper Augustus, the plant-based poisons, the Rembrandt sketch and the map showing the capital letter G. Finally, as he finishes his third beer, I tell him about the discovery of the coffin and the four flowers in Oude Kerk and how the prominent political profile of the latest victim, Daniel Raap, has prompted the night's rioting.'

'And the killers actually left one of these tulips on the roof of your boat?' he asks.

'In a flower box actually, with a load of other less rare tulips.'

He sniffs. 'Well, they can't be that rare if someone's scattering a bunch of them in the font of a church.'

'Someone valued the first Semper Augustus at about a million euros,' I said. 'But you're probably right. The more that appear, the less valuable they will be.'

'And no-one has seen this type of tulip since …?'

'For about 400 years.'

'Bloody hell. Well, it all sounds a bit overdone to me, darling. Not just the flower but the deliberate posing of the bodies – and you say that's the same as a Rembrandt sketch of a dead girl?'

'A dead immigrant girl. It all seems designed to get maximum publicity and point to a liberal pro-immigration pro-green agenda that's targeting particular right-wing activists and snuffing them out. And it's pouring petrol on a fire with the national elections coming up fast. It's just mad.'

Will yawns, stretches and smiles. 'You should have gone to Venice. I hear they've got canals there too. Anyway, I suppose you might get another book out of it! Now then, how many bunks are there on this tub? I don't suppose you've got around to sharing a bed with Nina yet?'

My friend, of course, is privy to my feelings for Nina and fails to understand why we aren't yet a couple. I have considerable sympathy for this view.

I settle him onto the couch in the saloon with a few blankets, turn out the lamps and lock the stern door. Finally, I scribble a note for Nina so she isn't surprised to find another man sleeping on board in the morning. I slip quietly into her room and leave the note under her watch on the bedside table. I take a few seconds to admire the profile of her face as it rests on two hands clasped in a prayer-like gesture. The pose makes her look breathtakingly beautiful, but with a child-like innocence. She will be pleased to discover Will is on board tomorrow. They are firm friends. But our holiday-a-deux seems to be over and I go to bed with a slightly sad and wistful feeling.

CHAPTER THIRTY-FIVE

The following morning's summit meeting at the Amsterdam offices of the Ministry of Justice and Security is so well attended that there aren't enough seats at the table. Most heads of department and the Minister's top senior civil servants are all present and correct. A buffet table filled with croissants and coffee has already been hoovered clean and an unseen pecking order banishes deputies and others to the soft seating around the edge of the conference room. The three senior police officers have gathered together to claim the far end of the table which gives the unfortunate impression of a self-defensive huddle. The two men are in uniform and sit either side of Beatrix, who isn't. She is quietly hoping that the overcrowded room combined with the stress of recent events won't prompt one of the sudden rushes of heat that occasionally sweep through her body these days.

'Good morning, everyone,' barks the Minister as his tall frame bursts into the room at precisely eight o'clock. His handsome angular face has rings of tiredness under the eyes which are slightly bloodshot. He waits a fraction of time after everyone has stood to greet him before telling them all to sit. He unthinkingly repeats the gesture he is famous for, running a hand through his thick shock of hair, before opening a folder in front of him.

'I'm sure, like me, you have all had a busy night and you have much still to do. However, it is imperative that you all understand the gravity of the situation facing our country.'

Beatrix sighs inwardly. *'None of us need a pep-talk or a lecture right now,'* she thinks to herself. *'Just let us bloody well get on with it.'*

'I repeat what I said on this morning's television and radio broadcasts. The events of last night were disgraceful and we will come down very hard on the perpetrators.' He glances down at a slip of paper. 'Two hundred injuries, many serious, and eleven officers left needing medical treatment, four still in hospital. Several million euros worth of damage, never mind the negative images abroad. Fifty-five people in custody.'

The First Chief Commissioner of Police coughs. 'Sixty-five at the latest count Minister. And we will round up more after studying the CCTV and mobile-camera units' pictures.'

The Minister frowns at the interruption. 'This is not good enough, ladies and gentlemen.'

Beatrix concedes that she isn't the only woman in the room this time, but notes that she is still chronically outnumbered.

'Our streets are on fire, literally, and there is a national election in just a couple of weeks.' Aha, thinks Beatrix. Now we're getting to the nub of it. 'The failure to capture or stop these so-called Tulip Murderers is leading to widespread anarchy. The murder of Daniel Raap was the last straw. We knew where the final body would be found thanks to the intelligence passed on by the British. Why weren't the perpetrators apprehended Dr van der Laen?'

Beatrix wisely decides not to argue about the distinction between the Q and G theories and nods at a technical operator. A picture appears on the room's large flat screen television. It shows four dark-suited pall bearers carrying a flower-strewn coffin towards the main door of Oude Kerk. 'As you can see, they hid in plain sight and surprised us by delivering the body to the church in broad daylight. The hearse had been stolen a couple of hours earlier and its plates had been changed. But, of course, the theft wasn't red flagged because we didn't know it was to be used in this way. We are trying to get facial matches, but the hats and sunglasses are disguising most of their features. We previously envisaged the killings to be the work of at least three people and we have now revised this to four.'

She looks around the room. She has everyone's close attention. 'For the first time, the victim was not killed with a plant-based poison.' She nods again and the picture changes. 'Mr Raap was shot in the back of the head while he was out hunting deer on his private estate. His private chef heard two shots in quick succession, the first being from Raap's own rifle. What you see on the screen are the fragments of a wooden bullet tip that were dug out of his skull.'

'Wooden?' demands the Minister.

'Yes Minister. We can only surmise that this, once again, is some kind of grim and highly theatrical declaration of responsibility – possibly by an environmental terrorist cell. I am advised that it would have been particularly difficult to pull off. Wooden bullets are not unheard of, of course. But they are primarily designed as less lethal weapons, like rubber bullets, to be used for crowd control. Either that, or they are fired as salutes or blanks for armies to use for training. Our firearms experts are on the case, but their preliminary advice is that a special one-off gun may have been fashioned for this purpose and that the killer would have needed to get quite close to the victim to be sure of a head shot like this. This is consistent with the highly planned and even professional nature of all of the killings. Needless to say, death was instantaneous.'

'We do not plan to make this detail public knowledge at the moment,' chips in the city's Chief Commissioner of police.

'Quite right,' snaps the Minister. 'This information doesn't leave this room. My God! it's unbelievable. Plant poisons, missing tulips and now wooden bullets. What else have we got?'

'We have the car and the coffin,' continues Beatrix. 'But based on the previous killings, we do not expect to find any fingerprints or traces of DNA. And we have been checking laboratories and universities across the Netherlands and Europe via Interpol to look for any recent and relevant work on lethal plant-based toxins. Next please.'

The Rembrandt picture of Elsje appears on the screen. 'You may have read in the newspapers about this social media post of a Rembrandt sketch with the hashtag #TulipMurders. It is too early to say if it is actually connected with the murders. However, as you can see, it closely mimics the pose of seven of the victims and it may contain some kind of pro-immigration message. We know the victims believed the opposite and were violently anti-immigration. We are trying to establish where this originated from.'

'It seems incredible,' says the Minister. 'Eight murders in eight days and we are not one bit wiser as to who is behind this. The Prime Minister has asked me if we expect another killing tonight – or even today. Your views please, ladies and gentlemen.'

There is an uncomfortable silence. 'Frankly, it's impossible to say, Minister,' says Beatrix calmly. 'However, if you want someone to put their neck on the line...'

The Minister interrupts. 'All of our necks are on the line Dr van der Laen.'

Beatrix decides to ignore him. 'I'd say it is less likely rather than more likely. I suspect the completion of the letter G, which may point to the green movement in some way, may have finally achieved its ambition with the general unrest last night. The murder of Raap also seems to feel like a full-stop of a kind - in terms of his profile and politics. I may be wrong of course.'

'This is what is so disturbing,' says the Minister, prodding his paperwork with the point of an index finger for emphasis. 'The fringe parties, especially the right, are piling in – portraying themselves as the martyrs, and the left as the guilty party, and we in the centre as useless. We must do better. We must hunt these people down quickly.'

'If I may, Minister?' All heads swivel to look at the Director of the country's General Intelligence and Security Service. 'Our counter terrorism operations have been on the highest alert since these killings began and our undercover operatives have been told to report any and all suspicions.'

'And to what effect?' demands the Minister brusquely.

'There is no concrete evidence so far, but we have done some theoretical analysis.'

'Theoretical,' mutters Beatrix in disgust. The two senior policemen flanking her flinch slightly.

'Perhaps, I could brief the Minister in private for the moment. As I say, it is purely theoretical.' The chief spy is smoothness and charm personified in spite of alienating almost every person in the room with his suggestion.

Beatrix can't help herself. 'Typhus!' It is a curious habit of the Dutch to use medical terms as swear words and she is no exception. 'Well … that's just … just bollocks,' she says. 'This is supposed to be a combined inquiry. If you've got something to say, just say it. Spit it out man.'

Most of the men around the table have met the former Queen Beatrix in person and they still find it hard to reconcile her physical resemblance to Amsterdam's senior murder detective. They find it doubly hard when their former Monarch's lookalike tells them off. This time, however, it is the Minister who steps in. 'I'll hear what the AIVD Director has to say in private and I shall make a judgement on how widely it is shared Dr van der Laen. You'll have to be satisfied with that for now.'

Beatrix opens her mouth to protest but feels the weight of her immediate boss's restraining hand on her forearm.

'Now, I want to know what our preparations are for any repeat of last night's disturbances?' continues the Minister. 'The floor is yours First Chief Commissioner.'

CHAPTER THIRTY-SIX

The three of us sleep-in after our very late night and it is ten o'clock when I am roused by voices and the clink of plates and cutlery in the galley. Nina is on an armchair in a towelling dressing gown with her legs tucked under her while Will is dressed in boxer shorts and a T-shirt and poaching eggs at the stove.

'Morning,' I yawn. 'Any tea in the pot?'

'Here he is,' says Will in an offensively cheerful voice. 'The creature from the dark lagoon – or the dark canal anyway. Tea, toast and eggs coming up.'

'Isn't it nice to see Will?' enthuses Nina. 'It was such a surprise when I saw your note. I got up straight away – although it was still gone half-past-nine. Eddie needs a walk.'

'I'll take him,' says Will instantly. 'Just as soon as I've had something to eat and got dressed. I don't want to cramp your style. I was just telling Nina, Jack, it was an impromptu decision to join you for a couple of days. I hope you don't mind. It seems a bit crazy in the cold light of day.'

I take a mug of tea from him and yawn. 'It's not a problem. It's good to see you.'

This may have sounded slightly grudging because Nina quickly wades in. 'It's a lovely, lovely surprise, Will. We can have some proper holiday fun together at last. Jack's been a little distracted by this spate of murders over here.'

'Yeah, he was telling me all about them last night. Sounds like some really weird stuff's been going on. And this rare tulip was actually left on this boat – amazing!'

'Yes, and one of the murder victims was left hanging under that bridge back there.' Nina points to the wooden drawbridge. 'He was a Roman Catholic priest.'

There is a pause in the conversation, and we all hear the sound of far-off police sirens. 'It was a bit mad out there last night,' says Nina. 'Street riots connected to the latest murder. The victim was a well-known right-wing politician and a billionaire.'

'Yes, Jack told me.'

'I had a walk up to the Dam and back afterwards,' I tell Nina. 'It was quite a mess. They'll still be clearing up this morning. In fact, you might be better finding a park for Eddie's walk. There was a lot of glass on the streets last night.'

'Righto,' says Will, wiping up the last remaining egg yolk with his bread. 'I'll be off. See you here later this morning. I'll bring some coffee back.'

He is dressed and off the boat within ten minutes. Nina is quiet after we've taken it in turns to shower and dress. 'What's the matter?'

'I don't think you were very welcoming to Will.'

'What? I sat up with him for two hours and plied him with beer and sandwiches last night. We did our catching up then.'

She shakes her head and wrinkles her nose. 'Nope. You need to try harder.'

'Okay,' I sigh. 'I am pleased to see him, honest. But this was supposed to be a holiday for just the two of us. I'm sorry, but it's not working out how I thought. We need to go back to your wish-list of things to see and do. Time's running out fast.'

She laughs. 'It's alright, Jack. I should expect to go on holiday with you and find myself in the middle of a murder investigation and city-wide riots! It is what it is. But let's try to have a few nice remaining days with Will.'

'It's a deal,' I say. 'So, what shall we do for the next hour?'

'Let's see if there's anything special happening,' she says, opening her laptop. I shuffle across alongside her to look at the screen.

I notice she has changed the image on her screensaver to a head and shoulders of Rembrandt. 'He's really got to you hasn't he.'

'Oh, Jack. He was a genius. Jodi was so interesting about him. Did you know he was a miser? His apprentices would paint coins on the floor and laugh when he tried to pick them up? Jodi was so eloquent about him. He was a true pioneer. He didn't just paint people as they looked. He painted who they were. And it was something completely new in art at the time. She said that's why his self-portraits are so amazing. They're honest attempts to get to grips with who he really was.'

I love her enthusiasm. 'I like the idea of him sketching Elsje. Even though he was at the end of his life – it somehow captures his humanity.'

'Yes, exactly.' Her hands hover over the keypad. 'I wonder…'

'What?'

'I was just wondering if there was any other connection between Rembrandt and what's been going on? Did he ever paint the Semper Augustus for example? We should have asked Jodi.'

'Google it,' I suggest and watch as she types Rembrandt and Tulp. An image of The Anatomy Lesson pops up before she realises she has mis-spelt Tulip. 'Damn it,' she says, and types in the search box for a second time. Rembrandt and Tulip.

This time a long list of advertisements for tulips being sold as *The Rembrandt Collection* comes up. It seems that his name can be attached to anything in the hope of a quick euro. Nina scrolls down to a section called *'People Ask.'* One of the first questions repeats Nina's original thought and reads: *'Did Rembrandt paint tulips?'*

She opens up the answer and reads it aloud. It seems to have been drafted by some kind of American algorithm. *'The bi-colour tulips had a base color of red, purple, pink and even brown. These colorful tulips became very popular and caused the first recorded speculative bubble known as tulipmania. The artist Rembrandt did not produce flower paintings.'*

'So, the answer is no. Nice try though,' I say. 'And pretty surprising really, considering their popularity at the time that he was painting.'

'He didn't go out of his way to be popular,' says Nina. 'He was his own man.'

'Just go back a minute,' I tell her. 'Type in Rembrandt and Tulp again, T-U-L-P, just like you did the first time.'

She looks puzzled but does as I ask. 'There look. D'you remember the painting's full name? *The Anatomy Lesson of Dr. Nicolaes Tulp*. We wondered if the doctor in the picture was related to Cornelius Tulp – our not-so-friendly tour guide.'

'That's right,' says Nina. 'So, Rembrandt never painted a tulip, but he did paint a Tulp!'

'Isn't that a bit weird?' I ask. 'That the two words should be so similar. There's just one letter difference.'

We examine the image of the painting in front of us. 'We'd never have seen it if it hadn't come over from The Hague on loan,' muses Nina.

Although there are eight men in the painting, all of the attention and lighting is focused on the corpse and the man carrying out the public autopsy, Dr. Nicolaes Tulp. Once again, I see the remarkable resemblance between the painting of the surgeon's face with its curled moustache, pointed beard and glittering, intelligent eyes, with the man who took us out on his boat.

'Can you find out a bit more about Nicolaes Tulp?' I ask. She enters his full name and finds Wikipedia to be the most-read entry. The opening section tell us he was born Claes Pieterszoon, the son of a prosperous linen merchant but changed his name to Tulp after becoming a doctor.

'I wonder why he did that?' I ask.

'Let's see what else there is,' says Nina, scrolling down the other entries.

Over the next half-hour we discover that his original birth name was a very common one in the Dutch provinces – much too common for the highly ambitious and upwardly mobile doctor. Having qualified as a *doctor mediciae* in 1617 he became well known for his warm bedside manner and passion for anatomical dissection. By the 1620s, the doctor had entered into city politics, and like all good politicians he looked for a way of becoming noticed more widely. And so, in 1621, he changed his name to Tulp – *"in order to associate himself with the fashionable and expensive Tulip flowers.*

'The crafty bugger,' I exclaim.

'It sounds like a very modern type of politics,' says Nina. 'It would be like a politician today changing their name to *Apple*!'

I laugh and we read on. Apparently, it wasn't enough to just change his name to Tulp. He hung a painting of a tulip above his door to announce his medical practice and chose a tulip as the main feature of his newly commissioned coat of arms and insignia. There are even records showing that a tulip was emblazoned on the side of the full-sized private coach which ferried him around the city to his wealthy clients.

'Amazing!' I say, 'the guy was obsessed by tulips. Tulp is the Dutch word for tulip and he used them for all of his branding – before branding even existed as a concept!'

'Tulips and self-promotion,' observes Nina. 'Look, he commissioned eight full-scale portraits of himself which eventually included The Anatomy Lesson by Rembrandt. It says here that Tulp would have paid the most to Rembrandt to secure the starring role.'

'Not exactly a shrinking violet then, is he?'

'Not a violet, no Jack. A tulip!' I groan and she reads on.

'He was a pretty impressive doctor for his time. He was the first person to describe migraine, discovered the effects of smoking tobacco on the lungs and he published some very successful medical books.'

'But he was a politician too?'

'Yes.' She reads on. 'He became Mayor of Amsterdam in 1654 and held the position for four terms. His son became a doctor and his daughter married Jan Six. He must be part of the famous Six family.' I look blank. 'There's a building on the Amstel which houses the Six Collection. It's one of the most famous private collections of old masters in the world.'

'So it's fair to say the Tulp family were loaded and probably continued to be for future generations?'

'You saw Cornelius Tulp's house on the Golden Bend. He pointed it out to us. It was one of those double-width mansions. If he's a descendant of Nicolaes Tulp, which seems more than likely to me, then, yes. I think you can fairly assume he was born with a golden spoon in his mouth to go with the house on the Golden Bend!'

'And he's continuing the family tradition of politics – with his Born-Again party.'

'I wonder what his ancestor's politics were?'

Nina bends to her screen again. 'There's a bit here from Simon Schama, the historian. It's quite funny really. Tulp strongly supported the Calvanist Church against the Roman Catholics and what was referred to as *'papist idolatory'*. He tried to crack down on the feast of St Nicholas and ban the sale of dolls, cookies and candles. But there was an insurrection of eleven-year-olds – and their parents – and the magistrates were forced to back down. Serves the old killjoy right!'

A thought occurs to me. 'I wonder if Jodi knows much more about him?'

'Well, why don't we ask her? She wanted to meet up with us for a drink. And it could be fun now Will is here too.'

'Good idea. Let's do some shopping at a deli after Will gets back with Eddie. We can have lunch on the roof. It's going to be a lovely day.'

'Good plan.' She brushes my cheek with her lips and bustles off, humming happily. It doesn't seem as though our holiday has been totally ruined…yet. And, in reality, Nina seems as interested in the mystery of the tulip murders as I am.

However, something is niggling at the back of my brain and, as I sit in the sun jotting down some notes of what has happened during our holiday, it comes back to me. I remember the other leading figure of Amsterdam in the 17th century who I came across when I was researching my short article – Adriaan Pauw. Pauw had been the fabulously wealthy gentleman botanist who planted out the Semper Augustus at his rural retreat, the castle in Heemstede. I remember that he used a mirror-sided gazebo to multiply the effect.

It sounds as if he was as obsessive as Cornelius Tulp when it came to the tulip flower – and he certainly had the funds to invest in his hobby. I wonder if their paths ever crossed. Is it possible Tulp could have been Pauw's physician? And could the distinguished man of science have helped Pauw crack the flower's secret and keep the rarest and most expensive tulip in history going for all of this time? It's an intriguing theory which I jot down. I make a mental note to discuss it with the Rembrandt historian, Jodi Luiken, when we see her.

CHAPTER THIRTY-SEVEN

Nina returns with a big grin on her face and confirmation that Jodi would love to escape from her little office for an extended lunch break on our houseboat. But the clock is ticking and there is still no sign of Will, so we leave him a note promising to be back by 11.30 a.m. and head off with a couple of small backpacks for provisions.

A nearby deli supplies us with delicious looking mixed salads, some fresh crusty bread and a selection of cold meats and cheeses. I also help myself to a few decent bottles of red and white wine and some cold beers. Finally, Nina swings into a cake shop on our way back and buys some very pretty cakes topped with glazed fruit. It's quite a warm sunny day and we are both full of the holiday spirit.

After returning to the boat, I fetch a couple more chairs from below and place them on the little deck that has been fixed to Flora's roof. There's a slight breeze so I peg a crisp white cloth to the table and fetch plates and cutlery while Nina unpacks the salads and prepares sharing platters of the meat and cheese. Then we both gather in the stern to wait for Will and our other lunch guest.

However, before either of them appears, a familiar classic

Porsche swings into a parking space near the mooring. 'The name's Bhalla, Gupta Bhalla!' says Nina naughtily.

The large frame of our man from the embassy clambers out of the low-slung sports car with a little less athleticism than 007 and Archi smooths down his grey two-piece suit. He gives us a wave and a smile and ambles towards the gangplank.

'Hello there,' he calls out. 'Lovely morning! Permission to come on board?'

'Permission granted,' calls Nina and he joins us in the stern where he politely shakes hands with me and ducks down to give Nina a peck on both cheeks.

'What brings you, Archi?' I ask.

'Ah yes, well, I was told about your part in the discovery of Daniel Raap's body at Oude Kerk. Better late than never. Hey ho, the Dutch authorities have got a lot on their plate, haven't they? The Ambassador has already been asked to write a report for the Foreign Secretary about the riots last night and the current state of politics in the Netherlands – although I didn't tell you that, of course. Chatham House rules again, heh?'

'That's hardly surprising Archi,' I say.

'We didn't play much of a part,' says Nina. 'We just happened to be wandering around the church and came across four of the famous tulips in the font. Well, Jack did. After that, the coffin containing Raap's body was found in a little side chapel.'

'Yes, yes. I know that. But you also spotted the Rembrandt sketch, didn't you? The police seem very interested in that. GCHQ has been trying to help them find the source of the Elsje posts. *And you turned out to be right about the location of the last victim.* Although it seems the killers mapped out a capital G rather than a Q, didn't they? Just like you told me. And that's driving everyone crazy with speculation that some kind of gang of green fanatics is responsible. It would all tie in with the tulips and the plant poisons, wouldn't it?'

'Just as I told you,' I remind him waspishly. I haven't quite forgiven him for his reluctance to pass my information on a second time. But Archi's eyes are glittering with excitement. I suppose all this must be more compelling than dealing with lost passports or drunken British stag parties. 'Er, is there anything you want from us Archi?' I ask.

'What? No, no. I don't think so. I just thought I'd call in and check you were both okay after all the recent hoo-ha. Make sure you were alright after the riots. That sort of thing you know?'

It sounds a bit lame to me. I suspect Archi fancied a morning out of the office on a nice spring day and another encounter with the lovely Nina. The lady in question is smiling broadly. 'I know,' she says. 'Why don't you join our little lunch party? A friend of ours has come over from England for a couple of days and Jodi Luiken from the Rembrandthuis is joining us too. We thought we'd eat on the roof. Nothing fancy, just some salad stuff and wine. We've got plenty of it, though.'

Archi looks like the fat little kid in class who is surprised to be picked for a playground kickabout. He beams with joy. 'Oh my gosh. That is terribly kind of you Nina! I would love to join you if that is okay.' He looks at his thin gold wristwatch. 'I don't need to be back at the office until two o'clock so, yes please, that would be wonderful.'

I fetch a fifth chair. The deck is getting a bit crowded, but we will just about squeeze around the little square metal table that is bolted to the roof. The three of us are sitting there with glasses of wine and exchanging greetings with an occasional passing boat when Will reappears with Eddie. He has a clinking plastic bag which he announces is a contribution to the boat's supplies of grog and he is quickly settled alongside Archi with a glass of wine. 'Sorry, forgot the coffee but it's a bit late for it now anyway,' he grins. 'Cheers all.'

Archi is fascinated and slightly starstruck to discover that Will is an actor and bubbles with enthusiastic questions about how he got into the profession and what he has been playing in recently. Will has always been Will's favourite topic of conversation and he happily chats away about a recent run of plays and a film audition he has just been invited to prepare for.

'Oh, my goodness,' says Archi. 'I often think I would have given acting a go if I hadn't been encouraged by my parents to join the Foreign Office.'

Will examines Archi's plump figure and slightly froglike face behind the thick glasses. The contrast with his own matinee-idol looks and well-proportioned frame couldn't be greater. 'Uh, yeah, well, there are lots of character actors out there. It's tough to make a living though. I'd stay where you are if you want my advice.'

Archi looks slightly crestfallen but immediately cheers up as another beautiful woman greets us from the bank and steps across to join us. I make all the introductions and quietly exchange a smile with Nina. Jodi Luiken is looking stunning. A wrap-around dress is tied at the waist. It accentuates her figure and her red wavy hair shimmers in the sun. She kisses each of us on the cheek and the two boys look slightly stunned.

'So, an actor, a spy and a journalist!' she laughs, showing her pearl-white teeth. 'What an interesting lunch this will be. Thanks, Jack,' she adds, taking a glass of chilled white wine from me. 'Good health.'

'Oh, no,' protests Archi. 'I'm not a spy...'

'And you're an expert in Rembrandt?' asks Will, leaning forward and arranging his handsome features into a look of ferocious interest.

Jodi waves an elegant hand which I notice is ringless. 'My PhD was in 17th century Dutch art. But I have tended to specialise in Rembrandt due to my current job. It isn't a hardship,' she laughs. 'I'm asked to speak at quite a few conferences – which means a lot of foreign travel. I like that. I like new experiences.'

'Me too,' says Will in a voice laden with hidden meaning.

'Yes. And me. And I like travelling too,' adds Archi in a rush.

I see Nina suppress a giggle before she asks me to give her a hand with fetching the food from the galley. 'Oh, my goodness,' she laughs when we are standing in front of the fridge. 'Poor Jodi. Will and Archi are positively salivating, and I don't think it's because they are hungry!'

'I think she can handle herself,' I say. 'But yes, she does look like she's stepped out of a Vermeer painting – or a copy of Vogue.'

'Oi, you,' she digs me in the ribs. 'Eyes front please.'

She laughs as I drop on one knee to the deck and begin singing *'I only have eyes for you...'*

'Get up, you idiot, and take these plates upstairs.'

Will and Archi amuse us with their competitive attempts to tell the best anecdotes, but my oldest friend is an accomplished raconteur and quickly elbows his way onto centre stage. He usually entertains Nina and me with stories of romantic scrapes and jealous husbands, but he is wise enough to avoid such topics with Jodi present. Nevertheless, he soon has us crying with laughter at accounts of the disasters which a hapless stage manager wreaked on his latest play before the run was cancelled at short notice in Leeds. 'And that freed me up to jump on Eurostar and join Jack and Nina for a short holiday,' he says with a grin.

'Lovely,' says Jodi.

'How lucky for you,' says Archi, although he doesn't sound as though he means it.

Nina steps in to cover the awkwardness. 'Have some more food guys. Jodi, Jack had some questions for you about Dr Nicolaes Tulp. Would you mind or don't you want to talk work?'

Jodi sparkles with pleasure. 'No of course, it's fine. You mean the famous Dr Tulp in *The Anatomy Lesson*, yes?'

'It's a Rembrandt masterpiece,' I explain to Will and Archi.

'We were reading about him,' explains Nina. 'And we were interested that he actually changed his name to Tulp because he had a thing about tulips.'

'Yes, sure. He was from a modest background but very, very ambitious. This was at a time when the Dutch Republic was moving away from the church and the monarchy. Our society was run by wealthy private citizens – and Tulp was an up-and-coming man of science at the time.'

'But his real name was Pieterszoons,' I say.

'Yes. And that was a common name. Much too common for Tulp. There were Claes Pieterszoons digging ditches and making bread all over the United Provinces. That would never do. I suspect he was a very vain man. Tulips were all the fashion at the time. They adorned all the homes of his wealthy clients and so he changed his name. He rebranded himself and chose a flower that was thought to be dignified, exotic and expensive. He wanted those values to be associated with himself. Then the Rembrandt painting was a sensational success. It established his reputation as the best physician in Amsterdam and a public figure of real significance. It was a triumphant exercise in self-promotion. This type of man would be a successful politician in any age.'

'Or a famous actor?' asks Will in mock innocence. We all burst into laughter, even Archi.

'Have you seen the picture, Will?' asks Jodi. 'It's on loan in Amsterdam at the moment.'

'We've seen it,' I chip in. 'Nina and me, I mean.'

'Perhaps you would show it to me?' says Will, topping up Jodi's glass and then Archi's as something of an afterthought.

'I would be glad to,' says Jodi immediately. Poor Archi looks crestfallen. 'But I warn you, I could talk about it for hours!' Will looks as though he will be more than happy to make this sacrifice.

'Can I ask you something else, Jodi?' I say. 'It relates to the Semper Augustus. That's the flower everyone thought had vanished in the 1600s,' I explain to Will.

'The one that's been turning up next to the bodies,' adds Nina.

'It occurred to me this morning. We know that there was a really wealthy merchant and politician called Adriaan Pauw who collected them at the time. Almost uniquely. Is there any chance that Pauw and Tulp's paths would have crossed?'

Jodi cocks her head on one side to think. 'Hmm... good question. I can't remember ever seeing anything to suggest such a thing. But it would be likely, wouldn't it? If they were both alive in Amsterdam at the same time. Pauw was one of the wealthiest and most powerful men in the city. He was Grand Pensionary I think, and Tulp was supposed to be the city's finest doctor. I need to check their dates. Wait a moment.'

She pulls out her mobile phone. 'Let's see. Nicolaes Tulp. Born 1593, Died 1674. Now then, Adriaan Pauw. He was born in 1585 and died in 1653. So, their lives certainly overlapped. What are you thinking, Jack?'

'It may be nothing. It sounds a bit mad.'

'Go on,' she urges.

'Well, I was just wondering if somehow it might explain how the Semper Augustus survived. Could the greatest ever collector of this tulip, with his unlimited funds, have commissioned his tulip-obsessed doctor and man of science to find a way of keeping it going for all this time? And if he did, could their descendants still be cultivating them? And could that explain their reappearance in some way?'

'And could there be another connection?' says Nina slowly. 'Rembrant painted Tulp – and made him famous. And Rembrandt also sketched Elsje, the picture of the dead girl whose pose exactly mirrors that of the Tulip Murder victims.'

Jodi rests her elbows on the table and looks at us both thoughtfully. 'I don't know about any surviving relatives of Adriaan Pauw,' she says. 'But there is a very famous Tulp who is alive and well in Amsterdam. He is very wealthy and a politician, the founder of the Born-Again party. He's called Cornelius, Cornelius Tulp.'

'Yes. We've actually met him and seen his house on Herengracht – from the outside,' says Nina excitedly. She gives a quick account of our encounter in the Waldorf Astoria and our subsequent boat trip and lunch.

'It's an intriguing theory,' says Jodi. 'If you like, I'll speak to a city archivist I know this afternoon. She'll know if Pauw and Tulp were connected in any way. But I'm not sure where all this really takes you?'

Archi has been following the conversation with a furrowed brow of concentration. 'Nor me to be honest. Are you suggesting the tulips may have come from surviving collections in the possession of Pauw or Tulp's descendants? Or that someone else has got hold of them?'

'It's just a flight of fancy,' I shrug.

'Jack loves cryptic crosswords and conspiracies,' says Nina.

'Well, I'd still really like to see that painting,' says Will shamelessly.

'And I need to get back to work,' adds Archi with an air of sad finality.

The lunch party breaks up in a flurry of handshakes and kisses. Archi presses his business card into the hands of Jodi and Will, and then takes me to one side. 'Look, Jack, there's been a slightly strange enquiry about you to the embassy, through an unofficial backchannel. I think you might be getting a visitor this afternoon. An official visitor if you know what I mean?'

'Not really Archi. No, I don't.'

'I can't tell you anymore. Just that I can vouch for them being who they say they are.'

'Archi. Stop being so bloody mysterious. What are you on about?'

He grips my arm. 'Just be co-operative. There's a good chap. Allies across the water and all that.'

Meanwhile, Will has managed to stay with Jodi and is talking quietly in her ear on dry land. She waits by the gangplank while he comes back to us. 'Er, Jodi's got to go back to the office for half an hour, but then she's offered to take me over to the Rijksmuseum.'

'That's nice of her,' deadpans Nina, while I roll my eyes at him.

'Yes, well. See you when I see you. My cultural education awaits.' He winks, grins and runs back to Jodi who gives us a wave and they stroll away together, talking and laughing as they go.

CHAPTER THIRTY-EIGHT

Nina and I are left to tidy away the remains of lunch and wash up. I tell her about Archi's strange parting message. 'Oh, what a silly ass,' she complains. 'Why didn't he just say what it was all about? Does this mean we have to wait around on the boat all afternoon?'

'Well, I don't see why we both need to. If you want to go for a wander, that's fine by me.'

Nina pops some of Archi's chewing-gum in her mouth. 'Hmm, I think I might. I'd like to find something tasteful to take back for Anna.'

'Well, Aunty Nina, I'd advise you to avoid the cannabis-flavoured gum. It really isn't a good look. I'm surprised that a well-brought up home counties girl like you has become so addicted.'

'I've told you, it's not addictive. It's just mildly flavoured, and I quite like it.'

I just shake my head sadly while she giggles naughtily and begins gathering her stuff together for an afternoon shopping expedition. Half an hour later, Eddie and I are both dozing in the saloon when there is a knock at the stern door. It opens before I have a chance to say anything, and a tall man bends to look in at me. It takes a moment for his eyes to adjust to the darkness of the boat's interior and for me to quiet Eddie's barking.

'Mr Johnson? Jack Johnson? May I come in and have a word? I think you may be expecting me?'

'If you mean Archi Gupta Bhalla warned me, then not really. He just said someone might pop in – but he didn't say who.'

The man moves closer towards me with an outstretched hand and a smile that doesn't quite reach a pair of shrewd and calculating eyes. 'I apologise. That was unnecessarily cloak and dagger.' The man is clearly Dutch but speaks excellent English. He is wearing a loose blue linen jacket with an open-necked pink shirt, chinos and loafers. Slightly incongruously, a flat cap completes his wardrobe, but when he takes it off, I can see his buzzcut hair is silvered with age. He looks to be in his mid-fifties and with a fit and hard physique. However, I confess to an Englishman's prejudice against his small leather man-bag.

'I am Colonel Joost Hartgers.' Having shaken my hand, he produces an identity card from an inside jacket pocket and offers it to me. The photograph matches, but it doesn't tell me much more. He registers my look of bafflement. 'I apologise. I am from the MIVD, our country's Military Intelligence and Security Service. I am a spook as I believe they call us in England.'

'Okay,' I say warily. 'You'd better take a seat. Tea? Coffee?'

'No thank you, I have some water.' He sits and I do the same with the table in between us. His cap, bag and a half-full plastic bottle of water are on it. 'Have you seen this today?' He pulls his phone out of the bag and shows me the screen. It displays a screengrab of the sketch of Elsje hanging dead on the post with the small axe suspended by her head. There is some new writing in Dutch on the Facebook post alongside #TulipMurders.

'It's Dutch. It translates as: *"Finally, Justice for Elsje,"* he tells me. 'There have already been a lot of enquiries from journalists about it. I believe it was you who noticed this post when it was first shared?'

'It was my friend Nina who noticed it. I'm on holiday with her. She's gone shopping.'

Hartgers nods. 'Very perceptive of her. What do you think the latest message means?'

'I haven't a clue,' I laugh. 'Maybe the word *"finally"* is indicating that the killings are over? The point has been made?'

The Colonel narrows his eyes and deep wrinkles fan out to either side. 'And what do you think the *"point"*, as you call it, is?'

I shake my head. 'I'm sorry, you're the man from the intelligence services, aren't you? How should I know? Elsje was an economic migrant. The Tulip Murder victims all seem to have been violently anti-immigration or anti-Islamic. Although, I'm not sure how that squares with all this other stuff about the Greens seeming to claim responsibility. The capital G, the tulips and the plant-based poisons.'

'You're right. It doesn't quite all hang together, does it?' He pauses but I allow him to end his own silence. 'Nevertheless, it seems to be having an effect. The question is whether it is the required effect or not. The latest polls show the far-right parties climbing sharply in popularity. They are attracting a lot of sympathy and there is considerable anger on their behalf. The far left – especially the Greens – are falling away sharply and the central coalition is also losing support in the run up to the election. It is being blamed for the failure to catch the killers. We could be dealing with a right-wing led coalition and even a right-wing majority government and prime minister if these trends continue.'

I lean forward. 'But that's what is so strange isn't it?' I ask. 'If the Greens or the far left are behind these murders – they're at risk of achieving precisely what they wouldn't want, aren't they?'

'Indeed, they are Mr Johnson.' Hartgers reaches into his man-bag again and extracts a folded piece of paper which he smooths out on the table in front of us and swivels to face me. 'Perhaps the extremists or fanatics responsible for these killings don't care what happens in the ballot box. Perhaps they just want the blood of their enemies? Or perhaps you are right and something else is going on here. The document in front of you is our version of your Official Secrets Act. I would like to discuss some intelligence with you and get your response to it. But first, you must agree not to share it any further. And you must do so in writing. Are you willing to do that, Mr Johnson?'

'Not even with Nina?'

'Not with her, nor with any other friend. Particularly the English journalist, Su Mortimer.' He pushes a pen towards me. 'So far, our background checks suggest you can be trusted. Is that so?'

'I really don't see how I can help you.'

'Perhaps you can't. However, there are strange forces at work and the stakes are very high. Eight people have been murdered, there is rioting across the country and turmoil in the election. We can't afford to ignore any possible avenue of investigation. Please sign the form, Mr Johnson.'

I do as he asks after a moment's thought. This isn't my war, and I don't think I have anything to lose by co-operating. He folds it away again and is no longer smiling with encouragement. 'Thank you. You can now be fined or even imprisoned if you reveal my confidential information,' he says.

'Welcome to the Netherlands,' I mutter.

'As you know, there have been an enormous number of social media posts surrounding these so-called Tulip Murders and we have been monitoring the activity closely. Much of it is clearly designed to raise the stakes and whip up strong feelings. Last night's riots might not have happened without such naked incitement.'

'You can't be surprised by that,' I say. 'It's the way of the world now, isn't it? It would be nice for Twitter to be used for civilised debate. But it's usually a poisonous 280 character rant in my experience.'

He pauses, as though weighing up whether to press ahead with his next words. 'Our experts, and our allies' experts, believe some of this social media is coming from Russia.'

'Allies like GCHQ in the UK?' I ask.

He's clearly surprised I know about the British involvement and raises an eyebrow before continuing. 'They certainly believe the Elsje image may have originated in Russia. And if it did, it may be further proof of their gangster-president trying to interfere in the elections of a Western democracy. We know all about

Russian dezinformatsia and their Internet Research Agency or IRA. It's a troll factory staffed by hundreds of young Russians in St Petersburg who carry out social media campaigns under false identities. We believe they are behind the Elsje posts and much else. It is very clever. It is deniable by the Russian government. It works by relying on the target countries' local and national media to magnify the impact of their online meddling. To act like a megaphone. This has been seen in the United States and the United Kingdom and now we believe we are seeing it here, in the Netherlands.'

'Why are you telling me this?' I ask, genuinely puzzled. It's all very fascinating but I can't see how I can help the man from the MIVD. He just looks at me with his head tilted to one side, like a teacher challenging a slow pupil to come up with the answer for himself. 'Unless ... unless you're saying that if the Russians are responsible for the Elsje posts, and they're stirring things up here, then maybe they're also responsible for the murders?'

'I'm not saying anything,' says Hartgers smoothly. 'You are. But we are talking about a country that sends GRU death squads across the world to hunt down and assassinate Chechens.'

'And it's also a country which sends hitmen to an English cathedral city where it spreads a bit of Novichok around to try to kill a double agent and his daughter.'

'Salisbury. Yes indeed.'

'And the same laboratories which produced the Novichok might also be used to provide an impressive range of plant-based poisons or even reinvent the Semper Augustus.'

'It's possible Mr Johnson. We can say no more than that.'

I shake my head. 'I think you're reaching. Unless you know something I don't? I know they've got form but so far, all you've got is a teenage troll causing mischief from his bedroom in St Petersburg. What you're suggesting is incredible.'

'There is more. We've got the laptop belonging to the murdered footballer Munt. He was lured to his death via an online dating app. It was an old-fashioned honeytrap.'

'Let me guess. You've traced that back to Russia too?'

He nods. 'Incredible means unbelievable. And without any proof, it remains unbelievable. It is our job to find this proof. So, why am I here? I am here for two reasons. Firstly, to ask if there is anything, anything at all which you have come across which might help us to pursue this Russian line of inquiry?'

I rack my brains, but nothing comes to mind. 'No. I'm sorry. I had a hunch about the location of the victims meaning something – mainly because they were joined by straight lines, horizontal and vertical, and were evenly spaced apart. And Nina noticed the Elsje post because of the dead girl's position on the gibbet, and because she had seen it in a Rembrandt art book recently. But that's it.'

'And what about the tulip found on your boat, Mr Johnson?'

'What? I don't know. A coincidence?'

'Really?' Hartgers has stiffened, his body language is much less friendly now. 'In my line of work, we learn to be suspicious of coincidences. Because the other reason I am here is to rule you in or out of what has been happening. Perhaps you have been involved and perhaps the tulip on your boat was a ruse to suggest your innocence when, perhaps, it does precisely the opposite? The murders began on the day you arrived in the city.'

I laugh in his face. 'What? You're seriously suggesting we're mixed up in all of this? You've checked me out, remember? I'm an English journalist on holiday with a friend. That's it.'

'And then you just happen to be the first to come across four tulips in the font at Oude Kerk?'

'I was there because it looked like being the location of the eighth victim,' I protest.

'And surprise, surprise, it was.'

I shake my head. He has remained very calm and collected but I am becoming really angry now. 'Christ, you people must be really desperate if you're trying to put me and Nina in the frame for all of this. I think you should piss off.'

He stares at me coldly. I refuse to blink. 'Your passport please Mr Johnson.'

'What?'

'Give me your passport, please.'

'Why?'

'I shall be holding onto it for a few days.'

'Go stuff yourself.'

He rests two clenched fists on the table in front of him. 'I have a couple of well-trained colleagues just outside. I can ask them to take it off you forcibly or you can give it to me. What shall it be?'

'I want to call the British embassy.'

'They are already fully in the loop and anxious to co-operate with us in any way possible. The passport. Now.' His eyes are unflinching.

I reach into my back pocket and throw the passport on the table. 'Fuck you.'

'Thank you,' he says, putting a card with his name and phone number next to it. 'As I said earlier, perhaps you can be trusted. Perhaps not. Don't try to leave the country and don't talk to anyone about this. Especially the press. You are now officially a person of interest to us and if you have to kick your heels in a prison cell while we get to the bottom of what's happened, then believe me, you will. You will find we are a little less patient and understanding than our colleagues in the police force. We have to be if, or when, our national security is at stake.'

The man's calmness is seriously intimidating. He puts my passport in his bag, replaces his cap and leaves the boat without shaking my hand or saying goodbye.

I am stunned. Twenty minutes ago, I was a harmless holidaymaker coming to the end of a fortnight's break in Amsterdam. Now, I am someone of interest to the Dutch military security services and my passport has been confiscated. How the hell did that happen?

CHAPTER THIRTY-NINE

Official Secrets Act or not, I usher Nina onto *Flora's* roof deck with two large gin and tonics as soon as she returns and tell her all about my scary visitor. 'He's actually taken your passport?' she says. 'That's outrageous!'

'I know. He said the British Embassy was already fully in the loop. But I think I'd better tell Archi what's happened and ask them to intervene, or protest, or do something.'

'Well. If there is a Russian connection, the governments will be co-operating like mad, won't they?' Her big, dark, beautiful eyes open wide with a sudden thought. 'Hey! You don't think he planted some kind of listening bug on the boat, do you? Is that why you brought me up here to tell me all about it?'

I hadn't considered the possibility, but now I'm forced to. 'No, I'm sure he didn't have the chance to do that. He was in my sight the whole time.'

'Did he leave anything behind?'

'Wait there!' I say and dash down into the boat before returning with the Colonel's largely empty water bottle. We both take turns to inspect it closely and Nina even unscrews the plastic cap and looks inside. I empty the last few drops into the canal.

'Look at us!' I say, laughing. 'This is bloody ridiculous.'

Nina looks suspiciously around our mooring. 'Well, I wouldn't be surprised if they were keeping you under observation.'

I shake my head in disbelief but can't help myself from looking around too. Everyday life seems to be going on as normal. 'I think they're just desperate. Well anyway, Eddie needs a proper walk. Are you too tired to join us after your shopping?'

'Of course not. I'm much younger than you, remember?'

We stroll across the Amstel and then go west and south until we find ourselves on the Herengracht and the fabulously grand Golden Bend with its double-width mansions.

'What's happening over there?' asks Nina. We pause and watch as a small crowd of young people in identical red t-shirts give a cheer as an impressive front door swings open and a man comes out onto the top step of a double staircase.

'It's Tulp!' Sure enough, we both recognise his figure and the house he pointed out to us during our boat trip.

We continue to look across the water after finding a metal table and chairs alongside a small van that is kitted out as a portable bar. Tulp seems to be making a speech of some kind from his doorstep and there is an occasional round-of-applause or a cheer as he does so.

'They must be his Born-Again party workers,' I say. 'He's probably getting them worked-up before they go out door-knocking and handing out leaflets.'

'They're quite young, aren't they?' says Nina.

'Yes. They look like university students. So much for this city's hippie culture, eh? Whatever happened to students marching to ban the bomb and fighting for civil rights? Are they really campaigning *against* immigration now?'

'Give the man your order, grandad.' I order a couple of beers from the waiter and we sip them as Tulp gets one last rousing cheer and the party-workers board two buses which head off in different directions. I notice that Tulp doesn't join them, and the wide front door swings shut behind him.

'Never mind the Russians,' I say after taking a big gulp of my drink. 'It's people like Tulp they should be worrying about. I still say the police should be trying to follow the trail of the Semper Augustus and asking that guy over there if he had an ancestor who was obsessed with tulips.'

Nina laughs. 'So, you know better than the combined intelligence of the Dutch police and security services do you, Jack? Did you tell your visitor about your theory? How Nicolaes Tulp and Adriaan Pauw might have met and cracked the tulip's secret?'

'No,' I admit. 'It never crossed my mind. I was too angry to think straight at the time.'

'And was that also because you think it would have sounded pretty weak?'

'A bit,' I concede grudgingly. 'I'm not sure where it would have led them anyway. He just wanted to know if we'd seen anything to support their own theory about the Russians being involved.'

'Well, you have to admit, after Salisbury anything is possible.'

'Yes. Yes, I know. It's just that all they have to go on is some internet troll making mischief.'

'But the honeytrap is a bit more damning,' she says thoughtfully. 'It sounds like someone tricked the footballer into a date which turned into an ambush.'

'That's true,' I concede. 'And maybe he wasn't telling me the whole story.'

'Did Jodi get back to you? She was going to find out if Tulp was Pauw's doctor.'

'No. I haven't heard from her. She's no doubt busy entertaining our mutual friend.'

Nina giggles and then, to my disgust, takes her gum out of her mouth, wraps it in some paper and puts it in the ashtray before unwrapping a fresh one. I shake my head sadly. 'That really is beneath you, you know. I bet chewing gum wasn't allowed at your posh boarding school.'

But she ignores me, rests her masticating chin on her cupped palms and stares at Tulp's home. The historic mansions on this spectacular stretch of canal are covered with classical pediments, columns and pilasters and decorated with vases, busts and marble scrolls. Many of them seem to have been converted into apartments, offices and banks or museums but Tulp's home looks intact. I can only guess at its eye-watering value. As one of the few remaining private houses on the most desirable part of the prestigious Lords' Canal, it must be astronomical. As I am watching, a street level door opens below and between the double staircase and a man hurries out and away.

'That must have been the separate entrance for the servants,' says Nina.

'It looks like it still is.'

We are still watching when the highly varnished prow of Tulp's Venetian motor launch pokes its nose out of the semi-circular opening at water level. I know that many Amsterdam homes belonged to wealthy merchants who also used their cellars to store precious goods and valuables from Asia. Presumably, the Tulp boat house leads to such a space.

The cabin curtains on the launch are drawn so we can't see if the man himself is on board. A tall, powerful-looking man in a black leather blouson is at the helm and the boat quickly cruises out of sight. 'Christ, you can smell the money from here,' I mutter into my empty beer glass. 'Another?'

'Why don't we see if Will and Jodi are free? Then we can make plans for this evening. I'd like to go out for dinner and perhaps they'll want to join us.'

I text Will. It turns out they're nearby and within ten minutes they are strolling towards us, hand-in-hand like a couple of love-smitten teenagers and with silly smiles on their faces. This is fast work, even by Will's well-practised standards.

'Hi, guys,' he says, putting a new round of beers onto the table after heading straight towards the mobile bar. 'The painting was amazing.'

Jodi smiles fondly at him. 'I think, perhaps, he pretended to be more interested than he was. It's hard to tell when you are talking to a professional actor.'

'No really. It was fascinating,' Will protests. '*The Anatomy Lesson of Dr. Nicolaes Tulp*. Jodi told me all about it and explained why Rembrandt was such a genius. It was awesome.'

'So, what have you two been doing?' Jodi asks us.

'Well, Jack has been talking to spies while I went shopping,' says Nina, 'Although we'll probably be killed for telling you that. And we've just been doing some spying for ourselves on the Tulp family home over there.' She points to the mansion opposite.

'What? You mean the guy in the painting lived in that place?' demands Will.

We think so. It would make sense for a house like that to be passed down over the centuries and stay in the same family for it to remain unaltered like that,' I reply. 'The current Tulp had some kind of mini political rally on his doorstep earlier on.'

'Ughh ... the Born-Again party. I despise them,' says Jodi with real feeling.

'And look. Can you see? He's even got a boat house straight off the canal. Jack thinks it probably leads into his cellars.'

'You missed his personal Venetian taxi. It went out about half-an-hour ago. It's the one he took us out to lunch in.'

'Before we were dumped for being rude about his politics,' adds Nina.

'I'm glad you were,' says Jodi firmly. 'I'd have been tempted to push him overboard.'

'Well, I'm afraid his party seems to be in the ascendancy at the moment. At least, according to my visitor.' I know I shouldn't, but I happily settle down to repeat my conversation with Colonel Hartgers from the MIVD. I feel the whole situation is too ridiculous for words and that there is no risk to me as long as the Russian angle doesn't get into the Dutch press.

'Wow. The Russians. That's big!' says Jodi after I finish.

'It's flaky,' I say. 'But even so, if you tell anyone and it gets into the press, I'll probably go to prison.'

'I'll visit you mate,' says Will with a grin. 'It'll be a doddle after our boarding school.'

'Don't worry. I'll stick to paintings rather than politics,' adds Jodi. 'But really? A team of Russian assassins? Why would they do this?'

'As Jack says, they did it in Salisbury,' says Nina.

'Yes, but that was to kill one of their double-agents, wasn't it?' asks Will. 'Why would they be taking out right-wingers over here?'

'Search me,' I say. 'Like I say, it feels pretty flaky and all they're basing it on is some internet trolling. At least, that's what they told me.'

'Well, I suppose they need to check everything out,' says Jodi.

'That's what the Colonel said too,' I admit. 'But taking my passport off me ... well that's pretty bloody out-of-order.'

'As you can tell, Jack's still a bit sore about it,' says Nina brightly. 'And so, I propose a nice dinner together this evening where the size of the bill can take his mind off it.'

There is general enthusiasm for this idea and Jodi books a restaurant she knows on a stretch of connected streets in the Jordaan known as 'Little Italy'. We agree to meet up later after dropping Eddie off at the boat. This will give Jodi a chance to wash and change and show Will her 'very tiny apartment'. Will seems very enthusiastic about this late afternoon property viewing and they hurry off into the sunset shortly afterwards.

CHAPTER FORTY

It has been another long and trying day for Dr Beatrix van der Laen and her deputy Robert Fruin. She has been given the courtesy of a brief call from the First Chief Commissioner of Police in the Netherlands who in turn has already been given the courtesy of an even briefer call from the Minister. The essence of both calls is to inform them of a possible Russian connection to the social media surrounding the internet images of Elsje as well as the Munt honeytrap. But nothing else is shared and the police are ordered to continue with their investigation and take all necessary precautions to stop a ninth murder and any more rioting.

Beatrix spends half an hour ranting to her immediate boss, the Commissioner of Police for Amsterdam, about the *"appalling lack of reciprocity"* and the arrogance of the AIVD. It makes her feel slightly better but achieves nothing of any real value.

'Alright then,' she says when she has calmed down and is finally alone with Robert. 'What have we got?'

Robert gloomily rattles off a list of dead ends. Never has the phrase been more appropriate. There is nothing new from forensics. They have drawn a blank on the wooden bullet or the special gun that must have fired it and the faces of the fake undertakers were too well-hidden to be identified or circulated. Divers had eventually found the sunglasses discarded by the bearded man in the gin boat – but a DNA check had drawn a blank. A search of Daniel Raap's private forest has identified a clearing where a muntjac was shot but they've come up with nothing else. An international search for laboratory work relating to plant poisons has found little to get excited about. The tulips, of course, are telling them nothing new and the country's leading horticultural experts remain baffled by the reappearance of Semper Augustus. And with the capital G now complete, there is no indication of where the next victim might be found – if indeed there is one. Leading Green politicians and environmental campaigners have been questioned, but they all have good lawyers and excellent alibis. 'All we've got that's new is this latest post of the Rembrandt sketch of Elsje and these new words. *"Finally, Justice for Elsje."'*

'Let's hope the word *finally* means what it says,' comments Beatrix.

'We'll have patrols out in real numbers again tonight,' says Robert. 'And the riot squads will be on standby. There's certainly been no sign of the politicians dialling down the rhetoric, so it could easily all kick-off again. I wouldn't want to be trying to balance our budget for all of this.'

Beatrix looks up at him. The only calculation she cares about is eight unsolved murders. Robert, in his sharp suit and with his impeccable grooming could pass as a successful accountant or management consultant. How can he be worrying about budgets at a time like this? Or is she just being old-fashioned? She is certainly feeling despondent at the moment. And this is so unlike her. She is usually so cheerful and upbeat. She wonders if it's time to retire and let someone younger take the reins. A nice new house in the country with a garden perhaps? She would get a great deal of money for her home in Amsterdam. It would certainly buy somewhere with a lot of land outside the city. And she could go travelling. The Far East, Africa …

'Beatrix. Beatrix.' She snaps out of her reverie. 'Are you alright?'

She rolls her head around on her neck tiredly and clutches the back of it. 'I'm sorry Robert, I was just thinking.

He smiles kindly. 'We've got the team meeting scheduled in an hour. They're all primed to do another root-and-branch review and report back to us on each murder. It's going to be a long afternoon, but maybe something will occur to you then.' He quickly corrects himself. 'To us.'

She doesn't hold out much hope but is grateful to him for trying. And then, she has decided, she will spend the night in her office until the early hours. She might as well. She wouldn't be able to sleep at home anyway. No, she will sit at police headquarters and wait for a call which she hopes will never come.

CHAPTER FORTY-ONE

'So,' I ask Jodi as our Italian waiter pours out four glasses of Chianti Classico in a bistro in Amsterdam's *Little Italy*. 'How come there aren't any clusters of restaurants in districts called *Little Holland* in the other cities of the world?'

'Jack,' chides Nina. 'Don't be rude!'

'No. It's a serious question,' says Jodi, smiling. 'Of course, there aren't any *Little Englands* either. Just English style boozers. But I accept, you get *Little Italys* all over the world.'

'And *Chinatowns*,' adds Will, helping himself to a breadstick and then remembering to offer them to Jodi and Nina.

Jodi smiles. 'No, you are right,' she says. 'I just don't understand why there isn't worldwide enthusiasm for our stodgy cuisine of potatoes and cabbage and heavily processed meats. After all, it is all so delicious and distinctive!' We all laugh. 'Did you know that despite being one of the smallest countries in Europe, we produce and eat nearly a third of the continent's French fries?'

'No!' says Nina in horror.

'Great mayonnaise though,' I chip in.

'But seriously...' continues Jodi. 'Perhaps our food is so bad because we were a coloniser for centuries. So, we adopted the cuisine of other countries rather than developing our own. We still have 180 different nationalities living here in Amsterdam. Perhaps the same is true for your country? What is there beyond fish and chips and a roast beef dinner that is typically British?'

'Korma Curry,' I say laughing.

'Spaghetti Bolognese,' adds Nina.

'Chicken Chow Mein,' says Will.

'Ha! You see. Indian, Italian and Chinese. I rest my case.'

'Fair enough,' I say. 'But maybe there will be fewer nationalities living here after the next elections.'

'Oh God. I pray not,' says Jodi. 'Can you imagine it. A far-right prime minister in power for the first time. I would be so ashamed of my country.' Her beautiful face is contorted and there is moisture in her lovely green eyes. Will puts a consoling hand over hers on the table.

'But these populist movements are everywhere,' I say in my own attempt to comfort her. 'Trump. Brexit. Le Pen in France. Everywhere you look there seems to be a crisis of confidence in democracy. I confess, I had no idea that it was happening here and I'm ashamed of my ignorance now.'

'I'm an academic and a historian,' says Jodi. 'And throughout history would-be dictators have thrived by identifying a common enemy. The Mexicans, The Muslims, even other Europeans. The Jews of course. What is that famous phrase? *"The only thing necessary for the triumph of evil is for good men to do nothing".*'

'JFK,' says Nina.

'That and a catchy slogan,' I say. '*Take Back Control. Make America Great Again. In the Name of The People.*'

'Well, I don't know about that, but the guy running Russia at the moment seems a pretty evil son-of-a-bitch,' says Will. 'Jodi and I were talking about your spook-visitor earlier.'

'Yes, and he's still got my passport and we're supposed to be going home shortly. I emailed Archi earlier to see if the embassy can do anything about it.'

'No more politics,' says Nina firmly after the waiter deposits our bruschetta starters. 'I know I keep saying this, but we're supposed to be on holiday remember?' We clink glasses and move onto a more general chat which ranges from recent films, living on canals and keeping fit to some more theatrical anecdotes from Will. At one stage the two women begin to discuss having children.

'My career has always come first so far,' says Jodi. 'That and the continuing absence of a suitable candidate to be a father.'

Nina laughs. 'Well, I don't have a career as such. But Adam and I had talked about having a family. He was my husband, but he died.'

Jodi looks sympathetic. 'Yes. Will told me he was a soldier. I am so sorry Nina.'

Will and I are following the conversation closely, but neither of us feels we have a right to contribute to it. I am fascinated. I haven't heard Nina talk about wishing to be a mother before.

'I have a niece. Anna. She has just started a degree at Oxford. Her mother, my sister-in-law is dead and so I feel very close to her.'

'But I guess that will never be like having your own daughter... or son,' says Jodi.

'No. I suppose not.'

'And we can't put off this decision forever, can we?'

'No. No we can't.'

There is an awkward silence which Jodi breaks. 'Did you know, we have a traditional nursery rhyme in the Netherlands. It goes: *The children in Holland take pleasure in making, What the children in England take pleasure in breaking.*'

'What? What on earth does that mean?' asks Will.

Jodi shrugs. 'I'm ashamed to say I don't know. Our two countries have been at war in the past. Perhaps it was just a bit of homegrown propaganda that has hung around.'

'Another bit of glib sloganeering that appeals to patriotic nationalism,' says Nina.

'Well,' I say. 'You could argue that it applies now to England's modern invasion of Amsterdam with stag parties and hen-dos. I imagine they break more than they make, and they aren't exactly reciprocated, are they?'

'Oh, my goodness that's true,' says Jodi. 'No-one wants them except some sleazy businesses. Do you know I saw an advert for a Canal Strip Boat recently that was aimed at stag parties. It was a private canal cruise offering striptease on board. We should do much more to dissuade these groups from coming.'

I entertain them with a story about Will arriving stark naked on the roof of my boat in the middle of the night in Oxford. It happened after a private acting engagement with a boat load of nudists had gone spectacularly wrong. But Will quickly takes over the story and carefully avoids any mention of the failed romance which prompted the incident in the first place. He clearly wants the beautiful and clever Jodi to think the best of him. I give him a knowing smirk and let him finish the heavily redacted story.

Nina finishes her dessert first and is fingering the petals of a plastic tulip in the centre of the table. 'That reminds me, Jodi. Did you find any evidence that Adriaan Pauw knew Nicholaes Tulp?'

'Oh my gosh, I'm so sorry Nina,' I completely forgot. 'Will and I were quite busy this afternoon.' The pair exchange a complicit smile. 'But I did send an email to my friend who works in the city archives and I know she sent me a reply. I haven't read it yet.' She peers at her phone and her forefinger skims the screen. 'Yes. Here we are. Let me see. She says she hasn't ever been asked about a connection between Pauw and Tulp before, but she was intrigued by their overlapping dates. Oh, listen to this. They're continuing to digitise the city's archives, which is a massive project, but she was able to do an online search of the two men. It came up with a letter in Pauw's family papers that mentions Tulp. She's forwarded it to me. Wait a minute and I'll open it. It's in Dutch obviously. Let me try to translate it.' She reads the letter from start to end without interruption.

February 1653

My Dearest Son,

If you are reading this letter, then I am dead. Do not grieve overlong for me. My immortal soul is safe in the keeping of our Almighty Father and I draw comfort that my time on earth has been one of public service and most beneficial to my fellow man and our nation's prosperity. I have been a practical fellow and I have raised you to be cut from the same cloth – and so to business.

The lawyer has my detailed will and testament with all of the papers and deeds which will be necessary for your succession as master of the House of Pauw. As my only surviving child you inherit everything – my title as Lord of Heemstede, the town of Heemstede and Heemstede Castle, the house in Amsterdam, the six trading boats and all of my paintings, tapestries, servants, and other possessions. Your mother's jewellery has been in her room at the castle since her death in 1648 and I commend you to loan it to your own good wife.

I have made arrangements for you to take my place as a Director of the United East India Company and I trust that, in time, you will follow the example of your grandfather and father and seek the high office of Mayor and Grand Pensionary. You may also be called upon to represent your country on diplomatic journeys and follow the example of your father who, as envoy of the States General to various foreign courts, negotiated peace with Spain after countless years of unprofitable war, and who most recently sought peace with England in spite of so much stubborn opposition and the strain it has placed on my health. The lawyer has my written guidance about all of these matters in his possession.

There is one more thing I wish you to do. My long and abiding passion for the extraordinary beauty of the tulip flower has been a mainstay of my life. My collection is unsurpassed and I charge you with its keeping as a living memorial to the late Lord of Heemstede and Keeper of the Great Seal of Holland.

Continue to cultivate the special flower according to my written instructions, but share them with no-one, not even your wife, just as I never told my beloved Anna, your mother.

Be especially cautious of the surgeon-doctor Tulp. He has been sniffing around me like a spaniel, pretending that his main concern is for my health – but all of the Dutch Republic knows of his obsession.

I beg God's forgiveness for being intemperate. Sixty-eight years on this earth, my many cares and my ill health have made me short tempered. I am proud of you my wonderful boy and I am sure you will repay my faith in you so that the Pauw family name will continue to be entwined in the glorious history of our country for hundreds of years to come.

Your loving father,

Adriaan Pauw,
Lord of Heemstede

'Wow,' I say.
'Gosh,' says Nina.
'What?' says Will.
'Don't you see?' I say. 'It's a deathbed letter from Adriaan Pauw to his son. It must have been attached to a will or something.'
'And it refers to a *"special flower"* – that has to be the Semper Augustus,' says Jodi.
'And he's telling his son to continue growing it according to his written instructions,' continues Nina.
'But he's also warning his son about Dr Tulp,' I add.
'The castle at Heemstede, the Pauw family seat, is no longer standing,' says Jodi. 'It's just a pile of stones. I went there once.'
'So, if there are no prominent members of the Pauw family still around...' says Nina thoughtfully.
'What?' asks Will again. He's clearly struggling to follow our thoughts and baffled by our growing excitement.
'Then maybe Dr. Tulp obtained Adriaan Pauw's secret papers ...' says Jodi.
'That's just speculation,' objects Nina.
'Sustained,' I say. 'But all the same, it's a possibility. As the letter says, Tulp was an obsessed man. He even changed his name, remember?'
I ask Jodi to read the letter again from start to finish and we continue to discuss its meaning until Will gives a yawn which would have been visible to an audience in the upper tier of a theatre. 'I'm sorry,' he says. 'I'm a bit knackered. Time to call it a day?'
My mind is still whirring with this new information, but the

others all stand and the waiter hurries over with the card machine.

'Penny for them?' says Nina as the four of us walk back to the boat for a quick nightcap. We are walking arm in arm behind Will and Jodi who are wrapped around each other even more tightly.

'If Tulp managed to get hold of Pauw's secret instructions on how to cultivate his special flower, then maybe they've been passed down through Tulp's ancestors rather than Pauw's,' I say.

'I know. I've been thinking the same,' says Nina.

'But you do realise where this takes us.'

'Straight to a possible connection between Cornelius Tulp and the Tulip Murders,' she answers straight away. 'But that's mad.'

We stop walking for a moment and look at each other. Jodi and Will continue to draw away from us. 'Is it?' I ask. 'He's standing for election and his party currently stand to gain the most from everyone pointing their fingers at the Greens and blaming the government.'

'But it's still all speculation,' protests Nina. We begin walking again. 'Surely this isn't enough to take to the police?'

I give this some consideration. What weight would Commissioner Beatrix van der Laen give to an old letter from the archives which simply proved that Tulp's famous ancestor was known to Adriaan Pauw? It didn't even mention the Semper Augustus by name. At this stage, we don't even know for certain that Cornelius Tulp was related to the famous doctor in Rembrandt's painting. There was a facial resemblance sure enough. But what else? Nina pulls me to a halt again and smiles up at me.

'Ok, so let's ask him.'

'What?'

'I know you pretty well by now, Jack,' she says. 'And you're just like Eddie when you get something between your teeth. You'll clamp on and worry away at it and you won't let it go. This is really bothering you, isn't it? So, let's just go and ask Tulp about it. What have we got to lose?'

'Just march up to his door and say …?'

'Just march up to his door and say good evening, Mr Cornelius Tulp – or as we say in England, Mr Cornelius Tulp. D'you remember us? Well Jack here wants to know if you've got a secret collection of Semper Augustus tulips seeing as your ancestor Dr Nicholaes Tulp was a bit of a tulip nerd and he was probably treating the man who had the finest collection of them in the 17th century, the Lord of Heemstede, Adriaan Pauw. And seeing as they've turned up alongside eight dead bodies all over Amsterdam, Jack thought you might like to give him a comment on it.'

I stop and look at her. 'Are you serious?'

'Sort of,' she laughs. 'You have become a bit obsessed by all this. No change there. So, let's just go and ask him. We know where he lives. It's only half past eight. And I'm sure he'll still be up.'

I'm not sure whether she's joking or not, but after a moment's hesitation, I decide to call her bluff. 'Alright then. You're on. You only live once.'

Nina buckles with laughter. 'You're bloody mad, Jack Johnson. But I do love you!'

Wow. There's definitely no going back now. I shout to Will, run to catch up with him and quickly explain what we're planning to do. 'Would you mind going on to the boat and letting Eddie out for a pee?' I ask. 'Make yourselves at home. There are the remains of a bottle of Japanese whisky somewhere. We won't be long. In fact, he'll probably just shut the door in our faces and we'll be straight back.'

Will shrugs. 'Well, it all sounds a bit mad to me mate, but sure. We'll see you later,' he says. He leans forward to whisper in my ear. 'But make sure you make a bit of noise before you come back into the boat.' I stand back to look at his face. He winks. 'You can't blame me Jack,' he says quietly. 'She's bloody gorgeous.

CHAPTER FORTY-TWO

Beatrix reaches across the table and pours another glass of wine from the chilled bottle of Montrachet in front of her. She is quietly impressed by her companion's choice of wine. She always keeps a couple of bottles of the white Burgundy at home for special occasions, but this was entirely Archi Gupta Bhalla's choice after he asked what she would like, and she told him to surprise her.

'This is delicious Archi, thank you.'

'It is completely my pleasure, Beatrix. It is a gesture of appreciation for agreeing to meet me at such short notice.' Actually, Beatrix is only too grateful for the excuse to escape from Amsterdam's central police station for an hour. It has been a soul-destroying afternoon going over and over the evidence with her team and arriving at no conclusions or even potential new avenues of investigation. She has never seen her team more downhearted and depressed and blames herself for failing to rally their spirits.

Fortunately, it is still all quiet on the streets and, so far this evening, there has been no new discovery of a body and a rare tulip. She therefore felt no pangs of guilt as she accepted Archi's invitation and slipped out, leaving Robert in charge but with instructions to call her immediately if the situation changed.

She sips her wine with real appreciation. It is a Puligny-Montrachet that the sommelier at this up-market wine bar has produced with a proud flourish from his cellar. She calculates its cost and wonders whether the British Embassy will be picking up the bill. She suspects not. She is all too familiar with the niggardly expenses policy of government departments. In which case, she calculates, Archi is probably paying more than a couple of hundred euros out of his own pocket for this particular vineyard and vintage.

Her sharp detective eyes appraise him closely. He is always well-tailored, and she has seen his classic sports car parked at the police station. She too likes classic cars and has recognised it as a Porsche 912 from the 1960s. It is in mint condition; his thick black glasses are recognisably Tom Ford and his watch is a Patek Phillipe. A private family income, she calculates. But that still doesn't explain why he is lavishing the prestigious white wine on her. What does he want? It couldn't be sex, could it? Don't be ridiculous. Pull yourself together Beatrix.

'Beatrix, I know you must be ridiculously busy so I'll cut to the chase if I may?'

'Of course, Archi.'

He coughs. 'I want to share something with you off the record. It may be something you already know. But I've been asked to um, raise it via a back channel as it were…'

Beatrix studies his face. It is plump and slightly ugly really, but she suspects that there is a good mind at work behind the unprepossessing exterior. He would be an easy man to underestimate, she thinks. 'Go ahead. Off the record it is.'

'Yes, well. I had an email from Jack Johnson earlier this evening – the Englishman who had the tulip on his boat and who found the four tulips at Oude Kerk.'

'Of course, I know who you are talking about,' says Beatrix. 'His girlfriend is called Nina.'

'Yes well, I'm not sure she's his girlfriend,' says Archi a little too quickly. Beatrix suppresses a knowing smile. 'Anyway, he had a visit from one of the chaps at MIVD today. I'd been told to warn him it was going to happen.'

Beatrix frowns. 'But why would MIVD be interested in him?' She feels a flash of anger that this information hasn't been shared with her by her supposed colleagues.

Archi takes a sip of wine from his glass and looks at her carefully. 'Off the record then, I suppose you know about the MIVD's suspicions about the Russians?'

Beatrix must now decide whether to pretend she knows more than she does, or risk being embarrassed about her ignorance. She opts for the truth. 'All I know is that the security services think some of the social media with the Tulip Murders hashtag has been coming from Russia in an attempt to stir the pot - particularly the Rembrandt sketch of the girl Elsje.'

Archi blows out his rounded cheeks in relief. 'Good. Excellent. And we've been using our own listening post at GCHQ to come to pretty much the same conclusions,' he says. 'But the senior spook who spoke to Johnson went much farther. He seems to have suggested the Russians might have had a hand in the murders – to destabilise your elections maybe. And to cap it off, he confiscated Johnson's passport. Johnson's furious of course. But they made him sign an official non-disclosure form.'

'And yet he still disclosed everything to you?' observes Beatrix.

'Yes, well. I imagine he felt it would be alright to speak to his own government about it in the circumstances.'

'I didn't know they were going to interview him,' she says with a hunch of her shoulders. 'Let's just say they are being less than forthcoming with us at the moment.'

'Yes, I see. That's a shame. But there are two issues here. Firstly, we're not too chuffed about an English citizen with a blameless record being dragged into the frame. The ambassador is worried about the optics if it gets out. I suspect he'll make unofficial representations tomorrow.'

'And the second?'

'And the second is this idea that the Russians might have carried out the murders. That would be an outrage on the same scale as the Salisbury poisonings. Even greater perhaps. It would be massive. Is there any reason to believe this to be true, Beatrix?'

So, this is the reason for the sudden meeting and the expensive wine. Perhaps the embassy will be picking up the bill after all. She pours some more into her glass to reassure herself that the English taxpayer isn't being ripped off. Then she shakes her head and lowers her voice.

'Honestly, Archi. I have no idea. If military intelligence has got any proof of this, I haven't seen it or heard a whisper about it. Frankly, I suspect they're more likely to share it with your people at MI6 than me. It's crazy but there it is. I'm on standby for another killing tonight and my colleagues are prepared for some more rioting. But it seems that MIVD is carrying the ball with the investigation now and the Minister is quite happy about giving it to them.' Archi looks genuinely crestfallen. 'I'm sorry I can't give you any more Archi. You'd be better off speaking to MIVD if you can.'

'Yes well. I don't think that's going to happen, do you?'

Beatrix leans forward. 'And are you absolutely certain Johnson has nothing to do with what's been going on? He seems to have been particularly adroit at being in the wrong place at the wrong time. And he's made some surprisingly educated guesses about what's been going on.'

'Yes, yes, we are certain about him,' says Archi automatically. 'Nevertheless, it might be an idea to look in on him this evening. Just to check-in and see the lay of the land as it were.'

Beatrix pats his hand. 'You do that, Archi. Make sure he hasn't done a runner – passport or no passport. And, of course, you can check that the lovely Nina is alright too. The woman who isn't his girlfriend.' Archi blushes slightly and Beatrix realises her teasing has hit home. She smiles kindly at him. 'Off you go now, but don't forget to pay the bill on your way out.'

It takes Archi less than five minutes to kiss Beatrix on both cheeks, settle their account with some plastic and hail a taxi to *Flora's* mooring. Beatrix asks herself, what the hell are MIVD up to? They're a law unto themselves. She sighs, congratulates herself on being left with almost half a bottle of the prestigious Chardonnay and pours another glass. It's not a Grand Cru of course, but it's extremely palatable. And it's going to be a long night so she might as well sit back in comfort, kick off her shoes, light a cigar and think about Dutch tulips, Russian internet trolls and English journalists.

CHAPTER FORTY-THREE

Most of Tulp's mansion looks dark and shuttered but there is a light in a couple of its tall windows to suggest that someone is at home. There is a metal bellpull in the shape of a lion's-head on one side of the imposing front door. I yank it and hear a jangling from somewhere inside the house. The door opens inwardly a short while afterwards and a tall, thick-set man in a black roll-necked sweater and black jeans scrutinises us. He is probably in his late twenties; he has close cropped brown hair and he looks more like a nightclub bouncer than a butler. This impression is reinforced by his muscular folded arms, the appearance of a black ear pod in one ear and the absence of a polite greeting,

'Good evening,' says Nina, stepping forward. 'We were wondering if Mr Tulp is home? We met him recently and we have something to discuss with him.'

The man continues to stand there impassively and without speaking. 'It's about the Semper Augustus tulips,' I add. 'The flowers which have been found with all of the dead bodies recently.' The man blinks for the first time since opening the door.

'I'm Jack Johnson and this is Nina Wilde,' I add. 'Mr Tulp does actually know us.'

'Wait,' orders the doorman. Then he turns and closes the door firmly behind him.

'Charming!' says Nina. 'Not even a please.'

'Well, at least he told us to wait rather than go away,' I reply. 'That suggests he might be coming back.'

'I feel sure I've seen him before somewhere,' says Nina.

We turn our back on the door at the top of the double staircase to admire the view across the Herengracht, back to the far bank where we were sitting earlier in the day. There is no longer any sign of the mobile bar. 'It really is a very swanky neighbourhood,' I say eventually. 'The city fathers knew what they were doing when they built this new canal district for themselves to live in.'

Nina checks her watch. 'It's been five minutes now. Try again.'

I pull the lion's-head and the bell jangles for a second time. A couple of minutes later I hear footsteps and the door opens. This time it is Cornelius Tulp himself. His chin, with its little pointed beard, is thrust forward challengingly and his eyes look fierce. 'What is this all about?'

Nina holds out a hand which he takes somewhat reluctantly and quickly releases. 'Hello again Mr Tulp. We're extremely sorry for calling on you without any notice. But since we've been here, Jack has become something of an expert on 17th century Tulips, and I've been studying Rembrandt and well, to cut a long story short, we were wondering if you are in fact a descendant of the famous Dr Nicholaes Tulp – the man featured in *The Anatomy Lesson*. Jack gets a bit obsessed sometimes, and so do I, and so I suggested we ask you directly. I hope you don't mind. It's a bit forward of us, I know. We've had a bit of a drink.' She giggles. 'But we were just passing and it's given us the Dutch courage to knock on your door.'

He frowns at her but is met with an encouraging smile. Just as I think the solid door is about to be slammed in our face, pride seems to overcome his hesitation and hostility. 'Yes of course. Dr Nicholaes Tulp is my ancestor through the male line. He was a great man. But what …?'

'I know it might sound far-fetched,' I say, cutting him off. 'But

I've been trying to work out how the Semper Augustus might have survived for all these years. And so, I wondered if Dr Tulp had somehow managed to get the secret of its cultivation from Adriaan Pauw, and whether that explained how it had miraculously reappeared recently? A document has just come to light which suggests Pauw was one of your ancestor's patients.'

Tulp's reaction is immediate and strange. He shoots out a hand and grips my upper arm tightly. 'Why would you ask such a thing? Do you dare to suggest I have had something to do with these so-called Tulip Murders?' He looks both angry and scared at the same time.

'No, no, not at all,' says Nina automatically.

But I can't help myself from responding to his instinctive panic. 'Well, do you? Maybe we should be getting the police to ask you all about Dr Nicolaes Tulp and Adriaan Pauw? What do you think Mr Tulp?'

His eyes have narrowed, and his face is creased with fury. A doorstep conversation is familiar territory for most journalists, and I've had enough similar conversations to judge when a door is about to be slammed in my face. I half-turn away to loosen his grip on my arm. But instead, he yanks me towards him and pulls me forward onto the marble floor of a large entrance hall. 'Come in,' he snaps over his shoulder at Nina. He slams the large door closed behind us and begins marching down a long hallway which is lined with oil paintings. The men in the portraits boast moustaches, beards and features which are very similar to those of our host. 'Follow me,' he orders. Nina and I exchange looks and then troop after him into a large drawing room filled with more paintings, oriental rugs and two ornate wooden settees which look Chinese. The soft lighting comes from a handful of lamps on polished wooden side tables.

'What a lovely room,' says Nina politely, as though we have just been invited in for tea.

'Sit,' he says. We do as he says. He does the same opposite us and puts both hands on his knees. 'Alright, say what you have to say.'

There seems to be a sub-text here which I am unclear about. It feels like a challenge to us to do our worst.

Nina coughs. 'It's just what Jack said. We know your ancestor Dr Tulp was obsessed with tulips. So much so that he changed his name and used the flower as his trademark.'

Tulp shrugs. He seems slightly calmer now. 'This is well known. It is in many history books. And the painting by Rembrandt helped to make him a very famous person.'

'So, we were wondering whether he might have come across Adriaan Pauw, the Grand Pensionary of Holland at the time?' I say. 'We were wondering whether he might have had Dr Tulp as his physician. And now, it seems, there is written proof of this in the city's archives.'

'So what?'

'So Pauw was famous as a fabulously wealthy collector of the broken tulip, Semper Augustus. The letter by Pauw to his son suggests he had found a way to prevent it dying off. It also suggests he was very suspicious of your distinguished ancestor. So, I wondered if, somehow, Dr Nicholaes obtained the secret and whether this explains how it has suddenly reappeared after all of this time.'

'But you have no proof of this?' demands Tulp. 'It is just the wild theory of two English tourists.'

I rear back in surprise. 'You make it sound like an accusation.'

'I know what you are doing, don't think I don't. You are trying to link my family's famous and respectable name, and me, to these terrible murders. I already know you don't like my politics.' He points a finger at me. 'Now, you are trying to spread vicious rumours in an attempt to undermine me and my party.'

'Well, that's a thing,' says Nina calmly. 'Until we came here tonight, it was just a bit of historical theorising. I suggested to Jack that we ask you about it just to shut him up. But now we're here it's making me wonder if there is more to this than meets the eye.' I look across at her. There is a slight bulge of gum showing in the cheek nearest to me. Where is she going with this? 'Maybe you *are* involved in what's been going on. You and the Russians.'

What!? Where the hell did that come from? I turn to stare at her, but her big dark eyes remain fixed on Tulp. Her voice is even and calm in marked contrast to the shrillness of Tulp. 'Because

I've just realised where I've seen your doorman before. He was one of the two men who removed your drunk dinner guest at the Waldorf wasn't he? The one who was leering all over me. You let his name slip during our lunch on your boat. Do you remember? He was called Leonid. That's a Russian name, isn't it? Like Leonid Brezhnev for example? Looks a bit like him too.'

My God! She's right. I remember our young bouncer at the door and another man effortlessly lifting the drunk man called Leonid and taking him back into the private dining room. And if Leonid is indeed a Russian, then perhaps Colonel Joost Hartgers of the MIVD is on the right track after all?

Tulp is smiling at her now, but it looks forced and one of his feet is tapping the floor furiously. 'You really are the most ill-mannered guest a person can have. You were rude during my lunch and now you are rude to me here, in my own home.'

'No, maybe she's right,' I say, leaning forward. 'There's a possible historical connection between your family and the rare tulips and, as Nina says, you've recently been entertaining a bunch of hard-looking Russians. So, maybe the so-called Tulip Murders are all about getting you and your Born-Again party into power in the Netherlands? Is that what's been going on?'

My mind is racing with the possibilities now. 'And maybe you've been deliberately pointing the finger of blame at the left-wingers? The greens and the pro-immigration lobby? You get the sympathy vote and the government is discredited. Is that what this is all about?'

Nina picks up the thread. 'And the Russians have also been helping you stir things up with their internet army of trolls.'

Tulp stands up abruptly. His features are twisted in anger. 'You are crazy, both of you,' he spits. 'This is… this is outrageous. You come uninvited into my home and call me a murderer and a traitor to my country. A traitor. Me? Cornelius Tulp. This is utterly vile and outrageous. Get out, get out both of you. And I warn you, if you repeat a word of this, my lawyers will make you pay many millions in compensation. I will bankrupt you both.'

I stay seated and put a hand on Nina's to keep her in her seat. I am certain our off-the-cuff riff has hit home. 'You might as well give up now Tulp,' I say. 'Guess who came to visit us on our boat this afternoon? A Colonel from the Dutch Secret Services.'

Tulp visually blanches at this. 'You're lying.'

'His name was Colonel Joost Hartgers of the MIVD.' I fish my wallet out of my back pocket. 'He left me his card actually, in exchange for my passport. Here it is.' Tulp snatches the card from my hand and stares at it. His eyes widen. 'He told me they were onto your Russian friends.'

'Why would he tell you that? An English journalist and his girlfriend? You're bluffing.'

So, I'm not *"lying"* anymore. I'm *"bluffing"*. It's a schoolboy error. People who accuse others of bluffing are actually revealing that they have something to hide. 'Not at all,' I say calmly. I have told the truth. Hartgers was suspicious of the Russians – but he had no idea that Tulp might be involved. And neither did I until tonight. Now I am certain of it. 'They're on to you and your chums Tulp. It's just a matter of time.'

'Get out. Get out of my house. Now.' Tulp's voice has risen to a shriek and there is a spittle of white phlegm in one corner of his mouth. 'I'm warning you – get out before I call the police.'

I stand and Nina does likewise. 'Really Tulp? I'm not so sure you will. But sure. We'll be off for now. Maybe it'll be us who call the police instead? Do you know Dr Beatrix van der Laen? The murder detective? We know her quite well. She seems a nice lady. I think she'll be very interested in what we've discovered today.'

'GET OUT. GET OUT.' He is still shouting as he yanks open the room's door and throws it wide.

I hold Nina's arm and steer her past Tulp, back into the long corridor which leads to the front door. I even feel his hot breath on my neck as we pass him. He is panting with emotion. I check over my shoulder. He's frantic to get us out of the house. I even feel his hand push the small of my back at one point.

The three of us have just moved into the marbled entrance hall when a pedimented door opens to one side. The big young doorman moves into the hall, only this time his appearance is slightly different. He is still dressed in black, and the earpiece is still in place. But now he is holding a matt black gun in his hand

and it is levelled directly at my chest.

CHAPTER FORTY-FOUR

The sight of the lethal weapon is so shocking and unreal, it makes me give an irrational giggle of disbelief. Another line of Chandler's runs through my head. 'When in doubt, have a man come into the room with a gun.' Only this isn't one of his hard-boiled thrillers. This is real life.

'What? What are you doing?' yelps Tulp. The man with the gun ignores him and jerks his head at me and Nina.

'Hands on the wall.' I look at the gun which is unwavering and turn to put both of my hands flat against the expensive wallpaper. Part of my brain registers the design of intricately intertwined tulips. Nina does the same alongside me and we turn our heads sideways to look at each other. Her face is saying, 'Wow, I didn't expect that,' and mine is trying to reply with, 'No, nor did I.'

I feel the man's foot kick against mine. He is urging me to spread my feet apart and then to slide them backwards until I am wholly relying on the wall to stay upright. He does the same with Nina. We are now shaped like two human buttresses and it would be easy for him to kick a leg away and send us crashing to the floor. But instead of doing this, he pats us down thoroughly and removes both of our mobile phones.

I'm not sure I can hold this vulnerable position for much longer and I cannot turn my head far enough to see if he is still standing directly behind us. It is Nina who makes the first move by simply moving her feet forwards, closer towards the wall and standing upright. I follow suit and we turn into the hall simultaneously. The gun is still pointing at us, but there is no sign of Tulp anymore. I assume he has fled back down the long corridor as we didn't hear the front door being opened.

'Through there,' says the doorman, jerking his head at another pedimented door, directly opposite the one he came through. Nina goes first and pulls the door open herself. I follow her into a small square room. It smells of bleach and contains an assortment of cleaning equipment – two vacuum cleaners and a cluster of brushes and mops. I notice it does not have a window. The door closes behind us, plunging us into instant darkness and I hear a key turning in the lock.

'Wait a minute,' says Nina, and after a moment the room bursts into a harsh neon light. There is a switch by the door which she must have noticed as he left. 'That's better.'

'Well done,' I say. 'Well, that all went pear-shaped a bit quickly!'

'I think we may have blundered into the truth.'

'I think you're right. There's no reason the Dutch authorities would suspect Tulp of working with the Russians to kill off his own people.'

'Although it makes perfect sense, doesn't it? It's swinging the election his way.'

'And there's no reason the police or the secret services would connect Tulp with the Semper Augustus, even though it's staring out at them from one of the most famous paintings in the world.'

'So, our theory must be right,' says Nina. 'He must still have a collection of them somewhere.'

'And he's been using them to get worldwide attention focused on what's been happening and to draw blame on the left and get the government accused of incompetence.'

We both fall silent – afraid to voice the implications of all of this for us. These people are very efficient killers and they won't shirk from doing whatever is necessary to fulfil their plan. They certainly won't let two English tourists get in their way. I stand and begin a careful inspection of our surroundings while Nina sits on the ground and watches me. It doesn't take long. We are in a small antechamber that leads off the main entrance hall. It is obviously used by the cleaning staff to store their things. There is no window, the ceiling is solid and the door is definitely locked shut. I try to peer through the keyhole, but the key has been left in and it's blocking any view of the entrance hall. I do another circuit of the small room, paying particular attention to the metal shelves which contain an array of cleaning agents, bleaches, sponges, cloths and dusters. In one corner of the room is a pile of old newspapers. I slump down onto the floor beside it. Nina is opposite me. Only a couple of metres separates our feet in the small room.

'I'm sorry. I've been so stupid and reckless. I've put you in serious danger.'

She momentarily stops chewing her gum. 'Don't be an idiot. If anyone's to blame, it's me. I was the one who suggested we just march up to Tulp's front door and ask him about his famous ancestor.'

'And I shouldn't have wound him up like that.'

'I was the one who clocked the Russian from the hotel remember? I should have kept my mouth shut.' We fall silent again. After a few minutes Nina whispers, 'Jack?'

'What is it?'

'Can I have a hug?'

I shuffle over on the floor next to her and wrap one arm around her far shoulder. She leans her head onto mine.

'We can't do anything for the moment. Let's just rest up,' I feel her gradually relaxing into the fold of my body.

I wonder if she realises how desperate our position is. If Tulp and his Russian friends have been responsible for eight consecutive murders and trying to sway an election, another couple of killings won't trouble them at all. The geo-political stakes are enormous. I assume they are out there now, making plans and deciding their next steps. We have no way of contacting the outside world and the outside world has no way of knowing what is going on in this grand mansion on the Golden Bend of the Herengracht.

But Will and Jodi know where we were going. I asked them to continue walking to our boat in order to let Eddie out. Tulp and his cronies have no knowledge of this. Will our two friends stay there and eventually become worried by our non-appearance? Or will they tumble into bed together on the boat, fall asleep with exhaustion and be oblivious to the rest of the world until morning? Or will they eventually lose patience and simply go on to Jodi's apartment? I think I know my friend well enough to put my money on the second or third options. I check my watch. It is 10.30 p.m. I estimate we have been in this room for half an hour now. So, if Will and Jodi do stay on the boat, and aren't too drunk with post-coital bliss, how late would it need to be before they started to get worried about us? Midnight maybe? But we could both be dead by then.

Should I warn Tulp that we are expected back on the boat by our friends? It might make him pause and buy us some time. Or it might put Will and Jodi in mortal danger too. I am mulling over this dilemma when I shift my position and feel the newspapers rustle slightly. And as I sit there, with a numb backside and arm, it reminds me of a trick my grandfather showed me as a boy. He told my mother to lock us both in my bedroom but leave the key in the lock. I can still remember her look of amazement when we both reappeared in the kitchen less than five minutes later.

'Nina. Nina. I've got an idea. Here. Stand up.' I remove a double-sided sheet of newspaper from the top of the pile and begin to search the shelves.

'What are you looking for?' she asks.

'Something small and sharp that I can poke through the keyhole.'

'What about this?' Nina has taken a wire coat hanger off the top shelf. I grab it, untwist the handle and straighten it out. Now I begin bending it both ways until it snaps in two, six inches from the end.

'What's the idea?' she asks.

'Stay quiet and pray,' I say. 'It's an old schoolboy trick.' I move over, drop to my knees and lay the sheet of newspaper flat on the floor. I slide it under the door until just an inch is left on our side. Then I slide it sideways, so it is close to the door jamb. I bend my head close to the handle and begin to poke my piece of wire into the keyhole. The plan is to work the key around until I can push it out. With luck it will land on the newspaper. Then I can pull it back under the door into our room and open the lock from the inside.

But anything can go wrong. The key might be impossible to poke out. It might not drop neatly onto the newspaper. The noise of it falling might alert someone. And the gap below the door might not be large enough to allow the key to pass through. But it's better than sitting around and doing nothing.

Nina has realised what I am trying to do and is kneeling alongside me. I can sense her holding her breath, willing me to succeed. It's an old-fashioned key and pretty loose in the lock so the wire manages to turn it round into a vertical position quite easily. Now I point the end of the wire at the very end of the key and push it forward slowly. It eases backwards until it tips downwards. One final nudge should do it. We both hear a metallic sound as it drops onto the floor of the hall and hold our breaths. Now I move the sheet of newspaper gently back into the centre of the door, hoping that any gap will be greatest there. I begin to pull it very slowly towards me. The sheet of paper is almost two-thirds through when the key appears at one edge. Nina pounces on it and looks at me with a huge grin, her eyes shining with excitement.

I hold a finger to my lips, take the key from her and place it in the lock. It turns quite easily and the door immediately begins to swing outwards. I hold it closed for the moment. We are standing now. I put my mouth close to Nina's ear and whisper. 'Make for the front door as quickly as possible. Ready?'

She nods. I pull the door open slightly and check the hall. There is no-one there. We both creep out and immediately turn left towards freedom and safety.

'Simple but ingenious. Obviously, we should have removed the key from the lock.' We hear this from the entrance to the corridor with the portraits in it and freeze. I contemplate making a dash for the handle of the front door, but the doorman has moved swiftly into the centre of the hall. He still has his gun and it's levelled directly at me from point blank range. He isn't smiling, unlike the man who has spoken. I turn and immediately recognise the bear-like man with his paunch and shock of thick grey-white hair that is swept back into a quiff.

'Leonid' breathes Nina.

CHAPTER FORTY-FIVE

I look at him closely. The last time we saw him his eyes were glazed and his red and sweaty face betrayed the intake of vast quantities of alcohol. Now, he looks sober, calm and totally in control of himself.

'Please, come with me.' He turns and heads off down the corridor. The gunman wags his pistol and we are forced to follow. This time, we go past the door to Tulp's impressive drawing room, cross a huge stone-floored kitchen and enter a kind of library. We must be at the rear of the house. It has a pair of large glass doors leading onto a garden terrace and most of the walls are lined with leather bound books. Leonid moves his bulk behind a large antique-looking desk and collapses heavily into a green leather chair. 'Please sit.' There are two similar chairs facing the desk and we claim one each. I look behind me. The doorman is standing in the open doorway and pointing the pistol at my back.

Leonid pulls open a drawer and puts a three-quarters full bottle of vodka onto the desk followed by a shot glass. He untwists the metal cap, pours out a couple of inches and downs it in one.

'Za Zdarovje,' he says, replacing the cap and chuckling. 'To your health.' He says. 'I heard all of your conversation with Tulp.' He speaks in a heavily accented bass rumble. 'He would have been an idiot to let you back out onto the street.'

'So, we were right,' I say. 'He's been working with you on the Tulip Murders.'

'I am Major General Leonid Petrov, a senior officer of the GRU, our country's military intelligence, and commander of an elite special services unit. This operation has taken more than a year of careful reconnaissance and planning and it was executed perfectly by three of our best operatives under my leadership.' He raises his eyes to the man at the door. 'But yes, Tulp identified the victims for us. They were all liabilities for his new party, in one way or another, and therefore they were expendable – or they were rivals of his in some way. They were martyrs for their cause. And now the Dutch far right is poised to take control of the Netherlands as a wave of disgust at the left-wing extremists takes hold and disquiet about uncontrolled immigration sweeps the country.' He chuckles to himself. 'It is clever is it not?'

'But what's in it for Russia?' asks Nina.

Leonid leans forward on his elbows. 'We are continually mistreated and conspired against by Western powers. We have been ever since the fall of the Berlin Wall. But now we have a president who is prepared to fight back.'

'By trying to destroy western democracies,' I say.

'Exactly, Mr Johnson! But from within. That is the genius of it all. A homebred authoritarian figure can ultimately inflict much greater damage on a democratic system than a remote foreign power can.' He laughs out loud. 'Trump achieved more chaos in America during his first term of office than we have achieved in 75 years of enmity with the US.'

'Your army of computer trolls helped Trump to get elected?' asks Nina.

Leonid shrugs. 'Their influence is exaggerated. But that is the point. When there is an information deluge, they don't need to hack their way into Western computer systems. They just need to stir the pot. The internet and your uncontrolled media do the rest. People don't know what information to trust any more. Is it Fake News or Real News? Who knows? And if people believe the

Kremlin is somehow behind all this, so much the better, even if we aren't. It makes them take us even more seriously.'

'You're just happy to create disruption and confusion?' I ask.

'Exactly! Being thought to affect the results is as good as actually affecting the results.'

He pours himself another generous shot of vodka. 'Look at Poland. It's a classic example of our success. You don't know the story? Okay.' He looks at his watch. 'We have a little time. The Law and Justice Party took over in 2015 precisely because of the mistrust and suspicion that was sweeping the country. A plane crashed in 2010 and ninety-six people were killed, including the party's founder. His twin brother told everyone it was a conspiracy and that the crash wasn't an accident.' He smiles conspiratorially. 'Maybe it was. Maybe it wasn't. But we helped to stir the pot and PiS swept to power. Now they've packed the courts with their own people and taken over Poland's main broadcaster. A potentially hostile country on our own doorstep is now all but finished as a Western democracy.' He grins and empties his glass in one go again.

'But that's terrible,' protests Nina.

Leonid points a blunt finger at her. 'You are naïve. Like a schoolgirl. Your democracies carry the seed of their own decline. You have diseased tissue, and you make it easy for us to put maggots on it. We make it even worse from within. Look at the so-called dream of a united Europe. It is collapsing before your eyes. And now, after Brexit, will come Nexit! A new government will take the Netherlands out of the EU. And as the EU crumbles, so will NATO eventually.'

'To be replaced with what?' demands Nina angrily. 'Your Communism wasn't the answer, was it? And nor is your gangster-president!'

'Enough!' Leonid bangs the leather-topped surface of the table with a clenched fist. 'Tulp called you rude and you are. You do not speak of our president in that way. He is a great man achieving great things for our country.'

'Piling up billions of roubles for himself and his mates, I say. 'Building palaces for themselves and ever bigger yachts while they imprison and torture any opposition at home.'

'And spread chaos abroad,' adds Nina.

Leonid is smiling. 'You still don't understand, do you? It is not just chaos we seek to create. When there is chaos, people seek simple solutions. They seek someone to blame – usually outsiders, immigrants and so on. New populist political figures become powerful, but they carry the seed of democratic destruction within them.'

'A bit like the Semper Augustus,' I say.

'Exactly!' He laughs and bangs the table again. 'Just like the rare tulip.'

'Except it survived, somehow,' says Nina.

Leonid sits back and rests his hands on his paunch. 'And that is really what brought you to Tulp's door this evening?' He shakes his head. 'Fate is a strange thing. Well, if it gives you any comfort you were right. He told me the whole story.'

He looks at his watch again. 'Adriaan Pauw had the largest collection of the famous flowers in the Netherlands. There were a few hundred of them in his castle's gardens and he used mirrors to make it look like there were many more. But he never sold them or shared them. He didn't need the money. Moreover, he had stumbled on the secret to overcoming the damage done to the bulbs by the virus. He noticed that the tulips that were planted near a quince tree were much healthier and more vigorous than the others – which continued to die away. The quince tree also comes from the middle east, just like the tulip. For some reason, the virus – which is spread by aphids – was arrested by a fungus in the roots of the quince tree. Scientists know all about this phenomenon now. There is a special name for it. But I forget it.'

'But how did Tulp's ancestors acquire the secret?' I ask.

'Hah. The Tulp doctor was treating Pauw on his deathbed. Before he died, Tulp saw a letter to Pauw's son. The silly old man hadn't trusted his lawyers with the secret instructions. Tulp's ancestor simply left the letter where it was, stole the instructions and a few of Pauw's bulbs and grew his own collection. It's out there,' Leonid jerks a thumb over his shoulder.

'What? In the garden? Here?' I ask incredulously.

'Yes, right here in the heart of Amsterdam. There is a hidden walled garden out there. The Tulps planted a small orchard of quince trees and ensured a plentiful supply of the right kind of aphids. The Tulp family has kept the tulip going in secret ever since. They were wealthy and successful enough. They never needed to cash them in. But now Tulp has done so – for power rather than money.' He shrugs. 'Although often, of course, they amount to the same thing.'

'But why did you put them by the bodies?' asks Nina.

I answer for him. 'Chaos and disruption.'

'Exactly!' he laughs. 'It guaranteed worldwide attention and gave another nudge of suspicion in the direction of the poor innocent Greens.'

'Just like the plant toxins,' says Nina.

'Developed in our Russian laboratories and brought over in diplomatic bags,' says Leonid with satisfaction. 'A nice touch, don't you think?'

'But why did you leave one on our boat?' I ask.

The bass rumble of a laugh again. 'It was Tulp's idea. He couldn't resist it after he picked you up in his boat and saw how close you were moored to the Groenburgwal Bridge. He thought it was an excellent joke after you annoyed him.'

'A joke?' says Nina indignantly. 'Eight people dead and he thinks leaving a tulip on our boat is a joke? He's sick in the head. You all are.'

The doorman says something tersely in Russian and Leonid nods at him. Then he puts both his palms flat on the table in a gesture of finality. 'Well, our work is almost done here. We need to join our two colleagues at Schipol Airport where we have seats on an overnight flight to Moscow.'

'And what happens to us now?' I ask. Nina looks at me with a sudden realisation. Leonid has been very open and frank with us about his identity, his country's tactics and the secret of the Semper Augustus. He can't be planning for us to survive the night.

'Now, you will follow me.'

We trail behind him, inhaling vodka fumes as the gunman follows behind us. However, this time Leonid pushes through a door just outside the library and we descend four flights of circular stone steps. Another door is opened, and an overpowering smell of chlorine hits us. Long neon lights blink on automatically. We must be under street level now and a large subterranean swimming pool stretches out in front of us.

It's an unexpected sight. And equally unexpected are the red flamed tulips complete with their stems and leaves floating on the surface of the water. There must be over a hundred of them in total. A green swimming-lane rope is stretched along the centre of the blue-tiled pool, dividing it into two halves. And suspended in the centre of it, with his arms and head hanging down across it, in exactly the same pose as poor Elsje, is the wide-eyed and very dead figure of Cornelius Tulp.

CHAPTER FORTY-SIX

I wrap an arm around Nina and look back at Leonid. 'You killed him? Why? Why would you do that? I thought you wanted to put him on the throne?'

'He would never have been king, just a helpful king-maker,' says Leonid. 'He signed his death warrant when he spoke to you. I had no idea he told you my name during your lunch. My operational name. But I realised we couldn't trust him any longer. He was weak, a liability. He might have talked under pressure. My country's involvement may be suspected, but it can never be proven. Not now.'

'Unlike Salisbury,' I say.

He dismisses my comment with a flick of his hand. 'A partial success. But it was not my operation. So, now we tie up all loose ends and leave with all of the essentials still in place. There is one more martyr for the cause – and a very high profile one. The other joint founder of the Born-Again party. That should be enough to guarantee the election for a far-right government don't you think?'

One more martyr? Or does he mean three? Are the two of us about to join Tulp in the pool? The sharp prod of the pistol in my back seems to confirm my fears. But instead of hearing it cocked, it pushes me along the side of the pool towards the deep end. In the centre of the wall facing the pool is a heavy metal door. It has already been swung open.

'Stop there,' orders Leonid. A gun has appeared in one of his hands too. Nina is standing beside me, our backs against the wall. He says something in Russian to the other man who immediately disappears through the doorway. We hear something metallic scraping which sounds like it could be another door. He reappears. A pistol is now trained on each of us.

'Alright. Take off your clothes,' says Leonid brusquely.

'What?' says Nina.

'Go fuck yourself,' I say.

'Take off your clothes,' repeats Leonid to Nina. 'Or I begin to shoot your boyfriend in a way that will guarantee a long and very painful death.' He looks at me. 'He will bleed out slowly on the floor.' Then he looks at me. 'Or I could do it the other way around if you like and start with her?'

I look into the eyes of both men. They are shark-like, cold and totally emotionless. Leonid sighs. 'Alright, I count to five and you will have to guess who I shoot in the belly first. I do it just to make a painful but fatal wound you understand. One. Two. Three...'

'Just do it Nina,' I mutter, bending to begin removing my shoes and socks. It takes less than sixty seconds for two piles of clothing to crumple in front of us on the tiled floor. Nina is magnificent. She makes no attempt to hide her modesty. She just stands there, her hands at her sides and a look of utter loathing in her eyes.

'Also, your watches,' orders Leonid, before motioning his gun towards the doorway. Nina goes first. It is a tiny windowless room with bare stone walls. There is another doorway on the opposite wall which seems to lead out onto some kind of wooden pontoon. I can hear a faint slopping sound of water. This must be the boathouse we saw from across the canal. 'Sit.' There is a metal-framed chair bolted to the floor of the little cell and, about a metre in front of it, a waist-high metal bar is sticking upright out of the ground. Nina sits on the chair with her hands in her lap.

A small copper pipe protrudes high up on the wall opposite

Nina and I am motioned to stand under it. Leonid reaches into a trouser pocket and pulls out two long black plastic ties. He loops one around Nina's wrist and the horizontal arm rest of the chair and pulls it tight. Then he secures the other wrist. She is breathing heavily and shivering and so am I. Our bare skin is prickling with the cold.

Leonid's partner swings the heavy metal door to the swimming pool shut with a clang and gloom instantly descends on us. He turns a key in the lock and pockets it. A torch with a narrow pencil beam is switched on behind Nina and Leonid's voice comes from above it.

'Welcome to Tulp's water-house, otherwise known as the *Drowning Cell*.' The beam of the torch travels around the perimeter of the room. 'He told me it is an exact replica of a seventeenth century form of punishment from a House of Correction in Amsterdam. Apparently, it was used to tame boys who refused to work. It is very simple really. The laziest boys were locked in the cell and water was allowed to flow into it. The boy needed to work the pump continuously or the cell would fill up and he would drown. Ingenious, is it not? Tulp was very amused by this notion and he used to enjoy showing it off to his dinner guests.'

'You sadistic bastard,' I growl. Leonid is now standing in the doorway to the boathouse. The second man must have turned on a tap somewhere. Water begins to flow out of the pipe above me and splash around the floor at my feet.

'Actually, Tulp felt it wouldn't have been seen as particularly barbaric at the time. People were being hung, drawn and quartered by the authorities, or put into sacks and thrown live into the river. Or they were having their tongues cut out or they were being garrotted on poles like poor little Elsje. You did well to spot her, by the way. But then someone was supposed to. Another little contribution to the stirring of the pot. This cell was just a gentle educational aid by comparison, a way of persuading the idle young to mend their ways.'

'Please...' says Nina.

'He also said it was a metaphor for the struggle by hard-working Dutch people to survive the rising sea waters and build their cities,' continues Leonid relentlessly. 'He really was quite boring about his wonderful ancestors and their amazing legacy. So now, he will be remembered as the final victim of the Tulip Murders. And the chaos continues with the bodies of two English holidaymakers found in the secret drowning cell at his home. That should prompt some amazing conspiracy theories don't you think? With a little help from us and the internet, of course. Perhaps you were both responsible for all the killings and decided on one dramatic double suicide to end it all.'

The beam of the torch rests on Nina's nakedness. 'A delightful last sight. I am told I was rude to you at the hotel and that I asked you for a kiss during our dinner with Tulp. I am sorry. Sometimes I drink too much vodka. Of course, I could just take a kiss now, couldn't I? Without asking your permission. But I won't. And I am sorry to make you strip. But I couldn't risk you stuffing rags into the water pipe, could I?'

'Wait,' shouts Nina. 'Wait. Please.' She looks up at me. 'Please may I have one last kiss from Jack?'

The torch beam shoots across to me. Leonid, or whatever his real name is, laughs. 'Why not? Deep down, we Russians have romantic souls. Quickly Mr Jack Johnson, one final kiss. And then you will try to use the pump to save your loved one. But you will become exhausted and then you both will drown."

I splash forward. The water is already approaching ankle height. I bend my head down to Nina's. I feel so grateful to her. We both need this last comforting touch of another human being. Our mouths meet. Her lips are open. I open mine too. And that is when I feel her tongue push a solid wad of chewing gum into mine. I almost gag in surprise. The torchlight has lingered on our faces during this exchange but now it goes out and the second door clangs shut. We are now in complete and utter blackness. I have only experienced a total blackness like this once before – during a tourist tour of a disused Welsh coalmine when our guide switched off the lights for a brief moment. But down there, deep in the bowels of the earth, it was oppressively silent too. Here, in the drowning cell, our heavy breathing is accompanied by the threatening splash of water.

I move forward to the metal bar sticking out of the ground and begin to rock it backwards and forwards, backwards and forwards. 'Jack. Jack. Have you got the gum?'

'Yes. I can guess what you're thinking. But I don't know if it'll hold back the water in the pipe. I'm just working the pump handle now.'

'Alright, listen to me, Jack.' Nina's voice is urgent but under control. 'We can try the pump again in a minute but let's try the gum first. Then I need you to try to bite through these ties. They're only plastic. I'm not going to drown tied to a chair. I'm just not. Do it for me, Jack. Please.'

'Alright. I'll try.' I hold my hands out in front of me, turn 180 degrees and splash towards the wall. The water is approaching my knees now. I reach the wall and jump up three or four times until my flailing hand brushes against the pipe. I catch my breath and gather my strength for one last jump. I have a good sense of where the pipe is now. This time, I am able to grip it and stay suspended for a moment before falling backwards. It would be impossible for me to hang there and place my other hand over the pipe for any length of time. I pull the gum out of my mouth, mould it into a moist ball and hold it ready in my left hand. Then I crouch low and spring upwards for a second time. My right hand grabs the pipe, but then it slips, and I fall backwards again.

'Jack?' says Nina out of the darkness.

'I can't do it,' I pant back at her.

'Please. Please just keep trying.'

I try to bring my breathing under control and go again. This time, my right hand holds tight to the protruding pipe. I brace my feet against the wall to steady myself and swing my left hand up to meet my right. Then I stuff the gum into the opening. My right arm feels like it is being pulled out of its socket, but I hang on grimly and use the thumb of my left hand to ram the gum further into the metal tube. Then I fall to earth and collapse onto my knees in the pooling water.

The flow of water immediately slows. I can still sense a trickle coming out, but the sound of splashing below is much quieter. Nina must hear it too.

'Well done, Jack. Quick now, the ties.' I splash back past the pumping handle until I feel Nina and the chair. Then I bend down onto both knees. This makes the cold water reach the top of my thighs. I feel the tight plastic and begin to gnaw it with my front teeth. It feels hard and unyielding. I sense Nina yelp as I pinch some of the flesh on the back of her hand. 'Keep going Jack. It doesn't matter if it hurts me.'

I turn my head sideways in order to move the tie backwards in my mouth where the jaw muscles are more powerful. I grind and grind until I feel a small nick in the plastic with my tongue. Now I use my arms as levers and try to tear the nick larger by ripping my head backwards. The tie breaks on the fourth attempt. But I sense that the sound of the water has changed again. It seems to be flowing more freely again. The pressure must have pushed the gum out of the pipe. I'll never find it again on the floor under all this water.

Nina puts her free hand on my head. 'The other one now Jack. Quickly.' I move my head across to the other wrist, locate the tie and this time I begin gnawing it with my molars straight away. It too breaks eventually after I yank and pull at it, shaking my head like a terrier with a rat. I stand upright. The water is definitely deeper now – just below my navel. Nina's hands are on both my shoulders. 'Well done, Jack! Now stand up and get back to the pump. We can take it in turns.' Her voice is still shaking but I take heart from her courage and clear thinking.

'Alright. But you stand on the chair for the moment,' I reply. I wade back and grope underwater for the pump handle. It is completely submerged now. I begin moving it forwards and backwards. Forwards and backwards. There is greater resistance than before, and it is harder to move. My back, arms and shoulders feel as though they're on fire. It's difficult to tell whether I am having any effect on the water level at all. The pump could even have been disconnected by the Russians in order to guarantee a quick double death and leave no loose ends. I stand upright, gulping for breath. Yes, now the water is at my waist. I have hardly slowed its rise at all. 'I don't think I'm having much effect,' I pant to Nina.

'Wait there. Let's see if both of us can do it.' I sense her wading towards me as the water is pushed between us. We stand either side of the rod and move it left and right, left and right.

'This is no good,' I shout. 'You need to push and pull from one end and I'll do the same from the other.' We readjust our positions and begin to rock the handle between us. It's definitely moving faster now, but Nina is a foot shorter than me so the water must have reached the height of her chest. It won't be long before she will have to bend her face into the water to reach the pump handle. I begin to count each movement in batches of ten. I may be imagining it, but the water seems to be holding level where it is. Holding level but failing to go back down. How much longer can we do this?

One, two, three, four, five, six, seven, eight, nine, ten. One, two, three, four, five, six, seven, eight, nine, ten. On and on it goes. How many times have we moved the handle? It must be above a thousand. I am too breathless now to count out loud. 'Count in your head,' I pant at her. My arms and shoulders are in agony. The coldness is numbing our minds and bodies. Christ. How much longer can we hope to do this? How can we even begin to do it all night? And even then, assuming we make it through to the morning, how long will it take for anyone to notice that we, or Tulp, are missing?

'Jack. Jack.' Nina sounds faint with tiredness. 'I can't go on Jack. I'm sorry.' She is breathing hard and gives an enormous racking sob which makes me reach forwards for her. I wrap her in my arms. 'I know. I know,' I whisper into her ear. 'Shush now. It's okay. Climb back up onto the chair.' I push her over to it and help her stand. 'Can you feel the ceiling above you?'

'Yes, I can just touch it,' she pants down at me.

An arm's length. This means there is roughly another two feet of headspace. I might be able to join her on the chair and hold her up for a while longer. Or should I try to return to the pump on my own? I choose the latter course of action for the moment. Climbing up onto the chair will just delay the inevitable – and not for very long. I grope under the water for the handle again and resume rocking it. My neck is burning with pain and the water has reached my upper chest. Forwards and backwards, forwards and backwards. But it is much harder to move on my own and I can sense the cold water continuing to creep up my skin.

Now it is at the bottom of my neck and I can't reach the handle without submerging my face under the water. It's hopeless. I abandon the task and retreat to the chair where Nina and I stand tightly clasped together. The blackness is all encompassing. The water is above my waist now, even though I am on the chair. I raise my arms and feel the ceiling. How much longer until the cell is full? Thirty minutes perhaps? I have lost all sense of time and there is no way of measuring it. My watch is lying with my clothes beyond the door. What crazed sadist invented this bloody thing? A *Drowning Cell*. And they inflicted it on children!

'I'm scared Jack.' Nina's teeth are chattering so much she can hardly get the words out. 'We're going to die, aren't we?'

I don't want her to give up hope, but I want her to be prepared. 'Yes. Yes, I think so. I'm so sorry.'

I feel her tighten her arms around my neck. I still have one arm braced up against the ceiling to hold us both steady. Her lips find mine and this time there is no gloopy plug of strawberry and cannabis flavoured gum to get in the way. 'I d-do love you, Jack. You do know that d-don't you?'

I squeeze her back and whisper in her ear. 'And I've loved you since the moment I first met you.'

'W-we've wasted so much time. We could have been so happy.'

'I have been happy, Nina. In a way I am now. Knowing that you love me just as I love you.'

She tries to laugh but it tails away into a shuddering sob. I kiss her again. But when I come up for air, I realise it is a fast-diminishing commodity. The water is now at my chest level and just below her neck. 'I'm going to have to hold you up,' I say. 'You're staying with me for as long as you can.'

She clasps both her arms around the back of my neck, and I feel her wrap her legs around my waist. I try to support her bottom with both my hands, but it feels much more precarious without at least one of my hands braced against the roof of the cell. I am just adjusting my position to try to hold her up one-handed, when there is a loud metallic banging sound. It is quickly followed by another and another and another.

'Hold on,' I tell Nina urgently and feel an extra tight squeeze of her legs around my waist. Suddenly the blackness turns grey and there is a whoosh as a torrent of water hurls the outer door of the boathouse open with a clang and floods out. The cell instantly begins to empty itself. We look down in the murky light and can just make out the smooth top of the wave of water as it pours through the open doorway into the boathouse. The level of water in the cell is getting lower and lower by the second.

'Bloody hell, I'm soaked,' complains a man's voice from beyond the doorway.

'Me too,' says another.

We are still standing on the chair, wrapped tightly around each other's naked bodies when the shocked faces of Will and Archi appear in the doorway and stare up at us.

'Oh, my goodness!' exclaims Archi.

'Bloody hell,' says Will grinning. 'Get a room you two!'

CHAPTER FORTY-SEVEN

The two of them are as drenched as Nina and me, although they are still fully clothed and we are still stark naked. They squelch into the room and help us down from the chair. My legs are almost too weak to stand and Nina is still holding onto me for dear life. Then they half drag us out of the *Drowning Cell* and into a small dock area with wooden pontoons and a brick ceiling. The only light is coming weakly through the boat house's semi-circular entrance onto the canal.

'Jack! Nina!' shouts a woman's voice. I peer through the gloom and can just make out Jodi sitting in the stern of a small wooden launch. 'My God!' She quickly climbs out and hurries towards us with an armful of blankets. 'Here, wrap these around you. All of you.' She enfolds Nina and begins to start rubbing some warmth into her. 'Will, you do the same to Jack,' she orders. 'Quickly now.'

Will begins rubbing the scratchy blanket into my aching back and shoulders. Nina is shivering, both from the shock and the cold. 'Thank you, thank you', she is saying, over and over again.

Archi is hopping from one foot to the other in front of us, his drenched bespoke suit clinging to him. 'Thank goodness you are alright. We've been trying both your phones for the last hour, but they're as dead as dodos.'

'What ... what time is it?' I stutter.

'It's just gone midnight,' says Will. I calculate we have been in the cell for about an hour. A nice round time for a terrified person to drown slowly. 'Archi came to the houseboat to check you were okay. We told him where you'd gone but when you didn't come back, and there was no answer on your phones, we began to get worried.'

'There was no answer at the front door, so the wonderful Jodi here borrowed a boat, and we came in via the boathouse,' continues Archi.

'There was a padlock on the door, but it came off after a few bangs with our anchor,' adds Will. 'But we weren't expecting Niagara Falls when we opened it. Let alone you two. What the hell has been going on?'

'It's called a *Drowning Cell*. And if you'd been ten minutes later, it would have worked,' I tell him.

'And Tulp put you in there?' says Archi in a horrified voice.

'My God, we must call the police at once. Is he still in the house?' asks Jodi.

'Tulp's in there. But he's dead,' says Nina. The colour is slowly returning to her cheeks. We all need to get somewhere warm and dry as quickly as possible.

'Tulp's dead?' asks Archi, his eyes round with surprise behind his misted glasses. 'But how?'

'How far is police HQ from here?' I ask Jodi. 'By boat.'

'What? Oh, not far. Five minutes at most.'

'I'll explain on the way,' I say. 'Please get us there as fast as you can.' Thankfully, they all pile into the boat without further discussion and the outboard engine springs into life with Jodi's first pull of the starting chord. We are soon belting along the Herengracht, swinging left down the little Leidsegracht and then turning right onto the meandering Singelgracht where the police headquarters building is located.

It's difficult to make myself heard above the noise of the engine during our ride, but I manage to shout into Archi's ear. 'It's the Russians. If we move quickly, we might get them.'

He widens his eyes at me but then nods purposefully. 'Faster, Jodi,' he urges her. I imagine our wash is disturbing the sleep of quite a few people on their boats, but that's just tough in the circumstances.

The duty sergeant behind the desk doesn't mess about. If it's just after twelve and four very wet English people and a Dutch woman are urgently demanding to speak to Dr Beatrix van der Laen. who is he to question it? Especially when four of them are wrapped in boat blankets and two of them appear to be naked underneath. This feels like a situation that is way above his pay grade. Besides, he knows Her Majesty is asleep on a cot in her office and her deputy Robert is still somewhere in the building too.

It takes another ten minutes before the two murder detectives and the surprise arrivals are all assembled in a conference room. Robert has taken one look at us and ordered a uniformed officer to bring hot drinks as quickly as possible. Nina is sitting on a chair next to me and holding my hand on the table. We are both still shivering.

However, as a journalist, one thing I can do is tell a story clearly and succinctly. I order the facts in my head as though I am writing an article. There are no interruptions as I give the room a brief account of everything that has happened and everything that was said after Nina and I first pulled the bell at Tulp's door. I realise time is of the essence and I don't dwell on the horror of the *Drowning Cell* - but the look on the others' faces tells me I don't need to.

'So, if you want to catch Leonid, or whatever his name is, and the other three killers, you need to be intercepting them at Schiphol before their plane leaves for Moscow,' I finish.

Impressively, Beatrix doesn't waste a single second by asking me any questions or trying to cross examine my account. Instead, she says, 'Please stay here for the moment,' and leaves the room with Robert close behind her.

'Umm ... I just need to speak to the office,' says Archi, moving over to the corner of the room. However, I suspect his mobile will have had too much of a drenching to let him do that.

I extend my arm around Nina's shoulder and pull her closer towards me. 'Are you okay?' I breathe into her hair, and I am rewarded with a little nod.

'I am now.'

'I'm going in search of more coffee,' says Jodi.

Will is seated at the table opposite me. 'That's quite a story,' he says quietly.

'We owe you one,' I reply.

'I was just trying to get into the house to find you,' he says. 'Obviously, we didn't know anything about the *Drowning Cell*. We were just sure you'd have rung to tell us you'd be so late coming back. It didn't feel right.' He nods over at Archi who is bent over his phone in frustration. 'He wasn't very happy about breaking into a respectable Dutchman's house with an anchor. But he doesn't really know about your talent for trouble, and I just asked myself what you would do in the same situation.'

'I thought you and Jodi might have been a bit preoccupied to worry about us,' I tell him with a smile and Nina gives a little giggle. That's a good sign.

Will looks slightly abashed. 'Well, I suppose we were for a bit after we gave Eddie a walk. But then Archi boy turned up. He'd been for a drink with the detective woman and wanted to check up on you.'

We all fall silent with our thoughts for a few minutes until the door opens. It's Robert and he is carrying a fresh tray of hot drinks.

'What's happening?' I ask him.

'We've informed MIVD and there's a combined operation underway at the airport,' he replies. 'Beatrix is on her way out there and I'm co-ordinating things from here. I'm sorry. I know you must be very tired. We have found some temporary clothing for you and then perhaps you can write down some statements? After that, we can drive you back to your boat, or wherever you want.'

The temporary clothing turns out to be some black all-in-one police overalls, but we are given fleece jackets and warm socks too. Some officers supervise our statements and Archi is then allowed a landline to speak to a duty officer at the British Embassy. After doing this, he appears to be much less stressed.

We end up in an interview suite with comfortable chairs where we turn out the light and try to doze. Jodi is snuggled up on Will's lap in one armchair while Nina and I are curled up together on a settee. Archi is alternately snoring and grunting in an armchair. The clock on the wall tells me it is 2 a.m. when the door opens again, and Robert comes into the room.

'I am sorry to wake you. You can leave now. We have a couple of cars waiting out front for you.'

'What's happened?' says Nina, rubbing her eyes. 'Did you get them?'

Robert sighs and I instantly know the answer. 'We grounded the Moscow flight and isolated all the passengers. But we were an hour too late. A private jet took four passengers out of Schiphol at half past midnight. It had a flight plan logged for Moscow.'

'They got away?' says Archi in disbelief.

Robert nods mournfully. 'But now, we can get you home. I'm waiting for a proper debrief with Beatrix. I am sure we will be in touch with you tomorrow. Thank you.'

Arrangements are made for Archi to be driven straight to the embassy, Will and Jodi to Jodi's apartment and Nina and I ask to be taken back to *Flora*.

'They got away,' repeats Nina as we make the short journey in the back of the marked police car. She is still holding my hand. She has barely let go of it since we emerged from the *Drowning Cell*. 'I can't believe it.'

'It was a well-run operation from the start to the finish,' I say. 'Carefully planned and flawlessly executed. All except for one thing.'

'What's that?'

'We survived to tell the tale.'

CHAPTER FORTY-EIGHT

Nina and I are slow to rise the following morning. Her head is resting on my chest when I open my eyes. The sun is streaming through the porthole and the room is as warm as Nina's bare skin against mine. It's like waking up in paradise after the nightmare of the previous evening. I lift a hand to check my watch, but my wrist is bare. Of course, it is still at Tulp's house. Presumably the police broke in last night to recover his body and turn the place over. It would have been a very long night for Beatrix and Robert. I wonder if they're still on duty and if the news has broken to the wider world yet? What would Su give to know about this latest development? Should I give her a tip-off? No. Not yet. Just lie here and relax. I breathe out slowly. I mustn't do anything to break the spell. Me and Nina - together at last.

A while later she begins to stir, flexes her neck muscles and opens her big dark eyes at me. 'Good morning, lover,' she says.

'Good morning, lover,' I reply. There is a scratching at the door. Eddie has heard our voices.

'I had the weirdest of dreams.'

'Hmm. Me too.'

'A pool full of tulips. Drowning cells and Russian spies. And a boat going fast through Amsterdam in the middle of the night?'

'That's weird. Me too. Or something like that.'

She gives an enormous yawn. 'And now here we are.'

'Yes, here we are.' Eddie is now making a dog yowl which roughly translates as, 'I know you're in there and it's time to get up.'

'Right. I'm going to make some coffee and say hello to Eddie. And then I am coming back to bed,' says Nina decisively.

'That sounds good,' I say beginning to sit upright. But she pushes me back down onto the pillow. 'No. You're not going anywhere. You stay there.'

'Yes, ma'am.' I am still smiling as she goes through the door, pulling on her robe. And the smile is still there when she comes back, a mug in each hand. But it freezes when I see her face and she raises and drops both shoulders in resignation. 'The police are here. We're wanted apparently.'

There is an unmarked police car on the towpath with a uniformed driver at the wheel and the smartly dressed man waiting in the boat's saloon says he is from the Ministry of Justice and Security. The Minister himself would be enormously grateful for a meeting with us both as soon as possible this morning. It is a matter of national importance.

He waits in the car while we dress, snatch some toast to go with our coffee and clip Eddie's lead to his collar. Then we are whisked through the city to a modern tower block which is labelled Rembrandt Tower and take a lift to the very top. We are asked to wait for a few minutes in a plush reception area where a secretary offers to look after Eddie. Nina makes it very clear he is staying with us and we are eventually ushered into an inner sanctum. The Minister's penthouse office boasts ultra-modern furnishings and floor to ceiling panes of glass which look out over the city.

A tall elegant looking man with thick, swept back hair comes to greet us with an outstretched hand and a politician's smile. 'Good morning Mr Johnson and Mrs Wilde. It is very kind of you to make the time to see me this morning. Particularly after your ordeal last night. Hello there. What a nice little dog. Please take a seat. May I offer you coffee? Tea?'

We each claim a black leather and chrome chair and decline the offer of a drink. The man who collected us takes a seat in the background with a notebook while the Minister sits opposite us.

'I have been fully briefed on the events of last night and your part in them,' he says, running his hand through his hair. 'And I have read your written statements.'

'We'd be dead if it wasn't for our friends,' says Nina.

'Yes of course, your friends. One of them is from the British Embassy is he not?'

I nod. I'm still not clear where this conversation is going.

He coughs. 'As you can imagine, the Dutch government is completely outraged that a Russian spy operation has been mounted on our sovereign territory with a clear attempt to influence our forthcoming election. It is totally and utterly unacceptable. Putin has completely overplayed his hand this time. Eight murders ... no, nine now if you include Tulp, and two attempted murders. Once this becomes known, our Western allies will be forced to make a co-ordinated response.'

'We haven't had a chance to see any news yet this morning. Is it out there yet?'

He combs back his hair with his fingers and coughs. 'No. Not yet. We are preparing for a press conference this afternoon when I shall be accompanied by the Prime Minister. We would prefer to take complete control of the news agenda in this instance.'

'Bit awkward though, them getting away like that.' I'm still quietly seething that the foreign murder squad has slipped through the net.

He automatically clenches one fist on his trouser leg. 'It was very disappointing. Very disappointing indeed. Of course, we are already making the strongest possible protests to Moscow and I imagine a number of their embassy officials will be expelled by the end of today – both from here and from other European capitals.'

'That'll teach them,' I say sarcastically.

'And of course, we shall be pressing for further sanctions.'

'You read what the man Leonid told me? They're conducting a clandestine war to destroy Western democracies from within.

And they really don't care if anyone gets in the way. Expelling a few diplomats won't make much difference.'

'Yes. Of course, we have long suspected as much. But it is very useful to have your first-hand testimony. We hope you will co-operate with AIVD and MI6 to identify the man who called himself Leonid? He is GRU obviously, the special forces arm of their military intelligence. And he was their team leader. We are trying to establish when he came into the country with the other three.'

Nina has been quiet up to now. 'I'm sure we'll co-operate as much as we can,' she says. 'These people tried to kill us too. They're barbarians.'

'Thank you, Mrs Wilde. I am very anxious to secure your co-operation.'

'So how are you going to get all of this back on track?' I ask. 'Full and frank disclosure?'

'We shall reveal everything about Tulp's involvement with the Russians and how their plan was to discredit the Green-Labour and liberal parties of our country in order to influence the election. However, I shall be candid with you, we are still concerned on two counts. Firstly, it may be too late to swing public opinion back to where it was; and secondly, all of this will create conspiracy theories which will swirl around for a long time to come. This is precisely what the Russians planned and what they want. No doubt, they will try to foment these theories further with their internet meddling. That is why it is important that there is no loss of confidence in the forces of law and order or our security services.' He pauses as though not quite sure how to go on.

'We're listening,' I say.

'Frankly, and confidentially, it is embarrassing that two English visitors have broken this case and delivered proof of the Russian involvement – however welcome that outcome is.'

'And even more embarrassing that you let the killers escape back to Moscow,' says Nina.

'Especially after you'd been told by us where they were going,' I say, twisting the knife.

'Nevertheless, it is in our country's best interest for the role of the police and our security services in resolving the case to be ... how can I put it? Upgraded.'

'And for our role to be ... how can I put it? Downgraded?' I ask, smiling at his bare-faced cheek. 'Why should we co-operate with this?'

'To prevent the extremists coming to power,' he says simply. 'My government and this Ministry have been heavily criticised for the handling of the Tulip Murders. Now, of course, we know what we were dealing with; ruthless, well-trained and well-resourced assassins from a major foreign power. It is vital that we claw back some credit.'

'And you need to do that in time for the election,' observes Nina.

'So, what's your proposed story?' I ask.

The Minister stands and starts pacing. I imagine he does this so that he doesn't have to meet our eyes. 'We will not lie. However, we do not propose drawing attention to your involvement at this stage either. We will simply state that our officers found Tulp dead in his swimming pool and narrowly missed arresting the Russian killers at Schiphol after they fled on a private plane. We will state that our intelligence sources already suspected their country's involvement due to diligent technical detective work on various social media posts...'

'Which we brought to the police's attention,' interrupts Nina.

'... and that those subsequent discoveries, such as Tulp's secret tulip garden, have confirmed he was working hand-in-glove with the Russians as a traitor to his country, until they, in turn, betrayed and executed him.'

'That still doesn't explain how you closed in on them,' I say.

He stops pacing and sighs. 'I know. And if you hadn't gone asking Tulp about the Semper Augustus and his family history, we might never have known the truth. It was a lucky break. For us I mean,' he adds hastily. 'I do not diminish the ordeal you went through. But we will not lie. We will simply say that we cannot give more operational details as it might compromise the work of our successful secret services and their associates. Of course, in this instance you would qualify as an associate.'

'You forget,' I say. 'It's not just us who you need to get on board for all this. We had our friends with us, including a British diplomat.'

'We are talking to your Embassy now and seeking the Ambassador's co-operation. There is talk of a new posting and a promotion for your friend – with his agreement of course. As for your two other friends, we would hope that you could persuade them to, um, to fall into line.' A young woman pokes her head around the office door and shakes a wristwatch at him before ducking back out again.

'I beg you to co-operate with this. We cannot stop you telling the whole story – although I would remind you that you signed our Official Secrets Act. You are a journalist and a book-writer. I know it is in your interest to reveal your involvement. But if you do, you risk giving the Russians and the right-wing extremists all that they want.'

'I need to think about this,' I say. 'We need some time.'

'Time is in short supply. I can give you ten minutes to discuss this,' he replies. 'As I said, we have a press conference scheduled for this afternoon and I need to brief the Prime Minister. Please remain here. I shall return shortly. Please think this through carefully but quickly.' He ushers the other man out of the door in front of him and then pauses. 'There's one other consideration. Your own safety. If you are publicly identified, then there may be no shortage of violent people, fanatics, who might seek some kind of retribution. You will be safer if you remain in the shadows.'

'What do you think?' asks Nina quietly, as soon as the door is closed.

'I don't like it, but I think he's probably right about the election. They need a big win if they're going to turn this situation around quickly. If they play it right, public opinion will be outraged at what the Russians have done, and the government could benefit from that.'

'And parading a couple of English tourists as the accidental heroes of the hour doesn't quite cut it, does it?' she asks. 'And the Russians know who we are – and if they find out that we survived the *Drowning Cell*, we could still be in some danger from them couldn't we? That's another argument for keeping our heads down.'

I shake my head. 'They'll find out that we're still alive soon enough. Especially if we aren't mentioned as a couple of corpses discovered in the house on the Golden Bend.'

'So, what do you want to do, Jack?'

I smile at her. 'Actually, there's nothing I'd rather do than to go back to bed with you for the rest of the day. But for the moment, help me find a bit of paper and a pen, would you?'

We leave Rembrandt Tower twenty minutes later. There is no longer a chauffeured police car waiting to take us back to *Flora*. But there is a carefully folded piece of paper in my back pocket. It is dated, timed and signed by Nina and me and the Dutch Minister of Justice and Security and his senior civil servant alongside an official ministerial stamp. The agreement, in my own handwriting, reads:

We, Jack Johnson and Angelina Wilde, undertake not to reveal our involvement in events at the mansion of Cornelius Tulp on the night of his death and the activities of a Russian execution squad in Amsterdam until at least two months after the Dutch parliamentary election takes place. We also agree to prevail on our friends Will Simpson and Jodi Luiken to do the same and will advise the Ministry of Justice and Security by 1 p.m. today if this is not possible.

In return for our unanimous agreement to the above, the Dutch government in turn agrees to.

1. *Commend Archi Gupta Bhalla to the British Embassy for his prompt thinking and helpful role in this affair.*
2. *Request the Metropolitan Museum of Art in New York return the two Rembrandt sketches of Elsje Christiaens to Amsterdam on temporary loan for public display in the city where she was executed.*
3. *Publish the secret of the successful propagation of the Semper Augustus tulip and ensure its continuing survival under controlled conditions.*
4. *Do and say nothing, either publicly or privately, to undermine my book about The Tulip Murders when it is eventually published.*
5. *Provide accommodation and hospitality for the four people*

named above at the Waldorf Astoria for the coming week.

CHAPTER FORTY-NINE

Point (5) on our list of demands had been cheekily added by Nina as an afterthought but the Dutch government didn't quibble for a moment and two of the hotel's best suites were quickly secured in our names. Our extended holiday in the lap of five-star luxury was a treat. Will made arrangements to delay his return to the UK for a week and Jodi proved to be an outstanding guide to her home city. We would meet over breakfast to plan a loose itinerary for the day and then we would drift apart and together, two lovestruck couples in a beautiful foreign city. Nina strictly rationed me to half-an-hour's examination of the news each morning. Then we got down to the serious business of eating, drinking, sight-seeing and the occasional retreat to our room where we were sustained by each other and room service.

Su tracked us down one evening. She suspected that we knew more than we were saying but she was forced to retreat without any profitable titbits. This was my story, and I wasn't about to share any more of it. Besides, we had made and signed an agreement with the government.

The election came and went shortly after we returned to our mooring in Oxford. The ruling centre-right coalition clung onto power and there was no change of Prime Minister. However, the Minister of Justice and Security found himself reshuffled into healthcare. This all happened in the wake of international outrage at the allegations of nine murders on Dutch soil by a Russian death squad. Diplomats were expelled, sanctions implemented and permits for travel cancelled. A few Russian oligarchs had their holiday plans disrupted.

The Russian government dismissed the Dutch claims as fantasy and demanded proof. The Dutch authorities provided video pictures from the airport of four men climbing onto a private plane and subsequently revealed Leonid's real name and rank. But otherwise, they hid behind the need to protect the anonymity of their security services and the secrecy of MIVD's operations. There was no mention whatsoever of our role in the affair.

Archi was hurried out of Amsterdam before we could say a proper goodbye, but he sent us a delighted email to say he had been promoted to a higher-ranking post in New Delhi and that his mother and father were 'over the bloody moon'. The email was headed *Chatham House Rules.*

Two other noteworthy things happened on our last day in Amsterdam. Beatrix van der Laen asked if she could meet us for a coffee. We suggested cocktails in the Vault Bar of the Waldorf instead and asked if she would bring Robert along too. At one point she took me aside to tell me she had decided to retire to the country. 'It is time for younger people to take over,' she said with a sad smile. 'I shall build a garden with lots of tulips in it and write my memoirs.' I gave her Su's email address in case she needed any help.

Finally, later that same evening, Nina insisted that we walk Eddie back to the Groenburgwal Bridge. We stood there, slightly befuddled by fine wine, breathing in the cool night air and staring along the canal towards *Flora.* Then Nina took something out of her coat pocket and gave it to me. It was a padlock. I turned it over. She had used red nail varnish to paint a capital J and a capital N on it.

I snapped it around another padlock that was fixed to the bridge and tossed the key into the canal. We kissed. The next day, we turned our faces back to England. I had a book to write.

AUTHOR'S NOTE

A reader of this book who is lucky enough to find themselves in Amsterdam will be able to trace almost all of its geographical features for themselves – including the eight locations of the Tulip Murder victims that form the shape of a capital letter G on a map of the city. The only part of the book's setting that is a complete invention is Tulp's mansion on the Golden Bend of the Herengracht complete with its boathouse and *Drowning Cell.*

I have also tried to be as accurate as possible about the historical events of the 17th century in the book. These include Rembrandt's life and works, the fame and value of the Semper Augustus, the short unhappy life and death of Elsje Christiaens, tulipmania and the existence of the *Drowning Cell*. The life histories of Adriaan Pauw and Dr Nicolaes Tulp are also accurately portrayed although I have come across no evidence that the two men ever met. I also hope that any present-day ancestors of Dr Tulp will forgive me for inventing his theft of the supposed *secret* of Semper Augustus.

I am very grateful to the horticultural historian Advolly Richmond for coming up with Mycorrhizal Association as a semi-plausible explanation for the broken tulip's survival.

All of the other contemporary characters featured in Tulip

Murders are entirely fictional with the exception of President Putin and some Dutch politicians who are briefly referenced. I have set Tulip Murders shortly after the covid outbreak and before the Russian invasion of Ukraine and the rebranding of Twitter as X. Meanwhile, a recent general election in the Netherlands saw Geert Wilders and his hard right Freedom Party (PVV) win the largest number of seats and plans to relocate the city's red-light district are advancing at pace.

Thanks also to my excellent proof-readers, David Birt, Karon Jamous, Andy Townend and, as always, my wife Helen. I am also deeply grateful to Amsterdam photographer David Lichtneker for the cover photograph, to Orphan Press for the cover design and to Michael Pearson and Tamar Lumsden of the excellent Pearsons Canal Companion series for the bespoke maps of Amsterdam.

The illustration of the Semper Augustus tulip is reproduced by kind permission of the Norton Simon Art Foundation (Great Tulip Book: Semper Augustus, 17th century. Gouache on paper, 30.8 x 20.0 cm).

The Rembrandt sketch is reproduced courtesy of the Metropolitan Museum of Art, Havemeyer Collection, bequest of Mrs H.O. Havemeyer 1929. It is by Rembrandt van Rijn (1606-69), *Elsje Christiaens hanging on the gibbet* (c. 1664), pen and wash with bistre.

The following books were invaluable in my research for The Tulip Murders: *The Tulip* by Anna Pavord, *The Embarrassment of Riches* by Simon Schama, Amsterdam, *A History of the World's Most Liberal City* by Russell Shorto, *Amsterdam, A Brief Life of the City* by Geert Mak, *Why the Dutch are Different* by Ben Coates, *My 'Dam Life* by Sean Condon, *The Amsterdam Canals* by Cris Toala Olivares, *Time Out* Amsterdam and Wikipedia.

This book is dedicated to my brother and my sisters Simon Griffee, Lorraine Wheeler and Janice Watt, who I love very much.

ABOUT THE AUTHOR

Andy Griffee

Andy Griffee is a former reporter, news producer and senior manager at the BBC who began writing crime fiction six years ago. The father of two lives in Worcestershire with his wife Helen and two Border terriers called Phoebe and Eddie. When he isn't reading or writing in his study overlooking the Malvern Hills, he is rearing rare breed pigs, struggling to keep a Mark 1 Triumph Spitfire on the road or walking his dogs along riverbanks and towpaths to seek inspiration for the next book.

PRAISE FOR AUTHOR

"A WELCOME NEW VOICE IN CRIME FICTION IMBUED WITH A REAL SENSE OF PLACE" (Canal Pushers)

- MARY PICKEN, LIVE AND DEADLY

"A CENTRAL CHARACTER WHO DREW ME RIGHT INTO HIS WORLD...ANDY GRIFFEE IS AN AUTHOR TO WATCH." (Canal Pushers)

- STEPHEN BOOTH, BESTSELLING AUTHOR OF THE COOPER & FRY SERIES.

"A MODERN AND GRITTY THRILLER TOLD WITH HUMOUR AND AN OBVIOUS PASSION FOR BOATING...SLIP YOUR MOORINGS AND HEAD DOWN TO YOUR LOCAL BOOKSHOP." (River Rats)

- GEORGINA MURPHY, THE LIBRARY DOOR

'GREAT FUSION OF THE STEAMY AND BUCOLIC, OXFORD FROM THE WATER IS A DIFFERENT PLACE FROM MORSE-LAND." (Oxford Blues)

- DOMINICK DONALD, SUNDAY TIMES BESTSELLING AUTHOR OF

BREATHE

"A THOROUGHLY ENGAGING MYSTERY THAT BUILDS TO AN UNEXPECTED CONCLUSION, ARGUABLY HIS BEST YET." (Oxford Blues)

- AMELIA HAMSON, WATERWAYS WORLD

THE JOHNSON & WILDE CRIME MYSTERY SERIES

Jack Johnson and his companion Nina Wilde have a talent for finding trouble as they tour the canals and rivers of the UK and beyond in Andy Griffee's series of thrilling tiller-thrillers.

Canal Pushers

Jack Johnson, a divorced and unemployed print journalist, is seeking a fresh start and decides to try living on a narrowboat. But he's a duffer with the sixty-four-foot boat until he meets the enigmatic Nina Wilde on the towpath and she comes to his rescue. A chance meeting with a young homeless man and his dog sets of a sequence of events that leads to a perilous chase across the Midlands canal network. Can Jack and Nina escape from a media manhunt and survive when a drugs gang and the mysterious Canal Pusher have them in their sights?

Oxford Blues

It is winter in Oxford and Jack has moved on to the River Isis in pursuit of Nina, whose niece is studying at the university. He's hoping their relationship will get a kick-start in the city of dreaming spires. But instead, it gets a kick in the teeth when Nina befriends Caleb Hopper, a handsome young American member of the university's rowing team. The body of Caleb's girlfriend has been dragged up from Iffley Lock by magnet fishermen and Jack is soon neck deep in a tale of drowned love and dirty business.

Devil's Den

A chance encounter in a local pub alerts Jack and Nina to a valuable secret in some nearby tunnels and so begins a perilous sequence of events, some of which are distinctly unworldly. Tarot cards are read and an illicit seance is organised. But the spooky underground gathering is rudely interrupted and a night-long ordeal begins as the complex of historic tunnels reveals more of its hidden secrets.

Printed in Great Britain
by Amazon

8d096823-8c88-4fc9-9d91-08d0f67c9d37R01